THE IRON VOW

Books by Julie Kagawa
available from Inkyard Press

Each series listed in reading order. Novellas complement the full-length novels but do not need to be read to enjoy the series.

The Iron Fey

The Iron King (special edition includes the "Winter's Passage"* novella)
The Iron Daughter (special edition includes the "Guide to the Iron Fey"*)
The Iron Queen (special edition includes the "Summer's Crossing"* novella)
The Iron Knight (special edition includes the "Iron's Prophecy"* novella)
The Iron Prince
The Iron Traitor
The Iron Warrior

The Iron Fey: Evenfall

Shadow's Legacy (ebook novella)
The Iron Raven
The Iron Sword
The Iron Vow

Shadow of the Fox

Shadow of the Fox
Soul of the Sword
Night of the Dragon

The Talon Saga

Talon
Rogue
Soldier
Legion
Inferno

Blood of Eden

Dawn of Eden (prequel novella+)
The Immortal Rules
The Eternity Cure
The Forever Song

*Also available as an ebook and in *The Iron Legends* anthology
+Available in the *'Til the World Ends* anthology by Julie Kagawa,
Ann Aguirre, and Karen Duvall

JULIE KAGAWA

THE IRON VOW

inkyard
PRESS

ISBN-13: 978-1-335-45366-2

The Iron Vow

For questions and comments about the quality of this book, please contact us at CustomerService@Harlequin.com.

Inkyard Press
22 Adelaide St. West, 41st Floor
Toronto, Ontario M5H 4E3, Canada
www.InkyardPress.com

Printed in U.S.A.

To Nick

PART
I

PRELUDE

Let me tell you a story.

The story of a girl who went into the land of faeries, met a prince, and fell in love.

She went on a journey to rescue her brother, and along the way, she learned many things about herself and the world around her. She learned her father was a faery king, which made her a faery princess. She discovered her best friend was a faery straight out of legend: Robin Goodfellow. Puck of the Summer Court. Once you meet him, you'll never forget him.

On the way to rescue her brother, the girl met many strange and fantastic creatures. One of them was a talking cat, who agreed to help her in exchange for a "small favor." The girl didn't know it at the time, but she had stumbled upon one of the wisest and most infuriating creatures in all of Faery, and without him, she probably would have wandered in circles until she fell into a dragon's cave or was eaten by a giant spider. If you are ever lost in the Nevernever, look for a gray cat with golden eyes, or call the name Grimalkin into the wind. Chances are, he'll hear you. He might ask for the impossible, but he'll always get you where you need to go.

But we're getting off track, aren't we? Let me start again, from the beginning.

The girl went into Faery completely unprepared, knowing nothing about any of the things that I just mentioned. It was there, in the Nevernever, that she met a Winter prince. His name was Ash, and he was the most beautiful, dangerous creature she had ever encountered. He was also the youngest son of Mab, Queen of the Winter Court, which made him her enemy. And the laws of the fey forbade them to be together. But the girl was young, and she didn't care. She loved him, and though it took him a while to admit it, the prince loved her, as well. They faced many trials: terrible monsters, faery wars, kings and queens trying to tear them apart. Despite every obstacle and law and ominous faery warning, they fought with all their hearts to be together. But, sadly, their happily-ever-after was not to be.

The girl became a queen. A queen of the fey in the Iron Kingdom, and the prince could no longer be with her in her new realm because it was poisonous to him. And so, the prince went on a quest himself, a journey to find a way to be with the queen forever. His quest took him all the way to the End of the World, and he had to face unspeakable challenges, but in the end, he was triumphant and returned to the girl he loved. She was still waiting for him, in her realm of iron, and finally, at long last, they could be together. But the story isn't over yet.

The girl and the prince got married, and after a time, had a son. They named him Keirran, and Keirran grew up to be a handsome prince himself. The Prince of the Iron Realm. The queen and her husband loved him very much, but a dark prophecy hung over the Iron Prince's head. A prophecy that said he would betray his kingdom and bring about the destruction of the entire world of Faery. The Iron Prince became friends with the queen's brother, Ethan, who was also grown up now, and

Ethan's beloved, a girl named Mackenzie St. James. The three of them had many adventures together in the land of the fey. But Keirran had fallen in love with a girl named Annwyl, a faery of the Summer Court, and the law said they could not be together. The Iron Prince tried to defy that law as his parents had done, but all his attempts failed. And so, as the prince gave into despair, the prophecy surrounding him came true. He betrayed his best friends, betrayed his parents and his kingdom, and tried to destroy the Nevernever.

A great war was fought, with the Iron Prince battling those he'd once called family. His parents were heartbroken, but they had to protect their kingdom from their own son. Many lives were lost, but in the end, the Iron Prince was saved by the very friends he had betrayed. Ethan, Kenzie, and the prince's own love, Annwyl, faced the Iron Prince behind enemy lines, and somehow, they were able to bring him back. But the final battle was not without loss and, sadly, Annwyl sacrificed her existence to save the prince she loved so much. The Iron Prince returned home to face the consequences of his actions, and as punishment, was forever exiled from the Nevernever. He became King of the Forgotten and went on to rule a realm known as the Between, swearing to protect the world he'd once tried to destroy.

But the story isn't over yet.

Several years after the great war, a monster appeared in the Between. A monster of nightmares that spread anger and fear to everything it touched. It threatened the Iron Prince's kingdom, and the Iron Prince knew he needed help. He sent two messengers to the Iron Realm to ask for aid: Robin Goodfellow and a mysterious faery called Nyx. Nyx was a kind of faery no one had ever seen before, but she was beautiful and a deadly fighter, and she helped Puck reach the queen and the Winter prince in the Iron Realm. Together, the Iron Queen and her family confronted the monster and discovered the terrible truth. Long, long ago, there was another realm of Faery known as Evenfall. And Evenfall was home to a whole species of faeries called the Evenfey. The Evenfey were very much like the faeries of the Nevernever, except they were born of darker dreams and nightmares. They were ruled by a powerful entity known as the Nightmare King. But then, a selfish faery known as the Lady decided to seal Evenfall away, cutting the Evenfey off from the rest of the world.

This made the Nightmare King very angry. He fell into a deep sleep, and he dreamed of revenge. Of darkness and destruction, and vengeance against all fey, the Nevernever, and the entire world.

Years passed. The king slept on. But eventually, the seal to Evenfall weakened. The Nightmare King was waking up, still filled with rage toward Faery and the Nevernever. And so, to save their world, the girl and her companions decided to step through the weakened seal into Evenfall. To find the Nightmare King and stop him. Whatever that meant.

They didn't know what awaited them on the other side. They didn't realize that what they would discover would cause them to question everything.

But the story isn't over yet.

In fact, this is just the beginning.

1

My name is Meghan Chase.

Queen of the Iron Fey. Ruler of the Iron Kingdom. Daughter of a human mother and the immortal faery king of the Summer Court. I have survived multiple wars, faced unspeakable evil, and stopped at least two End of the World prophecies.

None of that was quite as terrifying as where I stood right now.

The sky overhead was black. No stars, no moon. Trees surrounded us, bent and twisted as if in horrible pain. A flat gray luminance filtered through the trunks, turning them into skeletal silhouettes that seemed to move whenever you looked away. In the distance, I could make out things dangling from the branches: rotting cages and sacks that bulged as they swung lazily back and forth.

I shivered. *Remember those horror movies that you love so much? Well, congratulations, now you're in one.*

A chill traced my spine. *It* was still out there, searching for us. I could feel its presence, old and patient, prowling through the trees. The monster that had been waiting for us the moment we'd set foot in this strange, terrible world. An Elder Nightmare, vicious and nearly unstoppable, that had attacked us as soon as we'd arrived. We'd managed to fight it off and escape, but not unscathed.

Clenching my jaw, I pressed a hand to my elbow. Beneath the bloody cloth I'd wrapped around my arm, my bones throbbed with pain. But even that was a small inconvenience compared to the bigger problem. If things had been normal, I would have healed myself by now, my fey glamour naturally restoring torn flesh and broken bones, staving off complete exhaustion and keeping me on my feet. But things were far from normal, and dread, yawning and terrible, had settled deep in my stomach.

There was no glamour in this place. None. It was a wasteland, barren and empty of magic. I could feel the deadness in the air, in the ground, in the trees around us. It made me sick. The Nevernever—the land of the fey—pulsed with magic; glamour existed in every tree and rock and living creature. It fueled our power, our very existence. It flowed from the mortal world into Faery from human dreams and emotions. From their loves, their fears, their passions and creativity.

This was nothing.

This was Evenfall.

Evenfall. A mirror realm to the Nevernever, Evenfall had existed alongside Faery since the very beginning. It was home to the species of faery known as the Evenfey. These were the true bogeymen, the monsters in the darkness. The Nightmares that everyone feared. The ruler of Evenfall was the immortal, immensely powerful Nightmare King, and even the fey of the Nevernever feared him.

So much so that, in the age before the courts rose to power, the strongest fey in the Nevernever made the terrible decision to seal Evenfall away from the world. Worse, they erased all memories that Evenfall, the Nightmare King, and the Evenfey had existed at all. Cut off from the glamour of the real world and the Nevernever, the fey of Evenfall were doomed to slowly Fade into nonexistence. Starving and forgotten, the Nightmare King fell into a coma-like sleep, and the fey of Evenfall vanished from the world.

Until recently, when the Evenfey had begun appearing again. No one knew how, or why, though it was suspected that the rising anger, division, and hatred in the world had been strong enough to reach the Nightmare King in his sleep. We—myself, Ash, Puck, Grimalkin, and Nyx—had been called to a place known as InSite, where it was rumored that the Evenfey had been gathering. Deep beneath the building, we'd found a circle of Evenfey attempting to raise the Nightmare King from his slumber. We intervened, only to discover we'd been tricked. Destroying the seal did not stop the ritual as we'd hoped. Instead, it tore open the way to Evenfall. And every faery on this side of the Nevernever—Summer, Winter, Iron, and Forgotten alike—now remembered Evenfall and the Nightmare King.

With the opening of the seal, the Nightmare King had stirred. He was waking up, and if he did, he would take his revenge on the Nevernever and the fey who'd sealed off his world. The Lady and her circle, those faeries of old, were no longer alive, but the Nightmare King wouldn't care. He had gone mad in his dreams and would destroy the Nevernever, the courts, and possibly the real world as well.

We had to stop him. Even if the Nightmare King was unkillable, and our own powers were greatly diminished in his realm. Even though it meant traveling into Evenfall itself and seeing the exact horrors that awaited us on the other side.

A world with no glamour. A realm of Nightmares, where the fey were starved, twisted creatures from mankind's darkest emotions. Where the king's own nightmares had taken form and now roamed the land, preying on all they encountered. Somehow, we had to cross this nightmare world, find the Nightmare King, and either put him back to sleep or…

Or what? I frowned at my own thoughts. I didn't like the idea of killing him. What would happen to Evenfall if we did? What would happen to the rest of the Evenfey? I didn't know exactly what we would do when we found him, just knew that it was up to us—again—to save our world from destruction.

Even though we had no magic here.

I sensed his presence behind me before his strong but gentle touch warmed my back. Leaning into the caress, I glanced up. Ashallyn'darkmyr Tallyn, former prince of the Winter Court and my husband, gazed solemnly over my shoulder into the woods. His silver eyes scanned the shadows between the trunks, ever alert for threats, though the hand against my back was of silent support. I wanted to lean into him, to close my eyes and forget this terrible place existed. But I couldn't. A queen had to remain strong, even if the only ones to see it were her family and closest friends. I was the Iron Queen. In this empty world bereft of glamour and magic, I had to give them hope.

"It's still out there," Ash murmured behind me.

I nodded. "I haven't seen or heard it in a while, but I'm sure it's still stalking us." The Nightmare had chased us for a while after we had fled. Or, rather, when Keirran finally convinced the rest of us to retreat. It was not in the Iron Queen's nature to run away, even less so for a warrior son of Winter and the infamous jester of the Summer Court. Ash, Puck, and I probably would have fought the creature until we killed it or it tore us apart, but the Forgotten King had reminded us that we had an important mission to accomplish. If we died here, there would be no one to stop the Nightmare King from waking up, and the Nevernever—and possibly the real world as well—would be doomed. Realizing this, we finally retreated, and eventually lost the Nightmare in the twisted forest surrounding us.

I didn't like running away. Rulers of Faery did not give

ground to their enemies. And I hated the fact that I was weak now. But Keirran had been right. Our mission was too important to waste time fighting. We were here to stop the Nightmare King and save the Nevernever. And somehow, we would do that, with no glamour, no allies, and no idea of how to accomplish anything.

"Has Nyx returned yet?" Ash asked, interrupting my bleak musings.

I shook my head. "Not yet." The Evenfaery had left several minutes ago to scout the area, hoping to spot the Elder Nightmare before it found us. Nyx was unmatched at remaining unseen, and this was her world. We would have a better chance of avoiding the monster if we knew exactly where it was.

Cool fingers slid over my arm, brushing my elbow. "Come inside," Ash urged. "Nyx will be back when she's ready. There's nothing we can do until then."

"Yeah." I sighed and let him lead me back into the cave. It wasn't a large cavern, just a hole carved into a hillside, but it was sandy and dry and, most important, free of anything living in it.

A reddish-orange fire burned sullenly in the center of the cavern, lighting the interior. Puck sat cross-legged in front of it, feeding twigs into the flames. His bright red hair glowed in the flickering light, making it seem like his head was on fire. Opposite him, a fluffy gray cat lay comfortably on a flat rock, feet tucked into his chest, golden eyes half-closed in the dancing shadows.

I crouched in front of the small fire and spread my hands before it, letting the warmth seep into my cold fingers. "How's everyone holding up?" I asked.

Puck's green eyes met mine over the firelight. The gash on his forehead had stopped bleeding, though his left cheek still looked a bit bruised.

He shrugged and managed to dredge up his old devil-may-care grin. "Never better, princess. Who wouldn't want to go gallivanting through a literal nightmare world filled with horrific monsters and no magic? I'm thinking of setting up a lovely vacation home in that grove of trees with the screaming heads."

I gave a faint smile. Not even a literal nightmare world could stop Puck from making a joke about it. "Then you'd at least have a captive audience," I replied, making him snort. "Sleeping might be a challenge, though."

"Trust me, princess. No one is ever going to sleep in this place."

Ash knelt beside me, deliberately close. I resisted the urge to lean into him. "You managed to get a fire going, at least," he observed.

"Yeah." Puck snapped his fingers, and a tiny flame appeared over his thumb for a split second before he snuffed it out. "By virtue of being me. This is it, though. This is how much glamour I have left, and it ain't a lot. What about you two?"

Ash shook his head. "Mine is gone," he said grimly. "I used the last of it fighting the Nightmare."

"Princess?"

I sighed. "The same," I admitted. "It took nearly everything I had to re-seal the portal to Evenfall. I have maybe enough for one more big attack, and then everything will be drained completely. I know Keirran is in the same boat. I'm not sure about Nyx."

"So, we have no magic," Puck said. "No glamour, no power, and we are in the literal plane of Faery hell." He grimaced and scrubbed a hand through his crimson hair, making it stand on end. "Yeah, this is gonna be all kinds of fun."

I clenched a fist. They were both putting on brave faces, but even though he hid it well, I could sense Ash's fear. Without glamour, he was weaker; still a skilled and deadly swordsman, with a few natural Faery perks that made him more dangerous than the strongest human, but he would not be able to bring the awesome power of his Winter magic to bear. I knew he was worried, not for himself, but for the rest of us. His greatest fear was that he wouldn't be able to protect the ones he cared for.

I felt the same.

My hands shook. For so long now, I had felt the pulse of glamour in the very land around me. As a queen of Faery, I was connected to the Nevernever in ways that even the normal fey couldn't comprehend. I had forgotten what it was like…to be a normal human.

"So, what does this mean?" I asked. "We can't go back—if we open the portal again, the Nightmare King could wake up."

"No," Ash agreed. "We can't go back. We have to keep going, find the Nightmare King, and end the threat he represents. One way or another."

"It will not be as easy as that." On the rock, Grimalkin raised his head, blinking slowly. "Evenfall has been cut off from the glamour of the real world and the Nevernever," the cat explained. "I am not even sure how the realm has survived this long and not Faded away, much less the Evenfey themselves. But there is no natural glamour here, which means you will not be able to draw on the land to heal yourselves or fuel your powers. How do you propose to face the many Nightmares you will encounter, much less the Nightmare King himself?"

With a crunch of boots against rock, another figure stepped forward, firelight washing over his features. Silver hair and ice-blue eyes glimmered as Keirran, my son and the King of the Forgotten, melted out of the shadows to stand before us. Like his father, he was tall and graceful, with the pointed ears and sharp beauty of the fey, though his human blood softened his features somewhat.

"Nyx is returning," he said, gazing at the mouth of the cave. Puck rose quickly to his feet. I caught the flash of relief on his face, a surge of emotion he wasn't able to hide.

There was a ripple of moonlight at the cave entrance, and a slender figure dressed in black leather armor seemed to materialize from nothing. The Evenfey assassin glided noiselessly across the cavern, pale hair and yellow eyes glowing in the darkness. Not long ago, we had all thought Nyx to be a Forgotten, those faeries whose names and stories had faded from everyone's memories. Now, though, we knew the truth. Nyx was an Evenfaery. Evenfall, this nightmarish, magic-barren world, had once been her home.

"The Elder Nightmare is gone," she told us. "It left the edge of the forest and headed into the swamps. I don't think it's coming back."

Keirran nodded. "Good." He rubbed a hand over his forehead. "This is going to be hard enough without those monsters stalking us everywhere." His blue eyes regarded the Evenfaery and softened with sympathy and concern. "Are you all right, Nyx?"

"No." The Evenfaery shook her head. "Forgive me, your majesty, I am not. My memories of home are scattered, and some are just beginning to return, but…" Her gaze strayed to the mouth of the cave, and a haunted expression crossed her features. "Evenfall was not like this when I left. This is not the world I remember."

Puck moved quietly behind the assassin and slipped his arms around her waist. For once, his eyes were serious as he leaned in. "I know what it's like to be banished from home," he told her solemnly. "But I can't imagine coming back to the Nevernever and finding it…like *this*."

Nyx sighed, and one of her hands rose to rest over Puck's. "I had hope…for a moment," she murmured. "When the seal was broken and I remembered what had happened, I had hope that maybe Evenfall had endured, even after all this time. But deep down, I knew that was foolish. Evenfall…" She shook her head. "It is still lost to me. My home is still gone."

My jaw tightened. What had been done to the Evenfey was unforgivable. Nyx had been robbed of her memories, her world, and almost her entire existence because of what the Lady had done eons ago. And the worst part was, Nyx was right. We couldn't fix this. To unseal Evenfall was to release the Nightmare King on the Nevernever and the rest of the world.

"Maybe we could talk to him." Keirran sounded hopeful. "The Nightmare King. I know he's been asleep for a long time, and I know he wants revenge on the Nevernever, but if we could reason with him, maybe we could come to some sort of understanding."

"An understanding?" Grimalkin sniffed, fixing a bright gold gaze on all of us. "The Nightmare King is lost to madness," he said. "You saw him, did you not? In the final battle below In-Site? Even asleep and half-mad, he spoke to you through his Nightmare creature and warned of what would happen when he awoke. Do you not remember what he said?"

I did. I remembered that terrible moment when the hulking form of the Elder Nightmare turned, and I was suddenly staring into the eyes of something more ancient than I could comprehend.

"I will destroy all." Even asleep, the Nightmare King had made the ground tremble with his words. *"All dreams will die. This nightmare I find myself trapped in will finally end. I hear the ripples of the world above. I hear the voices calling. The screams, the anger, they pull me from this dream. Soon, I will be among them. Soon, all will know my rage. All will be darkness, and the ones who betrayed us will know nothing but terror. Wait for me, dreams. I will be there, soon."*

"If the Nightmare King wakes," Grimalkin went on, "there will be no reasoning with him. That Nightmare King wants only to destroy and cover the world in darkness. I am afraid that, should you meet him in the waking world, he will not hear you."

"So, the only solution is to kill him." Keirran did not sound happy.

"That, or find a way to keep him from waking up," Ash said. "Whatever we decide, we are going to have to find him, regardless. Nyx, is there someone who might know where the king is? Did Evenfall have a court?"

"It did," Nyx replied slowly. "Not in the sense that Summer and Winter have courts, but the king did rule Evenfall from his castle in the Forest of Mist."

"The Forest of Mist?" Puck repeated, and wrinkled his nose. "Typically, anything with *mist* in its description is either on some other weird plane of existence that doesn't conform to normal space or is an absolute pain in the ass to find."

"Have you ever been there, Nyx?" Keirran asked.

Nyx frowned. "Yes," she said, as if memories were just start‐ing to return. "I believe… I was at the castle a lot. I'm sorry, I am just starting to remember my life in Evenfall before the Lady, and some things are coming back slowly." The assassin seemed to ponder the situation before she gave a solemn nod. "We need to find the Nightmare King," she said. "That is the only certainty I know. I can guide you to the Forest of Mist to look for the castle, but I think it could be a long way. There is no guarantee the king will be there, but it is our best lead."

"That sounds like a plan," I said, and glanced out of the cave, where darkness still shrouded the land in night. "I would sug‐gest we wait until daylight, but I'm guessing the sun never rises in a realm of nightmares."

"You are very astute, your majesty," Nyx said, and Puck groaned.

"Oh, I just love it when there's no sun," he muttered, and blew out a gusty breath before looking up with a wide grin. "Okay, well, since we don't have to wait for a morning that will never arrive, I suppose there's nothing left but to get on with it."

"How has Evenfall survived with literally no glamour?" Keir‐ran wondered as we followed Nyx through a forest that looked like every horror movie set in a dark, creepy wood. Skeletal trunks crowded us, branches and twigs reaching out like claws, snagging hair and clothes. The sky overhead was pitch-black, but the spaces between the trunks were lit with a flat gray light, outlining silhouettes and eerie shapes in the trees. I lost count of the times I thought I saw a figure in the corner of my vision, only to find nothing there when I turned my head. It was *not*, I decided, like being in the wyldwood, the great tangle of forest surrounding the Faery courts. The wyldwood was dim and murky, with vivid splashes of color against a perpetual gray backdrop. It, too, played tricks on your eyes, making you see movement or figures that might or might not really be there. But walking through the wyldwood felt...*surreal* was the best way to describe it. Like you were in a dream. The wyldwood was alive; it was dangerous, beautiful, and forced you to pay attention to it.

This place felt dead. Lifeless.

"I don't know," Nyx replied in answer to Keirran's question. "When the Lady and her circle closed the way to Evenfall, they also erased it from everyone's memories. They intended for the realm to Fade, along with the Nightmare King and every Evenfaery who lived here. It *should* have Faded away. Without glamour to sustain it, I don't know how the realm survived." She gazed around at the haunting forest, a pained look crossing her face. "This...is all wrong," she murmured. "I am glad to be home, that Evenfall still exists, but...it shouldn't be here. The Evenfey shouldn't be here. We should have Faded long ago."

"Hey." Puck stepped up, placing a hand on her shoulder. His green eyes were surprisingly intense as Nyx turned to him. "What does it matter?" he asked. "Who cares *how* it survived— it did. It took the Lady's plans for genocide and spit in their face. And the Evenfey are still here. Despite everything, they're hanging on." One hand rose and pressed against her cheek. "So, no more talk of Fading, huh? You deserve to be here as much as anyone else. Evenfall survived, and the Evenfey still exist. Trying to figure out *why* things are in Faery is just a surefire way to give yourself a headache."

Nyx arched one silver brow, though she gave him a faint smile. "Is this your solution to most things, Goodfellow? Ignore them and pretend they don't exist?"

"Most things, yeah." Puck shrugged. "I was going to offer to shove glamour down your throat if you started to Fade, but I might've ended up with a knife in the eye. Or the groin. And that just sounded painful." Puck gave her a wry grimace before sobering. "You're not allowed to Fade on us," he told her. "If you start, just imagine me being sad and mopey for the rest of my life, until ice-boy gets so fed up he stabs an icicle through my heart to stop my whining."

Beside me, Ash snorted. "If that was a viable choice, I would've done it years ago," he muttered.

Nyx shook her head, then leaned forward and kissed Puck on the lips, very briefly. "I'll keep it in mind," she said in a soft voice, pulling back. "Though I will point out that, while we might not be in danger of Fading, without access to any glamour, things will be much more difficult."

"And yet, you continue to stand here and keep talking," Grimalkin said from atop an old stump, "instead of moving toward a solution. We will never find the Nightmare King if certain fey continue to…" He trailed off.

"Well, don't keep us in suspense, Furball," Puck said, turning toward the stump. "I assume you meant to say 'be distracted' but—oh, he's gone."

We all tensed, hands falling to our weapons. Everyone, even Nyx, knew that when the cat disappeared, something was coming.

Silence fell for several heartbeats. We backed into the shadows, watching and listening for sounds of pursuit.

My skin began to crawl. Something was moving through the distant trees. Something enormous and bulky that, impossibly, made no sound as it almost glided through the air. As it slid into the open, I bit my lip to keep the sudden fear and horror contained. I did not frighten easily anymore. I was Queen of the Iron Fey. I had lived in the Nevernever for a while now. Nowhere near as long as Ash or Puck, but I had seen my share of the weird, the scary, and the grotesque. I'd fought everything from dragons to trees to giant snakes. But this creature, much like the world around it, seemed to have come straight out of a nightmare.

It was longer than it was tall and had a body disturbingly reminiscent of a giant insect. Multiple jointed legs stuck out at strange angles, though when I looked closer, I realized they weren't legs at all but thin, bony arms with long fingers grasping at nothing as it crawled forward. The body itself looked pale and featureless, until I saw what it was made of.

Skulls, hundreds of them. Animal, human, and faery alike, all jumbled together into one massive, nightmarish beast of bones and teeth and empty eye sockets. Tendrils of hair and bits of fur trailed from the skulls, giving the creature a mangy appearance, and the smell of rot and grave dirt drifted toward us on the breeze. A distended neck, ending in the bleached skull of a horse, swung slowly from side to side.

Nobody moved. I don't think anyone breathed.

The skull-insect thing continued into the forest, its terrible body shockingly graceful as it glided over the ground. It moved like it was half wraith, half maggot, squirming forward but somehow barely touching the tops of the bushes as it crawled. Its long neck swung toward us, the horse skull disturbingly small against the bloated body, and an eerie sound, like a wail being muffled by pillows, emerged from the gaping jaws.

I clenched my teeth and did not move a muscle, despite the chills running up and down my arms. I could feel Ash tense beside me, his entire body coiled and ready to strike. The creature continued its distorted wriggling flight into the darkness until it was no longer visible, but nobody relaxed for several long minutes after it had disappeared.

"Okay," Puck whispered when we were sure the creature was well and truly gone. "What was *that*? Is this how it's going to be from now on? Every beastie we run into is some sort of awful Nightmare monstrosity?"

"Nyx?" Keirran looked at the assassin. "What are we dealing with? Was that a fey or something else?"

"I...don't know," Nyx said, sounding concerned and frustrated. "I'm sorry, your majesty. I don't think it was fey, but I've never seen it before." She stared in the direction the monster had disappeared, eyes narrowed. "There were always disturbing creatures in Evenfall, but nothing like that. Unless I've forgotten more than I realized. However..."

She gazed around the forest, furrowing her smooth brow. "I am starting to recognize this place. If we keep going, we'll reach the Sinking Swamp, and if I'm not mistaken, Stilt Town is close."

"A town," Ash repeated. "That could be helpful. But do you think anyone is still alive out here?"

"I don't know," Nyx replied. "But I would like to see for myself. If there are still Evenfey around, they would know more about what has happened to the realm in the time I've been gone. They might even know where the king is."

I nodded. "Then we should try to find it."

My heart was still pounding. Ash reached down and curled his hand around mine. I could feel the strength in his fingers, the silent comfort because he knew I was on edge, and I squeezed his hand. So far, Evenfall was proving to be horrifically disturbing, but at least Ash was with me. Nyx, Keirran, and Puck were here as well, and Grim would pop up eventually. We were always stronger when we were together.

A bone-chilling wail echoed from the direction the Nightmare had disappeared, making the hairs on my arms stand up. Silently, we followed Nyx into the trees, and the eerie moans faded into the night.

★ ★ ★

I smelled the swamp before we saw it, the pungent odor of stagnant water, mud, and rot. We came out of the trees to see the remains of a town spread before us. At one point, either the swamp had crept forward and swallowed most of the town, or it had sunk into the muck. Structures lay half-buried in mud and brackish water, rotting wood and thatched roofs poking up from the glassy surface. Another town had been built atop the skeletal remains, with walkways and platforms strung between the ruins, covering the surface of the water like a rickety web. It was a jumbled mess of shanty town, sunken village, and city on stilts, all dripping with moss, algae, and the clinging smell of bog water.

We stopped at the edge of the water, gazing at the cluster of dilapidated buildings before us. A rope bridge led from the forest into the town, the bottom planks barely clearing the surface of the water beneath. I was certain that my boots were going to be submerged trying to cross it.

"Oh," Puck remarked. "How charming. Really gives you that rustic, fishy, scum-covered feeling."

Nyx scanned the town with troubled eyes. "I think this is Stilt Town. It used to be the last settlement before you crossed into the swamp. But it wasn't like this before. The swamp has… grown."

"Does anyone still live here?" I asked, searching for movement atop the bridges, ladders, and platforms. "It looks like it's been abandoned."

"I see light," Keirran said, squinting as he gazed across the water. "Not much, just a candle or two, but that should mean someone in there is still alive, right?"

Before Nyx could answer, a chilling wail echoed from the forest behind us. It rose above the trees, several voices crying out in agony, before drifting away on the wind.

Puck flinched, and we all turned to stare at the darkness. "Don't look now," he muttered, as a rattling sound drifted to us through the branches. "But I think our monster friend is on to us."

Ash nodded. "Move," he ordered. "Everyone into the town."

We hurried across the bridge, which did indeed sink into the water under our weight, drenching my boots and the bottom of my coat. Across the bridge, the actual town became a labyrinth of walkways, structures, and narrow alleys between lean-tos. We ducked into one cramped, narrow corridor and peered back the way we'd come.

"I don't see anything," Keirran said. "Maybe it didn't notice us after all."

A cold wind, smelling of dust and rotting things, blew into the alley from the forest. As it did, the town around us...stirred. As if dozens of eyes suddenly turned our way. Beyond the lapping of water and the creaking of planks under our feet, I heard the faintest skittering sound.

"It's coming," Ash muttered, as that clammy chill raced up my back. He drew his sword, bathing the dark alleyway in the glowing blue light of the ice blade. "Everyone, spread out," he ordered. "It's one creature—it won't be able to follow us into tight spaces very well. Use that to your advantage, and we can slow it down."

A bloated, pale form rose out of the trees beyond the edge of the swamp. The Nightmare, looking like a hideous giant insect, swam through the air toward the town. Multiple jaws gaping, it let out a piercing wail that made my blood curdle, and shot toward us over the water.

"Go!" Ash said, and the five of us scattered. Puck and Keirran drew back, vanishing down another alley, and Nyx disappeared into the shadows. I turned and slipped between a pair of rickety buildings with Ash, drawing my sword as I did. He gave me a fierce, determined look over his shoulder, silently asking if I was ready. I met his gaze and nodded.

The Nightmare wailed as it came in, a hundred voices shrieking at once. Instinctively I reached for my glamour, opening myself up to the magic of Faery. The deadness in the air shocked me, reminding me that we were no longer in the Nevernever. This was Evenfall, and we were on our own.

With shocking speed, the Nightmare slammed into the space between buildings, reaching for us with a scream. Bony talons stretched into the alley, and Ash responded instantly, slashing the arm with his sword as it came in. As the Nightmare pulled back with a shriek, I darted forward, ducked beneath Ash's arm, and plunged my sword into one of the wailing skulls. The skull shattered, and a wisp of something dark rose from the fragments and dissipated on the breeze.

As it did, I caught the faintest hint of magic, like a familiar smell, before the wind blew it away. Whatever it was, this Nightmare possessed magic that was absent everywhere else.

The Nightmare recoiled, backing out of the alley while trying to cover its many faces with its arms. As it pulled back, it changed. The body pulsed and writhed, skulls shifting and reforming themselves, becoming narrow and thin. It no longer resembled a bloated maggot but a bony, long-armed centipede. The horse skull at the front opened its jaws with a chilling scream and plunged back into the alley with us.

I took a breath and felt the last of my glamour rise to the surface, making the air around me crackle. If this monster couldn't be killed by swords or blades, we would see how it fared with a bolt of lightning to the face.

A hand on my arm made me pause. "Wait," Ash told me as I glanced up at him. "Not yet. It's too cramped to fight in here. Fall back and regroup with the others."

I nodded, and we fled, retreating from the monstrous creature slithering toward us. The Nightmare skittered along the wall, rattling off planks and loose boards, long strands of hair snagging on nails and sharp edges.

Ash and I ducked and wove through narrow spaces and tight corridors, hearing the scrabble and screams of the monster behind us, until we reached an open platform over the dark waters of the swamp. Whirling around, we stood shoulder to shoulder, watching the Nightmare snap a pair of low-hanging beams as it spilled onto the platform. With a hiss, it reared up, skulls and bones towering over us, the horse head gaping as it slithered forward.

A trio of spinning crescents flew through the air and struck the creature's side, shattering skulls into a dozen bone fragments. With a screech the monster twisted around, just as Puck leaped from a nearby roof and bashed several skulls while Keir-ran stepped out to bring his sword smashing down through the creature's middle. More skulls shattered and burst apart, raining bone fragments everywhere, and more tendrils of darkness coiled into the air before writhing into nothing.

Ash and I lunged forward, striking with our blades, severing skulls and cutting through flailing arms, forcing it back. Darkness swirled around me, and rage poured from this creature, its poisonous glamour leaking into the air and making me gasp. The creature radiated the glamour of Evenfall; anger, fear, hatred, despair. Like the Elder Nightmares we'd fought before.

As I realized this, the Nightmare screamed. Rearing back, it exploded, skulls flying outward until it was no longer one mass but hundreds of swaying heads. Dozens of skulls stared down at us, held together by long black strands, like a hydra made of bones and hair.

As we backed away, I became aware of a new sound: a scratching, chittering noise, coming from all around us. Dozens of feet and claws scrabbled over wood as a swarm of small, furry bodies appeared on the tops of the buildings, bridges, and wooden platforms.

I drew in a sharp breath. They looked like rats. Enormous, bipedal rats with glowing red eyes, tattered ears, and long naked tails. Their hairless fingers clutched simple weapons, like spears, slings, and bows and arrows, and their red eyes shone with intelligence as they leaped and scuttled forward. Chittering madly, they bared long yellow incisors at the monstrous Nightmare looming overhead, and the Nightmare wailed, its swarm of heads weaving frantically as it tried keeping track of so many enemies.

Puck staggered back a pace, eyes wide as he stared at the army of rat things. "What in the world?" he gasped, his voice nearly lost in the storm of wailing, scrabbling claws, and aggressive squeaks. "What kind of Pied Piper hell is this? Now we have to deal with rats as well as hair horrors?"

"No!" Nyx dropped from seemingly nowhere, landing in a crouch beside us. "They're not enemies," she cautioned as she rose, gazing at the army of rats with a sudden recognition. "Don't hurt them," she called, as Puck and Keirran glanced at her in surprise. "They're Evenfey."

With a flurry of squeaks and chitters, the rat swarm attacked. Spears, darts, and stones flew at the Nightmare, some missing the frantically waving heads, but many striking true. Skulls cracked, fractured, and imploded from the storm of projectiles, releasing a mist of dark glamour into the air.

The Nightmare howled and thrashed, skulls striking out madly. I dodged one swooping head and lashed out at another, cutting through a dog skull and splitting it in half. Furry bodies were flung through the air as the flailing heads struck rats from their perches, sending them tumbling into the water or crashing into walls.

As more skulls were destroyed, the dark mist grew thick on the air. I reached out for it, and the pulse of glamour coursed through me, angry and choking. But it was magic, the Nightmare glamour of Evenfall, and my own powers rose up in response.

"Stranger!"

A raspy voice caught my attention. I turned and saw one of the rat creatures, crouched on a crate, peering up at me with beady red eyes.

"The heart," it squeaked, pointing back to the writhing Nightmare. "In the center. Destroy the heart, and the Nightmare will fall."

The rat leaped off the crate and scampered away, and I spun back toward the battle. The heads still swirled and lashed out frantically, striking rat and friend alike. But in the very center, where the hair and fur converged, I could see a cluster, a tangled knot throbbing with a faint light. With the storm of skulls around it, it would be nearly impossible to hit.

"Ash!" I called, smacking away a serpent head as it lunged at me, fangs gleaming. "We need to clear out the heads! Or at least give me a clear shot at the center!"

He nodded but didn't turn, busy dealing with four skulls at once. After striking down the last head, he darted to one side, circling the Nightmare. A swarm of heads followed him, and on the other side, Keirran and Puck baited a cloud of skulls into attacking them, leaving the center exposed.

The sky overhead flickered. Energy surged in the air, and I brought a spear of lightning straight down into the center of the monster. Bones and hair ignited, and planks burst into flame as strands of lightning pulsed outward. The Nightmare let out a horrific, ear-piercing scream, which cut off as its remaining skulls burst and rained bone fragments everywhere. The pulsing, hair-covered knot in the center flared, then exploded in a burst of shadow.

Glamour filled the air, a ripple of power and rage fluttering over me as the Nightmare died. The rats surrounding us rushed forward in a furry mob, swarming over the Nightmare's remains, snatching bone bits, clumps of fur, even strands of hair. For a split second, I wondered if they would take them as trophies, but then I saw they were *eating* them, stuffing them into their jaws one after another.

"Ew, I think I'm going to be sick," Puck muttered, appearing beside me. Keirran and Nyx joined us, watching the rat creatures gorge themselves on the Nightmare's remains. "This is... yup, definitely going to be sick. Excuse me while I hurl."

I shuddered, forcing myself not to turn away, as the grisly feast continued. In seconds, every part of the Nightmare was consumed, down to the tiniest bone chip. Slowly, the swarm turned, beady eyes glowing red in the darkness. Ears and noses twitching, they stared at us, curious and wary.

Remembering the one that had spoken to me, I stepped forward, causing several to skitter back and bare long yellow incisors. Ignoring the flashing teeth, I stood tall and met the beady gazes of two hundred rats. "We mean you no harm," I told the army before me. "My name is Meghan Chase, queen of the Iron territories in the Nevernever. Are you… Evenfey?"

Several of them blinked. Glances were exchanged, naked tails swishing over the planks as they chittered at each other. Finally, one edged forward. I couldn't tell if it was the same rat from before; they all looked pretty much the same. I did notice this one carried a spear and wore a necklace of teeth, but in the craziness of battle, I hadn't been concerned about what the rat who'd spoken to me was wearing.

"We are Skitterfolk," it told me in a creaky voice. "This is our town. What is the Nevernever?"

I blinked. "You've not heard of the Nevernever?"

"No," the rat, or Skitterfolk, confirmed. "You are strangers. You are new to us. You…" It raised its head, whiskers trembling as it sniffed the air in my direction. "You are not like us," it stated. "You have the magic. Like the king's offerings. But you are not like them, either."

"The king's offerings," I repeated. "Do you mean the Nightmares?"

"The king's offerings," the Skitterfolk insisted. It made a chittering sound, seeming frustrated that I didn't understand. "Strangers speak oddly. Skitterfolk do not know their words." It took a step back, raising one scaly claw. "Come. Come, and speak to our Palefur. She has the words to make you understand."

I glanced at the others. Puck shrugged. "Sounds like their version of an oracle or priestess," he said. "Either way, perhaps she can tell us what the heck is going on in Evenfall."

I nodded and turned back to the Skitterfolk. "Lead on, then."

The rats surrounded us, but I felt it was more out of curiosity than aggression. We followed them through the dilapidated, waterlogged city, crossing multiple bridges and swaying platforms, until we came to an old shack on the edge of town. It jutted over the water on stilts, looking like anything stronger than a sneeze would cause it to tumble into the swamp. Bones hung from the roof like wind chimes, and a tattered gray cloth had been drawn over the door.

The Skitterfolk leading us held up a claw. "Wait here," it told me. "Strangers are too big. Might cause the Palefur's house to fall into the swamp again. I will tell the Palefur you have come. If she is not sleeping, she will be out to meet you."

It turned and vanished through the door of the ancient hut. A few minutes later, the cloth parted, and a thin old rat stepped through. True to her name, her fur had turned pure white, though most of it had fallen out, showing scabby, wrinkled skin beneath. Her eyes were milky, and her withered claws were curled around a staff topped with a bird skull. She raised her head, nose twitching as she sniffed the air, and her lips curled back from her curved yellow teeth.

"Strangers," she said in a high-pitched, raspy voice. "They do not smell like us. They do not feel like us. I smell..." Her whiskers worked frantically as the rest of the horde watched in silence. "Glamour," she said at last. "That is not from the king. Strange magics." She sneezed, making several rats jump, then shook her head and peered sightlessly up at us. "Who are you?" she asked. "Where do you hail from?"

"We are not from Evenfall," I told her. "We come from the other realm. The Nevernever."

"The Nevernever," the Palefur stated. "I know not of this place. But there are legends. Stories of another time, about a world like and not like ours. Where the glamour did not need to be harvested—it was free to all. It flowed from the very ground, saturated the air, and the fey took it in with every breath they breathed."

A murmur went through the crowd behind us, but the Palefur snorted. "Fantasies," she said with a wave of one twisted claw.

"Stories and legends do not keep us alive. Maybe they did once, a long, long time ago. But now, there are no more stories. There is no more magic. And it does no good to dwell on what cannot be. This is the world we exist in now."

Nyx stepped forward, her gaze intense. "Your people said the Elder Nightmares were the king's offerings," she said. "What did they mean by that?"

"The king sleeps," the Palefur said. "Somewhere far away. Somewhere unknown and unreachable. But while he sleeps, he dreams. And his dreams manifest and roam this land. The strongest of these dreams are his offerings—what your kind call Elder Nightmares. They are for our survival, a bit of his own glamour to keep us alive. We hunt them, but the offerings, the Nightmares, hunt us as well."

"Isn't that dangerous?" Keirran asked. "What happens if you can't kill them?"

"We lose many Skitterfolk to the king's offerings," the Palefur said. "Each fight, each battle, more of us fall. But the Nightmares do not kill, no. They corrupt. They madden. They turn us into creatures like them. For each Skitterfolk that falls to an Elder Nightmare, a new creature is born, twisted and mad with hate. They turn on their former kin, and we are forced to destroy them for good. They are not the king's offerings. They do not have the power of the Elder Nightmares, but they are no longer fey."

"So, you have to hunt these Elder Nightmares for the glamour you need to live," I said, trying to follow along. "But the Elder Nightmares will turn normal fey into smaller, less powerful Nightmares if they kill them."

"That's not confusing at all," Puck muttered sarcastically.

"Yes." The Palefur bobbed her head. "The king's offerings are powerful. We lose many this way. But we would lose all if the Elder Nightmares disappeared. The king knows. He sleeps, and he delivers glamour to us the only way he can."

"So that is how the Evenfey have remained alive all this time," Nyx mused. "The Elder Nightmares are their source of glamour, but they have to kill them to release it."

"Yes," said the Palefur again. "The king takes care of his people, even though his dreams are terrible in their grief and rage. We have accepted it. We are grateful for his sacrifice, even though we must fight and kill to survive."

"Uh, not to alarm anyone," Puck said. "But...what happens if the king wakes up?"

The horde at our back broke into a storm of alarmed chittering and sounds of frightened dismay. The Palefur bared her yellow teeth at Puck.

"Do not speak of such things," she rasped. "The king is the only reason Evenfall exists. He is our lifeline—his offerings are the only source of glamour in this entire barren world. If he wakes, there will be no more Nightmares, and thus, we will all Fade and cease to exist."

I drew in a horrified breath. The gravity of the situation descended all at once, threatening to crush me. If the king's Nightmares were the only way the Evenfey could survive in a world empty of glamour and magic, what could we do? If we somehow killed the Nightmare King, the Evenfey would die. If he woke up, the Evenfey would Fade.

"Strangers." The Palefur was staring at us with blank eyes that were suddenly filled with a grim understanding. "You are not from this world," she mused. "You come from...the other place. A realm beyond Evenfall. But why have you come here, if the balance has not shifted? If your own world is not in danger?" She paused, long whiskers trembling for a moment, before she asked: "Does...does the Nightmare King wake?"

I swallowed. "Yes," I said simply, and the horde at my back broke into another cacophony of terrified squeaks and chitters. "Something happened in our world to cause a ripple effect that reached Evenfall and the king. He is waking up, and he threatens not only the existence of Evenfall, but our own world in the process. I don't want to endanger an entire realm of Evenfey, but I must keep my own world safe."

"The king must be kept asleep," the Palefur hissed, almost desperately. "He cannot be allowed to wake. Strange queen, you must find a way to put him back into his endless slumber, or we are all destined to Fade into nothingness."

"How?" Ash questioned. "How do we stop him? Is there a way to put him back to sleep?"

"I do not know." The old Palefur let out a long breath, seeming to shrink in on herself. "It has been many years since I have spoken to anyone from outside our haven. The Skitterfolk do not dream of grandeur. None of my own warriors have ventured beyond the swamp. I know only that if the king wakes, we are all lost."

"There must be someone who can tell us more about the king," I said. "Does this world have its version of oracles or seers? Someone who might know how to help us?"

"None that I am aware of, but..." The Palefur chewed a ragged claw in thought. "There was...a city, once," she said slowly, as if recalling something long forgotten. "In legend and story, it was a bastion of understanding. A hive of secrets and forbidden knowledge, where information was hoarded like gold, and words were used as currency. The greatest mass of information was said to exist at the very center, a collection of knowledge through the ages. Words written in languages no one can remember..." She paused, twitching her whiskers. "The city, if it still exists, might have the information you seek. Though the name of the city has been lost to time. I do not remember what it is called."

Nyx straightened. "Hollownest," she whispered. "I remember."

"Hollownest?" Puck frowned. "I don't think I like the sound of that." His nose wrinkled. "But then again, I don't like the sound of *any* of these places. Hollownest, the Sinking Swamp, the Forest of Mist. Is there one place in Evenfall with a happy-sounding name?"

"The library," Nyx said, ignoring Puck. "Hollownest has a massive library at the very center of the city, the largest and grandest in Evenfall. Back when I still lived here, fey would travel from all across the realm to seek the knowledge contained in the library. It was said that there was not an answer to any question the library did not have, if you had the patience to search for it. The librarians were very jealous of that knowledge, however. There were rumors that certain places within the halls were forbidden to everyone. That they held secrets no one should possess or understand."

"Sounds like a good place to learn how to put the Nightmare King back to sleep," Keirran said.

"If I can find it," Nyx said. "I...think I remember where Hollownest is. The city is in a part of Evenfall known as the Grave Lands. If we can make our way to the Grave Lands, we'll find the entrance to Hollownest."

"Then you already know where you must go," the Palefur said. "Find your way to Hollownest, if it still exists. Find the keepers of the forgotten lore. Beware the Elder Nightmares that roam the world, but also beware of those whom the Nightmares have slain, who now roam the land as Nightmares themselves."

She shot a split-second glance at her own people, clustered behind us, concern in her milky eyes as she shook her head. "It will not be safe for you to journey to Hollownest," she went on. "But it will not be safe for you anywhere. Rachitik," she said, glancing at the Skitterfolk who had brought us. After a moment, I realized that was his name. "Take the strangers to the old bridge over the sunken city. It is not the safest way out of the swamp, but it is the fastest."

The Skitterfolk from before stepped forward with a nod. "It will be done, Palefur."

"We appreciate your help," I told the ancient Skitterfolk. "If there is a way to keep the king in eternal sleep, we will find it. We will not let you and your people Fade into nothing."

"Perhaps you will at that." The pale rat opened her jaws in a yawn that bared all her cracked, yellow teeth. "I am going back to sleep," she announced. "In the endless nothing, I feel no hunger or pain. And if I Fade away while I slumber, that is the best any of us can hope for. Farewell, strangers. I wish you luck. Though your quest sounds impossible, I will hope that you will find a way to save this world, and us. And if you do reach the king, remember the Skitterfolk kindly. You might be the only ones who do."

She turned and slipped back into the dilapidated hut, naked tail sliding over the soggy planks as she ducked through the door and the curtain swished shut behind her.

The Skitterfolk—Rachitik—turned to us with a grave look. "Come," he said. "I will take you to the bridge."

"Sounds like a good plan to me," Puck said. "No offense, but three hundred pairs of beady red eyes staring at you like you're the last chocolate donut in the box is a little bit unnerving."

Rachitik didn't answer. He simply turned and padded away, his curved claws clicking over the rotting planks and his tail dragging behind him. With nothing left to do, we followed.

The red eyes of the Skitterfolk watched us the entire way.

3

WARNINGS OF WOLVES

Outside the Skitterfolk city, we stood at the edge of a swaying rope bridge over the swamp. The tattered-looking structure, covered in algae and vines, hung twenty or so feet over the surface of the water and looked like it might snap at any moment. But that wasn't the cause of the concern sweeping through me.

Beneath the bridge, a massive sinkhole had opened in the center of the swamp, swallowing trees, vegetation, and even buildings. I could see the tops of roofs and towers where structures had tumbled into the hole and had either gotten stuck in the middle or had lodged themselves against the sides. I couldn't see the bottom of the sinkhole, but I did know that I wasn't entirely thrilled with the idea of walking across a giant hole into the abyss.

"Oh, this looks fun," Puck commented, peering down into the pit. "A rope bridge across an endless crevice, how quaint. You *know* it's going to snap when we're in the very center of it, right? It could have hung there, perfectly functional and safe, for hundreds of years, until you decide to stroll across it and *boom*, that's the moment it decides to snap. Does that happen to anyone else, or just me?"

I looked around for our guide and found he had already fled, scurrying back to his city and his kin. I could still feel their eyes, watching us from hidden nooks and crannies.

Remember the Skitterfolk kindly, the Palefur had said. *You might be the only ones who do.*

I will, I promised silently. *I will not forget your people, and the help they offered. I will remember.*

Thankfully, despite Puck's claims, the bridge did not snap when we were in the middle of it, though walking across it was nerve-wracking. I had no magic now. I had used the last bit of my power fighting the Nightmare. From here on out, we would have to get by without glamour.

A furry gray cat waited for us on the other side, curled up on a log with his tail over his nose, apparently asleep. Gold eyes cracked open as we approached.

"Finally." Grimalkin sat up with a yawn and a flash of sharp teeth, before settling back to give us an impatient look. "I thought you might have gotten yourselves eaten by the rat things. Did you enjoy yourselves in the city of vermin? I was certainly not going to set one paw inside that place. The smell of filth was bad enough."

"Aw." Puck grinned. "Was our widdle kitty cat scared of the big mean rats? I guess I can't blame you—if I were a cat, that's the last place I'd want to go." One hand rose to scratch behind his head. "Getting eaten by rats would just be embarrassing."

Grimalkin sniffed. "I was simply trying to avoid acquiring fleas, Goodfellow," he said, and Puck quickly dropped his hand. "Regardless, I assume you were able to discern where we must go next?"

"Yes," I said, and glanced at Nyx. "The city of Hollownest, and its Great Library, is our next destination."

"Hollownest." Grimalkin thumped his tail in thought. "It sounds…familiar."

I frowned. "How is that possible, Grim?" I asked. "You've never been here before. Until a couple days ago, no one had even heard of Evenfall."

"Incorrect." The cait sith gave me a superior look. "Until recently, no one could *remember* Evenfall," he stated. "Because of the nature of the Lady's ritual, the memories of Evenfall, the Nightmare King, and the Evenfey were erased from everyone's minds. However, as I am sure our Evenfaery assassin has realized, some memories are beginning to return. This Hollownest does sound familiar to me. Perhaps I had heard of it before the Lady sealed off Evenfall and everyone's memories were lost."

"I keep forgetting how old you are, Grim," I told him, and the feline sniffed.

"And I am constantly reminded of how rude and inexperienced you all are," Grimalkin returned. "In any case, we know Hollownest is real. Whether or not it is still there is a different story."

Puck frowned. "Why do I get the feeling this isn't a normal city?" he asked. "Also, why do I get the feeling I'm not going to like the answer?"

"Because you're not," Nyx stated, and sighed. "The city of Hollownest is underground," she went on. "Deep underground. And the residents there are… Well, one of the oldest, most common human phobias is a fear of—"

"Oh no," Puck immediately said. "No. No, no, no. Are you telling me that this is a city full of giant bugs?"

"They are fey," Nyx replied. "They're Evenfey, so they're not animalistic. Everyone in Hollownest is very polite, actually. Or at least, they were when I lived here. And their Great Library is supposed to be the greatest collection of knowledge in Evenfall. But…yes. Essentially, we'll be going underground to meet a city's worth of intelligent giant insects."

"Oh," Puck said, and he suddenly looked rather pale. "Great. You know, maybe I'll stay here after all. That cozy cottage in the grove of screaming trees is sounding better and better."

"How long will it take us to reach Hollownest?" Keirran asked, ignoring Puck.

"I'm not entirely sure," Nyx replied. "Bear in mind, Hollownest is enormous. The actual city stretches for miles underground. There are multiple entrances scattered throughout Evenfall, but many of them are hidden. The entrances I know of might not be there anymore. And once we do find Hollownest, it might take us another day or two to reach the heart of the city, where the library is located."

"But you can get us there," Ash said.

The Evenfaery nodded. "I will get us into Hollownest," she assured him. "And we will find the library and ask its keepers for the knowledge of the Nightmare King. I just hope they'll have the answers we need."

I hoped so, as well.

Not long after we crossed the bridge, the swamps came to an end, to the relief of everyone in the party. The forest beyond the swamp was tangled and dark, with an eerie, constant haze that turned trees skeletal and accented the bleakness of the woods. It was oppressive in a way I couldn't put my finger on at first. Certainly, there were bleak, frightening places in the Nevernever. The farther I walked, however, the clearer the picture became. The forests of Faery, though they were still very dangerous, were alive, teeming with life and glamour. Even the human world had pockets of magic drifting around, glamour provided by the emotions and dreams of countless mortals. For most fey, being cut off or banished from the Nevernever was an eventual death sentence, as they would inevitably Fade into nothingness, but there was enough magic in the human world to sustain a faery for a while. How long depended on the faery's own strength and will to live, and some very strong fey were able to exist in the mortal realm for years, sometimes centuries, finding ways to glean their magic from somewhere without returning to Faery.

Evenfall felt dead. No, that wasn't exactly right. Evenfall felt like a shadow. Like a memory. Something that you could see, that you knew was there, but that had no substance. If I closed my eyes and really concentrated, pushing as deep into the land as I possibly could, I could feel a wisp of emotion. Something dark and painful, almost sad. But it was so faint, barely a breath of a thought, that it might have been my own fears and emotions coming to the surface. Evenfall was like a photograph, an image of a world that wasn't real. The hint of emotion I felt, whatever it was, might not have been there all.

I lost track of time. The sun never rose in Evenfall; the world remained perpetually dark, the sky without moon or stars to light the way. Nobody spoke much, not even Puck. Much like being in a nightmare, loud noises and drawing attention to yourself seemed dangerous. We followed Nyx as the Evenfaery wove an unerring path through the trees, a shadow that seemed perfectly at home in the looming woods of Evenfall. She was also vital to finding food in this strange, barren world, though what she returned with wasn't exactly what I would call appetizing. Mushrooms the color of flesh, covered in thin blue veins. Bulbous red fruit with cores made of teeth. Berries that looked like eyeballs, and so forth. Most of what she gave us, I would not even consider eating had she not insisted it was edible and safe. Still, I ate only when I had to, swallowed without tasting, and tried not to think about what I was putting in my mouth.

We were making our way through yet another forest, surrounded by shaggy black pines that eerily resembled some sort of furred monster themselves. It didn't help that the pine cones hanging from the branches were bone white, which only reinforced the image of bushy giants with crooked teeth looming above us.

The feeling of being watched crept over me. I caught a shadow from the corner of my eye, a ripple of movement in the trees, and turned my head. Of course, there was nothing there. Seconds later, it happened again.

"We're being stalked," Ash murmured beside me.

"Yes," Nyx said without turning around. "Keep moving. They're not going to attack quite yet. They might abandon the hunt if they decide we're too much trouble."

"What are they?" Keirran wondered. "Can we speak to them?"

"Wolflings," was the answer. "The Big Bad Wolf might be the most famous of humankind's fear of wolves, but he's not the only one. Here in Evenfall, we have our own versions." Nyx stared into the trees, golden eyes tracking the flitting shadows through the tangled undergrowth. "Normally, they're not dangerous. And they don't attack other fey without reason. But these are not normal times in Evenfall. I think we need to hope for the best and prepare for the worst."

"I don't like hurting wolves." Keirran sighed as a ghostly howl echoed from somewhere in the trees. "Real wolves in the human world don't attack people."

"Yeah, sadly, that's not true in the Nevernever," Puck said, pulling one of his daggers from nowhere. "The wolves we see in Faery are mankind's perceptions of them, however wrong they are. Take Big Bad, for example. Sure, he's all noble and friendly now, but a couple centuries ago, he ate a whole hamlet of farmers *and* their sheep. Nothing is black-and-white in Faery, princeling. Especially among those of us who can live forever." He shrugged. "What's that famous saying? In all stories, you either die the hero, or you live long enough to see yourself become the villain."

"That saying came from a Batman movie," Keirran said flatly.

"Doesn't make it false," Puck insisted, "and it happens to all of us, eventually. Even Yours Truly."

I frowned. Was that true? I had been living in Faery a long time now. Not as long as Ash or Puck, certainly, but long enough to build my kingdom and know the ins and outs of the Never-never. I thought of Mab and Oberon, faeries whose rule over their courts spanned millennia. Both had been cast as villains in many stories. Someday, would someone write a story about the wicked Iron Queen Meghan, who ruled her land with a tyran-nical fist and struck fear into the hearts of mortals and fey alike?

Another ghostly howl cut through the night, interrupting my musings. I could see them now, shadows gliding through the trees on all sides. With a resigned sigh, I drew my sword. I didn't want to fight, but I would not stand here and get torn apart by a pack of nightmare wolves, either.

"They're not attacking," Keirran mused, watching the tatters of shadow swirl around us. "Maybe they're trying to figure out how strong we are."

"Or maybe they're just picking out the weakest link," Puck added. "I guess that would be you, Furball...and he's already gone."

Ash stepped forward abruptly, his sword drawn but hanging loose at his side. "We are not prey," he said in a clear, firm voice. "There is no need for conflict between us. We don't wish to fight, but we will defend ourselves if we must. If you choose to attack us, your pack will not survive this encounter."

For a moment, there was no answer. The trees were eerily si-lent and still. I stood calmly next to Ash, watching the shadows, ready to bring up my sword if a pack of wolves rushed out at us.

There was a ripple of movement in the trees, and a creature emerged, seeming to melt out of the gloom. At first, it looked like a normal wolf: shaggy black pelt, lean body, furry ears and tail. It wasn't nearly as big as our Big Bad. In fact, it seemed a little small for a normal wolf. But as it drew closer, it gazed up at me, and the completely human eyes staring into mine made my stomach clench. For a split second, the darkness shifted, a bar of shadow sliding over its face, and I saw not a wolf but a hard-faced child on all fours, staring up at me. Only for a moment, a single heartbeat of shock, and then the creature was a normal wolf again.

I took a careful step forward, making sure to draw its attention but keeping my stance neutral. Nonaggressive. "I am Meghan Chase," I told it. "Ruler of the Iron Kingdom in the Nevernever. We don't want any trouble. We're just trying to pass through these woods."

The wolf regarded me with eyes that were still disturbingly human. Its muzzle wrinkled, lips curling back to reveal sharp white fangs. For another heartbeat, I saw the sneering face of the child overlaid with the canine. "Not one of us," it said in a breathy voice, and my jaw clenched at how young it sounded. "Not Nightmare. Not Evenfey. What are you?"

"Strangers to these lands," I replied. "We're trying to find our way to a city called Hollownest. Do you know of it?"

The wolf's ears flattened to its skull. It cringed, and the child cowered back like I was about to kick him. "Evil place," it growled. "Things crawl up from Hollownest. Searching, seeking. They can feel your heartbeat, hear your breath. If they catch you, they will drag you back with them. Into the earth, and the tunnels close behind them. Beneath the ground, they will bury you there. No one who goes beneath the earth comes out again."

"Well, this just gets better and better," Puck remarked, causing the wolf to bare its fangs at him. "I'm really looking forward to visiting Hollownest now."

"Where are these tunnels?" I asked the wolf. It shook its shaggy head.

"You cannot find them," it told me. "When the snatching things return underground, the earth closes behind them. Even if you dig until your paws are bloody, you will find only soil."

"So, the only way into Hollownest is to get grabbed by one of these insect body snatcher things?" Puck asked. "That's a great big *nope* for me. There has to be another way."

"There used to be entrances to the city throughout Evenfall," Nyx said, frowning thoughtfully as she stared at the wolf. "Hollownest used to be a place of knowledge, and fey traveled far to seek it out. Are there no clear paths into the city any longer?"

The wolf didn't answer right away. It gazed at Nyx with solemn human eyes, as if trying to figure her out. "You are different," it said at last. "I smell no strangeness inside you. You are like us, who must hunt the king's offerings to survive."

"This used to be my world," Nyx said quietly. "I was part of Evenfall, like you and your kin. But it was...different, when I lived here. I haven't been back in a long time."

The wolf's expression didn't change. "How long?" it asked.

"My memories are scattered," Nyx replied. "Many of them have faded, but now that I'm here, they're slowly coming back. I remember Hollownest as a thriving city of thousands. It was underground, but there were lush forests and icy caverns and lakes so deep no one had ever seen the bottom. It was hard to believe how big it was. All roads and paths eventually led to the very center of the city, where the Great Library held all the secrets of Faery collected over millennia." For a moment, she sounded wistful, her voice soft and distant. But then she shook herself and turned back to the wolf. "Those are my memories of Hollownest," she said. "Are they different from yours?"

The wolf stared at her in blatant disbelief, then gave a snort and bared its fangs. "Are you certain you have been here before?" it asked. "The city is empty, except for roaming Nightmares and the mad. No one goes there willingly, and those that are taken never return to the surface. It has been that way since before we can remember. The Hollownest you describe has never existed."

Puck scowled, but Nyx just gave a somewhat sad smile. "It was...a very long time ago," she murmured.

"Regardless," Ash broke in, "we need to get there. Is there

any way into the city without having to be dragged beneath the earth?"

Both wolf and child blinked at him. "If you truly wish to find Hollownest, you must travel to the sunken city," it replied. "In the center of an ancient temple, it is said there is a winding staircase without a bottom. Supposedly, it goes down to the void, but passes through Hollownest on its way. Beware, though. The sunken city is also full of Nightmares. Occasionally, one will stray beyond the borders, and our pack is able to bring it down. But within the land itself, there are too many Nightmares to handle. The risk of attracting more than one is very high. If you do reach the sunken city, tread carefully, lest the very earth collapse beneath your feet."

I nodded. "We appreciate your help," I told the wolf.

"We return to the hunt," it said, and the shadows around us melted back into the trees, making no sound as they did.

In seconds, the wolf creatures were gone, and we were alone.

I stood in the doorway of a ruined tower, gazing out into the endless night of Evenfall. It had been hours, or maybe days, since we had run into the Wolfling pack and learned that we needed to head toward the sunken city. Fortunately, Nyx knew where she was going, though she admitted to not remembering an entrance to Hollownest within the city itself. But Evenfall was different now, and it was the best lead we had, so we'd take it.

We encountered no more fey or Nightmares as we pushed through the forest. Eventually, we stumbled upon an ancient stone tower beside a cold mountain spring. After making sure nothing lived in the tower, we stopped to catch our breath. The tower was crumbling, and moss grew on the walls like a fuzzy carpet, but the second floor had a few beds that weren't completely disintegrated. To my complete delight, Puck even managed to scrounge up an extremely hard wheel of cheese, some rock-like bread, and a string of jerky packed in salt. In the mortal realm, any food in a tower this old would be rotten or nibbled away by rats or bugs. But time was a funny concept in Faery, and often didn't work the way you thought it should. It seemed Evenfall followed the same rules. Or lack thereof.

The bread was hard and tasteless, and the jerky strips were like chewing on salty leather, but it was leagues better than flesh mushrooms or eyeball berries. I would never complain about boring rations again.

Later, gazing out into the forest, I wondered what kind of normal creatures had roamed Evenfall, and if they still existed. I hadn't seen any deer or rabbits or even birds flitting about the forest as we traveled. Did the Evenfey need regular food, or did they survive completely on the glamour from killing Nightmares? I thought of the Skitterfolk, and the Wolfling pack we'd encountered. Both groups had been wary but helpful, not like the mobs of violent, maddened fey that had come pouring out of the unsealed portal into the Nevernever. The fey that the Elder Nightmares had killed and turned. Was that the fate of all Evenfey, eventually? Or would they simply Fade and cease to exist?

I felt a presence a moment before Ash slipped his arms around my waist from behind. He didn't say anything, just drew me to him and held me close. I closed my eyes and leaned against him, letting his solid presence soothe some of the tension pressing down from all sides. In the mad, chaotic sea that was everything Faery, no matter how stressed or angry or upset I was feeling, Ash was my rock.

"Where are Puck and the others?" I asked, keeping my voice barely above a murmur.

"Upstairs," was the equally quiet answer. "Currently in a debate about who should take watch tonight. I think all three are trying to convince the other two that they should try to get some sleep while they can."

I chuckled. "Who do you think will win that argument?"

"Given how stubborn those three are? Hard to say." Ash shook his head in amusement. "But I think it's fair to assume that the only one who will get any sleep tonight is Grimalkin."

I smiled at the ridiculous truth of that statement, then leaned into him with a sigh. "Well," I mused. "Here we are again."

"What do you mean?"

"We've done this before." I gestured out the doorway, indicating the eternal night beyond the frame. "Another prophecy. Another realm on the brink of destruction. And us, having to venture into the unknown to somehow stop the end of the world and save Faery."

"We do seem to end up at the forefront of all of these catastrophes," Ash agreed, sounding vaguely amused. "But this is no different from the war with the Iron fey or the Forgotten. Another type of fey has risen up to tear down the structure of what we know. It's either stop them, or be destroyed ourselves."

"But that's my point," I said. "This keeps happening, Ash. The Iron fey, the exiles, the Forgotten, and now the faeries of Evenfall. They were all part of the Nevernever once. None of them wanted what happened—they were trying to survive, too. If the Iron fey had been accepted by the courts from the beginning, would Machina have felt he had to destroy Summer and Winter to exist? If the Forgotten hadn't been ostracized and ignored, would they have turned to the Lady and her promises to save them? And the Evenfey have been hurt the most. The Lady and the sidhe of old sealed off their entire world, hoping the Nightmare King and all his subjects would Fade away. And for what? Because she *thought* he was going to destroy them. Because she was afraid that he was becoming too powerful. All of this misery has been caused by Faery fearing and shunning anything that is different."

Ash stroked my hair, cool fingers sliding through the strands. "I've seen it in Tir Na Nog as well," he murmured. "The eternal war between the Summer and Winter fey always leaves someone wronged or swearing vengeance. But we can't change the past, Meghan. What Machina and the courts and the Lady tried to accomplish...it's already done. We can only deal with the present as best we can and hope our actions can stop what others have set in motion."

I didn't reply, pondering what he had said and the events that had led us here. I knew he was right. The past was the past, and we could only keep moving forward. But there had to be *something* we could do to stop this kind of event from happening again. Faery didn't like change, especially the centuries-old, stuck-in-their-ways kings and queens of the Nevernever, whose laws existed simply because tradition dictated "this is how it has always been." But something had to give. Or were we destined to repeat the same mistakes for the rest of time, until one of these doomsday prophecies finally came true?

Maybe it already had.

I sighed and reached back, sliding my fingers into my husband's dark hair. "At least you're here," I mused. "I don't have to do this alone. I can stand against any monster and Nightmare if you're beside me."

"Always," Ash murmured, pressing his lips to the side of my neck. I turned in his arms and kissed him, feeling his arms tighten around me. In this world of horror and fighting for our lives, I would take advantage of these moments when I could; I didn't know how many we would have.

The quiet sound of someone discreetly clearing their throat broke us apart. I looked back to see Keirran at the bottom of the stairs, politely not staring at us. I sensed no discomfort from the King of the Forgotten; he had grown up seeing his parents' affection for one another and never had any reason to be embarrassed.

"I have been sent to inform you that Puck and Nyx have decided to take watch tonight," he said a bit wryly, fully sensing the irony that he, a king of Faery, had been sent to deliver this message by a jester and an assassin. "Currently, they are both outside, one on the rooftops, the other who knows where, and they strongly suggest that the three of us get some sleep while we can."

Ash snorted, showing how unlikely *that* would be. Keirran chose to ignore that.

"Also," he went on, "Nyx was able to remember a bit about the Grave Lands and wanted me to extend this warning. They are, as one would expect, a blasted, rocky place with many species of undead, skeletal-type fey wandering around. It might be difficult to distinguish between what is a fey and what is a Nightmare, but she cautions against attacking creatures solely because they look frightening."

I nodded. "We're not going to get into any fights if we can help it," I said, and he visibly relaxed. "We don't have access to any magic here, so if even a small Nightmare spots us and decides to attack, my plan is to run away and not engage. Discretion very much seems the better part of valor right now."

"I'm worried for Nyx," Keirran confessed. "Puck is, too. Without glamour, she could Fade away on us at any time."

"She's strong," Ash said. "And this is her world. She knows it far better than we do. Besides, Puck won't let that happen. If it comes to that, he'll poke and prod her to the point where she's so irritated she *can't* Fade away, even if she wants to."

Keirran nodded, but his brow furrowed, and the shadow hovering behind his eyes grew darker. He stared out the doorway into the forest, his jaw set and his lips pressed tightly together.

"Keirran," I prodded. "Something is bothering you. What's on your mind?"

"I…" He sighed. Shaking his head, he turned to us again. "I've been going through this scenario in my head again and again," he said in a bleak voice. "There's no good answer. There's no winning for any of us."

"What do you mean?" Ash asked.

"Evenfall relies on the king's Elder Nightmares to live," Keirran said. "Somehow, they're keeping the fey of this world alive when they should have Faded eons ago. If we kill the Nightmare King, we save the Nevernever, but the Evenfey will die because there will be no more Nightmares for them to hunt, and thus no more glamour. If we don't kill the king and he wakes up, he'll destroy the Nevernever and possibly take his vengeance on the mortal realm as well. Maybe we can put him back to sleep, but even that feels wrong. The Nightmare King and the Evenfey are victims of the Lady's callousness and fear. She sealed this world because she was afraid of the Nightmare King and his power. I can understand his anger—the Evenfey did nothing to deserve this. Making sure the king doesn't wake up just ensures Evenfall will continue on...like this. Where their only source of glamour comes from killing Nightmares. If we can't open the seal because that will wake the king, we're dooming the Evenfey to a life of misery and struggle. So..." Keirran made a frustrated, helpless gesture. "I don't know what to do. I don't see how any of this will have a happy ending."

"I know, Keirran," I admitted. And with that, the fear, uncertainty, and dread that had been plaguing me ever since I entered this world rose up like a tide. "Believe me, I want to make things right. What the Lady did was unspeakable. And the Evenfey shouldn't have to live like this. But the king *is* waking up," I went on. "And he does intend to destroy the Nevernever when he does. We can't allow that to happen, either."

"Maybe Grimalkin is wrong," Keirran said. His voice had gone very low, and I figured it was in case the cat was listening. "Hearing the Evenfey speak of the king...they think he's their savior, that he is the sole reason for their survival. That doesn't sound like someone who is lost to madness. Maybe there is a way we can reason with him."

"And if there isn't?" Ash wondered. "If we reach the Nightmare King, and he is too far gone to hear us?"

"Then we do what we must."

This last was from Nyx, who suddenly appeared in the doorway and surprised us all. Keirran turned to her in shocked amazement as the assassin slid into the room. "My king," she said, meeting his gaze. "I know you want to help us. I know you want to set things right in Evenfall. But I fear it could already be too late. You don't feel the land like I do. Evenfall..." Nyx sighed, gazing back at the looming forest, a pained expression crossing her face. "It feels dead," she stated. "Like it doesn't really exist at all." She paused a moment and took a few breaths, as if with that statement she was finally admitting a truth she hadn't wanted to see. "I honestly do not know how Evenfall has survived," she continued at last. "I was happy to be home at first, but...something feels wrong here. This is not the world I remember. I am starting to wonder if it's even real."

"Uh, the beasties we fought earlier were certainly real," Puck said, sauntering into room. "Unless the bruise that is my whole body is just my imagination." Seeing us, he gave a cheerful wave and a shrug. "I saw everyone was getting together and I didn't want to be left out, especially if there's a party. But I am confused as to why some of us seem to think the monsters we're fighting aren't real. They feel real enough to me."

"Even if they are," Nyx murmured, "what is left for us here? A realm that is dead, and a king who is lost to us."

"What are you saying, Nyx?" Keirran asked.

"That some things cannot be undone," the assassin said, though admitting it sounded painful for her. She stared at the floor, eyes unfocused, and when she looked up again, her gaze locked with Keirran's. "I agreed to lead you through Evenfall to find the Nightmare King," she said. "I did this knowing that he is very likely unkillable. That he has gone mad within his nightmares, and if he wakes, he will destroy the Nevernever and possibly the real world. And with all the fear, anger, and hatred being generated in the mortal realm, he would be powerful enough to do it. Even before Evenfall was sealed, the Nightmare King was more than fey. More than the ruler of a realm. He was, quite simply, a god."

Her gaze flickered to Puck for the briefest of moments. For a single heartbeat, regret and something deeper shone from her eyes, before they hardened once more. "We are very likely not coming back from this mission," she went on. "I knew that. I accepted it. But I still chose to lead you through Evenfall, because I knew that, even if the Nightmare King was unstoppable, you would do everything in your power to save the realm that could be saved. Right now, I am not certain Evenfall is that realm."

Keirran seemed stunned into silence. Even Puck gazed at the Evenfaery in surprise. Nyx took a quiet breath and let it out slowly before she spoke again.

"I know you will do the right thing," she said, looking at me now. "But when we stand before the Nightmare King, whatever we decide, there can be no hesitation. If we hesitate, all the realms will suffer for it. I am prepared to face my old king knowing I will most likely die. I will forfeit my existence to ensure Faery survives, if that is what is called for."

I met her gaze as Puck straightened and tensed. The eyes of the assassin were bleak but resolved. She had already made the choice to stand with the Nevernever to stop the Nightmare King, even if it meant turning her back on her home. Nyx was not Keirran. There was no wavering, no second thoughts, no hoping for an outcome that was impossible. She was coldly practical on what needed to be done, even if it was killing her on the inside.

"Nyx," Puck said quietly. "You don't have to do that."

"I am dedicated to seeing this through," the Evenfaery replied, still holding my gaze. "Whatever it takes."

Are you? was the assassin's silent question. Not a challenge. Just the quiet affirmation of where she stood. Nyx was expecting to die facing the Nightmare King. She wanted to make sure we were as committed.

"I am," I told her softly. "I will admit, I don't know the answer here, Nyx. I can't foresee what will happen when we find the Nightmare King. I know we cannot allow him to wake, and I know we have to help the Evenfey. But if the worst happens, I can tell you without hesitation, I *will* defend my world and those I love to the fullest extent of my power."

"We all will," Ash said. "You don't have to worry about that." His gaze flicked to Keirran, standing a few paces away. The Forgotten King's expression was conflicted, but as Nyx turned toward him, he took a deep breath, eyes hardening, and gave a single nod. "Yes," he said simply. "As you said, we do what we must. I have those I want to protect, too."

"Then perhaps we should stop wasting time with pointless sentiment," Grimalkin said, sauntering forward. Gazing around at us all, the cat sniffed and twitched his tail. "I had thought a path had already been chosen," he commented. "There is no use in lamenting the unknown, or what cannot be. Conversely, Forgotten King," he added, narrowing his eyes at Keirran, "I am *never* wrong. The Nightmare King must be dealt with, one way or another. If this ancient library truly holds the secrets of Evenfall, then perhaps it contains the secret to defeating him, as well."

"And if it doesn't?" Keirran challenged him.

"Then going there is still a better plan than rushing in blind and hoping to hit something along the way."

"Oh, I don't know." Puck sighed. "That's how my plans always go."

After a fitful rest, we left the tower, following Nyx through a forest that continuously mumbled or whispered words that were just faint enough to be audible. I lost track of the times I thought I heard my name somewhere in the trees. Gradually, the undergrowth began to thin, until the forest eventually ended at the edge of what I could only assume were the Grave Lands. As

Keirran had said, they were a flat, barren expanse with rocky outcroppings jutting from the earth like obsidian shards. The grass was dead and withered, and the few trees here were bent, twisted, and bare of leaves. Scattered throughout the plain, the skeletons of giant creatures poked from the ground like the remains of dinosaurs.

"Well, this is cheery," Puck remarked. "You know, I think I saw a picture of this place under the definition of the words *dismal* and *depressing*."

"It's called the Grave Lands," Keirran said. "Were you expecting butterflies and balloons?"

"Ah, you jest, princeling, but that would probably be even more terrifying."

Movement flickered among the rocks, and some kind of canine skeleton creature went trotting across the stony landscape. It paused and observed us with hollow eye sockets, the bones of its body bleached completely white, before it turned and hurried off. Its bony paws made faint clicking sounds over the rocks, until it slipped behind a boulder and disappeared.

We kept walking. The terrain didn't change over the next couple hours, the blasted, barren landscape continuing on. It wasn't until we walked past a field that vented steam from somewhere below the cracked earth that we saw something different.

The ruins of an ancient town, broken walls and crumbling watchtowers silhouetted against the horizon greeted us as we left the steaming plateau. From a distance, there were no lights, no columns of smoke, no smells or sounds or signs of life anywhere past the wall. This place, like many others before it, seemed abandoned.

Keirran glanced at Nyx. "Is this the sunken city?"

"I...don't know." The Evenfaery frowned as she observed the sprawling ruins. "It *was* a city, once. I seem to remember... lots of statues."

"Oh, and let me guess." Puck snorted. "Some of them came to life."

Nyx shook her head. "Not here," she said, completely serious. "You'd have to go to the village in the Staring Forest to experience that. Though I'd recommend you have quick reflexes—they come to life only when you're not looking, and they move very fast."

"Ah, you know what? That's okay." Puck shuddered. "I will be avoiding the 'I'll never sleep again' town."

As we drew closer to the ruined gates, the top of the watchtower seemed to move, a ripple flowing across the roof like a beast alerted to something's presence. Looking up, we saw the tower was covered in dozens of crows, silently watching us with beady eyes as we passed beneath.

"Oh, hey there!" Puck raised an arm in a cheerful wave. "My friends, how's it going? See anything interesting? Any good gossip lately?"

The crows stared at him in baleful silence. Puck sniffed. "Guess they haven't heard anything juicy."

We ducked beneath the gate, entering a broken city of ruined stones, shattered roads, and half-crumbled buildings. Skeletal structures rose into the air, some of them seeming to defy gravity as they loomed over us. I glanced between the rooftops and caught sight of a large structure that, for all intents and purposes, looked straight-up like a wizard's tower.

And like Nyx had said, the city was filled with statues. Stone figures, most of them broken and unrecognizable, stood on every corner, limbs and heads lying in the weeds. But even their numbers were small compared to the true residents of this place.

The crows. They were everywhere. Clusters of them perched on rooftops, on walls and pillars and exposed beams. They sat on headless statues or peered down from broken windows, muttering to each other. The air was filled with the sounds of grinding beaks and ruffling wings. Glassy black eyes watched our every move.

"I remember this place now," Nyx said. We had reached a square, surrounded by broken towers and the shells of buildings. An ancient fountain stood in the center, stagnant water filling the pool at the bottom. "I believe it was called Cruach at one point, though the Cruach I remember had fey living there."

Keirran, watching the clusters of birds perched overhead, narrowed his eyes. "Were there always this many crows hanging around?"

"Hey, there's nothing wrong with crows," Puck said. "Crows and ravens get a bad rap from mortals. Have you noticed in every spooky movie there's that ominous shot of the lone crow cawing from the trees?"

"Yes," Ash said dryly. "Must be that whole portent-of-death thing."

Keirran, still staring at the birds, shook his head. "I don't like the way they're watching us," he muttered. "I don't think these are normal crows—"

A section of crows perched on the corner of a building launched themselves into the air with a flurry of guttural cries. I jumped, then watched as the flock spiraled above the rooftops and began to descend toward us. We tensed, hands falling to weapons, as the crows swarmed the top of the fountain, cawing, wings and talons flailing, trying to find a spot to perch. For a moment, I couldn't see anything through the mass of flapping wings and feathers. Then, the cluster of birds seemed to fuse together into one. Bodies stilled, voices died, and a creature turned toward us atop the fountain. A lanky, humanoid crow, its arms ending in scaly talons, spread its dark wings for balance atop the stones and tilted its head at us, beady eyes sharp and curious.

"Food?"

Its raspy and guttural voice sent a warning tingle skittering up my spine. The eyes of the crow were bright with hunger. It shifted on the rocks, long talons leaving white gashes in the stone as it edged closer, opening and shutting its beak with a snap.

Puck stepped forward. "I got this," he told me, and smiled at the bird creature atop the fountain. "Hey, friend," he greeted it, and the crow turned hollow eyes on him. "We're just passing through, but I'm sure we can help each other. Check this out." He held up a hand, a black feather pinched between two fingers. "See? I'm one of you guys. Practically."

The crow stared at him, silent. Ash tensed behind me, his voice a warning. "Puck, look at the rooftops," he said.

I glanced up, and the glittering eyes of dozens more crow creatures stared back. Talons crushed the edges of the roofs and wings fluttered restlessly as the dark clusters of birds peered down at us with murderous intent.

"They're going to attack," Ash said, fingers curling around his sword hilt. "Everyone, be ready. They'll likely swoop down from above."

"Oh, fine." Puck sighed, daggers appearing in his hands. "Man, I hate to do this. Crows are usually smarter. But these guys don't look like they're going to listen to reason. Watch your eyes," he warned as the crow atop the fountain opened its beak with a hiss. "If I know crow tactics, they'll go for shiny things first."

My heart sank, but I stepped back with Ash and drew my sword. The dim light glittered off the bared blade, and the crows around us started to flap and flutter wildly.

"Stop!"

5

ANIRA

The voice rang out over the courtyard, coming from the sky, a moment before something dark swooped down and landed in front of the fountain. It looked like a massive crow before it rose, pushing back a feathered cowl, and the face of a beautiful woman stared out at us. Her jet-black hair looked like pinions, her eyes were like onyx stones, and a pair of dark wings settled behind her like a cloak.

The mutterings from the rooftops ceased, the fluttering stopped, and the crows became as still as gargoyles. The bird woman gazed around the now silent square, her eyes focusing on the crow perched atop the fountain. With a caw, the creature turned into a cluster of birds, which scattered into the air in every direction, shedding feathers that drifted lazily to the ground. In seconds the flock had vanished over the rooftops.

The woman turned to us. "I apologize for the crows," she said. Her voice was raspy but not guttural, and the gaze that met mine was sharp with intelligence. "Over the ages, they have become increasingly animalistic, to the point where they have almost forgotten how to be themselves. Please have mercy on them—they were not like this before."

"I'm glad you arrived when you did," I told her. "We didn't want to kill anyone. It isn't our intent to cause harm to your city."

"Not my city." The crow woman shook her head. "But we are all that are left. I am called Anira," she said. "I have not seen strangers pass through here in many, many ages. Where do you come from?"

"A place called the Nevernever," I said, and her thin brows shot up. "You have heard of it?"

"The other side of Evenfall," Anira whispered, sounding faint. "I thought it was a legend." Her sharp black eyes stared around at us, taking everyone in. "You have all come from the Nevernever?" she went on, sounding incredulous and hopeful at the same time. "I felt something several days ago, a change in the wind. Does that mean...the way is open?"

"I'm sorry," I told her, guilt stabbing me as her face fell. "The seal was broken, but only briefly. We had to close it again, to stop the Nightmare King from waking up."

Her expression turned to one of horror. "The king cannot wake up," she whispered. "If he does, the Nightmares will cease. And the crows will truly lose themselves forever." She gave us a sharp look, as if suddenly realizing something. "Is that why you are here in Evenfall?" she asked. "Do you wish to slay the Nightmare King and kill us all?"

"No." I shook my head. "We're trying to find a way to stop him that doesn't end in the destruction of the Evenfey *or* the Nevernever."

"We're looking for Hollownest," Nyx added. "We know the entrance is in the Grave Lands somewhere."

"You'll be looking for the Sunken City, then," the crow woman replied. "But without wings, it will be extremely difficult to get to, perhaps impossible." She touched a delicate hand to her chest. "I have flown over the Sunken City many times—it is a haven for Nightmares and those who have been destroyed by them. Many of my own crows have lingered too long above the city towers—you see the state of their minds, now. Besides the Nightmares, there are even worse horrors, things that crawl up from the earth, snatch the living, and burrow back into the depths. They can feel the vibrations of your passing and track your steps. Touching the ground in that city is a death sentence. You will not reach the entrance to Hollownest if you go in by foot."

"Would you be able to help us?" Keirran asked softly.

She regarded him thoughtfully, black eyes giving nothing away. "Come with me," she said, turning back to the rest of us. "It is not safe to talk here. The crows are listening. We will go to a place where we can speak freely." She paused, tilting her head at us in a very birdlike manner. "I...suppose we must walk there. This way."

We trailed the crow woman through the old city, following narrow corridors that snaked and twined through the stone like game trails through the forest. All around us, perched on roofs and fences and the shattered remains of ancient statues, the crows watched us pass, beady eyes flat and hungry as they stared down at us.

"Hey, come on, guys," Puck said as we passed the ruins of another old fountain. The statue in the center was impossible to see through the gang of black feathered bodies perched on it. "We're good, right? I love crows. I mean, I'm practically one of you."

The crows watched him balefully, then broke into a cacophony of guttural caws as they scattered. Puck watched them vanish into the city and behind the tops of the shattered rooftops, then grinned. "They'll come around eventually."

"Where are we going, if you don't mind?" Keirran asked the crow woman. She gave him another inscrutable look, then pointed a thin finger toward the rooftops overhead. To the tower in the center of the city.

Keirran followed the pointing finger and blinked. "Is that your home?"

"Our home," Anira replied. And from the dozens of crows circling overhead as she said this, she did not mean us. "We did not build it, of course. It was empty when I first came to this city. My mate said it once belonged to an old faery who liked to study the stars. We simply moved in."

"What happened to the stargazer?" Nyx asked.

"I do not know," Anira said. "The stargazer was here for a long time, according to the crows who came before. They did not like him. He kept cats, you see."

I suddenly realized Grimalkin was not with us and had not been for a while. Maybe that was a good thing, though. Anira the crow woman obviously did not hold any love for cats.

She led us to the base of the giant structure. Overhead, I could hear wood groaning faintly in the wind, as if the whole tower could topple at any moment. A simple door stood beneath an archway, but rubble had piled up in front of it, and the wood itself was rotting and cracked. Anira blinked at the doorframe, as if the state of it was new to her.

"I do not believe I have ever used this entrance," she murmured, sounding amused. "It has been decades since I have had to…walk…for any length of time. How does one get through a locked door? I don't think I've ever had to do that."

"Well, there are ways," Puck told her. "You can pick the lock, you can turn into something small and try squirming underneath, you can try using magic to get the door to change its mind about being locked—"

Ash stepped forward, put his shoulder to the wood, and bashed it open.

Puck rolled his eyes. "Or you can do that."

Beyond the frame, a series of rickety steps spiraled up into the dark. Many steps were broken, with large gaps between them. Even more than the tower, the whole thing looked ready to collapse at the barest whisper of a breeze.

"Hmm." Anira had not stepped through the frame with us and was peering up at the staircase from the doorway. "It looks so much taller from the ground," she mused. "Perhaps it is best if I leave you here and meet you at the top of the tower."

Stepping back from the door, she pulled up the cowl of her hood, and then her body twisted, seeming to collapse in on itself. It shrank down, shedding feathers, until a large crow raised its wings and flapped into the air. Swiftly, it rose above us until its feathery black body blended into the night and disappeared overhead.

Puck gave a wistful sigh. "She seems nice," he said. "You know, this place isn't so bad. I could definitely see myself staying here. Hanging out with the gang, soaring through the city on the wind currents, sharing carrion bits over firelight... It sounds kinda—"

Nyx turned her head and gave him an unreadable look. The smirk fell from his face. "Uh, I mean, except for the murder crows and the distinct lack of beautiful moon elf assassins, that is. I certainly don't have any intent to stay and hang out with... another crow... Wow, is it warm in here? Let's keep going."

We started up the creaking staircase, which was just as rickety as I'd feared. Every step groaned loudly, and in a few places, the entire staircase leaned or swayed to the side. I set my jaw and kept my steps as light as I could, hoping the inherent grace from my faery side would carry me through. Puck and Ash, though both were taller and bigger than me, demonstrated the unfair advantage of being faeries their whole lives, moving instinctively with the swaying stairs and making it look ridiculously simple. Keirran, too, navigated the staircase with the elegance of someone who had grown up in the Nevernever. Nyx, of course, didn't even make the steps squeak.

When we finally reached the top after climbing a short ladder and pushing back a trapdoor, we were greeted by a surprisingly cozy room. Overhead, a ring of catwalks and platforms encircled the room, leading to open windows with an unobstructed view of the night sky. On the ground floor, a tiny living area had been assembled with an armchair, a table, and several bookshelves that were mostly full. I noticed, as I gazed around the room, that there were no beds. Or at least, no human beds. There were, however, perches set up everywhere, jutting out of walls or standing on their own, feathers and questionable white splotches beneath. Thankfully, all the perches were empty, the flock of crows nowhere to be seen.

"Please excuse the mess." Anira came into view, back in her more human form. She watched patiently as we all crawled through the trapdoor into the room, then gestured at a very moth-eaten couch in the corner. "We can sit, if you like. Again, the concept of sitting in a chair is strange for me. But since I am fairly certain you do not want to perch, I do know how to seat myself."

I glanced at the moldy, white-spattered couch and smiled. "We can stand."

The crow woman nodded. "I appreciate that you would come here," she began. "Given the nature of the other crows, I am glad that you would trust me at all. Are you truly from…the other side? What is the mirror realm called again?"

"The Nevernever," Keirran said. "And yes, we do come from there. Well…" He glanced at Nyx. "Not all of us."

"Yes," agreed the crow woman, looking at Nyx as well. "I feel you are the same as the rest of us who call this world home. These strangers possess lingering magic, but you…you have that same emptiness within. And yet you have been to this Nevernever." She cocked her head again, looking distinctly birdlike. "What is it like, this other world?"

Nyx gave a sad smile. "I could tell you," she said, not unkindly. "But it won't change what happened here. It won't return Evenfall to the way it was."

"No." Anira's thin shoulders slumped. "You are right," she whispered. "And if I cannot see this other world, what is the use in pining for it?" She sighed, pushed back her feathery hair, and looked at me again. "I can help you, queen of the other world. If you wish to travel to the heart of the Sunken City where the entrance to Hollownest lies, you will need more than bravery, luck, and magic. The ground is too treacherous to venture far into the city." She raised her arms. "You will need wings."

"Oh, is that all?" Puck grinned at the rest of us. "That doesn't sound too hard. Some of us *have* wings."

"Only if you use your own glamour," I reminded him. "Which none of us have right now. Or at least, not enough to matter."

He shrugged. "It doesn't take much to become a bird, princess. Try exploding into a few dozen that scatter in every direction. *That* takes talent."

From the corner of my vision, I saw Ash roll his eyes before looking at Anira. "Are you saying you can give us the ability to fly into the Sunken City?" he asked.

"Yes," she confirmed. "But I fear there is a condition, and a favor that comes with it. Right now, I don't have the magic necessary to grant you wings. It will take a lot of glamour—a lot of power—to give all five of you—"

"Four," Puck reminded her, holding up that number of fingers. "Just four." The fingers switched to a thumb, pointing at himself. "Don't worry about Yours Truly."

"To give the *four* of you," Anira corrected herself, "the ability to fly. Magic does not come naturally to the fey of this world. I have the skills, the ability, and the willingness to do this, but I don't have the power. There is only one way to retrieve the glamour needed for this venture."

She paused, and the room was silent for a moment, before Ash raised his head.

"We have to kill a Nightmare."

Anira nodded. "I am sorry. But it is the only way. The king's offerings are terrible and dangerous, but if you are able to slay one, they do release an extensive amount of magic and glamour. Enough for me to grant all of you the ability to fly."

Puck groaned. "Oh, great. That's what I wanted to do with my weekend—fight a nearly unkillable monster in a world where I don't have the ability to heal." He gave the rest of us a mock disgusted look. "You know, I blame all of you for this. Why haven't any of you learned how to become a bird? It's so useful."

"So we have to kill a Nightmare," Keirran mused. "Do you know where we can find such a creature?" he asked Anira. "I know they wander the land, but will we have to travel all the way to the Sunken City to run into one?"

She shook her head. "There is one...not far from here," she said, in a voice that made Ash narrow his eyes. "It makes its lair in a nearby park, but sometimes it comes aboveground to prey on us. Many years ago, I lost my mate to this Nightmare. I have wanted it destroyed ever since, but neither I nor the crows who live here are strong enough to kill it ourselves."

"So that's why you're willing to help us," Ash said. "You want us to kill this Nightmare for you."

"I want to help you," Anira said, looking straight at Ash, "because this world is dying. Or perhaps it is already dead. I have not known another existence, but..." Her brow furrowed, her eyes becoming haunted as she gazed at us. "But I see you, I hear your stories, and for the first time, I feel something else. I feel hope." She shook her head, feathers ruffling softly against her face. "I don't even know what I hope for," she admitted. "I cannot imagine a world that is different. But whatever it is, whatever that looks like, it has to be better than this." She raised an arm, indicating the walls around us, the sickly moon peering through the shattered windows. "We are but shadows," she whispered. "Everything in this world is Fading or losing itself. Deep down, I have always sensed that there was something missing. That this can't be all there is." She stood straighter, chin raised, gazing at Ash. "That is why I want to help."

He gave her a solemn nod of respect and looked at me. I stepped forward, drawing her gaze. "We will kill this Nightmare for you," I told the crow woman, who slumped in relief. "And you will give us the ability to fly into the Sunken City, is that the bargain?"

"Yes," whispered the crow woman. "A favor for a favor. Those are the right words, yes? That is how it works in your world, as well?"

Puck sighed. "More or less," he groaned. "Just give me a second to powder my nose so it can be smashed in a second time tonight."

6

ANIRA'S NIGHTMARE

We left the stargazer's tower, heading down the creaking stairwell and back into the city streets. The crows were waiting for us, perched on rooftops and crumbling walls and the dozens of broken statues scattered everywhere throughout the city. Low mutters and guttural caws filled the air as we emerged from the tower, and baleful eyes glared down at us from every angle.

"Feeling a bit unwelcome again," Puck said, frowning at a pair of birds watching us from the branches of a dead tree. "You sure we can't come to an understanding? If you guys just got to know me, you would like me."

"Why are you so concerned about the crow population in this city?" Nyx wanted to know. Despite her serious look, she sounded amused. "This is not the Nevernever, Puck. And those are Evenfey, not normal crows."

"I know that. It's the principle of the thing."

"Anira said she'd meet us when we reached the ground level,"

Keirran said, gazing around at the slowly gathering birds. "I hope she gets here soon—we seem to be attracting a lot of attention."

A lone crow suddenly swooped down from atop the tower and landed on a broken fence post with a caw. Ruffling its feathers, it gazed around at the mobs of other crows perched everywhere and let out a very harsh, guttural cry. Several of the other birds took to the air, flapping away over the rooftops, and the rest of them turned their gazes from us, as if interested in other things.

I smiled and nodded at the crow, which cocked its head at us in a familiar, birdlike manner. "All right, Anira," I said. "Lead on. We'll follow you."

The crow turned, raised her wings, and fluttered away down the street.

We trailed Anira through the city, keeping our gaze overhead as she flitted from statues to pillars to corners of ruined buildings. None of the other crows bothered us, though they still watched us with barely restrained hunger and hostility, muttering or growling under their breath as we passed. As we went deeper into the city, however, the crows disappeared. I wasn't quite sure when it happened, just that we were walking down an alley, following Anira, and when I looked up again, every branch and rooftop was empty.

"The crows are gone," Ash muttered at about the same time. "They're scared of this part of the city."

"Yes," Nyx agreed. "We're close."

We came to what looked like it had been a small city park. Buildings and ruins disappeared entirely, and the ground became overgrown, weeds and brambles pushing up and choking everything. In the center of the overgrown park, a pond glimmered in the moonlight, but the waters were scummy, covered in algae and slime.

The crow that was Anira landed on a snapped tree limb, ruffled her feathers, and smoothly changed into her more human form. "There," she whispered, pointing with a trembling finger at the glimmering black waters. "That's where the Night-mare makes its lair."

"The lake?" Puck asked.

She nodded. "When you have killed it, bring me its head. It should hold enough glamour for me to complete the ritual that will allow you to fly."

"You're not staying, I take it," Ash said.

"I…" She trembled violently. "I am not a fighter. And I have seen what this Nightmare is capable of. I am sorry, but I must leave this fight to you. Please do not die."

"Die?" Puck grinned. "Obviously, you don't know us very well."

A cold wind blew across the pond, rustling the brambles around us. I smelled rot and decay and mold, but also something that reminded me vaguely of…wet fur.

Anira stiffened. "It is coming," she whispered, sounding ter-rified. "It is coming. Forgive me!"

In an explosion of feathers, she changed into a crow and flapped away into the darkness.

Keirran looked toward the lake, grimaced, and drew his sword. "Fighting another Nightmare," he muttered. "I don't think I'm ever going to enjoy this."

"Oh, why not, princeling?" Puck brandished his daggers and grinned. "You don't like getting your head stomped in by the nastiest, scariest, creepiest monsters ever to come out of the mind of the literal Nightmare King? Can't imagine why."

Cautiously, we walked toward the black waters. A ragged mist hung over the surface, trailing tendrils of fog that writhed into the air. As we watched, the mist scattered, as if blown away by a strong wind. The waters close to the bank started to bubble, and I put a hand on my sword hilt, ready for whatever horrific monster exploded from beneath the surface.

A cat walked out of the lake.

We all paused in wary confusion. The feline was skinny,

emaciated, its short fur dripping wet and fallen out in places. Its eyes were bulging and white, its jaws hanging slack. It looked like a drowned cat, come back to life for revenge on the person who killed it. An extremely long tail trailed behind it, and for a moment, I thought the tail was so long it continued back into the waters of the lake. But then the tail twitched, flinging away water drops, and the illusion was lost.

"Uhhhh..." Puck's voice broke the wary silence. "Okay, I'm just gonna come out and say it, then. What the hell is this? Is this the super scary Nightmare Anira was so afraid of? A dead cat? I mean..." He gazed down at the feline and wrinkled his nose. "It's a little disturbing, sure, and I bet Furball would think it's an unholy abomination, but I wouldn't call it a Nightmare. Though I guess cats *are* nightmares to most birds."

The dead cat hissed at him. Most of its teeth, I saw, were rotted out of its head, and the bones of one front paw showed through its fur. It crouched to spring away or attack, and a glittering shard of ice flashed through the air, striking the creature through the head and impaling it to the earth. I blinked and glanced at Ash, but it was Keirran who lowered his arm.

"We had to kill it," he said as his gaze met mine. "I wanted to put it out of its misery quickly. That is, however, the very last of my glamour. I won't be throwing anything else."

The cat slid down the icicle. Its body seemed to dissolve, flesh and skin peeling away, until only the skeletal remains of a cat were left, still speared through by the melting ice.

Puck snorted. "Easiest Nightmare we've ever killed," he said cheerfully. "Who's ready to head back and tell Anira the good news?"

Nyx frowned at him. "You know that wasn't the real Nightmare, Goodfellow," she said. "That's not the end of it."

"Oh, I know." Puck sighed. "I was just hoping."

The waters of the lake shuddered. Tiny ripples grew to larger waves that caused the scum and algae on the surface to bob wildly. Dark water splashed over the banks, and we all took a step back, as something huge emerged from the depths.

A bulky form pushed itself out of the water and lurched toward us, and I frowned. It looked like an enormous burlap bag, dripping with algae and bound with frayed rope. The sack itself wriggled and pulsed, as if hundreds of creatures trapped within were fighting to get out. Faint cries could be heard coming from the bag, desperate screams and yowls, making my stomach curl.

A head rose out of the water, bony and terrible, the half-rotted skull of a gigantic cat. White pinprick eyes peered from hollow eye sockets, yellow fangs jutted from exposed bone, and bits of wet fur clung to it as the massive head turned toward us and bared its teeth.

Nyx shook her head as the enormous Nightmare beast opened its bony jaws with a wail that made my teeth vibrate. "Does this count as Nightmare-worthy, Goodfellow?"

"Um, yep yep." Puck backed up, raising his daggers. "Definitely Nightmare-worthy. Completely, disturbingly, I-didn't-need-to-sleep-ever-again Nightmare-worthy."

The giant cat thing stepped onto the bank. Bony paws and hooked talons sank into the mud at the edge of the water. Algae hung from its body like green ropes, dripping water to the ground as it prowled forward. Behind the head, the burlap sack that was its body continued to writhe and throb, the muffled voices of hundreds of cats echoing in the damp air.

Beside me, Ash raised his sword. "Keirran, you're with me," he said. "We're going straight in. Goodfellow, Nyx, hit it hard while it's distracted with us. Meghan…?"

I nodded and took a quick breath to calm my heart. "I'll back you up."

The Nightmare cat screamed, a shriek that seemed to pierce right through my skull. It pounced, claws ripping deep gouges in the earth, but Ash and Keirran were already moving. Springing forward, they both dodged aside as the Nightmare lunged, ice blade and steel sword striking in unison. Keirran's weapon struck the monster's front leg as it swiped at him, and Ash's blade shot forward, hitting the creature in the side of the throat. Both weapons struck bone, leaving gashes across the surface of the skeleton, but not seeming to harm it. The Nightmare cat spun with feline grace, lashing out at Keirran, and the Forgotten King twisted away as those claws raked at him.

As it went after my son, I raced forward, leaped at the cat, and drove the point of my steel sword deep into the glowing eye socket. The tip struck the back of the skull, and the monster cat screeched as it whirled on me. This close, it stank of rot and death and wet fur, and I stifled the urge to gag as I retreated from the lashing talons.

With a yell, Puck dropped onto the monster's head from above and sank his daggers into the furry half of the decaying skull. They plunged deep, and when he pulled them out again, black ooze clung to the blades. "Oh, gross!" he yelped, leaping off as the Nightmare reared up with a shriek that sounded more enraged than hurt. Rolling to his feet, Puck shook his blades violently. "Ew, Nightmare brain juice, that's just nasty. Well, looks like the ambush is out."

The Nightmare stalked forward. Keirran lunged in, joining us as his sword clanged off the bony part of the cat's skull, making it hiss and shake its head. "I hate fighting undead things," he muttered as we leaped away from the questing claws. "You can never seem to hurt them. How do you kill something that's already a corpse?"

"Look for weak spots," I replied, dodging a talon and cutting my sword at the monster's chest. At the burlap bag that made up its body. The cat's head poked out of the top, but except for its limbs and tail, everything else was hidden in the sack. "The Nightmare in Stilt Town had a heart we had to destroy. Maybe it's the same here. Head, heart, brain, core, something like that."

"Well, it's definitely not following the 'stab them in the brain' rule," Puck stated, ducking beneath a bony claw. "What's that saying for a zombie apocalypse? 'If you don't see a hole in the corpse's head, put one there'? I don't think it applies to this big ugly."

The cat leaped back as my sword stabbed toward its body, and its blank, hollow-eyed glare turned on me. It opened its jaws with a scream, just as Ash came in from the side, leaped toward its skull, and brought his sword slashing down on its neck. The ice blade sheared cleanly through the spine, and the Nightmare gave one last yowl before its head dropped heavily to the ground, landing with a splat in the mud. Its jaws clenched and unclenched, as if trying to scream in rage, but then the pinprick lights in its eye sockets dimmed, and the head finally stopped moving. The headless body staggered, and we backed away, waiting for it to fall.

It did not fall.

Bony claws crushed the ground beneath it as the Nightmare regained its balance, rising up once more. It was now nothing more than a bulging sack with limbs and a tail, but the front of the sack turned toward us, severed spine poking through the top, and lunged.

"Okay, so strike 'remove head from body' off the list," Puck yelped as we scattered. The Nightmare followed us, slashing and raking wildly with its claws, seemingly enraged now that its head was gone. Puck danced around it, just barely avoiding the talons slashing inches from his head and face. "And I don't see anything that looks like a heart on the outside. I guess we're going to have to cut this thing open and see what the squishy inside is made of."

Keirran grimaced. "I don't think it's going to be anything pleasant."

He and Puck darted toward its middle, but the Nightmare leaped back, twisting its body out of reach. "Oh ho, I don't think the kitty wants us to pat its tummy." Puck grinned evilly as he circled around. "What's the matter, cat? Is the kitty ticklish?"

The Nightmare backed up, the front of the bag swinging from side to side, as if trying to keep an eye on all of us at once. Ash lunged forward, and the Nightmare spun toward him, lashing out with both claws. The talons screeched off the raised ice blade, and Ash drew back from the assault. But the Nightmare's right flank was fully exposed now, giving Puck the chance to dart forward and bring his daggers slicing across the bulging, wriggling sack.

A spray of clear liquid burst from the gash, arcing into the air, and Puck leaped back with a yell. Clapping a hand to his arm, he staggered away, jaw clenched in pain, making my stomach drop.

"Puck!"

We rushed to his side. The Nightmare was backing away, shaking and swinging its "head" wildly. Spatters of that clear liquid hit the ground, and where they did, the mud instantly bubbled and steamed. Puck slumped against a tree, gritting his teeth, one hand still cradling his arm. Steam writhed between his fingers, and the air around him smelled of decay and rot.

"Son of a bitch," he gritted out, and carefully pulled his hand away. The sleeve of his hoodie had been seared away, the edges blackened as if burned, or melted, and the skin beneath was a stark, angry red. "That kitty has some really nasty acid reflux."

Ash handed him the dagger he'd dropped. "Can you still fight?"

Puck winced. "Yep," he wheezed. "Though I'm not looking forward to slicing that thing open again. Really missing those daggers you can throw around, ice-boy."

Ash's face tightened, and he gazed at the Nightmare, still raging at the edge of the lake. "I don't have much glamour left," he muttered, raising his arm. "But I'll try."

"Ash, no." I pulled his arm down. "Conserve what you have," I told him. "You might need it later to heal. Or to save your life." His gaze was solemn as it met mine, but he dropped his arm and nodded. I took a breath and looked at the Nightmare. "We have to cut it open," I said, feeling the others' eyes on me as I raised my sword. "We'll just have to be really careful."

The Nightmare turned toward us. Bile or acid or whatever it was dripped from the gash in its side and ran from the front of the bag, making the ground steam below it. The sack was writhing feverishly, as if the cut to the fabric had incensed or made frantic whatever was inside. It stalked forward, and we tensed as it loomed closer, the smell of death and rot nearly choking us.

The monster gathered itself to lunge, and a pair of spinning crescents made of moonlight flashed through the air like shooting stars. They struck the Nightmare in the side, tearing through the thick canvas and continuing out the other side in a spray of clear fluid. The monster staggered, making heaving motions as if it was about to vomit, and the gash in the fabric widened.

Nyx dropped into view, seeming to appear from nowhere and making Puck start. "There you are," he breathed as she strode to his side, her golden eyes shadowed with concern. "Perfect timing as usual. What would it take for me to have my daggers just poof into my hands whenever I need them?"

The assassin's slender fingers gently touched his arm, her gaze probing. "Join the Order and spend the next two hundred years learning lunar magic," she replied absently. "And then survive initiation where your entire Order hunts you down through the night. If you live through that, you'll receive your bond blades. If not, you weren't skilled enough to join the Order in the first place."

"Oh," Puck said, and from his tone, he obviously hadn't expected an answer. "Is that all?"

"Everyone." Keirran's voice was a warning. He was staring at the still-heaving Nightmare, watching the tear in the side get wider and wider. The smell of death, decay and rotting flesh intensified, making my stomach churn. "I think it's about to get worse."

With a tearing, ripping sound, the burlap bag split open, and *things* spilled forth into the mud and grass. Cats. Dozens of them, maybe hundreds, the bodies making wet splats as they slid onto the ground like fish. Their fur was drenched and slick, plastered to their bodies, their eyes bulging and white.

"Oh," Puck said, sounding sick and breathless at the same time. "Drowned cats. Lots of drowned cats, and they're looking at us. You were right, princeling. This is far, far worse than the Nightmare."

The growing pile of wet, squirming cats broke apart. Staggering and clawing themselves to their feet, they gazed at us with frenzied eyes, then rushed forward with eerie screams and yowls. The wave of reeking bodies leaped up and crashed down on us, their shrieks ringing in our ears.

I slashed several from the air, seeing everyone else do the same, and dead cats rained down around us. But there were hundreds of them, coming from every direction. Furry bodies landed on me, wet and disgusting, sinking sharp claws and teeth into my skin. Being bitten by a cat is not fun; being bitten by a half dozen reeking of wet fur and decay was nightmare-inducing. Claws raked at me, and my eyes stung from the stench. It was hard to breathe through the noxious cloud surrounding us.

Around me, I saw the others striking down cats by the handful, Ash wading to my side so that we stood together against the throng. But there were always more. Dozens of dead cats flinging themselves at us, screaming and wailing. If we'd been in the Nevernever, a few pulses of lightning, ice, and Summer glamour from the four of us would've cleared out the horde in seconds. But there was no magic to draw on in Evenfall, and our reserves were very low. The last time we had been in Faery, we had stood against a literal army of enemies, and I had used the last of my magic to seal the way to Evenfall so the Nightmares could not pour through into the Nevernever. We had already been exhausted, our glamour nearly drained, before we had even set foot in this nightmare realm.

"Ugh, they just keep coming," Puck said, smacking a cat out of the air with the back of his arm. A mangy yellow creature landed on his back, half its fur fallen out, and sank its teeth into his neck, making him yelp. "Ow! No, bad kitty!" he yelled, wrenching the cat away by the scruff and flinging it back into the horde. "No touchie!"

"What is controlling them?" Ash wondered, blocking a cat leaping at my face with his sword. The feline slid down the blade and latched onto his wrist, biting and clawing, and he flung it away. "This was one creature. Usually there's a single power that controls them all like Meghan said. The heart or brain or core of everything."

"Unless Evenfall Nightmares don't play by the same rules," Puck added. "If they don't, I'm going to be annoyed. No one likes cheaters, especially unstoppable undead ones."

The cats were getting more numerous and more aggressive, clawing each other out of the way to get to us. Their screams and wails rang in my ears, and both dead and undead felines piled up near our feet. Blood from numerous gashes and puncture wounds ran down my skin, seeping into my clothes.

And then, through the swarm of shrieking, raging cats, I saw a lone feline sitting where the giant skull had fallen. It was shaggy and gray, with a raggedly bushy tail and a single golden eye, staring at us balefully. For one horrific, sickening moment, I thought it was Grimalkin. That somehow, something had finally gotten to our disappearing furry guide, and he had become part of this Nightmare.

No. That can't be Grim. I won't believe it.

At my side, Ash gave a start. He had seen it, too.

"That's it," he muttered. "The heart of the Nightmare." With a grimace, he reached back and tore a cat off his shoulders. "We kill it, the rest of these things will die."

"You hope," Puck broke in, dancing around leaping, flailing cats. "I'm not sure anything in this twisted place makes sense, ice-boy. But it's a better plan than what we've got now, which is trying not to become chew toys—ow! That is *not* a good place for kitty claws."

I ducked a reeking orange cat, feeling its talons catch strands of my hair as it flew by, and contemplated the distance between us and the Grimalkin look-alike. A literal carpet of writhing, undead felines stood between us.

Then Nyx slashed three cats apart and, in the half second that she was clear, leaped straight up into the air, drawing back her arm. Her crescent blade left her hand, spinning in a lethal circle, and flew at the gray cat seated on the giant skull. It happened in the space of a blink, but at the last second the gray cat sprang out of the way, and the moonlight blade passed over the skull before vanishing in a shiver of light, returning to its owner.

The undead Grimalkin curled its muzzle back in a hiss, baring yellow fangs, and the throngs of cats around us retreated. Turning, they clawed and swarmed and writhed their way back to the gray cat, before flowing over him and the skull like a carpet of ants. Both the gray cat and the bony head vanished into the mound, which started to writhe and surge.

"Oh, great," Puck muttered, watching the mound of dead cats wriggle over each other, yowling. "What horrible thing is going to happen now?"

The skull emerged as the cats peeled back from it. Slowly, it rose off the ground, still attached to the mound of writhing felines, which twisted and formed into the shape of the giant cat. Its body composed of the hundreds of drowned smaller creatures clinging to each other with claws and teeth, the huge feline turned toward us once more and opened its bony jaws in a wail.

"Oh, come on, how does this keep getting worse?" Puck

groaned. "Could we have the horde of tiny undead cats back, please?"

The Nightmare lunged. It didn't move like a normal cat, more like a mix between a feline and a snake, its body distending to unnatural lengths as it came at us. A limb slashed at Keirran, who cut it from the air, severing it. Immediately, the dead cats that made up the leg scattered and darted back to the body, before being swallowed by the writhing mass once more. Keirran shook his head as he backed away.

"No good. This will take forever if we have to kill them one at a time."

Nyx's blades flashed, and three more cats fell from the whole, but the spaces were instantly filled in by the others, making her frown. "He's right. There has to be a way to take them out all at once."

All at once. I clenched a fist, reaching for my magic, feeling the emptiness around me. Nothing there. I pushed deeper, searching inside myself, digging farther than I ever had before. I was half fey, and Queen of the Iron Realm. There had to be something left.

Deep within, power flickered to life. The very last of my magic, buried so deep it was woven into my essence. If I used it here, there would truly be nothing left. I would be more human than faery, unable to use glamour at all, until I was back in the Nevernever.

So be it. We have to defeat this monster. I will do whatever it takes.

Reaching down, I took hold of that magic, pulling it into the open. It hurt as I tore it loose, like I had ripped it out of my soul, but I dragged it free and shaped it into what I wanted. The air around me crackled as lightning and energy sparked into existence. I caught Ash's sharp look, his expression of surprise and alarm, but ignored it as I raised my arm, lightning snapping in my fingers, and narrowed my gaze at the Nightmare beast.

The giant cat screamed, crouching down to attack, the dead

cats that made up its body all staring at me with glassy white eyes. I set my jaw, then hurled the strand of lightning and magic at the charging Nightmare.

The bolt struck the creature in the chest, ripping through it in an explosion of dead cats. The skull let out a shriek, falling to the earth, as dozens of rotted, burned bodies flew through the air, scattering in the grass. As the huge body melted away, wailing and yowling, I could see the gray cat in the very center, single eye blazing with fury as its protective cocoon vanished. It glared at me and hissed, just as Keirran lunged through the massacre of squirming cats and sliced the head from its neck with one swipe of his blade.

My legs gave out as the last vestiges of strength keeping me upright vanished. I sank to my knees in the grass, unable to catch my breath, seeing darkness crawling along the edges of my vision. The hundreds of screaming, howling cats shuddered and collapsed to the mud, becoming lifeless bodies that began to steam. Tendrils of darkness rose into the air, and I could suddenly feel the glamour coming off the vanishing Nightmares. It flowed around me, wriggling like worms against my skin and tainted with fear, despair, and fury. The glamour of the Nightmare King. For a moment, I wondered if I could absorb it and use the magic of Evenfall and the Elder Nightmares, but then I remembered the chilling visage of the Winter King staring down at me, and shuddered. The Nightmare glamour flowed past me and dissolved on the wind.

"Meghan!"

I looked up, and Ash was suddenly there, eyes bright with concern as he knelt in front of me. He looked a bit stronger, I noted in relief, though that thought faded as his hands gripped my shoulders, silver eyes boring into mine.

"What happened?" he asked, his gaze concerned and the tiniest bit angry. "Are you all right? That wasn't your normal magic."

"I'm fine, Ash." I put a hand on his arm, feeling it shake with either fear or anger. "I'm sorry. I know I told everyone to conserve what little magic we have, but I am queen—it's my responsibility to keep everyone safe."

The grip on my shoulders tightened, not painfully, but firm. "Not at the expense of your own life," he snapped. "If you have nothing left, no magic at all, you could start to Fade like the rest of us."

"I'm part human," I told him. "I'm not going to Fade."

"It still might've killed you, princess." Surprisingly, even Puck sounded slightly angry with me, green eyes narrowed as he gazed down at us. "And we are in a place where the biggest problem isn't the freaky Nightmare monsters—though they're pretty nasty, too—the biggest problem is that we've run out of glamour, there's no way to get more—for us, at least—and everything we run into is trying to ruin our day. Fading is a very real possibility for some of us, and that is stressful enough without your best friends making the stupidly brave decision that they have to save everyone. That goes for you, too, ice-boy." He shot a wry glance at my husband. "This place is awful enough without having to worry about people Fading away or dying on me, and you are all too virtuous for your own damn good."

Ash raised a brow. "I seem to remember someone very recently commenting that saving the world was a good way to kick the bucket," he said.

"Right. And I am very happy that we didn't have to, after all. So, can we *all* agree not to do the stupid Ultimate Noble Sacrifice thing unless the world is about to explode?"

Ash looked at me. I sighed, letting my shoulders slump. "You're right," I told them both. I put a hand on Ash's chest, feeling his heart race beneath his shirt. "I'm sorry. We can't be reckless here. The rest of Faery is counting on us."

"A wise decision, Iron Queen," said a slow, familiar voice, and my heart leaped. "I myself have never understood this party's willingness to throw their lives away at the drop of a hat."

"Grimalkin!" I exclaimed, as Ash pulled me gently to my feet. The cait sith sat on a large rock, out of the mud and wet grass. Though his voice was calm, his tail flicked agitatedly from side to side, and his claws were fully extended. "You're here. I'm glad you're all right."

"Mm? Why would I not be?" Grimalkin twitched an ear, then cast a disdainful glance at where the Nightmare had fallen, the bleached cat skull still lying in the weeds. "Surely you did not think that *I* could be a part of that abomination," he said, curling a lip with a flash of sharp fangs. "I find that rather offensive."

Gazing down at the giant skull, Keirran sheathed his sword. He had politely ignored or pretended not to see the three of us talking, knowing Puck and Ash were the only ones who could chastise the Iron Queen and get away with it. "Anira said to bring her the Nightmare's head," he stated, glancing up at us. "Do you think this is what she meant?"

Puck gazed at the monstrous feline skull and wrinkled his nose. "If it is, I think we're gonna need a cart."

"No." Walking a few paces away, Nyx paused and knelt in the weeds, fingers reaching for something hidden in the grass. When she rose, she held a much smaller skull between her fingers. Even from here, I could feel the glamour pulsing from it. Dark tendrils rose from between the fangs and empty eye sockets as Nyx held the skull at arm's length, observing it solemnly. "I think this is what she was looking for."

7

GROWING WINGS

When we pushed our way through the trapdoor into her chambers at the top of the tower, Anira was sitting on the armchair. She was not seated in the actual chair, however, but perched on one of the arms, looking tense as we climbed into the room.

"You're back!" she cried, straightening quickly. "I'm so relieved. I thought I might have sent you to your deaths. Did you…" She blinked quickly, looking around at all of us. "Did you really manage to slay that horrible Nightmare?"

"After getting nearly clawed to death? Yeah," Puck replied, grimacing a little. He held up his hand, where several long, thin scratches could still be seen, crisscrossing his skin. "Cat scratches are the absolute worse, by the way. Like death by a thousand paper cuts."

Anira shuddered. "But it is gone now," she whispered. "The Nightmare is gone." She took a deep breath, closing her eyes. "My mate has been avenged. I can rest easy at last." Opening her eyes, she cocked her head once more. "Did you get the skull?"

Keirran stepped forward, solemnly holding out the cat skull. It still throbbed with an almost menacing air, ragged wisps of glamour curling off it to coil into nothingness. Anira's eyes widened, and she very reverently took the skull from Keirran, holding it in both hands.

"The king's offering," she murmured. "I will make good use of it." Glancing at me, she cocked her head in that curious, birdlike manner. "When do you wish to go to the Sunken City?" she asked.

"As soon as we can," I told her, and the crow woman nodded.

"It will take me a little while to prepare the ritual," she said, and gestured to the sofa behind us. "Please, make yourselves at home. I will call for you when it is ready."

Clutching the skull, she hurried away, climbed one of the ladders that led to the hanging platforms high overhead, and disappeared from sight.

Puck let out a tired groan. "I don't know about you all, but I could sleep for a month," he said, turning toward the couch Anira had indicated. "Assuming we do stop the Nightmare King, I think my next destination is somewhere sunny and cheerful. Maybe a nice beach where the scariest things to worry about are sand fleas." He started to drop onto the sofa, saw the suspicious white spatters on the end, and moved to the other side, only to find Grimalkin had claimed that end and was lying there with his feet tucked beneath him. "Oh, hey, Furball, you're here. Glad you decided to join us this time. Did lurking in the shadows with all the grumpy city crows get to be too much for you? Or did you finally decide you missed our company?"

Grimalkin sniffed. "I simply did not wish to alarm the crow Evenfaery, who had been traumatized by cats," he stated. "If she panicked and flew away because she saw a predator in her sanctuary, I doubt that would have benefited our mission. Birds are rather flighty creatures, you know."

Puck snorted a laugh. "That was a terrible pun, Furball. I approve."

"I was not..." Grimalkin sighed. "Regardless," he went on, looking at the rest of us, "I did not wish to say anything until I was sure, but..." He gazed around the chamber, his tail beating thoughtfully against the cushions. "I am almost certain I have been here before. Not in this room, per se, but in this city. It has changed, of course, but some parts of it feel...familiar."

"How is that possible?" Ash wondered.

"I am older than you, Winter prince," Grimalkin said in a serious voice. "Older than any in this room, save perhaps the Evenfaery. I have been around for a long time. And there are things that even I have forgotten. You were not yet realized when the Lady ruled Faery. You were not there when the way to Evenfall was closed. Evenfall and the Nevernever were not always separated. There was a time when fey from both realms traveled back and forth between them at will."

"Yes," Nyx confirmed. "He is right. I myself got stuck on the Nevernever side when the Lady closed the way to Evenfall. It makes me wonder—did any fey from the Nevernever get trapped here in Evenfall? Did they also lose their homes and their world?"

"I doubt we will ever know," Grimalkin said. "Unless they, too, have adapted to survive in a world without glamour. The point is, memories are starting to surface again. The longer I am here, the more familiar this becomes."

"Well, wouldn't that be a twist," Puck said. "If our dear old Furball turned out to be an Evenfaery all along."

"I am *not* Evenfey," Grimalkin went on with certainty. "I know that for a fact. The Nevernever and the wyldwood have always been my territory. But I am starting to realize that I have been to Evenfall before. And that certain places are becoming more and more recognizable. I suspect it is only a matter of time before we remember everything." He looked to Nyx as he said this, then yawned. "In any case, do what you must here—grow wings, turn into sparrows, whatever it is the crow has planned. Rest assured, when the time is right, I will find you in the Sunken City. Do not worry about me."

Before I could answer, there was a flutter of wings overhead. We all glanced up as Anira landed nearby and became human in a flurry of feathers and dust.

"It is almost ready," she announced. Furtively, I shot a glance at the end of the couch, but Grimalkin was no longer there. Anira didn't seem to realize there had been a cat on her furniture moments before as she stepped forward and held out a hand. "I just need a strand of hair from each of you," she said. "And then we can begin."

"Ooh, strands of hair," Puck said. "How very classic. This sounds like a transformation spell. At least it's not calling for toe or fingernails—I always found that slightly disgusting." He waved an airy hand with a grin. "Again, don't worry about me. I've got just enough glamour left to make myself a bird one more time."

Anira didn't answer, waiting patiently until we had all placed our own hair strands into her palm. Black, white, silver, blond. Closing her fingers around them like bird talons, she took a step back. "This way, please," she instructed us. "We need to go to the topmost platform, closest to the open windows."

We followed her across the room and up several decaying ladders, until we reached the very top of the hanging platforms. Not far overhead, a sliver of a moon shone through the open windows. At our feet, a white circle had been painted across the platform, runic symbols etched over the wood. The cat skull sat in the very center, still giving off faint tendrils of magic that writhed into the air and vanished.

Anira knelt in the center with the skull and instructed us to do the same around the edges. "This will take most of the magic stored in the skull," she said as we settled around the circle. "So, I will only be able to do this ritual once. If something goes wrong, you will have to destroy another Nightmare for me to attempt it a second time."

"Yeah, I vote we not do that again," Puck said. "My quota for getting chewed on by undead Nightmare cats has been exceeded. I'm good for the next century, I think."

"Once I give you the ability to fly," Anira went on, ignoring Puck, "you must travel due north. Straight as the crow flies, as some would say." A tiny smile crossed her lips, as if she found that secretly amusing, before it faded. "You'll know the Sunken City when you see it."

"All right," I said. "Whenever you're ready. What do you need us to do?"

Anira shook her head. "Nothing," she whispered, and placed both hands on the cat skull, closing her eyes. "This might feel slightly...disorienting," she warned, and clenched her fingers, digging her claws into the skull. The skull cracked, then split down the middle, spilling a rush of dark glamour into the air.

I tensed. I could feel the magic swirling around us, centered on the kneeling form in the middle of the circle. Anira's eyes were still closed, and she was whispering things under her breath, words that rippled with power.

My skin suddenly felt too tight, my bones shrinking and contorting in on themselves. I recognized the beginning of a transformation and gritted my teeth as the magic began pulling my body out of place. My hands turned scaly, long talons curling from my fingertips. My skin split open, and black feathers crawled up my arms, spreading up my neck and over my face. I fell forward, feeling my back tear open as something large and feathery pushed its way out, flapping madly. Closing my eyes, I held my breath against the vertigo and waited for it to be over.

The room stopped spinning, and the magic wrenching and twisting my body finally ceased. I opened my eyes and found myself much closer to the floor than when we started. Blinking, I looked around for the others. Three pairs of beady eyes stared back as the flock of crows met my gaze, fluttering their wings and shaking their heads in confusion.

"Oh, look at you all," Puck crooned, still sitting cross-legged on the platform. From my new perspective, he seemed much larger than before. "You all look so cute—ow! Knock it off, ice-boy," he said as one of the crows hopped forward and pecked his arm. "I just wanted to admire this for a second, you're such a handsome—ow, *ow!* Okay, okay, I'm changing, too. Geez."

Glamour rippled, and Puck shrank down until he was a glossy black bird perched on the edge of the platform. Flapping his wings, the much larger raven raised his head and glared at crow-Ash, as if daring him to try something now.

"It is done." Anira gazed down at us all with a smile, as if pleased to see us as birds. "I have kept my end of the bargain, Queen of the Iron Realm," she told me. "I have given you the ability to fly into the Sunken City and avoid the Nightmares that roam the streets, and the snatchers that burrow up from the ground. This form will not be permanent," she said, answering my immediate unspoken question. "You are free to return to your old bodies at any time, should you wish it. But be warned, once you return, the magic that sustains this form will be used up, and you will be unable to change back into crows. Do you understand?"

I tried to answer, but my throat couldn't form the human words, and all that emerged from my beak was a raspy caw. Anira, however, seemed to understand, for she nodded and rose, turning her gaze to the window.

"The others will not bother you now," she said. "To them, you will be just another part of the flock. You should be able to leave the city at any time. To enter Hollownest, look for the ruins of the cathedral in the center of the Sunken City—it leads straight to the underground."

She turned back, bowing her head to us all. "Fey of the other realm, you have my gratitude. For killing the Nightmare, avenging my mate, and freeing this part of the city from the fear it caused. I wish you luck on your journey. I do not know what you will do, or what you *can* do, to stop the Nightmare King from waking. But I do know that something must be done. This world will not last much longer on its own. I will leave you now, with an old crow mantra to take with you on your journey. May the winds always be at your back, your eyes always see the way forward, and your luck never abandon you when you need it most. Farewell, other realm creatures. I hope the winds bring you back to us someday."

With that, Anira bowed, turned into a crow, and flew out an open window in a flurry of feathers and one final caw. Swooping over the rooftops, she disappeared.

I blinked and looked at the four other birds perched with me on the platform. I still couldn't talk to them; I tried, and only a garbled caw came out. But the raven stepped forward and ruffled his feathers at me. It was definitely Puck; he had the confident air of being completely comfortable in this skin, as if he had done this thousands of times before. With a caw, he strutted to the edge of the platform and glanced back to make sure we were all following.

Puck crouched briefly, then launched himself into the air, soaring out the open window as easily as walking. I followed, feeling a brief flare of uncertainty as I had never done this before. I hoped my crow brain would just know what to do instinctively as I raised my wings and sprang into the air after Puck.

Thankfully, it did.

I soared upwards, wings pumping furiously as I gained altitude, seeing the wall of the clock tower rush toward me. My heart jumped to my throat, but I angled toward the window and darted through, feeling a blast of cold night air as I swooped into the open sky. The city spread out below me, looking much smaller from above. This was not the first time I had flown above a city; back home in Mag Tuiredh, I was quite the accomplished Glider jockey. But there was a difference between flying *on* something and flying under your own power. This... was completely freeing. I suddenly understood why Puck's preferred other form was a raven.

Puck's silhouette turned and swooped past me with a playful caw, as if he was teasing my lack of crow-ishness. At the same time, a second crow zipped by, barely missing him and causing him to wobble in midair. He looked up as the other crow, probably Nyx, glanced back with a smug, challenging gaze before soaring on. Puck let out a raspy cry and shot after her, and the two birds, one large and one small, went spinning away into the distance.

I glanced over as another crow glided down beside me, avian features expressionless as he flew straight ahead. Ash, apparently, did not find being a crow exciting, and looked like he would rather get this whole thing over with quickly. Keirran trailed us, and as always, it was difficult to tell what he was thinking, especially as a crow.

Briefly, I thought of Grimalkin, and hoped the cat would be able to find us again. But he had never failed us before, always popping up in the least likely places at the most opportune times. His timing was perfect. Even in a place like Evenfall, I trusted I would see the cait sith again.

With Ash and Keirran beside me, and Puck and Nyx flying circles around each other ahead, we pointed our beaks north and soared into the open sky.

8

THE SUNKEN CITY

You will know the Sunken City as soon as you see it, Anira had told us.

She was right.

From the name, I had thought the city and the lands around it might be in a giant swamp where the structures had slowly sunk into the mud. I thought it also might be underwater, though Anira had said the Nightmares walked on land through the city, and the snatchers burrowed up from beneath, so that was unlikely.

It was neither underwater nor in a swamp.

The city had literally sunk into the earth. As if tunnels or a giant termite nest had run underneath the streets, and all had collapsed in one massive, catastrophic event that swallowed buildings and toppled structures. Tops of stone towers poked out of the ground like broken teeth, and though grass and moss had grown over everything, the destruction the earthquake or whatever catastrophe had caused it was massive and devastating. The city was enormous, with miles of sunken stone buildings and crumbled roads carving jagged scars through the stone and rock.

Nightmares were everywhere.

From high above, I could see huge forms, lumbering and terrifying, moving through the broken streets. The ground wasn't swarming with them, exactly, but there were more Nightmares here than I had ever seen before. Some were gigantic, like the king's horrific Elder Nightmares, some were long and snaky, some more skeletal or insect-like. But they were all grotesque, bizarre, terrifying. Anira had been right; trying to navigate the city from the ground would have been very difficult. At the very least, every Nightmare we ran into would have slowed us down, and time was ticking away.

As we soared over the buildings, I saw what had to be the entrance to Hollownest.

In the center of the city, where multiple roads converged into an enormous square, a massive cathedral stood. Or, the ruins of a massive cathedral, anyway. It reminded me a little of Notre-Dame, with towering stone walls, soaring turrets, and leering gargoyles perched on corners and hanging off ledges. Fully half of the walls had crumbled, however, with towers and turrets lying shattered in the roads, spilling rubble everywhere. As we soared over the ruined structure, the cause of its collapse became inherently clear. An enormous sinkhole had opened in the very center of the cathedral, plunging into absolute darkness.

As I gazed down into that pit of nothing, my crow stomach contracted. Somewhere below these ruined streets lay another city, even larger and more sprawling than this one. An underground society of fey who burrowed through the earth like insects, who had a whole civilization living in a place that never saw the sun.

Actually, the entire realm of Evenfall never saw the sun—as far as I knew, it was a world of perpetual night—but the thought of being trapped underground in a city that ran for miles made me feel very claustrophobic.

All right, I thought as we circled the cathedral, gliding between the pointed towers. Even collapsed and broken, the giant structure was still impressive. *We found the entrance to Hollownest. So, how are we going in? Can I perch on a tower, I wonder? How does landing work?*

Aiming for the top of a tower, I tried coming in for a landing. Again, my crow brain seemed to know exactly what to do. My legs extended, talons opening, wings beating backwards to slow my descent. I landed atop a stone block with barely a jolt, feeling a momentary stab of relief and pride that it had been so easy.

Ash and Keirran dropped beside me, wings fluttering as they landed before folding them to their backs. Talons clicking on the stone, I walked to the edge of the tower and peered down into the gaping hole, which looked like the mouth of some gigantic beast.

I shivered, and the feathers on the back of my neck rose. I didn't know why, but it felt like I *was* staring down the gullet of some massive creature lurking just below the pit with its jaws open. I took a step back from the edge and nearly ran into Ash, who cocked his head at me in a very birdlike manner.

Opening his beak, he let out a guttural caw.

Can you understand me?

I straightened. *Yes,* I answered, though what came out of my beak was another raspy cry. *Does that mean we can talk to each other like this?*

Seems that way.

With a defiant caw, Puck swooped down and landed on the very edge of the tower, shaking himself in a cloud of feathers and dust. He seemed to be fully enjoying himself, fluffing his feathers and giving us a sideways look.

See? I told you, this is the best. But man, you guys make terrible crows. Ow! Nyx landed gracefully beside him and pecked him in the side with a sharp beak. *Present company excluded, of course, geez.*

Nyx ruffled her feathers. *I take it this is the cathedral Anira was talking about*, she said, cocking her head at the huge stone ruins. *I don't remember an entrance to Hollownest right here, but I suppose that sinkhole will take us into the underground.*

Keirran's talons clicked against the stone as he stepped to the edge of the platform and peered down. *Do you think we can just fly down into the hole?* he wondered.

One way to find out. Puck hopped to the edge of the stones, spread his wings, and grinned back at us. *Race you to the bottom!* And he dove straight down, toward the gaping abyss.

Puck! Hold on!

I dove after him, hearing Ash and the others take flight behind me. The five of us easily soared through the air, wind rushing through my wingtips, heading straight for the opening to the underground city.

As we swooped towards the towers, the feathers on the back of my neck rose again. Instinctively, I veered away, pulling out of my plunging dive, and saw something large and black hurtle past me before wheeling around as well.

I felt a stab of fear through my crow heart. A bird hovered in the sky overhead, beating ragged black wings that shed feathers with every flap. It was humanoid, like Anira, but its body was emaciated and skeletal, thin bones standing out through dark feathers. Scaly hands ended in black talons a foot long, and the head was a bleached bird skull. In baleful silence, it stared at me through hollow eye sockets before opening its beak in a silent scream and lunging down again.

I veered aside, swooping out of the way, and saw a mass of black bodies flying at us from the cathedral. They swarmed from the towers, wings beating as they soared upward, talons and beaks open to rend and tear.

Puck and the others scattered, veering away from the cathedral and dodging the Nightmare birds as they came in. I caught an air current and glided upward, feeling the hooked claws of one of the monsters graze my tail as it swiped at me. Flapping my wings, I headed for one of the towers, feeling two of the Nightmares give chase. A narrow window slit loomed before me in the wall of stone; folding my wings, I dove through the opening, my wings brushing the sides as I swept through. The two Nightmare birds didn't crash headfirst into the stone wall, but they did swerve aside at the last moment and slow down, giving me the chance to flap back toward the others. I saw my friends wheeling through the air to stay ahead of the Nightmare birds, diving and swooping to avoid the claws swiping at them.

We can't fight these things in the air, I realized. *We're going to have to land to have any chance of surviving this.*

I shot forward with a defiant caw, causing several of the Nightmare birds to turn and fly toward me, dark eye sockets blank and staring. Folding my wings again, I plunged toward the open floor that fell away into the sinkhole. As the ground rushed at me, I hoped I had timed this correctly. If I ran into the stones at full speed, not only would that really hurt, but Puck would never let me hear the end of it.

Let's hope this works. I am done being a bird.

The magic responded almost instantly, flaring through my body. I felt myself grow larger, wings, talons, and feathers disappearing as my own form took their place. I hit the ground on my feet, stumbled forward a few steps, then whirled and drew my blade. The steel edge struck the center of a Nightmare bird as it swooped in, and a jolt raced up my arms as I sheared the spindly monster in half. The second one behind it slashed me, talons clawing at my face, and I drove the point of my sword through its chest. The momentum impaled the monster halfway down the blade, and it exploded in a swirl of black feathers and tiny bird skulls.

Stepping back, I looked up and saw several more winged

Nightmares descending in a black cloud. As they came toward me, a single crow soared above them, changed into the familiar form of a Winter fey, and dropped straight down through the mass with his ice blade drawn. Feathers and skulls flew outward as Ash cut through three Nightmares on his way down, then landed beside me in a graceful crouch.

"Ash." Despite the situation and the swarm of approaching Nightmare birds, I gave my husband a mock frown. "I appreciate the timely and very flashy entrance, but I really didn't need a rescue."

"I know." Ash offered a faint smile as he rose. "Force of habit," he said. "It's very difficult for me to watch you stand in front of a charging monster without wanting to jump between. Besides…" He glanced up, raising his sword as the rest of the birds came in. "We fight better together than apart. My place will always be at your side, even here in Evenfall."

A Nightmare bird lunged at me, and Ash's blade cut it in half before it knew it was dead. Feathers and bird skulls rained down on me, and I winced. "Not the most romantic date I've been on," I said, slashing a pair of birds from the air, avoiding the talons that raked at my face.

Ash snorted. "I'll try to add a candlelight dinner next time."

A pair of spinning crescent blades sliced another bird into pieces, and a moment later Keirran vaulted over a crumbling wall and slammed his weapon into a Nightmare stalking in from the side. "Where is Puck?" he asked, almost shouting to be heard over the sound of beating wings. The flock of Nightmare birds was growing larger, as more dropped down from the surrounding ruins. I couldn't see anything through the swarm of black, withered bodies and flapping wings.

With a *caw* that echoed even over the Nightmares, a raven swooped down in a streak of black, changed to Puck in an explosion of feathers, and crushed a Nightmare beneath him as he dropped into our midst.

"Ta-da. I'm here." He swiped at a Nightmare with his dagger, making it recoil with a hiss, and frowned at me. "And, conversely, I am not happy that I am no longer a bird. I like being a bird, and now I can't be a bird anymore."

"Stop griping and start killing, Puck," Ash snapped.

"Fine, ice-boy, but I won't be happy about that, either."

The swarm of Nightmares closed in. We stood our ground, guarding each other's backs as we cut spindly bodies from the air, dodging raking claws and snapping beaks. For a few seconds, minutes, hours, it was complete chaos. I lost myself in the rhythm of battle; slash, stab, parry, dodge, feeling my friends around me do the same. The Nightmare birds were relentless, vicious, seemingly mindless opponents, not caring if their brothers were killed or if they were diving right into a sword point. They kept attacking, and we kept killing them, until the stones at our feet were covered with feathers and bird skulls.

A tremor went through the ground.

Stones rippled under my feet, pebbles bouncing away from us, bird skulls clicking against each other. For a moment, the flock of Nightmares circling us…stopped. Wings beating, they hovered, frozen as if afraid to move.

Ash set his jaw and moved closer to me, silver eyes hard. "Something big is coming," he muttered.

The earth shuddered again, rocks bounding across the stones to fall into the hole, and with a flurry of feathers and flapping wings, the Nightmares scattered. Like a flock of startled pigeons, they swiftly flew into the air, dispersing in all directions, as something massive rose from the sinkhole. It looked like a cross between a snake and a lamprey, with pinkish-yellow skin and a circular, sucking mouth filled with jagged teeth. Long, thin tentacles covered its entire body, waving wildly around it. Looking closer, I saw hooks and fingers attached to the ends as the tentacles lashed out, snatching a pair of Nightmares from the air. The bird monsters flapped and thrashed wildly as they vanished into the gaping maw, and then the jaws closed with a horrific grinding sound.

Puck blew out a breath. "Okay, I'm kinda glad I didn't go flying into that hole," he muttered. "That would've been a nasty surprise."

The worm swallowed, then turned its huge, bloated body toward us. Its jaws opened, showing rows of razor fangs. It let out a high-pitched scream, and then dozens of tentacles flew toward us over the ground.

"Meghan, Keirran, stay close!" Ash lunged forward, blade sweeping in front of him, cutting several grasping tendrils from the air. Keirran and I did the same, lashing out at the writhing limbs that snaked around us, slicing them in half. The ends dropped to the ground, long fingers twitching like dying birds. One of the hands flipped over and began crawling across the stones like a spider, before I stomped down hard and crushed it beneath my heel.

"No, no, no!" Puck let out a yelp, leaping back and slashing wildly with his daggers. "Bad tentacle worm, no touchie! Gah!" He jumped as Nyx appeared, slicing apart the tendrils around him in a flurry of moonlight blades. "Oh, there's my beautiful assassin bodyguard. Did you get jealous that so many things wanted to touch me?"

Nyx was too busy cutting at tentacles to answer, but the look she gave him was scathing.

The tentacle drew back, writhing in frustration. Glaring at us from the sinkhole, the huge worm shifted its great bloated body, seeming to settle farther into the hole. The tentacles swayed around it, but the worm itself didn't move.

"Uh, what's it doing?" Puck muttered to no one in particular. "Whatever it is, I don't like it."

A rumble went through the ground directly under our feet, and before I could move, the earth crumbled beneath me. Pale hands shot into the air, latching on to my arms and clothes. I gave a yell as I was dragged under, and the earth closed over my head.

Something grabbed my wrist before it was dragged beneath the ground, yanking me to a stop. I felt myself being pulled upward, though my eyes were closed against the press of dirt against my lids.

My head broke the surface, and I gasped, opening my eyes. Ash knelt in front of me, his face tight with concentration as he pulled me from the ground. The others stood around us, torn between helping and fending off the dozens of hands rising from the ground.

Ash dropped his sword and held out his arm to me. "Give me your other hand," he gritted out. Grimacing, I freed my arm from the dirt and gripped his wrist. The hands still clinging to me tried to drag me down, but Ash didn't relent or let go. My arms and shoulders started to burn with pain, my muscles feeling like rubber bands on the verge of snapping.

With a rumble of breaking stone, more hands and tentacles shot into the air around us. "Ash, behind you!" I cried as a tendril with clawed fingers sank into his arm. He clenched his teeth, bracing himself as the fingers curled around him, but he couldn't attack it without letting go of me.

"Hey! No touchie my friends!" Puck's dagger sliced down, cutting the tendril away from Ash. "Ice-boy, if you could hurry that up, we'd all appreciate it—it's getting a little handsy down here."

"I'm trying," Ash growled. "Hang on, Meghan."

"Oh, trust me. I am."

More hands broke through the surface, snaking out wildly. Puck gave a yelp as one snagged the back of his shirt. Another pair latched on to Ash's shoulders, making him duck his head as they started to drag him under.

Something flashed by us, a glowing streak that cut through the tentacles clinging to Ash. Another zipped by Puck, severing two more. And then the air was filled with spinning circles of light, flying through the air and striking the Nightmare worm. The monster reared back and wailed, the tentacles along its body flailing as the glowing disks cut them apart.

The things dragging me down abruptly let go, and the tension in my arms and shoulders vanished. Ash pulled me out of the ground, yanking me to him, as the Nightmare worm gave another shriek and disappeared into the sinkhole.

Silence fell. The five of us stood there, panting and gazing around in wary confusion, waiting for whatever had released that storm of spinning daggers to reveal itself.

"Are you all right?" Ash whispered to me. I could feel his heart racing beneath his shirt, the tension in his arms, which were locked around me.

I nodded. "I'm fine," I whispered back. "I'm okay, Ash. Still here."

"Well, I guess now we know what those 'snatchers' are," Puck said, still gazing around warily. "That's one mystery solved. Now we just have to figure out whose light show made the big caterpillar go away. It was kinda weird how they all looked like Nyx's..."

He trailed off. I pulled back from Ash and gazed around, then stiffened. Feeling him go rigid as well.

Several fey had melted out of the shadows and were now surrounding us, though they were so still, it was hard to see them at first. They were slender and graceful, with black leather armor, silver hair, and curved blades seemingly made from moonlight. Golden eyes shimmered in the darkness between us, and they all appeared to be staring, not at me, or Ash, or Puck, but at Nyx.

"Who are you?"

Nyx let out a ragged breath and took a halting step back, eyes widening, as a single faery stepped away from the rest, coming to stand before us. Even before she turned to face us, my stomach dropped away with the shock.

Another Nyx stared at us, the look in her golden eyes one of suspicion and disbelief, her deadly moonlight blades gleaming in her hands.

9

OTHER NYX

I stared at the faery before us, momentarily unable to speak.
It...was Nyx. Not someone that looked like Nyx, a twin or
a sister or something like that. No, this *was* our Evenfaery assassin. The two of them looked identical, but it was more than
that. It was the way she moved, the calm, lethal air surrounding
her that was indistinguishable from our own Nyx. This wasn't
a look-alike; this was the real thing.

Which was completely and utterly confusing. To everyone.

"What...the hell," Puck breathed.

The group of silver-haired fey ignored him. All were staring
at our Nyx, looking just as confused and wary as the rest of us.
The second Nyx stepped forward, golden eyes hard.

"Who are you?" she asked again.

"I...am Nyx," the assassin replied simply. "Member of the first
unit, leader of the Order of the Crescent Blades." She paused,
tilting her head at her clone. "But I assume that is the answer
you would have given me, had I asked first."

One of the other fey came forward, his expression stony. He

was lean and handsome, with golden eyes like Nyx and silver hair that reached his shoulders. "She's an imposter," he said to Other Nyx. "Maybe this is some kind of new Nightmare that takes our own form. We should kill them all, before more show up."

Seeing the other faery, a tremor went through our Nyx. Not because of his words. Because she knew him. I saw the recognition in her golden eyes, right before the blood drained from her face, something I had never seen happen to her.

Puck noticed as well and stepped protectively closer, his own expression suddenly dangerous. But Other Nyx shook her head.

"No," she almost whispered. "They're not Nightmares, but they're not Evenfey, either. They remind me of...of the Lady and her circle." She looked at us again, and the sudden, desperate hope in her eyes was heartbreaking. "Did...did you come from the Nevernever?" she whispered. "Is the way finally open?"

My throat closed. "I'm sorry," I told her. "The seal was broken, very briefly, but we had to close it again."

"You sealed it." This did not come from Nyx, but from the male standing beside her. "The way out of this hell was open, and you closed it again. Do you know how long it's been?" he asked me. "How long we've been trapped here, slowly dying, fighting the Nightmares just to exist?" His gold eyes narrowed, and he indicated the ruined city around us. "Do you like what you see? This is the world you created. When your kind sealed us away and forgot about us!"

"Varyn." Other Nyx put a hand on his arm. "If they've come from the Nevernever, then something must've happened," she reasoned. "That they remember us at all means that the Lady's spell is broken. That itself is reason to hope."

Other Nyx's gaze was on Varyn, so she didn't see Puck stiffen. His hands clenched at his sides, and a hard, dangerous look crossed his face. A nervous flutter went through my stomach.

Puck and Nyx knew this faery. Or had at least heard of him. And judging from what I was seeing here, he was part of Nyx's past.

I suddenly had a terrible, sinking suspicion of who Varyn was.

Thankfully, neither assassin seemed to notice the sudden change in Robin Goodfellow. Other Nyx's gaze shifted to me, and she looked so much like our Nyx that I forgot it wasn't her for just a moment. "Why are you here, fey of the Nevernever?" she asked. "Why have you come to Evenfall?"

Oh, Puck, I thought. *I'm sorry. But we can't jeopardize the mission, even if Varyn is part of Nyx's past. Whatever happened, I hope you both can work it out.*

"The Nightmare King is waking up," I told Other Nyx, and all of them froze. "That is why we had to seal the portal again—the glamour influx from the Nevernever and the real world was enough to rouse him from his sleep. He is starting to wake, and if he awakens fully, he'll destroy the Nevernever with his vengeance."

"So, it's to save your own world that you're here." Varyn's voice was flat. "You didn't come because you suddenly remembered the Evenfey. You came to stop the Nightmare King from destroying your own Nevernever. To save yourselves."

"To save both our worlds," Ash responded, his voice cold. "Because if your king wakes up, the Nightmares providing you with glamour will cease to exist, and the Evenfey will Fade along with them."

"How convenient for you."

"Enough, Varyn." Other Nyx shot him a firm look, and the Evenfaery assassin relented. Which was good, because by the look on Puck's face, he was a breath away from saying or doing something that might've ended in a fight. "They are not our enemies," Other Nyx went on. "They are not the Lady, or the sidhe of her circle. And even if they were, I will welcome any who are here to aid us. Even if they have betrayed us in the past.

Even…" Her gaze shifted to our Nyx. "Even if I don't understand how I am seeing myself staring back at me."

"Yeah, I'm a little concerned about that, too," Puck added loudly. "Forget the Nightmare King for a sec—there are two Nyxes standing here. Does anyone have any idea *why* that is? How can there be two of them?"

Another rumble went through the ground, making everyone tense. I bent my knees, ready to leap away should the earth shift below my feet, or the ground erupt with grasping hands. Thankfully, the shaking didn't last long, nor did any tentacles burst out from below. As the rumbles faded away, I took a quiet breath of relief, but I still felt extremely exposed standing out in the open. Apparently, I wasn't the only one.

"It is not safe to talk here," Other Nyx said, glancing warily at the sinkhole. "We'll attract too much attention. There are still Elder Nightmares wandering about." She turned her gaze to me, pausing a moment, as if struggling to come to a decision. "If you think you can trust us," she began, "we'll take you to a place that is safe. It is underground, and the Nightmares can't follow where we're going. Maybe Gilleas will have an answer for us."

"That would be appreciated," I said, and shot a furtive glance at our Nyx. She still stood in the same spot as if frozen, her back rigid and her expression unreadable. Puck hovered beside her, and though he wore a lazy smirk, I knew it was one of his dangerous ones. "Answers would be nice. For all our sakes. My name is Meghan Chase, Queen of the Iron Fey," I went on, and saw Varyn's eyes narrow. "This is my husband Ash, my friend Puck, and my son Keirran, King of the Forgotten. You already know Nyx."

Other Nyx gave a somber nod. "You know me," she said with a glance at her twin. "But regardless… I am Nyx, leader of the Order of Crescent Blades. This is Varyn, my husband and second-in-command, and the rest of my unit can introduce themselves later if they wish." The male assassin offered a brisk nod, and the dozen or so figures still waiting in the shadows bowed. "The Order is at your service," Other Nyx went on, turning back to me. "We protect the city and everyone here from the Nightmares." She shot a look at the assassin beside her. "No matter who steps inside its borders."

The Evenfey did not use roads, traveling the city entirely by rooftops. The reasons were evident; Nightmares roamed the streets and narrow back alleys below us, most of them smaller than the monstrous Elder Nightmare we had seen before, but still creatures I did not want to run into. And there was the constant threat of the giant Nightmare worm, reaching up from the ground and dragging us under. Here on the rooftops, we were safe from its snatching tentacles.

"Why do you stay here?" Keirran asked Other Nyx. "Not that I'm ungrateful you showed up when you did, but I wouldn't think anyone could live here safely."

"We protect the city," Other Nyx replied. "Not this one, but the one below it. Hollownest. There are those who still live there—the original residents of Hollownest—who have not Faded or turned into Nightmares. And through the years, other fey have found their way to Hollownest as well. Maybe they heard rumors of the library, or maybe they were just looking for a safe place to live. But as you saw, the roads and the ruins above are dangerous. If anyone wants to find Hollownest, they have to fight their way through the Nightmares. We try to get to them before the Nightmares do."

"I see."

"We've collected quite the eccentric population now," Other Nyx went on, the hint of a smile crossing her face. "And of course, there is Gilleas, the historian at the heart of the city. If you have come from the Nevernever, he will be very interested in meeting you."

"Why is that?" Keirran wondered.

"Because he has been trying to find a way out of Evenfall for centuries," Other Nyx replied. "Ever since he found the library, he's been consumed with opening the seal and releasing us all. But no matter what he tries, nothing works. We cannot leave Evenfall, and it has been so long. Most of us have given up hope, and the rest have forgotten that there was another realm at all. Evenfall is all they know now. But Gilleas keeps trying."

I shook my head, feeling that familiar prickle of sympathy, anger, and guilt. "I'm sorry," I murmured. "Had we known there was an entire second realm of Faery right under our noses…" I made a helpless gesture. "I don't know what would've happened, and there's no use in speculating, but I hope we would have been here sooner."

"You said you were a queen." It was Varyn who spoke, drawing both Ash's and Puck's warning gaze. Though the assassin's voice wasn't hostile, it wasn't exactly friendly, either. "Are you part of the Lady's circle, then?" he asked. "Does she rule the Nevernever now?"

"The Lady is gone," I told him. "She and the fey who sealed off Evenfall no longer exist in the Nevernever."

"Hmm." Varyn's faintly hostile air faded a bit. "Well, I would be lying if I said I'm not pleased to hear that," he said begrudgingly. "But who rules the Nevernever now? You?"

"It's complicated," I told him, seeing Other Nyx watching us now, listening intently. I sighed and tried to explain the current political state of the Nevernever. "There are four formal courts within the Nevernever," I began. "Summer, Winter, Iron, and the Forgotten in the Between. Each of these are considered different territories, and a different monarch presides over each of them. There is also the wyldwood, which surrounds the courts but is ruled by none, and the Deep Wyld across the River of Dreams."

"So many territories." Varyn's voice turned rather disbelieving. "How many kings and queens of Faery *are* there?" he asked.

"Currently? Five," I said, making him blow out an incredulous breath. "And those are the 'official' titles. That's not counting certain self-proclaimed Exile Queens."

"It's amazing that they can live so close to each other without fighting," Varyn muttered. "If they're anything like the Lady, I'm surprised they haven't torn the Nevernever apart."

"Oh, they keep trying," Puck said with a smirk. "Lucky for them, we're there to stop the worst catastrophes."

"It has been a very long time since the Lady became the First Queen of Faery," Keirran added softly. "A lot has happened since then."

We continued through—or rather, *over*—the ruined city, traversing rooftops and hopping over exposed walls. Several blocks from the cathedral, Other Nyx paused, then dropped to the edge of a stone culvert below us. She ducked into the stone tunnel, and we followed her through a series of damp underground passageways, until we reached a dead end. A wooden hatch was set in the ground, and as the assassin pried it up with a rope handle, I peeked inside, expecting a stairwell or ladder descending into the underground. Instead, a stone chute slid away into utter darkness, like a playground slide from hell. My heart started a loud thump in my chest.

"This is one of the entrances to Hollownest," Other Nyx told us. "And there are no easy shortcuts. We'll be entering a point in the city known as the Crossroad Maze. It's one of the more dangerous places to come in because of its proximity to the ruins and all the Nightmares on the surface, so be on your guard. Nightmares sometimes make it down to the city and are known to wander the Crossroads, and we haven't done a sweep in a while." She started to go down the chute, but paused, as if just remembering something else. "It is also very easy to get lost in the Crossroads, so I'd suggest you stay close," she added. "The Crossroads branch out to every part of Hollownest, to deep places even we have not set foot in. If you go down the wrong path, you could end up on the other side of the city, or worse."

"Noted," I said with a nod. "We'll stay close."

The assassin turned and vanished gracefully down the chute, disappearing in the blink of an eye. Varyn glanced at us and made a gesture for us to follow.

"Go ahead," he told me. "We'll bring up the rear and guard your back. There are still Nightmares roaming around. Wouldn't want any of them to grab you if we're not there."

"Hmm, scary Nightmare monster behind me, or creepy assassin with a knife—not sure which one I'd prefer." Puck's voice was a challenge, and I frowned at him. "Also, it's cute that you think we need your protection. Why don't you head on down first? We insist."

In the shadows of his hood, Varyn's lips curled into a smirk. "If you're afraid, I can tell Nyx we need to take the long way down."

Puck snorted. "Please. I've jumped into more deep dark holes than you've stabbed things with a knife," he returned. "I'm just a little leery of you coming down behind me. In case you 'accidentally' stab me in the back."

"Oh, don't worry." Varyn's tone was suddenly dangerous. "When I stab things, it's never by accident."

"What is happening here?" I asked, drawing both their attention. "We're wasting time. Puck, this isn't getting us any closer to Hollownest."

"Sorry, princess." Puck grinned, not sounding the least bit apologetic, and gestured at the chute. "After you."

I stepped forward, gripped the edge of the stone chute, and peered down. The slide dropped away into complete blackness. With Varyn's comment about us needing protection still fresh in my mind, I hopped into the chute and pushed off without hesitation, beginning a fast slide through utter darkness.

After what felt like far too long, the chute came to a sudden and abrupt end. My heart sprang up and lodged in my throat, but thankfully, innate faery reflexes took over. I dropped several feet before landing in a crouch on solid ground, managing not to fall or break my ankles on the hard dirt floor. Straightening, I took a deep breath and waited for my heartbeat to return to normal.

"You made it." Other Nyx stood several feet away, perfectly blending into the shadows except for her eyes and the faint glow of her silver hair. "Good." She glanced at the hole above me, and a faint smile crossed her face. "You might want to take a few steps back before the others come through. I've had a couple instances where I didn't move fast enough, and Varyn nearly landed on my head."

Quickly, I backed away, gazing around to see where we had landed. It appeared to be a simple tunnel, a large tube of earth and stone running into the darkness in both directions. Smaller tunnels branched off to either side, reminding me of a large termite nest or anthill. I imagined huge grubs or insects appearing in those tunnels, pale bodies and black shiny jaws gleaming as they squirmed or skittered toward us.

I shivered and pushed those visions aside. Nyx had mentioned that Hollownest was home to several insect-like fey, so I should be prepared to see them. The idea did creep me out the tiniest bit, however.

A few moments later, Ash and then Keirran came down the chute, each landing gracefully on his feet at the bottom. Puck and finally Nyx followed, the former hitting the dirt with a grunt, the latter making no sound at all.

"Well, that was fun." Puck dusted off his hands and looked back up the chute, wrinkling his nose. "Better than Splash Mountain at Disneyland."

Other Nyx blinked at him, obviously having no idea what he was talking about. Our Nyx just shook her head. I remembered the words up top, the sudden hostility between Puck and

Varyn, and hoped it would not become a thing. Whenever Puck took a dislike to something, it was usually for good reason, but it also tended to stick. We couldn't afford that here.

The rest of the assassins joined us, with Varyn being the last to drop in. Straightening, he turned to Nyx with a solemn, respectful nod. "I checked the tunnel before coming down," he told her. "It's clear of Nightmares. And the hatch is locked. We should be good to go."

"Wrong Nyx, Varyn," our Nyx said quietly.

Varyn stiffened and glanced at the assassin leader, then back to our Nyx. With a frown, he turned and strode toward Other Nyx, leaving our Nyx gazing after him with a strange, almost mournful look on her face.

This earned a scowl from Puck. With a few strides, he walked over to our Nyx, slipped an arm around her shoulders, and leaned in, whispering in her ear. I didn't know what he said, but whatever it was, a faintly exasperated look crossed Nyx's face as she shook her head.

Varyn's expression darkened even more. "Something you want to say to me, Neverfey?" he challenged.

"Oh, so many things," Puck responded, an evil smirk creeping across his face. "But they can wait until we're out of danger. Don't worry, though," he went on. "When the time comes, I'll be sure to tell you *everything*. When you've earned it."

I stifled a groan. Too late. It had already become a thing.

"Let's go." Other Nyx, sensing the obvious tension rising between the two faeries, turned and beckoned for us to follow. "Kyn and Ayaen will scout the path ahead. The rest of the unit will follow at a distance so we don't have any Nightmares surprising us from behind. Everyone stay together, and keep alert. It's a long walk to Hollownest."

10

Moving through the tunnels, I quickly realized Other Nyx was right; it was a gigantic labyrinth down here. Without her guiding the way, we would've become hopelessly lost. Everything looked the same: earthen tunnels snaking their way into the shadows, roots hanging from the ceiling, and dead vines clinging to the walls. The ground was peppered with pale white-and-brown mushrooms that pulsed with a subtle light, keeping the passages from being completely black.

As we turned a corner, Other Nyx abruptly stopped, raising a hand for the rest of us to halt as well. We paused, listening, as the sound of shifting earth began filtering into the tunnel. Something was coming toward us down one of the side passages—something large. I dropped a hand to my sword, feeling Ash move close, as the noises grew louder and a pair of huge, shiny black eyes emerged from the tunnel, then blinked at us in surprise.

I repressed a shiver. The thing looked like a cross between a faery and a giant pill bug. It had an oval, segmented body, huge eyes, and a pair of thin antennae that waved curiously in our direction. But four of its "legs" were actually extremely thin arms with long-fingered hands at the ends, and its shiny black gaze observed us with sleepy intelligence. A pair of mandibles wiggled, and a soft, almost clicking voice emerged between them.

"Oh, the over dwellers." It was odd to hear such a cultured voice coming from a giant insect; I saw Puck staring at it with thinly veiled alarm. "Are you on your way back to the city?"

Other Nyx gave a respectful nod. "Yes. We have visitors who need to speak to Gilleas," she told it. "Are the Crossroads clear?"

"No Nightmares wander the Crossroads at this time," was the reply. "At least, not in the places I have been. I have felt no vibrations through the soil except yours." The pill bug faery's antennae twitched in our direction. "They smell strange," it stated, its voice still calm, almost dreamy. "They are like us, and they are not like us. How can that be?"

"They are not from the city," Other Nyx said. "They come from…a place that is very far from here."

The pill bug blinked at us slowly. "The over world is strange," it said. "I do not know how your kind does not fear falling into the sky." It twitched its antennae, then began to pull back into the hole. "I return to my den, to forget thoughts of open space. Farewell, over dwellers. Burrow safely."

It vanished back into the tunnel, its long antennae the last things we saw, and disappeared.

Puck gave an exaggerated shudder. "Yay, giant bugs," he said. "I love feeling like I'm two centimeters tall. I'm not even going to guess how many creepy crawlies live in a place like this."

"Thousands," Varyn said immediately. "But don't worry," he added with a faint smile. "You won't ever see most of them. Just remember—they're always close, in the walls, under your feet, in the dirt over your head."

"You know, someone once told me you had a good sense of

humor," Puck said, frowning at the Evenfey assassin. "Clearly they needed to get out more."

Keirran looked at Other Nyx. "I hope we are not invading anyone's territory," he said.

"That was one of the tunnelfolk," Other Nyx told him. "They are perfectly harmless and cause no trouble for anyone. Even if you attack them, the most they will do is curl up into a ball and hope you go away. There are…more aggressive folk, but they inhabit the wilder, deeper sections of Hollownest. It is likely we will not run into them."

"Oh, good." Puck rubbed his arms. "Aggressive bugs, that's what I wanted to hear. Just let me know if we're ever in fire ant or giant spider territory."

We continued through the narrow passages. After a long time, the claustrophobic tunnel we were in opened up into an enormous cavern. Far overhead, I could see bulbous white spheres that glowed like tiny moons. The pathways turned into narrow stone bridges that dropped away to either side. Peering cautiously over the edge, I was surprised to be able to see the bottom, a forest of enormous, glowing blue mushrooms and luminescent moss. Creatures moved between the mushroom stalks, but they were too far away to see clearly.

"We're coming up to the Fungal Paths now," Other Nyx told us. "Fair warning, it is one of the larger territories of Hollownest. Fortunately, this is a very well traversed road, and everyone here knows who we are. We shouldn't run into any trouble, but you never know in the tunnels."

"This is beautiful," I mused, gazing at the multitude of softly glowing plants everywhere around us. Tiny motes drifted through the air, mingling with fireflies. I had seen glowing forests before—the wyldwood and the Deep Wyld both had their share of luminescent vegetation—but nothing like this. "It's hard to believe this is underground."

"Hard to believe this is still Evenfall," Puck added. "'Cause this looks like somebody's bad mushroom dream—whoa!"

At the edge of the trail, a cluster of purple ferns rippled, fronds parting as something rose from the bushes. A massive, caterpillar-type creature with a bulbous yellow body and neon-blue spines bristling from its back, holding a spear in one of its six arms. A shockingly human face turned to stare at Puck, brows rising as if *he* were the oddity.

"Oh, hey there," Puck greeted it, raising a hand as he took several large steps back. The point of the spear followed him, though the creature didn't lunge or attack. "Friend? Um, shouldn't you be in a certain book with a Cheshire cat and an angry queen?"

The caterpillar creature frowned at Puck, then turned to gaze at Other Nyx and Varyn. The look on its strangely human face was a question.

Other Nyx raised her hand in a calming gesture. "It's all right," the assassin told it. "Stand down. They're with us."

The caterpillar's spines bristled, but it lowered its spear. Slowly, the bright blue spikes covering its body retracted, seeming to melt into its flesh, until they were completely gone. Its skin changed from yellow to the bright purple of the fern it was hiding in, and after a last glare at Puck, the creature sank back beneath the fronds, blending in with the plant until it was virtually invisible.

Puck let out a nervous chuckle. "Just when I think I'm getting used to the place," he muttered. "I was actually thinking, 'Oh, this spot is nice and not terribly creepy.' And then something pops up that's just a giant *nope* for me."

Ash looked at Varyn and Other Nyx. "Sentries, I take it?" he asked.

"Road guards," Varyn replied with a shrug. "They know not to engage or attack the Nightmares, but they do take note of anything strange or out of place that travels the Fungal Paths and pass on the intel to us. You're lucky—if they think something could be a threat to the city, they usually don't ask questions. And they're excellent ambush fighters." He glanced at Puck, the tiniest of smirks crossing his face. "Quick word of advice—don't get pricked. Even if you survive, you'll suffer from vivid hallucinations for the rest of your life."

"Uh-huh," Puck said, crossing his arms with a faint smirk of his own. "And you would know all about pricks, wouldn't you?"

Thankfully, Varyn and the other assassins didn't seem to get what Puck was talking about, though Varyn's eyes did narrow in confused suspicion. I shot Puck a warning glare, and he shrugged.

Other Nyx gazed between Varyn and Puck, her expression unreadable, before she turned away. "Let's keep moving," she said. "We're almost there."

I didn't know what I expected the city of Hollownest to be. Perhaps a series of interconnected tunnels, like the world's biggest anthill. Perhaps an enormous insect mound or beehive, the walls swarming with many-legged creatures. I did not expect it to be a sprawling mass of roads and structures in a cavern so large you could not see the ceiling. The buildings of the city were strange: cylindrical earthen pillars rising into the darkness, with thousands of windows and doors lining the smooth edges. Bridges and walkways spanned nearly every level, and wooden platforms circled the spires. Below the looming spires were hundreds of smaller domed buildings with bulging round windows and oval doors.

Despite the vastness of the city and the towering structures above us, Hollownest was eerily silent and empty. It had the same terrible silence as a postapocalyptic zombie city, with barren streets that had once been filled with bustling crowds and traffic. A few lone creatures wandered the sidewalks, and I suspected even more lurked in places I could not see. But this was a dead city. I wondered what it had been like when Evenfall was alive.

"O-kay," Puck breathed. He inhaled and then exhaled slowly before turning to us and dropping his voice. "I'm gonna be honest here. I am not enjoying this. I do not like the look of this place. I do not like that there are millions of dark little holes, everywhere, that could hide millions of insects. And I really don't like the fact that that centipede scorpion thing over there is staring at me."

I glanced over and saw a creature with pincers and a dark carapace slide quickly into the shadows of an alley, disappearing too fast for me to get a good look at it.

"Yep, definitely not enjoying this." Puck shuddered, rubbing his arms. "So, where is this Great Library, anyway?" he wondered. "'Cause right now, I'm hoping it's close."

Other Nyx glanced back, then gestured straight ahead of us. "It's right there." She pointed it out. "You can see the library from anywhere in Hollownest."

We looked up. In the center of the city, a massive spire rose above the skyline, towering over the smaller buildings beneath. Glowing, pod-like windows marched up the sides until they vanished into the shadows above, and the roof was lost in the darkness.

"Is the library at the top?" Keirran wondered, shielding his eyes as he stared up at the spire.

Varyn shook his head. "No, the entire tower *is* the library," he said. "From the ground floor to the very top of the spire, the walls are lined with books, tomes, scrolls, and anything else you can keep knowledge in. It is said that even the historians of old never uncovered all the secrets contained in the Great Library, that there are places and books that have sat untouched for centuries."

"Wow," I mused, staring at the rising walls and trying to

imagine them completely filled with books. "I know several faeries who would spend their entire lives in such a place."

Other Nyx chuckled. "I know several faeries who already do," she told us. "Come. Gilleas will be waiting."

No one bothered us as we walked down the curving streets toward the Great Library at the center. Occasionally, there was movement in the shadows and the sounds of legs scuttling away, but the creatures never came into full view.

"I take it Hollownest has not always been this way?" Ash asked Other Nyx, who shook her head.

"No. At one point it was a city of millions, all living beneath the over world, as they called it. They were content to remain in Hollownest and never venture aboveground." Her smooth brow creased as she continued. "All that changed when Evenfall was sealed away. We weren't yet here in Hollownest, but I heard that, for a while, it was chaos. Everything you would expect to happen to a large city during a catastrophe. Mass exodus. Faeries turning on each other. Fire and blood and death. It's amazing anything survived."

"I heard that the old historians turned to some very dangerous rituals to preserve the library and all its contents," Varyn added. "No one knows what they did, but the library survived, even though the historians are gone. There are stories now that if anyone steals or damages a book belonging to the library, that fey vanishes, and no one ever sees them again."

"Is that true?" Keirran wanted to know.

The assassin shrugged. "I am not about to test those rumors."

"I remember this," our Nyx whispered.

We all turned to look at her. Through the entire journey, she had stayed near the back of the group, as far from Other Nyx and Varyn as she could. She had not said a word to either of them, particularly Varyn, as if hoping she would be forgotten. Now she gazed around the city with a pained expression on her face, her golden eyes haunted.

"I remember Hollownest," she said again. "But it wasn't like this. It's so empty now. When I visited the city, there was no part of Hollownest that wasn't moving, no place that was barren of activity. The buzzing of wings was so loud and so constant, you could feel the vibrations in your teeth."

Puck grimaced. "Funnily enough, that's not really a great selling point."

"Those are my memories as well," Other Nyx said, staring hard at her twin. "From very, very long ago. I remember when the city was at its peak. But this city is new to you. Where have you been since Evenfall was sealed away?"

"I..." Nyx paused. I could see her gather herself, compose her expression, before turning to face her mirror image. "My Order and I became trapped on the Nevernever side when the Lady closed Evenfall," she said. "Because our memories of Evenfall and what happened were sealed as well, we served her as the First Queen of Faery for a very long time."

"You served the Lady." Varyn could not hide his disgust. "The one who sealed us away. The one who destroyed Evenfall."

"*We* served the Lady," Nyx corrected him. "You, me, our entire Order. We were her spies and assassins. Those she deemed 'problematic' or 'unforgivable'—we made them disappear. I killed...so many for her." For a moment, Nyx faltered, an anguished look crossing her face, before it hardened again. "We killed for her," Nyx went on, "and we didn't question. Not once did I think she was the cause of my unending emptiness. The constant sensation that...something was missing. That something wasn't right."

My stomach clenched. Varyn still looked angry and disbelieving, but Other Nyx gazed at her counterpart with sympathy in her eyes and stepped forward.

"You said we were all there, serving the Lady." Other Nyx's voice was soft. She glanced at Varyn and the other assassins before turning to her twin again. "That our Order became trapped in the Nevernever when Evenfall was sealed. That means that there was another Varyn, correct? A second version of all of us? Where are they now?"

Nyx hesitated, then closed her eyes. "Gone," she stated simply. "Of the Order, everyone who was trapped in the Nevernever either died or Faded away. I'm the only one left."

She was hiding something. I could hear it in her voice. I saw it in Puck's expression as he stiffened beside her. A heaviness filled me as several things very quickly made sense. Puck's hostility toward Varyn. Nyx's shock at seeing him again. Something had happened between Nyx and her old Order, the real Order. Something that she did not want to reveal to the Evenfey before us.

"Gone," Varyn repeated, and crossed his arms. "Interesting that you're the only one left," he said. "Are you sure something didn't happen to us all while we were serving the Lady? How do you know you're even real?"

"Hey." Puck stepped forward, eyes narrowed dangerously. "That's not a very nice question," he said. "I would ask the same, because from where I'm standing, you're the shadow, not her. You died in our world, remember? So, who is the real imposter here?"

"*Puck,*" I said, as Other Nyx firmly put out an arm, stopping Varyn from moving forward. "Varyn, enough," she snapped at the same time. "Stand down."

"But—"

"I..." Nyx visibly trembled. My heart went out to her, even as Puck moved up beside the assassin, still glaring at the others. "I don't know," she whispered. "There was a point where... I was either asleep or gone from the world. When I woke up, a long time had passed, and everything had changed. The Lady was dead. There was a new King of the Forgotten." She glanced at Keirran, standing quietly behind us and watching this scene play out. I snuck a peek at my son and saw pain and guilt in his eyes as he gazed at Nyx. "Nothing was the same," Nyx went on. "There were courts, and new rulers and…everything I knew was different. And for the second time, I felt like I didn't belong in the world."

She swallowed, raising a hand to her face, as if expecting it to be transparent. "Maybe… I am just a memory," she mused. "Something that Faery dreamed into existence, or someone's memories brought back to life." Her fingers curled into a fist. "There can't be two of us," she said, her voice hard. "One of us here is real, and the other…is just a shadow—"

"Nyx. Stop." Puck's hand closed over hers. She blinked and glanced at him, and he gave her a tiny, wry smile. "This is Faery," he said. "We were *all* dreamed into existence. We could all Fade away if we're not remembered. You, me, the entire Nevernever. So, who's to say whether or not any of us really exist?"

"It doesn't matter now," Other Nyx said firmly. Stepping forward, she leveled a hard gaze at Varyn, who met it only for a moment before glancing away. "We're all on the same side," the Evenfaery went on. "The Nightmares are the ones we need to fight, not each other. Maybe Gilleas will have an answer for us." Glancing at Puck and Nyx, a strange expression flickered through her eyes. As if seeing a version of herself with Robin Goodfellow was odd for her. But she didn't comment on it, and her voice was quietly understanding as she added, "If you are ready, we can keep going."

11

THE LIBRARIAN OF HOLLOWNEST

The Great Library was even bigger once we got close, rising to an impossible height. From a distance, it had looked narrow and skinny, but the cylindrical base was far bigger than I had first imagined. Gazing up at the hundreds of pod-like windows, I tried to envision each one as a floor full of books and couldn't. The amount of books it would take to fill that entire building was simply staggering.

There was a large stone stairway that led to the front doors, but Other Nyx continued past it. "We don't use the front entrance," she explained, perhaps sensing my puzzled look as we walked by. "There are guards that patrol the first floor, and they don't like strangers in the library. They know us, but it's easier to bypass them entirely. The route we'll be taking leads directly to Gilleas's lab."

"A lab?" Keirran echoed. "I thought Gilleas was a librarian or a historian."

"He is both of those things," Other Nyx replied. "But he has also been trying to unlock the secrets of Evenfall for centuries.

Studying rituals, running complex magical equations, creating magical formulas." Her nose wrinkled in an exact parody of our Nyx. "I don't understand any of it, but Gilleas is really more of a researcher and an inventor than a historian. And the bottom floor of the library has become his lab. No one is allowed down there, sometimes not even us. But hopefully he won't have the back entrance sealed like last time."

"What if he does?" Ash wanted to know. Other Nyx shook her head.

"Then I'll send Varyn or one of my people through the front doors to remind him to open it again," the assassin replied. "It won't be the first time he's lost himself in his work."

Around the back of a building, we came to what looked like the entrance to a cellar, wooden doors lying on the rocky ground. Varyn bent down and yanked up the hatch, revealing a stairwell that dropped into the unknown.

"Oh, look at that," Puck commented. "More deep dark holes. And I thought we were at the very bottom."

Varyn didn't even look at him. He hadn't said anything since the confrontation in the street, and I suspected that, for now at least, he had decided to pretend Puck didn't exist. Probably a good thing; I was going to have a talk with Puck when we were alone. Antagonizing our only allies in a world of horrific monsters and Nightmare beasts didn't seem like a great idea.

Even if Puck knew something about Varyn that I did not.

Other Nyx shook her head. "Not even close, I'm afraid," she answered. "There's a whole undercity below Hollownest, and caverns and tunnels that go even deeper than that. No one really knows what lies at the bottom of the world, but sometimes creatures crawl up from the depths that are not entirely...pleasant. Or sane."

At the bottom of the stairwell was another section of claustrophobic earthen tunnels resembling a giant insect nest. Which didn't surprise me but made Puck very nervous. Fortunately, we didn't have to go far. A wooden ladder led back up to the surface, and this time we emerged into a small, dimly lit room. The walls were covered in shelves, boxes, and hundreds of books. Many of them weren't placed nicely but tossed haphazardly on the shelves or even the floor. I tried not to step on or knock over any book stacks as we all crowded into the room.

Other Nyx gazed around at the chaos and shook her head. "Gilleas isn't the most organized of fey," she said, walking to a thin wooden door on the opposite wall. "But the good news is, we're almost there. If this door isn't sealed."

It was not sealed and gave a strident creak as Other Nyx pulled it open. As she swung it back, a hissing sound came through the frame, sounding like a cat that had been startled.

"And my shadow nemesis returns," rasped a breathy, somehow familiar voice on the other side, making chills run up my back. Beside me, Ash straightened, his whole body going tense. "Why must they constantly appear just when I am in the middle of an equation? Every time they open that door, I fear I must start all over again."

Varyn rolled his eyes. "It's not our fault your door creaks, Gilleas," he said, ducking through the frame with Other Nyx. Numbly, I followed, entering a large room that was mostly books and shelves. Parchments and scrolls were scattered everywhere, and the air was heavy with the smell of ink.

Near the back of the room sat an enormous wooden desk, though you'd be hard pressed to see the desk beneath the piles of books, scrolls, paper, and inkwells. But the creature who had risen from the stool and was gliding toward us drew all my attention.

It was unnaturally thin, with arms that nearly reached the floor and long fingers ending in points. Its body appeared to be made of shadow, like a silhouette come to life, and on its head, a bleached deer skull gleamed brightly against the pitch-black of its body.

It was the same creature we had fought on our side of the world, the Evenfaery that had lured us to InSite and tricked us into breaking the seal to Evenfall. The creature responsible for stirring the Nightmare King by flooding the mortal world with anger and hate. Why was it here? Especially since, in our final encounter deep in the bowels of InSite, our Nyx had killed it.

"Oh, what the hell," Puck burst out. "This creepy guy again? Don't tell me we're going to have to fight him here, too."

"As usual, your incredible shortsightedness is both impressive and disturbing," said another slow, instantly familiar voice, making me gasp. Behind the spindly Evenfey, two bright golden eyes turned to watch us come through the door.

"Grimalkin," Keirran exclaimed as the cat materialized on the desk, twitching his tail. "You're *here*? But how did you…" He stopped, shrugging his shoulders in a resigned manner. "Never mind, I'm not going to ask stupid questions."

"A wise decision, Forgotten King. At least one of you has learned a bit of sense."

"You can all relax, you know," the thin, deer-headed creature said, holding out a very long, spindly arm. "I have been expecting you ever since Grimalkin arrived at my lab. He told me what you have been through, and he told me that my appearance might be alarming, since…"

It paused. Our Nyx had come forward, her expression not cold or hostile, but grim. As if she was on the brink of some terrible realization that hadn't yet revealed itself, but when it did, it would be devastating. "I…remember you," she whispered, as those empty sockets stared at her. "Your name sounded familiar. I didn't recognize you back at InSite, but I know who you are now."

"Yes." The Evenfaery nodded. "And I know you, Nyx of the Crescent Order. Or, I know this world's version of you." Its deer skull briefly turned in Other Nyx's direction, before swinging back to observe us again. "Before the Lady sealed us away,

I was the king's advisor, Gilleas of the Nightmare Court." He turned and nodded at me. "It is a pleasure to meet you, Queen of the Iron Fey."

I took a slow breath to absorb everything we had just learned. I still didn't know what was happening here, but in this world, the deer-headed faery was Gilleas, not the enemy we had fought below InSite. "Has Grimalkin told you everything, then?"

"No." The raspy voice sounded faintly amused as he shook his head. "As usual, our furry sage has deemed it wiser to withhold certain information until we are all present to hear it. Apparently, he wishes to tell the story only once."

"As usual?" Puck repeated. "Not that I'm arguing with you, but it sounds like you two already know each other."

"What an observant statement, Goodfellow," Grimalkin said from the desk, punctuating it with a yawn. "I am almost surprised."

"I have met Grimalkin before," Gilleas said, confirming what everyone already suspected. "Before the Lady sealed us away, I remember having long conversations with him in the wyldwood, and in Evenfall itself. I do not recognize any of you," he went on, gazing at the rest of us, until his gaze landed on Nyx. "With one exception, of course. The king's protectors. The Order of the Crescent Blades. I know you. I have known your organization for a long time."

"That doesn't explain why there are two of us," Nyx said, with a quick glance at her twin. "Or how you can be here when..."

The Evenfaery known as Gilleas tilted his skull head.

"When you killed me," he finished softly. "Back at InSite."

Nyx didn't flinch, but she did sink a little further into her hood. Puck groaned and ran both hands through his hair. "Okay, I feel like my head is gonna explode," he said, looking at the rest of us. "If anyone wants to throw out an explanation that actually makes sense, I'd really appreciate it."

"I have my theories," Gilleas rasped. "But that is all they are—theories."

"There is one explanation—" Grimalkin began.

"No," Gilleas said, whirling on him. "No, I will not accept that."

"Accept it or not, it is the only viable answer."

Gilleas seemed agitated now, glancing back at us. "I would like to hear your story first," he said. "From the beginning. Before we can solve the equation, we first must know the problem." He glanced around his extraordinarily cluttered space and made a hopeless gesture with his hands. "It seems my chairs were eaten again. Please, sit or stand wherever you are comfortable."

The only chair in the room was the stool in front of Gilleas's desk, and the floor was pretty much covered in books and clutter, so sitting was not an option. Near the door, Other Nyx made a furtive gesture with two fingers, and the other assassins save Varyn turned and melted from the room, giving us a little more space. Gilleas himself turned and crossed the room to his desk, brushed away the scrolls he'd been writing on, and sat atop the surface. Lacing long fingers under his sharp, bony chin, he nodded at me. "Begin," he rasped, "whenever you are ready."

We left nothing out.

Starting from the moment Puck and Nyx showed up in the Iron Kingdom with news that a deadly new threat had been seen in the Nevernever. Sometimes Keirran would take over the narrative, telling the story of how one Elder Nightmare had attacked Touchstone, and the chaos that came after. Gilleas listened intently, stopping us to ask questions about things he did not understand. Which, unfortunately, since he had been trapped in Evenfall for so long, was a lot. When we got to the part with InSite, and how we'd met another version of him trying to open the seal to Evenfall, his demeanor turned even more serious.

"And are you sure of what you encountered?" he asked, holding up one thin talon, as he had done many times throughout the story. "I am sorry, and I do not wish to doubt, but are you certain this faery was me?"

"Yes," Nyx stated, very quietly. She had been silent up until now, withdrawn into her hood and lurking in a patch of shadow. "It was you, Gilleas. You and the faery we met at InSite were the same." Her gaze flickered to Other Nyx, also listening silently in the corner. "Just like we are the same."

This seemed to trouble him greatly. One claw rose to his face, his claws scraping against bone. "It cannot be," he whispered, and his voice trembled as he spoke. "It *cannot* be. But then, why have none of my equations worked? Why do they fail when I know they are perfect? At least one of them should have yielded results, but all my efforts are for naught. It makes no sense. Unless…"

Abruptly, his hollow gaze went to Other Nyx. "Do you remember how you returned to Evenfall before the way was sealed?" he asked.

The Evenfaery blinked, frowning. "I…no," she answered, shaking her head. "It's one of those things I can never remember. We were in the Nevernever, tracking down the Lady, trying to stop her ritual before it happened. We'd found and killed a few of the high sidhe, but we never found *her*." Other Nyx's frown deepened, a flash of pain going through her golden eyes before she continued. "The next thing I remember is being back in Evenfall, in the palace of the Nightmare Court. But it was different. The palace was crawling with Nightmares, and we had to flee. Eventually, we made our way here, looking for answers. You know the rest."

"It is the same for me," Gilleas whispered. "I was also in the Nevernever that day, looking for the Lady. Or for anyone who would listen. And then…there is a gap where I remember nothing. I don't know how I returned to Evenfall, but I also found myself back in the palace, and it was full of Nightmares. And I could sense something deep within the palace, something angry and powerful. Unfortunately, with the number of Nightmares, I too had to withdraw. Only I came straight here, to the Great Library, intending to find answers. I have found more questions and frustrations than anything else." He paused, and then, almost as if he feared the answer, turned to our Nyx again and asked, "Shadow of our shadow, do you remember what happened to you when the way to Evenfall was sealed?"

"I do now," Nyx said softly. "We became trapped on the other side, in the Nevernever. I remember meeting the Lady, and being confused, because I didn't remember Evenfall or how I got there, or even who I was speaking to. I just knew something terrible had happened. But we ended up serving the Lady as the First Queen, until... I guess I Faded away or fell asleep, because the world was different when I woke up."

Gilleas visibly trembled. "No," he whispered, holding his head in both hands. "If this is true, everything I have worked for, everything I have tried to accomplish, has been for nothing."

"You know I am right." Grimalkin's voice echoed in the room, low and somehow terrible. "The theory makes sense. You have to face the truth, no matter how painful."

"Gilleas, what is he talking about?" Other Nyx asked, looking at the historian.

The thin faery was silent for a long moment, and then he slowly raised his head, his voice shaking. "We never returned to Evenfall," Gilleas whispered. "Because, on that day, we became trapped on the Nevernever side when the seal was created. You—" he continued, turning to Other Nyx "—and your Order went on to serve the First Queen of Faery. I...apparently went mad, created a place called InSite in the human world... and eventually died, at the hands of a fellow Evenfaery."

"You're...not making sense, Gilleas," Other Nyx said, her voice a little shaky. "We're standing right here, having this conversation. I'm afraid I don't understand what you're implying."

"It is this." Grimalkin sat up, golden eyes solemn as he stared at everyone in the room. "Imagine that Evenfall has been sealed off by the Lady and her circle. Imagine that, cut off from the magic of the Nevernever and the mortal realm, Evenfall, and all the faeries therein, Fade away into nothing. Until only the Nightmare King, the most powerful fey of all, is left. And in his fury and rage and grief, he falls into an endless sleep, and he dreams. Of his world. Of his people. And because the Nightmare King is able to do so, the dream manifests, and becomes reality. Of a sort. Evenfall is gone. But the world of the Dream remains. And the king finds ways of delivering his own glamour to his people in the form of Nightmares. Because he is the Nightmare King, and even his dreams cannot be pleasant ones."

"That's…" Varyn's voice was a rasp, a growl, as the assassin shook his head violently. "Impossible," he finished. "So, you're saying…"

"None of us are real," Gilleas breathed, barely audible even in the stunned silence. His long fingers uncurled in front of him as he stared down at his shaking hands. "Evenfall is gone. We have all Faded away. This—everything we know—is only a dream. We are all but dreams in the endless nightmare of the king."

PART

II

INTERLUDE

Now, the story of the girl who went into Faeryland is more complicated than it first appears. Many would think that the tale began on her sixteenth birthday, the day her little brother was kidnapped by the fey and a changeling was left in his place. But truthfully, it began years before, on yet another birthday.

The day her father vanished from the world without a trace.

"What do you want to do today, sweetie?" the girl's father asked. "Mommy is out shopping, so we have a couple hours together, just the two of us. It's your special day, so we can do whatever you want."

The little girl considered this. Normally, her daddy had to work and didn't get to stay home, so this was exciting. "The park," she decided. She liked playing on the swings and slides and running around without being told to stop. "But first, play me a song. The one that I like."

"A song?" Her daddy pretended to be surprised. "And what song is that?"

She scowled at him. It was her special day; he was supposed to do what she wanted. "You know which one, Daddy."

"I do?" He walked to their old piano and pushed back the lid. The little girl trailed eagerly and climbed onto the bench as he sat down. She loved listening to him, but lately, he had been so busy with work, he hardly ever played for her anymore. "Is it this one?" He started plunking a tune called "Chopsticks."

"No!" She frowned. "Not that one."

"No?" He grinned and switched songs, but this one was gloomy and sad. "Is it this one?"

"Daddy!"

He laughed. Picking her up, he set her on his lap, then stretched his fingers and put them on the keys. "Okay." He smiled mischievously. "I *think* what you're talking about is this song right here…"

And he finally played the right one.

It was called "Butterfly," and it was a song he'd written just for her. Bright and bouncy and cheerful, it always made her happy inside. Sometimes she would dance to the song, spinning and spinning as the music flowed around her. And sometimes, though not often, she would see strange things from the corners of her eyes: tiny flitting things with wings, or faces watching from the windows. They were always gone when she looked again, so she figured it was the magic from her daddy's music.

"Again!" she cried as the tune came to an end. Her daddy laughed and shook his head.

"Again? I've already played it three times. Besides, I thought you wanted to go to the park today."

Oh, right. She did. She liked the park, and they didn't get to go very often. Mommy didn't like being outside. She always seemed slightly nervous whenever they were outdoors and away from people. In fact, that was why she wanted to go today; Daddy was far more likely to take her to the park if Mommy wasn't there.

"Can I get bread?" she asked, sliding off the piano bench. "I want to feed the ducks." Her daddy sighed and picked her up in one arm.

"I suppose," he told her, and gently tapped her nose with his finger. "As long as you promise not to bring home frogs in your pocket. Mommy was not happy with all the mud she had to clean up last time."

The little girl promised, and a few minutes later, she and her daddy arrived at the park. It was a small, quiet little park not too far from their house, but surrounded by trees so that it felt like they were in the woods. There was a simple playground with a slide and a swing, a couple picnic tables, and a round green pond that held a sizable population of turtles and salamanders, and a little family of ducks.

There wasn't anyone else at the park that day, just the little girl and her daddy, but she didn't mind. She liked running around, being pushed on the swing, and swooping down the slide into his arms at the bottom.

Later, after she got bored with swinging and sliding, she and her daddy stood on the bank of the pond, tossing bread crusts into the water and watching the ducks zoom over to snatch them up. Around them, the breeze stilled, the branches of the trees going silent. It was suddenly very quiet; only the splash of water and the soft babble of ducks could be heard. As the little girl tossed her last crumb to a duckling, she looked down and saw something in the water's reflection.

A lady, watching her from the other side of the pond.

Blinking, the little girl looked up, but there was nothing on the far side of the water. She and her daddy were alone.

"Sorry, ducks, that's all the bread I have." Her daddy tossed his last crust into the water and dusted off his hands. The ducks swarmed around him for a moment more, quacking, then glided away when they realized he didn't have any more food. "Well, you ready to go home, sweetie?" he asked, glancing at his watch. "Mommy should be back by now."

She was about to answer when a faint jingling sound reached her ears, making her jerk up. The ice cream truck didn't stop here very often, but she'd know its cheerful melody anywhere. And suddenly, she wanted an ice cream more than anything in the world. "Can I get a Creamsicle?" she asked her daddy, who laughed.

"Ice cream? Now? You're going to have cake tonight, you know."

"Please?" the little girl begged. "I won't spoil my dinner. Please, Daddy?"

He chuckled again, but then a strange look crossed his face. Straightening, he gazed slowly around the pond, as if he could hear something the little girl couldn't.

The jingles were already beginning to draw away. Impatient, the little girl tugged on his sleeve. "Daddy?"

He shook himself. "Oh... Meghan." His voice was strange, his eyes still on the pond in front of them. But he dug into his pocket, pulled out a green bill, and handed it to her. "Here you go," he murmured without looking down. "Better hurry or you'll miss the truck."

For a moment, she almost didn't go. Why was he acting weird all of a sudden? But then, she remembered ice cream, and how badly she wanted it right then. She snatched the bill from his fingers and hurried away, across the park, toward the tantalizing jingle coming from the parking lot at the bottom of the hill.

But when she reached the parking lot, there was no truck. There were no vehicles at all except their own yellow station wagon, sitting alone in the space. Confused, the little girl gazed around, wondering why she was there. There was a dollar in her hand that her daddy had given her, for...something. Where was he?

Suddenly frightened, she turned and ran back toward the pond. As she sprinted up the hill, she heard someone singing.

★ ★ ★

The rest of the story is a little scary, and some of the details are not pleasant, so I won't go into them now. But that day, the little girl's father disappeared from her life for a while. For a long time, the little girl and her mommy were alone. And the girl was afraid. Because now she knew, even if it was just subconsciously, that something was out there. Something she couldn't understand. Something that was coming for her.

Eventually, the little girl got a new family—a new father—and a few years after that, a new brother. And though she loved her new family very much, she never gave up hope that she would find her real daddy again, someday. She kept hoping that he would come home.

And when she discovered the other world, suddenly she understood what might have happened, all those years ago at the pond. And she held out hope that, somewhere in the strange, frightening world, her father was there. Waiting for her.

It took a long time, and the girl went through many struggles, but because she never lost hope, eventually, she found her father again.

Hope is a powerful thing. It keeps us from giving in to despair. It keeps us from giving up. The fey might tell you that hoping for what cannot be is foolish, but in the Nevernever, even when the situation might seem desperate or impossible, holding on to hope can make the difference between lying down in defeat and finding the strength to carry on. Sometimes, you won't have strength or will or magic when the Nevernever throws its worst at you.

Sometimes, hope will be all you have to rely on...and it will have to be enough.

12

THE DREAMS OF THE KING

For a few heartbeats after Gilleas spoke, there was only silence. "No," Varyn said at last. His voice trembled, and he staggered back from Gilleas. "No, that...that can't be true. I've lived in Evenfall my whole life. I remember...everything. What you're implying..." He trailed off, looking desperately at Other Nyx, as if her denial would somehow make it right. "We're real," he insisted, still staring hard at the other assassin. "Gilleas is wrong. He has to be wrong."

Slowly, Other Nyx shook her head. "It...it makes sense," she whispered, and her eyes strayed to her twin, who met her gaze silently. "I have wondered for a long time now...how Evenfall could have survived. How we could still be here. Even with the glamour from the king's Nightmares, it seemed...improbable. But even before, that memory gap has always troubled me. And now, I have proof staring me in the face. Evenfall *didn't* survive. The Lady won, and I...never made it home." She gazed at Varyn, her expression softening with grief and pain. "None of us did."

I dragged in a shaky breath. This whole situation was so surreal; I was having trouble making sense of it all. But if what I was hearing was true, the entire realm of Evenfall, and all the fey we had met so far, were nothing but shadow and memory. My insides roiled; I felt faintly sick. I couldn't even imagine what Nyx and the Evenfey were going through, the sense that their whole world, their entire existence, was a lie. Nothing made sense. How were we even here? We *were* real. "Are you sure about this, Grimalkin?" I asked the cait sith. My voice came out shaky, and I swallowed hard. "We don't have any real evidence of what Evenfall could be—this is a theory."

"A theory, yes." Grimalkin's tone was unapologetic. "But a true one. Gilleas knows, as do I."

"He is right." The thin Evenfaery rose slowly, painfully, and turned to his desk. One claw touched an open book on the corner almost fearfully. "For years, I wondered why I could not find the way to open Evenfall, to end this world of nightmares. My rituals and calculations...they should have worked." The talons pulled the book off the desk, flipping through the pages with feverish intensity. "And yet, no matter what I tried, I was met with failure after failure."

He slammed the book on the desk, splayed claws holding it open to a certain page. "I kept trying," he continued. "I knew there had to be a way. Twice, I almost succeeded. There were two instances that should have worked. I remember them clearly. The first, I traveled to the place I believed was the location of the actual seal. Where, on the other side, the Lady and her circle had performed the ritual that would damn us all.

"It was a deadly place," Gilleas went on, "swarming with fey who had been turned into Nightmares or had gone mad from the lack of glamour. They seemed attracted to one spot, one small circle of land that had nothing on it. Could they somehow sense the real world on the other side? I was willing to bet that this was the place where, if I could just put a tiny crack in the seal, it would break. Or at least, glamour would start to flow into Evenfall again. But getting to that place was extremely difficult. I spent a long time raising an army, gathering those brave or skilled or desperate enough to make the journey with me. I assured them it would work. I all but promised them I would break the seal and return Evenfall to what it used to be. They believed me, or they wanted so much to believe me that they risked their existence for the chance. When I thought I had the numbers, we charged the site of the seal. The Nightmares came at us, so many of them. I lost...so many." Gilleas covered his face with a talon. "But we struggled and clawed and fought our way to that one spot, and those who remained continued to fight while I performed the ritual.

"I thought it would work." With a sharp crackle, Gilleas's talons crumpled the pages beneath it, before he hurled the book to the floor. "I poured everything I could into that spell. Everything I had learned and researched and struggled with since the day I found the library. I knew it was correct. I knew it would work...and yet, it didn't. The fey who had made the journey, who had agreed to protect and defend me, who sacrificed themselves to give me the chance to open Evenfall...they were dying around me. And I could not make it work. Not even by the smallest of cracks. No matter what I tried, I could not affect the seal.

"In the end, I was forced to flee," Gilleas finished, and from the shakiness of his voice, I suspected he was on the verge of breaking down. "I left them all," he whispered. "When my entire force was slaughtered to the last faery, and I was the only one left, I ran. I fled with my failure, with the guilt of letting those brave warriors die for nothing. I returned to the library, furious and grieving, wondering what I had done wrong. Why hadn't it worked?" He snatched the book off the floor, digging his claws into the pages as he shook it. "It should have worked. I vowed that next time I attempted such a thing, I would put only myself in danger. But it was years, decades later, that I worked up the courage for a second attempt.

"This time," Gilleas went on, "I took no chances. I did my research. I learned everything I could, not only about the seal, but about Evenfall and the Nightmare King. By that time, more fey were starting to trickle into Hollownest from the over world. Perhaps they were drawn to legends of the library, whispers of a safe haven relatively free of the Nightmares. Or perhaps they were seeking answers themselves." One talon gestured in Other Nyx's direction. "It was around this time that our moon elf warrior and her Order showed up, fighting their way through the monsters and Nightmares to reach the city. They provided a measure of safety for those looking to reach Hollownest and continued to protect those who made it this far, while ensuring that my work was not disturbed, of course."

Against the wall, Other Nyx gave Gilleas a tiny, solemn nod of respect, which he returned before turning back to us.

"At this point in time," Gilleas went on, "whispers began to reach me, even deep in the Great Library. No one had seen the king in years. But we all knew it was his Nightmares that provided us the glamour we needed to survive. No one had been to the palace, or what remained of it, since the Lady sealed us away. It was a death trap, crawling with the largest, most vicious of Elder Nightmares. But there were also rumors that, in the ancient throne room that no one could get to, the king slept his endless sleep. I became obsessed with that knowledge. I began to think that, if only I could reach the king, even though he dreamed, I might learn the secret to freeing Evenfall. And so, I began the journey across the realm to the king's palace. And this time, I went alone.

"It was a miracle that I found the palace," Gilleas continued. "And an even bigger miracle that I reached the throne room alive. I saw Nightmares that chilled me to the core, creatures that have scarred me from the inside, that I see in my mind's eye even now. I nearly perished many, many times, but somehow, I made it to the throne room, to the seat of the king."

Gilleas stopped. His claws curled into themselves, and he began to shake. "I will never forget," he whispered. "The throne sat empty. The king wasn't there. I had made the journey for nothing."

A flicker of dread went through me. Our entire plan, such as it was, consisted of tracking down the Nightmare King. If Gilleas had already been to his castle and the king was not there, where else could we go? How were we going to find him?

"I couldn't go back," Gilleas continued, unaware of my bleak thoughts. "The Elder Nightmares knew I was there. I had only minutes before they would find me. I could hear them approaching, and I knew I was not going to survive.

"And then." Gilleas raised his head. "I saw a door. At the back of the throne room. In itself, this was nothing. The palace has hundreds, thousands, of doors. But I had lived at the palace for a long, long time. I remembered everything about it. And I knew that this door was out of place. It was not there before. Which was odd, because—save for the Nightmares—the rest of the palace was as I remembered. Except for this. When had this door appeared? Where did it lead?

"Unfortunately, I did not have time to wonder or to research any of my theories," Gilleas said. "The Nightmares had found me. They flooded the throne room, and all I could do was run. Of course, there was nowhere *to* run...except to the door at the back of the throne room. I reached the door, and as I opened it, I felt...something. For just a moment, I saw what was on the other side. Then, I stepped through the doorway, and..."

Gilleas stopped again. "I found myself back here," he whispered, raising his talons to the room around us. "At the library, as if I had never made the journey at all. Before this, I could not tell you what happened when I went through the door, why I suddenly vanished and reappeared somewhere else, but... I think

I know the reason now. That doorway, wherever it went, it led to a place that was outside the king's dream. But I could not leave the Dream, because I am part of it. I am not real, and I cannot exist outside his dream world. None of us can."

"I don't understand," I said. "We have seen Nightmares in the Between, and the fallen Evenfey in the real world. A whole army of Evenfey breached the portal and entered the Nevernever. How can they exist if they're part of the king's dreams?"

"The Elder Nightmares are glamour made manifest," Gilleas replied dully. "They are not fey, but they can turn Evenfey into weaker versions of themselves. And they can leave this dream world because they are still part of the Nightmare King, his glamour and emotions and memories, though once on the other side, I suspect they will eventually Fade. But for us—for those who Faded away and were reborn from the king's memories—there is no escape. We are part of the Dream, part of the nightmare. We cannot exist outside it, because we are not real."

Silence fell once more. Everyone, even Puck and Varyn, were lost in their own thoughts, trying to process what had been revealed. I didn't know what to feel, or say, or do. It was like a hole had opened inside me, yawning and terrible. We had come to Evenfall to stop the Nightmare King. We had found a whole world on the other side, filled with unspeakable terrors and living Nightmares. But the Evenfey lived here, too. Faeries like Nyx, Varyn, Anira, the wolflings, the Skitterfolk. And somehow, against all odds, with no glamour and no magic to sustain them, they had survived.

Only, they hadn't. According to Gilleas and Grimalkin, they weren't real at all. The entire realm of Evenfall was nothing but a dream, a memory, from the mind of the Nightmare King. And when he woke up, the world of the Dream would vanish, as would everyone we had met on our journey thus far.

"No." It was Varyn who spoke first. The Evenfaery lifted his head to glare at Gilleas, though more than a hint of desperation shone through his golden eyes. "I can't accept this," he said. "I have memories that go back hundreds of years. I still feel…everything. Pain and grief and anger and—" he shot a split-second glance at Other Nyx, leaning against a shelf "—other emotions. I know I'm real. You can't tell me that I am nothing, that I'm just a figment of my king's imagination."

No one answered him, either to agree with or deny his claims. Varyn glared at us all, then turned and stalked to one of the bookshelves in the corner. And silence throbbed in the room once more.

"So," Puck said at last, his voice unusually subdued. "What do we do now?"

I took a deep breath and raised my head. "We won't know anything for certain," I told the room, "until we find the Nightmare King. He is at the heart of everything. He is the one we need to seek out. Perhaps there is still a way to save this world."

But Gilleas shook his bony head. "This world," he whispered, "is not real. It was never real. You cannot save something that does not exist. If the king wakes and his dream disappears, then so be it." He bowed his head, thin shoulders slumping in defeat. "It will happen eventually. No dream can last forever. Everything I have done has been for nothing."

"No," Keirran said, surprising us all. "You're wrong."

We turned to him. The Forgotten King stood there with his jaw set and his eyes hard with determination. "Even if it is true," Keirran said fiercely, "that Evenfall is gone and this world is just a dream, it's still worth saving. Like Puck said earlier, we were *all* just dreams, once. The Iron fey didn't exist until humans dreamed them into reality. Machina, the original Iron King, created a whole kingdom from the aspirations of mortals. It's the same for Oberon, Titania, Mab, Puck, the entire Nevernever. Faery exists because of mortal belief—it ebbs and flows with the dreams and imagination of humanity. And it fades when humans no longer remember."

"This is different," Gilleas said. "You are still real. Individual fey might vanish if they are forgotten for too long, but the Nevernever still exists. It will not simply disappear if one person wakes up from a dream. We are nothing but shadows, memories who have not yet realized their world is a lie."

"You are more than that," Keirran said stubbornly. "You have your own dreams, and fears, and aspirations. You've worked so hard to free Evenfall. Nyx—" he glanced at the other assassin in the corner "—wants to protect the fey who live here. Anira grieved the loss of her mate for years. The Skitterfolk depend on each other to survive." He clenched his fists. "Everyone I've seen, everyone I have met, talked to, interacted with, has proven to me that this world and those who live in it are worth saving."

"I agree with Keirran," Ash said. "This might be a dream, but I cannot tell the difference between this world and the real world. If this Evenfall vanishes and everyone disappears, it will be a tragedy."

"Seconded, ice-boy," Puck chimed in. His gaze first went to Nyx, then to her twin against the shelf. "If the people here are anything like the originals, there's no way I'm letting them vanish. We're going to save them. Or at least, we're going to make sure the king never wakes up."

"How?" Gilleas asked. "How do you intend to save something that is not there? That will vanish the moment the king opens his eyes? Or perishes?"

"The door in the throne room," I said. "You told us that it might lead out of the Dream. If we can get through the door, I bet the Nightmare King will be on the other side."

"You will never get there," the Evenfaery stated. "You do not know this world. The palace of the Nightmare King is not a place one can simply walk to if you do not know the way. And now, the palace and the surrounding area are swarming with Elder Nightmares. They are not like the ones you have seen so far. These are infinitely more powerful. It was only through luck and knowledge of the palace that I found my way to the throne room the first time, and even then, I nearly lost my life." Gilleas gave me a scrutinizing look, hollow eyes seeing far too much. "How do you intend to fight your way past the Nightmares? You have no glamour, no magic, and no power. How do you even intend to find the palace?"

"I will lead them there."

Other Nyx's voice echoed softly in the lull. She raised her head, watching us with solemn gold eyes. "I know the way," she went on. "Varyn and I will take them to the palace, and we will protect them from the Nightmares once we arrive."

"Foolish." Gilleas shook his bony head once more. "Everyone here is reacting on emotion alone and not thinking things through. Shadow warrior, you will be taking them to their deaths," he told Other Nyx. "Even if they are very powerful in their own realms, this is Evenfall. If they have no magic and no glamour, they will not stand a chance against the Elder Nightmares."

"Then how do we get the magic?" I asked. "The Evenfey survive by taking the glamour from the king's offerings. We've seen them do it, and I've felt the glamour from the Nightmares we've killed. Can we do the same?"

Other Nyx blinked. You could tell she was confused by either the question, or that we had no idea how to do such a thing. "All fey can use the Nightmare glamour," she said. "I don't see any reason why you wouldn't be able to harvest it, as well."

"We're not Evenfey," Ash said. "We're from the Nevernever, where the courts rule the realms. I am not able to use Summer glamour, and the same goes for Puck and Winter magic. Only Meghan and Keirran are able to use multiple glamours, and they're both part human."

"Not necessarily." This time, it was Grimalkin who spoke, sitting up on the desk to peer at us. "Glamour is a strange thing nowadays," he said. "It did not have a label before. There was not Summer or Winter, Seelie or Unseelie magic. They came about with the creation of the courts, as did the fey who wielded them. At its core, glamour comes from and is made up of emotion. The passion and heat of Summer. The fury and ice of Winter. But if you trace it back far enough, all magic was the same. And fear, which is the Nightmare glamour, is universal. *If*—" and the cat looked directly at Ash "—you do not lose yourselves in the emotion. If you can accept the fear and the grief and the rage, and not let it consume you."

"I almost did, once," Ash said in a very low voice. "I don't know if I can afford to risk that again."

"It is harder for some of us," Grimalkin acknowledged. "It is more difficult to remain in control when your very nature leans toward violence and anger and ruthlessness. But it is possible to use the Nightmare glamour of Evenfall and not lose yourself in the process. And you *will* need to use it, if we are going to find our way to the Nightmare King."

Ash sighed but gave a single nod. I met his gaze, seeing the hesitancy there, the fear of losing himself, before his eyes hardened with determination. "If that is what it takes," he said quietly.

I'm not worried, I thought at him, hoping he could see it in my eyes. *You're strong, Ash. You've already proven that you are more than your Unseelie heritage. Whatever comes of using this Nightmare glamour, we'll face it together.*

"So, it's decided, then," Other Nyx said. "We will take you to the palace of the Nightmare King. And we will help you fight your way through whatever Nightmares stand in your path."

"Why?" Gilleas almost whispered. His deer skull rose slowly to stare at Other Nyx. "Leader of the Order, I have never known you to be impulsive," he told the assassin. "You know virtually nothing of these strangers, only that they come from the outside world. Now that we know the truth, why do we even bother? None of this is real. You are not real." He gestured at

Varyn, still seething by the bookshelves. "Your kin are not real. This city, this library full of knowledge and secrets, is not real. What these strangers wish to accomplish is impossible. We are but a dream, and one day, the king will wake, or he will die. It is inevitable. Why delay our fate?"

"Because I am tired, Gilleas." Other Nyx looked at the Evenfaery, weariness and resignation settling over her like a cloak. "I am tired of living in a world that is dying. Of fighting every day for my own existence. Of watching those I care about Fade, or turn into monsters I must then put down. I might not be real, but I remember what this world used to be, what *I* used to be. And I know that something has to give. That Evenfall and the king will not be able to sustain us much longer.

"I know you feel your work has been wasted," Other Nyx went on, her gaze sympathetic as she watched Gilleas. "But that's not true. It gave the rest of us hope. In this living nightmare, when giving up and letting despair take us would have been easier, you gave us a reason to fight. To keep existing. In the hope that, one day, we will see the outside world again."

"But it was a lie," Gilleas protested. "I gave you false hope."

"No." Other Nyx firmly shook her head. "There is no such thing in Evenfall. We all hope for something better. And I will continue to hold out the hope that I will see the other side again. Which is why I will aid these strangers, because even if we fail, that belief will keep me going until the Dream ends and we all disappear."

"Come with us, Gilleas." It was Varyn's voice, shocking us all once more. The assassin moved into the center, golden eyes hard and fixed on the ancient Evenfaery. "You know more about Evenfall than anyone save the king. You know the secrets of the palace, and you've already found your way to the throne room once. You can either help us, or you can sit here and wait for the Dream to end, and for nonexistence to claim you." He put a fist to his chest, anger and determination sparking in his gaze.

"I, for one, will fight the Fading of the Dream as long as I can. Even if it means helping the thrice-cursed fey who did this to us in the first place."

It wasn't correct, or fair, for him to blame us, but I understood his anger. And now was not the time for division. "We would appreciate your aid, Gilleas," I said. "If there is a way to save Evenfall, we will find it. But we're going to need all the help we can get."

Gilleas was silent, thinking. Finally, he sighed, bowing his head. "Perhaps I am wrong," he murmured, more to himself now. "Perhaps these strangers will succeed where I have failed for millennia. My life's work was for naught but…they have come from the other side. They are here in the Dream, and the Nevernever is aware again of Evenfall. We are no longer forgotten. Perhaps it will be enough."

He nodded to himself, then looked up at me. "Very well. I will join you then, queen of the Nevernever," he said. "It might be impossible, but if you can somehow save Evenfall, then perhaps my work will have meant something after all."

"I am not the queen of the Nevernever," I told him. "I am *a* queen of Faery, but I am not like the Lady. And I am grateful, Gilleas. If there is a way to save Evenfall, we will find it. And we will bring you all home, I promise."

Gilleas and the rest of the Evenfey regarded me in awed, somber silence. I, as a queen no less, had just evoked one of the sacred vows of Faery. One did not use the word *promise* without being absolutely certain they meant to carry it through. Fey who broke their word could unravel, lose themselves, and cease to exist, so making a vow was deadly serious in Faery. It seemed the rules in Evenfall were the same.

The Evenfey were not that different from us, after all.

Before anyone could say anything more, Keirran stepped forward, his expression somber. "I will add to that," he told the Evenfey, who gazed at him in surprise. "I knew the Lady," Keirran continued, "more personally than anyone here except Nyx. When she returned to the Nevernever, determined to take back her throne, I was at her side. I fought for her, and nearly destroyed Faery in the process."

He said this calmly, though I saw the veiled anguish and guilt in his eyes as he faced the Evenfey before us, and my throat closed up. He still hadn't forgiven himself for what he had done in the war with the Forgotten. Perhaps he never would. I wished it could be different. Keirran had done terrible things, and his actions had left scars in Faery that would never heal, but I didn't want my son to carry the burden of his mistakes with him his entire immortal life.

"I know what the Lady was capable of," Keirran went on. "How far she was willing to go to achieve her goals. She became the First Queen after erasing an entire world from existence. She was ready to destroy another to reclaim what she had lost. I am ashamed of the part I played in bringing her to power a second time, but what she has done to Evenfall is unforgivable. So let me, as King of the Forgotten, also make the promise to set things right, whatever it takes. If there is a way, I swear I will find it. I wish I could promise you more."

"Enough." Gilleas held up a slender hand. "Please," he rasped. "No more. No more promises. No more vows. It is too much. We are grateful, but I do not want to see the death of any who came to help us. Queen of..." He hesitated, looking at me. "I am sorry. If I am not to call you 'queen of Faery,' what is your proper title?" he asked.

"The Iron Queen," I replied softly. "Or, just call me Meghan."

"Iron Queen." Gilleas nodded and bowed his head. "If we are to attempt this journey, I will be honest with you. As you are, you and your companions will not be strong enough to reach the king's palace. Not with the amount of Elder Nightmares surrounding it. Not even the Order will be able to get through on their own. The path I took is not possible with multiple people. The only way to that door in the palace is to face the Nightmares."

I nodded. "We're going to need magic, then. More than we have."

"We can teach you," Other Nyx said. "We can show you how to harvest and use the Nightmare glamour, but that means…"

"We're going to have to kill some Nightmares," Ash finished, and she nodded.

"The small ones are not enough," she went on. "Only the Elder Nightmares will have the amount of power that you're looking for. The older and stronger they are, the more magic you'll receive. Of course, going after the strongest Nightmares will be extremely dangerous. And the worst part is, if they kill you, you'll become one of them yourself. So be very certain that this is the path you want to take. We can lead you to the Nightmares, we can even help you defeat them, but it could be deadly, for all of us."

"If you're willing to help us, we will be very grateful," I told the other assassin. "But this is something that we have to do. We'll need to be at our full power, or close to it, if we want to face the Nightmare King."

She nodded gravely. "As you wish. Varyn…" She glanced at her husband, who straightened. "Go to the others. Explain what we'll be doing. I'm leaving them all behind to guard the city, but you and I will go to help Gilleas and the Iron Queen."

Varyn didn't look entirely pleased, but he didn't argue, slipping out the door and vanishing from sight.

Gilleas let out a long sigh and turned back to me. "If I am to embark on this journey to the palace, I will need time to prepare," he said. "Allow me to refresh my knowledge of certain things, gather a few books, and I will be ready. I assume we will be heading to the Howling Peaks first?" he asked, looking at Other Nyx.

"It's the closest lair of a named Nightmare," the Evenfaery replied. "I'm not looking forward to it, either, but it seems time is of the essence. The Wailing One is one of the few Elder Nightmares I know of."

"I will see if I can find anything on her." Gilleas sighed. "The Wailing One has been around…for a very, very long time. I'm sure there are a few legends surrounding her."

"Oh, great," said Puck. He had been so quiet this whole time, I was starting to worry about him. "A Nightmare called the Wailing One. Why do I get the feeling I'm going to need earplugs?"

The Great Library was well named, I found. After deciding our next course of action, Gilleas excused himself, saying he had research to do. He invited us to make ourselves at home but warned us not to venture too high up into the library.

I discovered what he meant by "high up" a minute later.

Following him through a small door in the wall, we entered the main library, and for a moment, all I could do was stare.

The room we entered was massive and circular, an enormous tube that went straight up. There was no ceiling, or at least, none that I could see. Instead, hundreds, maybe thousands, of ladders and catwalks crisscrossed the space overhead, looking like a spiderweb of wood and rope. Along the walls, spiraling up as far as I could see, were rows and rows and rows of books. Tiny figures moved along the catwalks and scurried up and down the ladders, too far away to see clearly, though I caught flashes of huge eyes and papery wings. On the ground floor, another maze of shelves loomed around us, dim and shadowy. Beyond the aisles, I could hear the rustle of paper, the whisper of books being slid back into place, and the soft pattering of feet, though I never saw the fey responsible.

"Hopefully this will not take long," Gilleas said, weaving through the aisles to the center of the room. A massive pillar, filled with child-sized holes, rose into the air like an enormous termite mound. Gilleas walked around the pillar and tapped lightly on the walls with his long, pointed fingers.

"The Wailing One," he said into one of the holes. His voice echoed, seeming to reverberate up the pillar and exit through the dozens of openings above us. "Named Elder Nightmare who makes her lair in the Howling Peaks. I need any information available—myth, story, or actual facts. As soon as possible, please."

For a moment, there was nothing. Then, with the flutter of wings, a trio of creatures flew out of the pillar through one of the many holes. From the brief glimpse I caught of them, they looked like piskies, but more mothlike than the dragonfly-winged fey I was used to. Their green, softly glowing wings were wide and papery, their eyes black and bulbous, and feathery antenna could be seen curling from their foreheads. They flitted into the air, leaving trails of glowing dust in their wake, and disappeared into the endless space above us.

"The Keepers of Words," Gilleas explained with a wave of his talon. "They know every book, every tome and scroll and tablet, that is kept within these walls. The only challenge is being specific enough in your request to make them understand what you are looking for."

"Huh," Puck remarked, watching the moth creatures fly through the room, a sly grin on his face. "So, what would happen if I just shouted 'cats' into one of these holes here?"

"You would be crushed under a virtual landslide of books and texts," Gilleas said flatly. "And the keepers would be extremely annoyed. Please refrain from aggravating them—they have perfect memories and would remember your request forever."

With a soft flutter, one of the moth creatures spiraled down, a leather-bound journal in its arms. Gilleas raised a hand, and the keeper dropped the book into his talons before flitting off again.

"Before we start out, I will do a little research on the Elder Nightmare we must face," the spindly Evenfaery told me. "I don't know how much I will learn, but even a little preparation is better than none."

"Of course," I told him. "Take your time, Gilleas."

"Maybe not *too* much time," Puck echoed, and glanced at me. "I mean, I know certain people who can get lost in a book and completely forget they were supposed to meet their best friend that afternoon."

"I will send a messenger for you when I am done," Gilleas replied, and looked around at the rest of us. The naked deer skull did not give away any emotion, but I could feel his hesitancy. "Feel free to use the library, but remember, be as specific as you can when requesting aid from the Keepers of Words. I once spent the entire night trying to get out of my lab after the keepers dropped every book they had on 'ritual knives' in front of my door."

Another pair of fey drifted down, one handing Gilleas a book, the other a rolled-up sheet of parchment. Tucking all three texts under one long arm, Gilleas nodded to us once more and glided off, the pointed tips of his legs making virtually no noise on the wooden floor. I glanced around and noted that Other Nyx had vanished as well. Grimalkin, unsurprisingly, was gone, so it was just me and those I had come into Evenfall with. Ash, Keirran, Nyx, and Puck.

Puck watched Gilleas leave, then shot an evil grin at the pillar once more. "How about cheeses, then?" he asked no one in particular. "How much information do you think this place has on cheese?"

"Puck." I sighed, but at that moment, our Nyx let out a quiet breath and turned away, and immediately Puck's attention shifted to the assassin.

"Nyx." He took a step toward her, his joking demeanor gone. "You okay?"

"Evenfall is gone." Nyx didn't turn around, and her voice was flat. "It really did Fade away. None of this is real. I…" She paused, then turned to glance back at us, her expression carefully neutral. "I'm sorry. I…need some time to think."

"Nyx, wait," Puck began, but the Evenfaery slipped into one of the mazelike aisles surrounding us and vanished from sight, like her counterpart.

"Dammit." Puck winced running both hands through his hair, and gave us a hopeless look. "You know, normally I'm better at this sort of thing," he admitted, scratching the back of his head, "but I think if I try to cheer her up now, she's just going to stab me. Honestly, I…don't even know what I could say to her."

"Is that the reason?" Ash asked, making Puck blink at him in confusion. "You've been acting strange, Goodfellow," Ash went on. "Ever since we met the other Nyx and Varyn. You're not usually this antagonistic to those who are trying to help us." His eyes narrowed, and he glanced in the direction Nyx had vanished. "Is there something about Varyn we don't know?"

"Yeah, you could say that, but…" Puck's lips tightened. "It's not my story to tell," he said, crossing his arms. "Let's just say I don't trust the guy. And I hate what running into him again is doing to Nyx. I don't know if she wants to see me right now, or if it's better if I leave her alone." He raked his fingers through his hair again, a pained look crossing his face. "This is a pretty screwed-up situation all around."

It was, and we would have to deal with the Varyn/Nyx situation eventually, but right now, one of our friends had just learned something devastating about herself and her world. "Go after her, Puck," I urged. "Don't try to cheer her up or say anything funny. You don't have to say anything at all. Just let her know you're there."

"Yeah." Puck looked down the shadowy aisle. "I... Yeah. That's... I'll do that."

He walked into the aisle after Nyx, turned a corner, and disappeared from sight. Leaving me to wonder what terrible secret he was keeping from us. There had to be a reason that Puck didn't trust Varyn. What did he know about the Evenfaery? Would it put us or the mission in danger?

I sighed, knowing there was nothing we could do about it now. "I hope they'll be all right," I murmured. "This has to be a shock for them."

"For everyone," Keirran said, his brow furrowed in sympathy. "I can't imagine what the Evenfey are thinking right now. Suddenly realizing that their whole world is..." He trailed off for a moment, eyes tightening even further. "How could the Lady do this to them?"

Ash turned to me, and in the dimness of the library, his silver gaze suddenly knew far too much. "What about you?" he asked. "How are you holding up?"

I'm fine, I started to say automatically, but the words caught in my throat. My mind was racing, thinking of Gilleas, Other Nyx, Varyn, and the terrible truth of Evenfall.

A dream. We were inside the Dream of the Nightmare King. His last-ditch, certainly desperate, attempt to keep his world and his people alive. I remembered Grimalkin's warning from earlier regarding the ruler of this world. That the Nightmare King had gone mad with his dreams and forced slumber and now knew only rage, grief, and destruction.

But that didn't quite make sense with the story I knew now. The Evenfey revered the Nightmare King; they didn't speak of him as some terrible demigod of violence and anger. Unless he had changed and was no longer the king they knew.

I was floundering. In the past, even when we had been on

an impossible mission, facing impossible odds, the path had always been clear. Fight the invading army. Defeat the one who led them. Find the Scepter and bring it back to Faery. Go into the Iron Realm and kill the Iron King. But now, the path wasn't just unclear, it wasn't there at all. I had no idea what we could do, for Evenfall, the dreams that lived here, even the Nightmare King himself. If we killed him, the Dream would end. Mad or not, if the king woke up, the Dream would end. The only other option was to make certain the king remained asleep and dreaming, but that didn't feel like a good solution, either. Would the Nightmare King just remain in perpetual slumber, dreaming of his lost world and people, for eternity?

Ash calmly took my hand and, after a quick glance at Keirran, who gave us a nod, led me into an aisle away from the main pillar. I followed until we were in an isolated corner, surrounded by narrow shelves of books. A moth-eaten sofa was shoved against the wall, a softly glowing lamp sitting on a stand beside it. Ash stood in front of me, silver eyes soft, his gaze questioning. If it had been anyone else, I would have banished the frustrated tears starting to form behind my lids. Let the mask of the Iron Queen fall into place. But with him, it was useless to hide anything, even if I'd wanted to.

"What are you thinking?" he asked softly.

"I just… I feel lost, Ash," I admitted. "I don't know how we're going to fix this. I'm concerned about Puck and Nyx, and what they might know about Varyn. And I'm terrified of what Keirran might do to save them all."

"I know," Ash said. "I'm worried about them, too. But there's nothing we can do about Varyn, and Keirran knows not to promise the impossible anymore. He has learned from what happened with the Forgotten and the Lady. I heard what he said earlier. 'If there is a way to save Evenfall, we will find it. I wish I could promise you more.' He knows that what we're attempting might not be possible, and he gave himself enough of an out—barely—to not break his promise should we fail. As for the rest of it…" He sighed. "Whatever happens, we'll get through it. We'll find a way, together."

"How are you so calm?" I asked him. "You always have a plan, Ash. But there's no good solution here. We're going in blind, hoping that we can save this world, somehow."

"I would always prefer to have a plan," Ash agreed. "Puck never stopped to think things through, and it got us into the stupidest situations. I try to avoid that, if possible." A smirk crossed his face, before he sobered again. "If there's one thing I've learned from being with you, it's that, sometimes, hope is all we have. Against the Iron King, against Ferrum, against the Lady, and even Keirran. Even in the darkest moments, what carried us through wasn't a grand plan or elaborate scheme, it was our faith in each other. That holds true here, as well."

I leaned into him, closing my eyes, and he drew me close. "I hope we can do this," I whispered. "For everyone's sake. For Keirran, and Nyx, and all the fey that are trapped in this dream. I hope, somehow, we can pull this off one more time."

"We can't go back," Ash murmured. "We can only go forward. I don't know if it's possible to save Evenfall, but I do know that we are all going to try. The first step is killing this Elder Nightmare and becoming strong enough to challenge the rest of them. Let's concentrate on that, before we worry about the Nightmare King."

"I don't trust them."

I opened my eyes. I had found a chair in an isolated corner within the maze of shelves and had settled down with a book to pass the time, but I must've dozed off. Voices murmured somewhere in the labyrinth of aisles, though I couldn't tell where they were coming from. I recognized Varyn's low tone, however, which meant he was probably talking to Other Nyx.

"They're from the Nevernever," the Evenfaery went on, the

disgust in his voice evident. "They're the same kind of fey as the Lady and her circle. Even if what Gilleas says is…is true…" He stumbled over the words, as if loath to say them out loud. "Even if this is just a dream, why should we trust the outsiders? They know nothing of life in Evenfall. You and I, we've seen the Nightmares, and what they do. Every day, we strive to keep our kin safe. We risk our lives fighting a war that we will never win. I've lost more brothers to the Nightmares than I want to remember. And now we have to keep these outsiders safe, in the hopes that they will somehow reach the Nightmare King and restore this world?" Varyn made a noise of contempt. "Even if they could, what's to stop them from running off and leaving us the moment they see what a real Nightmare can do?"

"Varyn." Other Nyx's voice was sympathetic. "I know you're angry. Trust me, I know. I was there the night the Lady convinced the others to seal us away. Or…real me was, I guess." Like Varyn, she faltered over the words, before continuing on. "That night," she whispered, "I looked into the Lady's eyes, and there was no remorse staring back at me. She was utterly dedicated to erasing us from existence. In her eyes, we were monsters. I don't think these fey are the same."

"Real you," Varyn muttered, and made another noise of disgust. "You *are* real to me, you know that, right? This other Nyx… I don't recognize her at all. She served the Lady in the other world, and that did something, changed her somehow. I don't know what happened to the rest of us in the Nevernever, where 'other me' went, but she's hiding something. She and that Goodfellow both." I could almost hear Varyn curling his lip at Puck's name. "I don't trust her," he finished. "She is not the faery I fell in love with."

"I hope not." Other Nyx sounded vaguely amused. "That would be rather awkward."

A short, almost surprised chuckle. "You are always so pragmatic." Varyn sighed. "Nothing fazes you. Even when the world is unraveling around us."

"I'm not," Other Nyx said. "You know that. I act calm because I must, as leader of this Order. Even when I'm faced with the impossible, I can't afford to look weak." I heard a rustle and assumed she'd leaned back against a bookshelf. "I admit, when I first saw her, in the ruins of the city, I thought she was a shadow. A memory or a piece of me, somehow bought into existence in the other world. But, as it turns out, *I'm* the shadow. We all are.

"But this is our world," Other Nyx went on before Varyn could protest. "This is the only life we've known for hundreds of years. I'll do whatever it takes to save it, if it can be saved. Even if it means protecting the very fey who did this to us in the first place. If there is the slightest chance I can give Gilleas, the Order, you, everyone, back your lives, I will do whatever is required."

Varyn let out a long breath. "All right," he said. "You win. I'll try not to antagonize these strangers, even that Goodfellow." His voice hardened, becoming dangerous again. "But if they betray us or leave us to fight the Wailing One alone, they won't make it back to the Nevernever. I'll make sure of that, personally."

I listened as Varyn and Other Nyx walked away, feeling a heavy weight settle in my stomach. Hundreds of years. For hundreds of years, they had been in Evenfall, living their lives. Fighting the Nightmares. This world, as terrible and horrific as it was, was real to them. We had to save it.

Somehow.

"Meghan?"

Ash appeared, moving soundlessly into the aisle. Seeing me, the expression on my face, his eyes narrowed with concern, and he walked swiftly to my side.

"Is something wrong?" he asked softly.

"No. I'm all right," I told him, and glanced back at the shelf. "Just...accidentally eavesdropping when I shouldn't be."

"Oh?" He reached out and drew me close. "Discover anything good?"

"Good? No." I leaned into him, feeling his arms around me, and wished I could lie down and forget everything, even for a couple hours. "Varyn doesn't trust us," I muttered, "Puck doesn't trust Varyn, and our Nyx is hiding something." I shook my head. "Not a great way to start a journey together."

"Should we be concerned?"

"If Nyx thought Varyn was truly a threat, she would tell us," I responded. "At least, I hope she would. I'm guessing something happened between her and Varyn in the real world, but I don't know how much it's going to affect the mission."

"We'll keep an eye on them," Ash said, running his hands up my back. "But it's not something that we can fix. The three of them are going to have to figure it out themselves."

A soft buzz interrupted us. I looked up to see one of the keepers had drifted down and was hovering a few feet away, watching us. Ash turned his head, and I could feel his vague amusement as the small fey twitched an antenna in our direction and gave another disapproving buzz.

"Do you think it's here to scold us about inappropriateness in the library?" I whispered to Ash, who gave a soft snort under his breath.

"If it is, I don't care," he replied, not moving or letting me go. "You're a queen and my wife, not a first date. It's going to have to overlook a few things."

The keeper fluttered down and, after a slight hesitation and a glare at Ash, held a folded piece of paper out to me. I took it, and the tiny faery immediately flapped off, particles of glowing dust falling softly to the ground as it flitted away over a bookshelf and out of sight.

I flipped open the note, scanning the lines of neat, extremely thin handwriting scrawled across the page.

I have researched our quarry and have read all that the keepers can find on the subject, which sadly is not much. I believe I am ready to depart whenever you are. Meet me back at the central pillar, and I will share what I have learned.—Gilleas

"All right." I took a quick breath, and Ash's grip tightened for a brief moment before he stepped away. "I guess it's time to go."

Gilleas was waiting for us at the center of the library as he'd said, his lean, shadowy form resembling a scar along the pillar. He held a book in his hand and was turning pages with one long talon, his deer skull head moving rhythmically back and forth as he read. As I walked up with Ash, the skull rose, hollow eye sockets fixing on me.

"The Wailing One," he said by way of greeting. "Not the oldest Nightmare, or the most powerful, but perhaps one of the most dangerous. This is going to be quite the endeavor for you all."

"We are up to the challenge," said Other Nyx's voice, and I realized she and Varyn were already there. They had our Nyx's innate talent for blending into anything to remain unseen. "Nightmares, even named Nightmares, can be killed. We just have to be careful, and strategic, in our approach."

"Elder Nightmares care nothing for strategy," Gilleas warned. "Some are unpredictable and beast-like. Some are eerily intelligent themselves." He held up the book he was reading. "The Wailing One has garnered quite the reputation for driving fey mad and turning them into Nightmares without even touching them. I do hope, for your sake, that whatever strategy you employ is a sound one. There are no more Wishing Trees in Evenfall, and the jinn and their kind have gone extinct. Wishing is for fools, and blind hope is dangerous."

"It is better than the alternative," Varyn broke in, frowning at Gilleas. "I will not sit here and wait for nonexistence. I would rather die having a fighting chance than wait for the king to wake up and for everything to disappear."

"I am not suggesting otherwise," Gilleas said, the hollow pits of his eyes seeming to glare at Varyn. "I am merely pointing out that the Wailing One is not an opponent to take lightly, and that wishing for a happy outcome is a futile, fatal endeavor. We must face reality if we are going to succeed."

Varyn's golden eyes narrowed, and he seemed ready to snap something in return, when a yelp sounded outside the aisle, drawing everyone's attention.

Nyx appeared, easing into view from the shadows and looking both amused and exasperated at the same time. It was obvious she was not the one we'd heard, as a moment later Puck stepped into the circle, ducking his head as a keeper fluttered by and hurled a pencil that lodged in his hair. "Ow, come on, stop it already," he grumbled, pulling it free. "It's not my fault you couldn't find much. Dropping encyclopedias on my head seems a bit drastic." A wadded-up paper ball came flying at his face, and he swatted it away. "All right, I get it! Not welcome in the library. That didn't take long."

14

BONE COLLECTORS AND PALE RIDERS

We left Hollownest by a different way than we came in, following Other Nyx, Varyn, and the Order as they took us through the city streets and into another series of tunnels. This time, the passages were filled with huge, bulbous mushrooms that pulsed and throbbed like they had a heartbeat. Pale, glowing bulbs hung from the ceiling on thin green roots, and the air reeked of rot and decay. Farther off the path, strange forms could be seen below the fat mushroom stalks. They were covered in a carpet of slimy moss and flowers, but some of the lumps appeared as if figures were sleeping beneath the layer of fungus. It was hard to tell with the glowing lights and pulsating mushrooms, but sometimes they seemed to move.

"Don't poke those," Gilleas warned Puck, who was reaching for one of the mushroom pods a few feet from the path. "Unless you want it to burst and cover you with spores. Which will not be pleasant, I assure you."

"Oh?" Puck grinned and gave the pod a sideways look. "Well, now I'm just curious."

"Go ahead, then," Varyn said, waving an arm at the lumps beneath the mushrooms. "Put it to the test. See if it goes well for you."

"I would very much advise against that." Gilleas glared at the assassin before glancing back at Puck. "The spores will put you into an endless slumber. You will fall asleep indefinitely, like those other 'curious minds' did, and the fungus and worms will feast on your blood until you're nothing but a husk."

Puck pulled his arm back. "Yep, this place is horrible," he announced. "I can't wait to get aboveground again. Also, if a certain Scowly Faery tells you to do something, do the opposite. Good to know."

Varyn just smirked, unrepentant. Ahead of us, Other Nyx paused, gazing down a path that snaked into the forest of mushrooms and glowing lights. "We'll have to pass through here," she told us, making Puck wrinkle his nose. "Just don't touch any plants, the mushrooms especially, and you'll be fine. Single file is probably best. Just in case."

We did as she instructed. I was careful to keep my fingers clasped firmly in front of me and remain in the middle of the path. The mushrooms made low gurgling sounds as we walked beneath them. They smelled faintly of rotten meat. I was relieved when we left the forest of fungi and entered the narrow dirt-and-stone passageways again.

After an indefinite amount of time walking through claustrophobia-inducing tunnels, Other Nyx stopped at a wooden ladder outlined in hazy light filtering down from a distant circle of open air, high overhead.

"The well is still intact," she murmured, gazing toward the ceiling. "Good. This should take us to the surface."

"Interesting choice," Gilleas mused, also peering up at the distant hole. "Doesn't this lead to the Rattling Wood?"

"Yes, but it's the closest exit from the underground," Other

Nyx replied. "And the Rattling Wood isn't dangerous anymore, since *he* is no longer there."

"He?" Ash wondered.

"There was a faery who used to live there," Gilleas explained, "who could make travel through the forest...interesting. There is a reason it is called the Rattling Wood."

"Hey, I don't care if we're going to a place called Slaughter Woods or the Forest of Exploding Faces." Puck swiftly moved to the ladder. "As long as we're getting out of here. No offense, but I've hit my creepy-crawly limit for the next millennium."

"Ah, fresh air at last," Puck exclaimed once we had climbed out of the well. Straightening, he put his arms over his head and stretched with a yawn. "It's so nice not to have dirt and bugs hanging over my head or falling into my hair." He looked up, his smile fading as he gazed around. "Even if we did land in a dark, spooky...unfriendly-looking...forest. There are skull trees over there. And the well is made of bones. Where exactly are we, now?"

I tried not to shiver as I climbed over the edge of the well, which was indeed made of old yellow bones. A forest stretched out around us, quiet and foreboding. The trunks and branches were made of skulls, stacked on top of each other and held in place by a mysterious force. Glistening red vines dangled from the tree canopy, tangled with bones and more skulls. My feet hit the ground and sank a little into a pink, spongy substance that looked like packed intestines. Red blades of grass grew in clumps through the forest; I brushed against one and felt a stinging sensation as the grass sliced open my pant leg and left a paper-thin gash across my calf.

"Avoid touching the grass, if you can," Other Nyx warned a second too late. "The trees are harmless, but the grass will take the skin off your ankles if you're not careful."

"Welcome to the Rattling Wood," Varyn added with a hard

smile. "One of the safer places in the Sunken Lands, if you can believe it." A transparent skull, lit with green flame, floated out of the trees and drifted past his head. I tensed, but the Evenfey barely reacted. "At least we shouldn't run into the Bone Collector."

That didn't sound pleasant, whatever it was. "I take it the Bone Collector is who you were talking about earlier," I said. "Is this another Nightmare?"

Other Nyx shook her head. "No, but if he was, I think I would rather attempt to take on the Wailing One. The Bone Collector is an Evenfaery. Legends say he killed so many faeries and creatures, he built a forest from the bones of his victims. This entire area—" she gestured to the trees around us "—is his work."

"Oh," Puck remarked. "Well, that's not disturbing at all. And what lovely landscaping—does he have a business card? I can think of several fey in the wyldwood who would love to have him as a gardener."

"Business card," Varyn repeated, frowning. "What is that?"

An exasperated feline sigh came from an old stump, and Grimalkin suddenly appeared. "I advise you to ignore at least eighty percent of what comes out of Goodfellow's mouth," he said. "That is what the rest of us have learned to do."

Puck sniffed and glanced at our Nyx. "I just don't get any respect."

The faintest of smiles crossed the Evenfaery's lips, which was good to see. I didn't know what had happened between her and Puck in the library, but she did seem more or less back to normal. I worried for her, as I did everyone, but if anyone could bring her back to her old self, it would be Puck.

Ash looked at Varyn and Other Nyx. "So, if we do run into this Bone Collector, will it be a fight?"

"No." Other Nyx shook her head. "The Bone Collector is

gone. He is a very old Evenfaery, and it would be dangerous to run into him, but he hasn't been seen in centuries."

I didn't answer, relieved and secretly thinking that the constant terror and horrifying landscapes of Evenfall were beginning to wear on me. While it was true that the Nevernever had its share of scary, traumatizing places, it could also be stunningly beautiful. I missed the sunlight of Arcadia, the frozen beauty of Tir Na Nog, and the surreal twilight of the wyldwood. And of course, I missed the Iron Realm. I missed Mag Tuiredh and the Iron palace and all the strange and wonderful fey who called the Iron Realm their home. I knew beauty was in the eye of the beholder, but I wondered if there were any places in Evenfall that were not completely and utterly terrifying.

We started through the Rattling Wood, following a narrow trail that avoided most of the grass clusters, though walking on the soft, squishy ground wasn't pleasant. As the forest's name suggested, every time a faint breeze came through, the trees would rattle, branches and skulls clattering in the wind. The small, glowing green skulls floating through the branches trailed us down the paths, chattering softly. Gilleas and Other Nyx told us to ignore them, though we soon attracted a swarm of incorporeal skulls, zipping through the air around us. They reminded me of will-o'-the-wisps, glowing balls of light that would lead travelers off the path to become lost in the forest or swamps. These seemed a bit more persistent, chittering in our ears as they followed us down the trail, but like will-o'-the-wisps, they eventually became bored with the lack of attention and drifted off into the trees.

"I take it nothing else lives in these woods?" Keirran asked Gilleas, deftly avoiding a clump of razor grass poking through the path we were on. The Evenfaery shook his antlered head.

"No, the fear of the Bone Collector is too strong, even now. No one dares to venture into the Rattling Wood—there are stories that even the Nightmares avoid it."

"Gee, I wonder why," Puck said, making a great show of gazing around. "I mean, look at this lovely flesh mound with all the bone spines poking up from it. Who wouldn't see that and think, wow, that's something I would really love to... Oh, geez, it's moving. It's moving!"

The earth trembled, skulls and branches rattling like mad, as the mound shifted and rose up, sloughing away from the giant form beneath. A creature emerged, bulky and skeletal at the same time, a hulking mass of raw flesh and exposed bone, its face gaunt and terrifying. Its claws were like sickles, its hunched back crowned with bony protrusions, and two pinpricks of orange light glimmered through the dark holes of its eyes.

"Pardon me," a deep, guttural voice intoned as the monster loomed over us. The politeness of the phrase coming from such a huge, terrifying creature startled me. "I don't mean to be rude, but is that magic I smell?"

"Bone Collector." Gilleas took a step back, his voice breathless and alarmed. "The stories say you Faded."

"No." The creature waved a bony claw. "My apologies. Not Faded. Just asleep. The world had become...boring. Hunting had lost all meaning. The Nightmares... I could kill them, and I did, but what was the point? They have no bones, no blood, no fear or awe or terror. I grew weary of killing Nightmares. Nor did I wish to hunt my fellow Evenfey. That would make me just like them, wouldn't it?" The monster sighed, huge shoulders slumping in tired resignation. "So, I decided to sleep. Lose myself in oblivion for a bit. Perhaps when I woke up, the world would be different. I see it is not different, but there is something present that was not here before."

Its gaunt face swung toward us, away from the Evenfey, and the orange pinpricks of its eyes gleamed as they focused on me. "Please excuse my rudeness," it said, "but you are not Evenfey. I remember the smell of human. I remember what magic smells like. And you…three of you—" it corrected itself, glancing at Ash and Keirran now as well "—smell of both. Which means you are more than shadows and glamour." It raised one pointed talon and scratched the side of its face. "Am I correct in assuming you have come from…oh, what was the name again? The Nevernever?"

"Yes," I breathed, as the monster tilted its head at me. "We have come from the Nevernever. We're trying to undo what the Lady caused when she sealed Evenfall away from the rest of the world." I did not tell it that this world was only a dream. If this huge creature took the news poorly, I did not want to see what would come of it.

The Bone Collector pondered that. "And where are you headed now, on this quest to save the world you doomed?" it asked candidly.

"To the Wailing One," Other Nyx replied. "A named Elder Nightmare."

"Ah, yes." The Bone Collector nodded. "If you slay it, you will absorb its glamour and make yourselves more powerful. A sound first step." It tilted its head the other way. "But that means that you have no magic now, correct?"

"We have enough to defend ourselves," Varyn said, his voice hard. The Bone Collector took a step back, clasping its talons together like two battling spiders.

"Oh, dear. It appears I have made everyone uncomfortable. My apologies. It was not my intent to frighten or offend. I *do* intend to kill you all, but I would much rather be polite and up-front about it."

Now everyone tensed. Hands dropped to weapons, and moonlight blades appeared in the hands of both Nyxes. The Bone Collector sighed again.

"Oh, come now. It's not so bad." The Bone Collector's demeanor was perfectly polite and nonthreatening, which somehow made it ten times worse. "Once I get started, it does not even hurt that much. The worst part will be when I tear your spines out through your backs, but it really is over in an eyeblink."

"Yeah, sorry, but I'm rather partial to my spine," Puck said, taking a step back with his daggers in hand. "It's one of my favorite bones. Next to my ribs and my skull and my pelvis and... well, all of them, really."

"Mm, I do enjoy a good pelvis," the Bone Collector mused.

"Bone Collector." Keirran stepped forward, unafraid as that gaunt face swung around to him. "If you kill us here, there will be none that come after," he told the monster. "We will be the last. And then, there will be another eternity of nothing, or the king will wake up and everything will Fade. But if we leave this place, if we can reach the king, we have a chance to save Evenfall."

The Bone Collector made a guttural, scraping sound that I realized was a chuckle. "Save Evenfall," it repeated. "Forgive me, I mean no offense, but if I remember correctly, it was the fey of the Nevernever who decided that we no longer deserved to exist."

"So, this is revenge," Ash said. The Bone Collector waved his claw.

"Oh, goodness, no. Please do not get the wrong idea. I am not going to kill you out of vengeance. Revenge is such a distasteful motive, don't you agree? No, this is just...it has been so long since I have had the chance to create anything. Since strangers who are neither Nightmare nor Evenfey crossed into my forest. This is nothing personal, believe me." Raising its head, it nodded to Other Nyx, Varyn, and Gilleas, standing tensely to the side. "You may go," he told them. "As I said before, I do not hunt my own. And you..." It glanced at our Nyx with a puzzled frown. "You are...different. But you are also Evenfey. You may go, as well. Or you can stay and watch. I do recommend you leave, however. The deboning process can be...unsettling."

Nyx didn't hesitate. "No," she said, and strode to Puck's side, moonlight blades still in hand. "You want the Nevernever fey, you fight me, as well."

"And me," Other Nyx chimed in. Varyn didn't echo her words. In fact, he seemed more than inclined to let the Bone Collector fight us, but once Other Nyx spoke, he moved close to her, weapons at the ready. "The Order stands with the fey of the Nevernever," Other Nyx told the monster. "You attack them, you fight us all."

"Hmm." The Bone Collector regarded us curiously, seemingly undisturbed. "What an unexpected wrinkle this is," it said. "And you are certain I cannot convince you otherwise? What of you?" he asked Gilleas, still waiting a few feet from the rest of the group, as if hoping to be overlooked and ignored. "Do you also stand with these outsiders? These interlopers to our lands? These fey who are not like us?"

Gilleas sighed. "We are all fey," he said in a weary voice. "The Nevernever. Evenfall. The Deep Wyld. The Dreaming Dark. They are all part of Faery. We were born from mortal dreams, and we die if we are forgotten. A long time ago, a group of fey tried to separate us. They made us outsiders. They made us 'other.' They used that as a justification to make us disappear. And we suffered greatly for it. These fey—" he turned his naked skull in our direction "—are trying to do the opposite. They heard what the Lady and her circle did all those years ago, and rather than pretend we don't exist, they came into our world to set things right. They are trying to bring Evenfall and the Nevernever together again." His raspy voice grew sharper, almost hissing. "And it is very difficult to accomplish this when certain faeries who shall remain nameless decide that, rather than giving them a chance to correct the past, they would rather flay them alive because they are *bored*."

"Ah." The Bone Collector took a step back. I couldn't be certain, but its gaunt face and hulking posture looked almost chastened. "That is an excellent point, I will admit. I do miss my creations, though." It studied us thoughtfully. "Such beautiful bone structures—it would be a shame to let them go to waste. Are you sure these outsiders can even accomplish what they say they are going to do? I have fought Nightmares before. They are fearsome foes, and no offense, but you are all, shall we say, vertically challenged?" An almost affectionately amused look crept over the skeletal face, which was both odd and terrifying. "None of you are very big, is what I am trying to say."

"Size does not always equal strength," Ash said, his body positioned in front of me and the looming Bone Collector. "There are many tales of the small bringing down giants and dragons."

"Yes," echoed Varyn, still standing protectively beside Other Nyx. Though of the two of them, I was almost sure she was the more lethal fighter. "It is dangerous to underestimate your opponent, no matter their size."

"You don't say." The Bone Collector drummed long talons against its leg. "A group of magic-less fey against one me, hmm. Quite frankly, I am tempted to put that theory to the test. However..." it went on, and gave a long, almost sulky sigh. "Your friend with the beautiful skull does make a compelling argument. I suppose I can let you go, with all your lovely bones still intact. Unless one of you would like to make a donation?" it added, looking hopeful. "I'm sure there are parts you don't need, or use as often? A rib? A vertebra? I'll even take a toe or a finger—you have ten of them. Surely you can spare a couple."

"Ah, no, no I'm pretty attached to all my toes," Puck said. "And they're quite attached to me. I'd like to keep it that way."

The Bone Collector pouted. "Oh, well." It sighed. "That's unfortunate, though it is what I expected. No one wants to give up their bones, it seems. A pity. They are so beautiful, to be hidden away behind flesh and blood." It sniffed, then took a lurching step back, tipping an imaginary hat with its long, pointed claws. "Well, if you will excuse me, then. Not to be rude, but I think I will be going back to sleep now. Have a good trip to the

Wailing One's keep. You will start to hear her from the edges of the forest. On bad days, that shrill voice penetrates my dreams."

"You could come with us," I offered, making Puck blink at me. I ignored him. The Bone Collector might have been grotesque and terrifying, but I sensed he was strong. And despite his appearance and disturbing appetite for bones, he seemed like a faery that was trustworthy...once he had decided not to kill you. "Help us fight and kill the Elder Nightmare. We would share a portion of the magic with you."

But the Bone Collector shook his head. "I am tired," it said. "And killing Nightmares has no appeal for me anymore. I was hoping to wake up and find the world as it had been. But except for you strangers, nothing has changed in Evenfall. Only now, I hear rumors that the king is starting to stir. If this is true, if he does wake up and the Nightmares cease, I would rather drift quietly into oblivion without knowing it.

"Maybe you can save us," it continued, giving me a strange, sad smile that was both chilling and heartbreaking. "Maybe you will find the way to bring us back to the Nevernever and the rest of Faery. Until then, I will dream of the day where Evenfall is whole once more. So, goodbye, and good luck. Perhaps one day we will meet again, and you will not be quite as attached to your bones as you are right now."

And with that, the huge Bone Collector turned and lumbered away into the trees. I watched as it shambled back to the hole it had left in the earth, stepped into the shallow crater, and sank to the ground, folding in on itself like a marionette being put back in a box. As it did, the spongy, glistening earth around the hole began to shift and rise, seeming to flow upwards, until it had covered the hulking Bone Collector once more. Only its spine poked out of the ground, bony protrusions jutting into the air, as they had when we first saw it. Within a few seconds, the ancient faery had disappeared, sinking back into the earth to return to sleep, and we were alone again.

"Well," said Grimalkin's voice. "How unexpected. I thought that at least one of you would end up bartering away a finger to leave this place without a fight. It seems even the Bone Collector is weary of existing in Evenfall. Or should I say, even the Dream is growing weary."

"You could've stuck around this time, Furball," Puck said, frowning at the cait sith. "I thought this kind of bargaining crap was your favorite thing. Or was the big scary Bone Collector too much even for you?"

Grimalkin sniffed. "*My* bones were in no danger, Goodfellow. Perhaps next time you could accept the offer and donate your bottom jaw? That would be quite good for everyone."

Varyn laughed, making Puck scowl even more. "Oh, hilarious, Furball. You only *think* your bones are in no danger."

Gilleas shook his head. "Come," he rasped, taking a step back from the looming mound that was the Bone Collector. "It is quite the distance to the edge of the wood, and we still have a long journey after that."

"How long?" Keirran asked, looking faintly confused. "The Bone Collector told us it could hear the Wailing One's voice in its dreams."

"Yes," Gilleas said gravely. "I am not surprised it could." At Keirran's continued puzzled look, he raised one shoulder in a shrug. "You will see what I mean when we get there."

We began hearing the voice not long after.

The Rattling Wood was never completely silent. Even a faint breeze could set the branches and dangling skulls chattering like grotesque wind chimes. In a stronger wind, the noise was almost deafening, hundreds of skulls clacking their jaws in a parody of laughter. As was often the case in Faery, there were several instances where I thought I heard my name being called through the clamorous racket.

But then, as the trees began to thin and the ground under my feet grew slowly firmer, I did start to hear a voice. Faint at first, barely a whisper through the sound of rattling bones. Sometimes it grew louder, sometimes it faded away altogether. But the farther we traveled, the clearer it became. There were no words. No names being called. No threats or vows of revenge. Just a constant, breathless sobbing, punctuated by high-pitched wails or moans.

"Man, someone is seriously unhappy," Puck muttered. "Did anyone think to bring any earplugs?" He raised both hands and pointed his fingers at the sides of his head. "If not, it's okay. I'll just shove a dagger through my ear canals."

"I take it that's the Wailing One." Keirran shivered, his eyes haunted. "It sounds like she's in agony. How can her voice carry this far? I can barely hear it, and it still feels like someone is raking their nails across the inside of my skull."

"That is the nature of the Wailing One," Gilleas told him. He raised his head, listening as the faint cries carried through the swaying branches. "She is not subtle. You can hear her misery for miles. Sadly, it will only get worse the closer we get to Howling Keep."

"Tell us about this Nightmare," Ash said. "I would have studied it myself, had I known what to look for. What are its strengths? Does it have any weaknesses? The more we know about our enemy, the better chance we'll have."

Gilleas seemed pleased with his statement, for he gave Ash a respectful nod. "Ah, yes. Someone who appreciates the fine art of research. I wish more had your insight, and the patience to study a subject before confronting it."

"We would," Other Nyx said in a flat voice, "but someone keeps shooing us out of the library and asking why we're not out protecting the city."

"Yes, well." Gilleas sniffed and chose not to answer that. "The Wailing One," he went on, turning to Ash again. "The Wailing One is a very old Nightmare. Some say she is one of the first Elder Nightmares to walk Evenfall. Just like us, the Nightmares grow more powerful when they are named, when they are remembered, and when stories are told about them. In the long ages that Evenfall has been sealed away, her stories have grown. One of the more common legends is that the Wailing One is the Nightmare King's great grief, his terrible sorrow at what Evenfall had become, and his regret that he was unable to save his people. The legend goes on to say that, as long as we can hear her, the king still grieves for us and Evenfall.

"Howling Keep is the Wailing One's territory," Gilleas continued. "It lies at the top of the Soulshard Cliffs, and it will be a dangerous journey to even reach the castle at the top. The area is swarming with smaller Nightmares, and even a few Elders. But the most dangerous of all is the Wailing One, who waits at the top of the keep. Whose cries of rage and sorrow can be heard for miles in every direction."

"Sounds like a blast," Puck muttered. "Really wishing I had earplugs now."

The Rattling Woods eventually came to an end, and what lay beyond the forest of bones and chattering skulls took me by surprise. Rolling plains spread out before us, with honest-to-God grass sweeping across the surface. No bones, no bodies, no silhouettes of roaming Nightmares against the horizon. The strangest things were the dozens, maybe hundreds, of broken stone statues scattered everywhere in the grass. Not small figures, either; these monuments were enormous. A hand that was twice as big as I was jutted out from a slope, fingers pointing toward the sky. A titan face lay half-buried in the grass, its expression twisted into a mask of either grief or rage. Overhead, the sky was a strange silvery blue, a crescent moon shining through wisps of ragged clouds that curled across the sky like wraiths.

"Oh, well, this is positively peaceful," Puck commented, gazing down the grassy slope. "Until those statues come to life and try to squish us, anyway."

"Do not concern yourself with those, Goodfellow." With a flash of gray fur, Grimalkin leaped onto a rock, the moonlight shining off his plumed tail as it waved back and forth. "The statues are not the things you need to worry about."

A shivering howl echoed over the plains, making me shiver. I hadn't forgotten about the Wailing One, but the agonized sobbing would ebb and flow with the night, fading away for several minutes before it returned, stronger and louder than before. The eerie cry drifted on the wind, seeming to come from the distant jagged peaks on the horizon.

"The Soulshard Mountains," Gilleas said as he strode forward, his hollow gaze on the distant peaks. "That is our next destination. We will need to use caution while crossing the plains, however. This used to be Pale Rider territory. I am not certain any of them are still around, but these are their hunting grounds, so let us be careful."

"What are these Pale Riders?" Keirran asked as we made our way down the slope onto the plains. A cold breeze hissed through the grass, blowing away the smell of rot that clung to my hair from the Rattling Wood. I inhaled the icy sharpness, feeling it burn my throat and lungs, strangely cleansing in a way.

"Exactly what they sound like," Varyn told Keirran. "They're elite hunters that used to roam these lands, searching for prey. Completely ruthless, utterly unmerciful. But don't worry, they never appear on clear nights. The only time you'll see them, briefly, before they kill you, is when the fog rolls in."

I glanced at the clear night sky. There didn't seem to be a trace of fog in the air or in the rolling hills, though I knew how quickly that could change in Faery. "Let's hope the weather holds, then."

We started across the plains. The bitterly cold wind blew

across the grass and howled as it passed through giant stone structures, mingling with the constant, distant cries of the Wailing One. I found myself wishing for my furred, glamour-lined coat, or at least a hooded cloak, as the breeze easily sliced through cloth and turned my skin numb. Still, I had been to Tir Na Nog and Winter's territory many times, where any non-Winter faery was never warm, no matter how many layers they had on. If I could spend an entire Elysium in Mab's absurdly frigid palace, I could endure the slightly freezing winds of Evenfall.

"Brr," Puck said. He gave an exaggerated shiver, rubbing his arms. "Has anyone else's nose gone numb? No? Just me, then?" He sighed and shook his head. "Man, I miss the sun. I don't know how you Evenfey can stand never seeing that giant ball of glorious warmth." He closed his eyes and flung out his arms, as if feeling the sunlight on his face, then dropped them with a sigh. "I guess you don't know what you're missing, but still."

Other Nyx cocked her head at him. "What makes you think we've never seen the sun?" she asked.

"Uh, because I've never seen it here, ever?" Puck replied. "Because everything is always dark and gloomy and dead-of-night spooky? Because a giant ball of fire is kinda hard to miss, and it never seems to rise over this creepy land of nightmares? Also, you yourself told me you were a nocturnal fey who didn't like the sun. Or, at least, other you did." He faltered, looking guiltily at both Nyxes now. "I mean, I remember a conversation where someone told me they lost their magic in the sun."

"That is true," our Nyx said, sounding faintly amused. "But that doesn't mean I never saw the sun in Evenfall."

"Not all nightmares take place in the dark," Gilleas added, turning his skull head to look at Puck. "Some parts of Evenfall are very sunny and bright. The Lake of Reflections, for example. Or Maw-burrough, the city of tongues. At least, they would be, if they still exist. I admit, I have not been to either in...centuries?"

He scratched the bottom of his jaw with his talons. "I have been underground for far too long."

"Well, I'd say you need to get out more, get some sun on your face, but...ya know." Puck shrugged. "Seeing as that's not an option, at least you're getting some air. Some fresh, invigorating, freeze-your-balls-off air, that is. Which might not last for much longer, because I think I see fog coming in behind us."

Everyone stopped and turned around. Sure enough, in the distance, a thick blanket of fog was creeping steadily over the rolling hills. It was coming fast, far faster than normal fog. I glanced behind us and saw the plains stretching away in every direction. There were no trees, no large rocks or anything that resembled cover.

"Can we outrun it?" Keirran wondered.

Varyn glanced at him with narrowed eyes. I remembered his words to Other Nyx in the library and suspected the Evenfaery was waiting for us to run away. "No, that's what they want," he told Keirran. "To separate us so we become lost in the fog, and they can pick us off one by one. No one has been able to outrun the Pale Riders once they've caught their scent. You can flee if you want, but they'll cut you down in a heartbeat. Our best option is to stand and fight."

Ash immediately pulled his weapon, and the chill of the ice blade joined the sharp wind. "How many?" he asked.

Nyx called her moonlight daggers to her hands, as did Other Nyx a moment later. "Probably a dozen," Other Nyx said. "Maybe more. The riders always hunt in packs."

"If there is a group of them, then we'll need to defend from all sides," Ash went on. "Everyone, stand in a circle. Back-to-back. Gilleas can be in the center, unless he wishes to fight."

"No, no." The Evenfaery immediately slid to the center of the ring. "I am a scholar and a historian—I have never been a warrior. I will leave the violence to those better suited for it than I."

"Are these Nightmares?" Keirran wondered, turning to stand beside Nyx and Puck, his blade held in front of him. I stood next to Ash, Puck on my other side, and took a calming breath to prepare for the battle ahead. The fog was very close now, though I couldn't hear anything within the blanket of white. The Pale Riders, whatever they were, made no noise at all as they came.

Other Nyx shook her head. "They're Evenfey," she replied. "But we haven't seen the Pale Riders in a long time. We don't know if they've changed, gone mad, or have become lesser Nightmares. No one has ever met them outside of the fog."

"Well, I guess we're about to find out," Puck said as the edge of the fog bank swept toward us. "'Cause here they come."

I braced myself as the sea of white rolled over us, damp and cold. Misty tendrils landed on my skin, clinging like chilly spiderwebs. Sounds were muffled, and even the screams of the Wailing One seemed to come from very far away. I peered into the swirling white, but other than the vague shapes of broken statues, I couldn't see anything in the mist.

And then, a section of fog seemed to disentangle from the rest. Before I even knew what was happening, it resolved itself into some strange, four-legged beast with wispy white fur that floated around it. It was vaguely doglike, but its head and muzzle were hidden beneath its fur, though I thought I saw a flash of very sharp, pointed fangs as it swung toward me. A figure sat atop the beast, wrapped in pale cloth, its long arms covered in strips of gauze so that no skin was visible through the wrappings. Much like its mount, its head was nearly impossible to see through the cloth that had been wrapped around it, but long silvery hair emerged between the strips and floated around its face. It carried a spear in one hand, the point angled toward the ground as it materialized from the fog.

Its appearance was so sudden that I barely got my sword between myself and the silent beast that emerged from the mist.

But before I could either attack or defend, the creature bounded past me, vanishing into the curtain of white once more.

Another rider came out of the fog; it too went leaping past us to be swallowed by the mist. I caught flashes of movement as they circled us, bounding in and out of the fog like fish through water, but they weren't attacking.

"Harrying tactics," Keirran murmured, somewhere at my back. "Is this normal for them?"

From within the circle formed by our bodies, Gilleas blew out a raspy breath. "I don't know," he answered, sounding faintly exasperated by the fact. "I didn't think to research the Pale Riders before we began our journey."

"This feels more like they're testing us," Ash murmured. His voice was calm, but the body next to mine was coiled to strike at a moment's notice. His eyes constantly scanned the swirling fog. If anything got too close or came out of the fog at him, it would meet the lethal edge of an ice blade, and probably would be dead before it realized what had happened. "They're probing our defenses, trying to find where we're the weakest."

Several more riders passed us, bounding out of the fog, just out of reach of our weapons. They were very fast, and in the swirling mist, it was impossible to predict where they'd come from next. Briefly, I wondered how different this encounter would be if we had our magic. If Puck could disperse the fog with a strong wind, if Ash and Keirran were able to freeze the riders in their tracks, and if I could send out a lightning strand that would ricochet to each and every one of them. Still, none of them were attacking yet. Maybe this didn't need to end in violence, after all.

"What do you want?" I called into the roiling mists around us. "If you aren't going to attack, stop bouncing around and talk to us. We mean no harm, but we will defend ourselves if we have to."

The frantic swirling of the mist gradually calmed. Slowly, it began receding, coiling back until it revealed a circle of Pale Riders surrounding us. There were at least a dozen, nearly identical, pale hair and fur floating around them in an ethereal manner.

One of the mounts padded forward. Its rider was a little taller than the others, wearing a helm whose top half resembled a wolf skull. Cold blue eyes peered down at me through the strips covering its face, the pupils vertical slits like a cat's.

"You are not afraid." The rider's voice was as faint and wispy as the tendrils of fog surrounding us. "You do not fear the riders. Your pack is strong, but you do not attack. Why?"

"There is no need," I told it. "We are not your enemies. But we have to cross these lands to reach the mountains beyond."

"Those are cursed peaks," the rider whispered. "You will find more dangerous things than riders wandering those crags. Do you not hear the screams? The Wailing One sees all who would enter her territory."

"We know," I told it. "But we still need to reach the Howling Peaks. If you let us pass, we'll be on our way."

The rider's mount stepped forward. Ash tensed beside me, and I noted that the beast's front paws had splayed fingers tipped with extremely long black claws. Its head rose, strands of fur parting to reveal a long muzzle and curved fangs. It snuffed at me like a curious dog, and through the tangle of fur that covered its face, I saw the glimmer of an icy-blue eye.

"You are not from Evenfall," the rider said as its mount stepped back again. "You are the outsiders we have heard about." Its head turned slightly, observing the rest of my companions behind me. "Our Whisper wishes to speak with you. We were told to search the Mistless Valley until we found the ones from the other side. Will you come with us to see her? I can promise no hunter in my pack will harm you while you are within our territory.

"The Whisper speaks only when it is of great importance,"

the rider went on as I hesitated. "She is silent until there is something urgent that must be said. That she asked for you means
that it is vital for you to speak with her."

"Where is your territory?" Gilleas wondered. "In what I have
read of the Pale Riders—which is not much, understand—I've
never heard of them having a permanent home."

"We do," said the rider. "It is not far."

Puck snorted. "Oh, well, that's very nonspecific. And not
suspicious at all."

"We will not force you to come with us," the rider went on,
"but know that you will not be able to find your way out of
the fog. Without us, you will wander, and may never find your
way back to the Mistless Valley."

"Um, you know that ultimatum is just as bad the other, right?"

I looked at Ash, who gave a tiny nod. It seemed we weren't
going to leave the valley unless we agreed to the terms of the
riders. "Very well," I said. "Take us to your Whisper, then. If
she wants to help us, we'll take all we can get."

The rider's mount sidled forward, until I could reach out and
touch the wispy body. The long fur drifted around me, shockingly light and silken as it brushed my skin. Without any no-
ticeable command from its rider, the beast lay down in front of
me. It was a large creature; even lying down, I was eye-level
with its shoulder. The rider itself peered down from the creature's back, then extended one thin, bandaged arm, fingers un-
curling as it held them out to me.

I stifled a grimace. "I don't suppose we could have our own
mounts?" I asked as politely as I could, hoping I wouldn't offend them. It wasn't that I distrusted the riders, not exactly, but
sitting on a beast in front of a strange faery was pressing the
bounds of comfort. "I would much rather have control of my
own mount, if possible."

The rider didn't lower his arm. "They would not listen to you,"
he said in a matter-of-fact voice. "To tame a mistwarg, you must

weave your own essence with theirs on the night of a dark moon. We do not control them with bridle or bit or saddle—they simply know what we want and execute it. If you try to mount a mistwarg without this bond, it will either vanish, or it will tear you apart. But do not worry. You and your companions will be perfectly safe with us, I assure you."

I sighed, giving Ash an apologetic look. He didn't look happy about the situation, but he met my gaze and nodded. Turning back, I reached out, grasped the rider's long, icy fingers, and let him lift me onto the back of the mistwarg.

Settling in front of the rider, I squeezed with my knees and sank both hands into long, pale fur. The creature beneath me didn't feel entirely solid; I could see the fur in my hands, feel the tickle of feathery tips brushing against my skin, but I didn't seem to be holding on to anything but air.

Glancing around, I saw the rest of my group seated atop the mistwargs with varying degrees of tension and discomfort. Gilleas in particular looked extremely uncomfortable, his tall, lanky form and spindly legs making him appear like some kind of giant insect crouched atop the warg.

I wonder what Grimalkin thinks of this. I doubted we would see the cat while we were in the presence of the riders, and I really couldn't blame him.

My mistwarg rose to its feet without so much as a lurch. "Do not worry," its rider said. "Rend is fast, but I will not let you fall." The mistwarg's head tilted, one blue eye gazing back at us at the sound of its name. "Rend," the rider said again, and a long arm slid firmly around my waist. "Home."

The mistwarg sprang forward, and I lurched backwards as my grip on the creature's fur suddenly came loose, my fingers passing through the strands like they weren't there. Clenching my jaw, I leaned forward, trying to grip with my knees and keep my balance without needing to grab anything. After the initial lunge, however, the mistwarg set a steady, bounding lope through the fog. It made no noise, no grunts or pants or sounds of paws hitting the ground. Both warg and rider were as silent as the surrounding fog, as was the rest of the pack behind us. I had to keep glancing over my shoulder to make sure we weren't alone, that the rest of them were still there, as we continued our eerie ride through the mist.

15

THE WHISPER'S WARNING

The fog didn't let up. No matter how far we traveled, it remained at the same opacity: thick and muffling. It reminded me of the Between—endless fog and mist, completely silent surroundings. But unlike the Between, this wasn't an endless void. I could see shapes in the fog, scattered trees and bushes, large outcroppings of rock, broken statues half-buried in the grass. The ground beneath the silent pads of the warg was grassy and solid. I began to wonder if the mist traveled with the Pale Riders, appearing whenever they did, or if we had somehow slipped into another world, passing through the fog into their realm.

After an indefinite amount of time, I glanced down and noticed that the thick grass of the plains had been replaced with shattered rock and dirt. Jagged cliffs and stony outcroppings rose into the air, towering over us. It seemed we had left the plains and entered a ravine or a mountainous region. I wondered how close we were to the Howling Peaks. I could still hear the chilling cries of the Wailing One through the fog, though it was impossible to tell how far away they were or even which direction they were coming from.

The rocky walls got closer as the path beneath us grew even more narrow. Sometimes, the passage was so tight I could have reached out and run my fingers along the stone. I caught fleeting glimpses of other paths in the mountain, cracks or crevasses snaking off into the mist. Once, I was almost sure I saw something enormous and many-legged, crouched between two craggy walls as we rode by, making my stomach lurch. I tried not to imagine what kind of Nightmares roamed these treacherous paths or crawled along the walls overhead. If I had just seen what I thought I'd seen, Puck would not be a happy camper.

"Where are we?" I asked the Pale Rider. My voice echoed weirdly in the silence of the canyon, muffled by the fog and crushing walls.

"The maze," was the reply. It didn't elaborate.

The gaping mouth of a cave opened in front of us. My heart nearly stopped, but the mistwarg bounded straight into the opening without slowing down, plunging into absolute darkness.

I clutched the warg's fur in my fists, forgetting that it was insubstantial and feeling it dissolve between my fingers. I couldn't see anything between the darkness and clinging fog, but the rider didn't seem concerned as its mount plowed ahead, swerving and making turns without commands, the walls and ceiling swooping dangerously close. Thankfully, the wild ride didn't last long; a hazy sphere of light appeared ahead of us, showing the end of the tunnel, and I took a breath of relief as we sprang through.

Beneath me, the mistwarg slowed, going from a bounding run to an easy trot. Sneaking a quick glance over my shoulder, I saw all my companions were still there, seated atop their mounts as the wargs padded silently from the tunnel. Ash caught my gaze from his seat behind his Pale Rider, his jaw set and his expression carefully blank. Clearly, he was having just as much fun as I was.

"We are home," my rider said.

Straightening, I looked up as the edges of the fog rolled back just a little to reveal a small grove in the mist. Trees were scattered around us, tendrils of mist caught in their branches, and long blades of grass brushed my boots as we padded into the open. As the fog continued to roll back, I could see the tall, crumbled silhouettes of stone ruins, overgrown with trees and vines, surrounding the grove. Tattered cloth banners hung from some of the towers, and wooden platforms and walkways connected several of the ruins. Figures ghosted between them, riders and mistwargs moving silently between the stones like ragged wraiths.

My mistwarg came to a stop a few yards from a half-ruined gatehouse, and the Pale Rider slid from its back. As it held out an arm to help me down, two other riders emerged from behind the gate and prowled forward with spears held at their sides.

"You bring the strangers." The voice was soft and raspy, nearly identical to that of the rider standing beside me. "The Whisper is waiting for them at the falls. She has bidden us to send you to her when you arrive."

"Understood."

The two guards padded away, and the figure next to me turned to watch the rest of his pack come in. Once his mistwarg had stopped moving, Ash immediately swung from its back and strode up to me.

"You're all right?" he asked once he was close enough that only I could hear him.

I nodded. "Kind of a wild ride." I futilely tried smoothing down my hair, which was in tangles from riding a bouncing mistwarg across the plains. "You didn't happen to see a giant spider crawling around those mountain paths, did you?"

He grimaced. "And its mate. I wasn't going to say anything to Puck."

"Probably a good idea."

"If you two are talking about the massive creepy-crawly near the caves, you can save your breath." Puck sauntered up, his red hair looking even wilder than usual. "I saw it. And I will be avoiding the mountains from now on."

"This way." The rider walked by us, neither impressed nor amused by our banter. "The Whisper is waiting for us."

We followed the rider through the base, ducking beneath wooden platforms and around enormous stone pillars. Riders and mistwargs stared at us, their blue eyes giving nothing away. Except for our own footsteps and the howling of wind through the peaks surrounding the grove, the camp was deathly quiet. Conversations were held in whispers, and even the silvery flames of small campfires scattered throughout the camp made no sound. Only the distant moaning of the Wailing One could be heard, constant and unbreaking, in the peaks towering overhead.

The Pale Rider took us through the camp and continued into the forest. Like the camp, the woods were eerily quiet and still. Fog crept between roots and hovered over the grass, and I didn't glimpse any wildlife flitting in the branches or slipping through the trees. I wondered if the animals were all shy and scared with the riders being so close, or if, like the riders themselves, they had perfected the art of not making any noise at all.

And then I began to hear a faint sound coming through the trees. A whisper of noise, low and constant. After a moment, I recognized the sound of falling water.

The trees opened up, and we stepped into a clearing surrounded by cliffs. Across the stones, directly in front of us, a waterfall tumbled into a shallow pool, though even the noise of the falls seemed muffled and indistinct. Mist drifted up from the churning water, partially hiding the pale figure seated on a stone before the falls.

I blinked. I hadn't even seen the figure at first; hunched and pale, it blended into the falls and rising mist. From this distance, it was hard to make out what was person and what was coiling spray from the waterfall.

"The Whisper," the Pale Rider said. It had stopped at the edge of the trees, indicating that the next part of the journey would be made without it. "She waits for you. Go to her, but do not touch the water."

As we drew closer to the waterfall and the figure seated on the rock, a scent came to me, sharp and somehow cloying, burning my nose and making my eyes water. I coughed, causing Ash to turn to me in alarm, placing a gentle hand on my back as I heaved.

"Meghan?"

"I'm fine." I gagged, then took a quick breath to open my throat. Unfortunately, that only made it worse, and I coughed for a good few seconds before getting myself under control again. Maybe it was my half-human side that was reacting this way, but it did not like whatever was coming off the water. Glancing up, I saw everyone watching me in concern, from Ash to Puck to Gilleas to the three assassins, staring at me with wide gold eyes. "Sorry," I told them all, wiping the tears streaming down my face. "I don't know what that was, but it was awful."

You taste the tears of the Wailing One.

The voice was a breath in my ears, coming to me even over the muted roar of the falls. In the rising mist and fog, I couldn't see the figure move, but there was no question as to who was speaking to us.

The bitter rage of the Wailing One, the Whisper continued. *The agony of failure and despair.* Two thin, wrapped arms emerged from beneath the ragged shawl, indicating the pool around us. *Her grief is so great, her tears flow down the mountain, seeping into the land, poisoning everything they touch. They collect here, at this pool, and the land cries with her as the tears soak through the very rock and dirt at our feet.*

"Ew," Puck remarked. "So, I'm hearing that taking a nice refreshing dive in the pool is out."

I saw your coming, the Whisper went on, ignoring Puck. The head shifted, and I caught the glimmer of a blue eye through the silvery strands, peering at me. *I saw you in the fog, making your way to the Howling Peaks. I saw the Wailing One as well. She knows you are coming. She is waiting for you.*

"Is that why you called us here?" Gilleas asked. "To tell us that the Nightmare knows we are coming? Sadly, we cannot allow that to stop us."

I saw two paths, the Whisper said, and I was unsure if this was a response to Gilleas's question or not. *In one, you ignored my riders and continued. You made your way to the top of the Howling Peaks, where the Nightmare waited for you. And one by one, you fell. You were not able to defeat her. And the world unraveled.*

The other path led you here, the Whisper told us, as a chill ran up my spine. *To this pool, to me. And when you left, the path before you grew hazy and unclear, and you vanished into the fog.*

"What does that mean?" I asked.

It means I do not know what became of you once you departed this pool, the Whisper replied. *It means the outcome is yet to be determined.*

"Because of something you are going to tell us," Ash guessed.

I do not know, the Whisper replied. *It is unclear whether my words will have any effect on the outcome. But I can tell you this. Named Elder Nightmares are very powerful, and nearly immortal. There is only way to kill one—find and destroy the essence of their core. Whatever that might be. It will not be attached to the Nightmare. It could be hidden very far away. But you must destroy the core before you can slay the Elder Nightmare.*

"Uh," Puck said, frowning. "I'm just gonna go ahead and say the thing everyone is thinking right now—what?"

That is all I can tell you, said the Whisper. *That is all the mist can provide. When you face the Wailing One in her castle atop the Howling Peaks, you must find the essence of the Nightmare's core. Only when you destroy it will you have a chance to slay the Wailing One for good.* She hunched her shoulders, drawing her arms beneath her tangle of wispy hair. *That is all I have to say.*

"Yeah." Puck crossed his arms. "I'm just going to mention it again. *What?*"

But the Whisper didn't answer. She bowed her head, long hair falling to cover her face, and didn't say another word. I remembered the Pale Rider's words about the Whisper, that she spoke only when she had something important to convey.

I guess she had delivered her message and was done speaking for a while.

After a lingering moment of silence, we turned and headed back to the edge of the forest, feeling the gaze of the Whisper on our backs the entire way.

The Pale Rider waited for us at the edge of the woods, both mount and rider nearly indistinguishable from the mist itself. "The Whisper has spoken," he said, regarding us all with an icy gaze. "Consider yourselves both lucky and cursed. Many never hear her voice." He tilted his head, wispy strands of hair floating around him. "Now that you have heard the Whisper, what is your next destination?"

"The Howling Peaks," I said. "To the lair of the Wailing One."

He nodded. "The climb will be treacherous," he said. "I cannot take you all the way to the Nightmare's castle, but I will show you the path up the mountain. Beware, though. Once you are through the fog, you are beyond our territory. Many Nightmares and Elder Nightmares roam those peaks, and our own warriors rarely venture into the mountains."

"We appreciate your help," I told the rider. "If you do speak to the Whisper, please convey my gratitude for the information she revealed. It was very important."

"Yes," agreed the rider. "The Whisper never speaks without

need. Seasons pass, and her voice is never heard. But, come…" He took a step back, melting halfway into the fog with barely a thought. "Your time with us is at an end. Follow me, and I will show you the path to the Wailing One."

INTERLUDE

The girl who lost her father and hoped for years to find him did find other friends along the way. Not many, for people seemed to forget she existed once she left their presence, but those she did find, she kept close.

Her best friend, for example, seemed as if he'd always been there. Always a part of her childhood, conjured out of nothing, like a dream whose beginning she couldn't remember. But later, after myriad adventures, heartbreak, and reconciliation, she finally got the story of how they met out of him.

Or at least, this is how *he* told it.

Puck did not want to go to the human world.

Normally, he liked visiting the mortal realm; there were so many oblivious humans, living their oblivious human lives, doing oblivious human things. So gullible, ignorant, naive. They were always fun to play with.

Today, however, he had a mission. A very long mission, involving a mortal girl who was not completely human, who didn't know she was not completely human. And she could never find out. That would be his job for the next decade or so. Hang around this mortal girl, protect her from anything "strange" that might appear to hurt her, and make sure she never realized what she really was. It didn't sound fun at all.

He would just have to make his own fun.

The schoolyard was noisy and crowded, full of shrieking human children running around like wild puppies. Sitting on the outer wall, Puck swung his heels against the brick and watched the crowd of mortals swarming the play yard. He had glamoured himself to look like them: a human child around eight or nine years old, with a missing front tooth and his red hair hanging in his eyes. But no one would notice him until he wanted to be noticed. And right now, that seemed like a good thing.

Puck usually liked hanging around children, or at least, small children. Very young humans could still see the fey. Toddlers still believed in magic, imaginary friends, and monsters under the bed, until they grew up a bit and "forgot" about them. But this bunch was a bit too old to be able to see through glamour anymore. Probably just as well. He wasn't here to play; he had a job to do.

He scanned the schoolyard, watching small groups of children swing on the monkey bars, or stand in a circle throwing balls at a child in the middle. Oberon had given him a description of the girl, but none of these children seemed to be the one he was looking for. He'd thought waiting near the playground where all the other kids were playing was a no-brainer, but the girl he was waiting for had other ideas, apparently.

"Well, this is boring," Puck finally muttered to no one in particular. "Where is this kid?"

Hopping down from the wall, he went looking for her.

Wandering around the building, he walked past smaller groups of children, circling all the way to the back, until he came to an isolated part of the schoolyard. There was nothing back here but a few shady trees and a peeling picnic table that was probably for teachers and staff.

Voices caught his attention. A few yards away, a large boy had trapped a smaller kid against the wall and was looming over him menacingly.

"Where's your money, Brian?" the taller human demanded, shoving a thick finger into the smaller boy's chest. "You still owe me from last week. Lemme have it."

The skinny boy cringed. "I don't have anything," he responded. "I swear. My mom stopped giving me money after I kept 'losing' it."

"You're a liar," the other said, and pushed Brian's shoulder, shoving him back into the wall. "Turn out your pockets."

"No!"

"Okay." Smirking, the bully grabbed the human by the collar and dragged him off the wall. His other hand clenched into a fist. "Guess I'll have to do it for you, then."

Watching this, Puck shook his head. Humans never changed. In any era, in any country, in nearly any age, they still bullied, attacked, dominated, and preyed on their own. For a moment, he considered stepping in, if only for the opportunity to cause a little chaos. But he wasn't here for this; he had another human to find. Besides, if the skinny kid couldn't stand up for himself, he would never get anywhere in life.

With a shrug, he turned away, intent on continuing his search, when another voice rang out, stopping him.

"What are you guys doing?"

Puck blinked. A third child had appeared, walking out from beneath one of the trees, a book tucked under one arm. She was smaller than the two boys, with shoulder-length blond hair and large blue eyes. When she saw what was going on, her lips thinned, and she stepped forward.

"Hey, leave him alone," she snapped. "I'm going to tell the teacher."

Puck smiled. Well, that was fortunate. The girl he was looking for had finally decided to show up. Even if he hadn't known what she looked like, he would have recognized her instantly. She had her father's silver-blond hair, and her facial features were slightly too elegant to be purely human. Only another faery would recognize her for what she was, a half fey, but to him, it was blindingly obvious. This was the daughter of his Summer King.

Which meant he was going to have to protect her and keep her away from everything Faery until her mortal life came to an end.

Fun.

The bully turned, and his mouth thinned dangerously. Striding forward, he shoved the girl to the ground and loomed over her as she cried out in pain and fury. The smaller boy against the wall immediately took off, sprinting around the building and out of sight. "You keep your mouth shut," the bully threatened, clenching his fist. "I'm not afraid to hit a girl."

Okay, then. Puck's eyes narrowed, and a flare of glamour went through the air. *Big mistake, pal. Let the games begin.*

Puck's body exploded into a cloud of black feathers, and he shot into the air as a large black bird. Swooping from the sky, he plunged toward the bully and flew into his face, beating him with his wings and screaming the cries of an enraged raven. The boy recoiled, raising his arms and swatting feebly, but Puck clung to him easily, cawing and screeching. Scratches appeared on the boy's forearms as Puck continued his attack, pecking at the boy's face and buffeting him with his wings.

With a cry, the bully turned to run. But he was too busy shielding his head to watch where he was going. Tripping on a loose rock, he pitched forward and fell face-first in the dirt. The breath left his lungs in a painful expulsion, and he gasped airlessly, mouth gaping.

That should do it. Gleefully satisfied, Puck backed off to let the human go, but suddenly a blow from behind knocked him from the sky. Stunned, he fluttered around to see the girl standing over him, her book raised to smack him again.

"Get out of here!" she cried, aiming another swat in his direction. "Go on! Shoo!"

Ow! What the heck? Puck dodged the second blow, flapping backwards into the sky with a caw. Stepping forward, the girl placed herself between him and the boy gasping in the dirt, the book held in front of her like a shield.

Gazing down at the human he was supposed to protect for the next decade or so, Puck shook his head in disbelief. *Are you serious?*

"Shoo," she told him again. "Go on, bird. Get out of here."

Well, this was unexpected. But he certainly wasn't going to attack the human he was supposed to watch over. Even if she had whacked him with a book. With a last caw, Puck turned and flapped away, soaring into the branches of a nearby tree. Perching on a limb, he watched the girl turn and kneel next to the bully, holding out a hand.

"Are you all right?"

Unsurprisingly, the ungrateful little snot smacked away the offered hand and lurched to his feet, caught halfway between bursting into tears and snarling in her face. Wiping his eyes, he staggered off around the corner of the school building and vanished from sight.

Puck ruffled his feathers. He wasn't worried that the brat would run off to tell a teacher; the kid would forget everything that had happened to him before he reached any grown-ups. Even if a teacher asked him about the scratches on his arms and the bruises on his forehead, he wouldn't remember anything. That was the nature of dealing with the fey.

But the girl might remember.

Alone, Oberon's half-human daughter pulled herself upright, then picked up the book that she'd dropped in the dirt. She sniffed, pushing a strand of hair behind one ear, then gazed in the direction Puck had flown. For just a moment, she stared at him with curious blue eyes, as if wondering whether she should call out to the bird in the branches. But then she turned, brushed the dirt off her knees, and headed around the building after the boy.

Watching her, Puck felt a strange glow of curiosity, disbelief, and…something else. Something that he wouldn't be able to put his finger on for many years. Maybe admiration, maybe the start of something even greater. But from that moment on, he knew, somehow, that his life would never be the same.

Empathy is a difficult thing for the fey to understand. It requires putting yourself in someone else's shoes, trying to see things from their perspective, and the fey are terrible at sympathizing with any perspective not their own. This isn't entirely their fault; faeries are born into the world without a conscience, so they have nothing to tell them that what they are doing is wrong, selfish, or hurtful. In a world where cruelty and capriciousness are the norm, it can seem like a weakness to show kindness, to look beyond the exterior and see the heart of the matter. Especially if you are dealing with an enemy or someone who wishes you harm. But it is never a mistake to be kind, and you never know…someday it might save you from a giant raven attack.

Or it might change the mind of one of the greatest pranksters in the world.

16

INTO THE MOUNTAINS

The fog ended at the base of the mountain.

"This is where I leave you," the Pale Rider stated, stopping his mount at the edge of the mist. Several paces beyond, a sheer wall of jagged rock, earth, and stone rose into the night sky. A narrow trail, barely wide enough for a single person and seemingly carved right into the rock, snaked its way up the cliffs. The wailing was much closer now, echoing off the mountain walls and rising into the wind.

"The moment you step onto that path, you will be in the Wailing One's territory," the rider continued. Its mount shifted, as if being this close to the cliffs made it anxious. "Remember," the rider went on, gesturing to a trickle of water flowing down the side of a rock. "No matter how thirsty or wounded you become, do not touch the water—it is a poison. Those who fall into the water or try to drink it suffer unimaginable torment.

"I wish you luck, strangers," the rider continued, as his mount began silently backing away into the wall of mist. "You will not see us again. But if you do manage to kill the Wailing One and bring silence back to these peaks, we will sing your triumph to the winds. Farewell."

A ragged curtain of white drifted between us, hiding the rider from view, and when the mist cleared, both rider and mount were gone.

Puck snorted. "Someone's been taking lessons from Furball."

"Do not be ridiculous, Goodfellow," said the cait sith's voice behind us. "I am far more subtle than that."

He was, of course, sitting on a rock at the edge of the trail, staring at us with haughty disdain. "I do not see why you had to go chasing after dogs," Grimalkin said, his tail thumping an agitated rhythm on the rock. "Even if the Whisper did speak to you, you are going to smell like one for days. But at least we are back on track. I trust that whatever the Whisper told you was useful."

Other Nyx titled her head at him. "You are from the Never-never," she said, looking puzzled as Grimalkin gave her a lazy glance. "You have never been to the Howling Peaks, or seen the Pale Riders. How is it you know about the Whisper?"

Grimalkin yawned. "I am a cat."

He hopped down from the boulder and sauntered up the trail without looking back. Other Nyx glanced at me.

I gave her a wry smile and shook my head. "You'll get used to it."

Ash took my hand, cool fingers curling around mine. Together, with Grim and the assassins leading the way and Gilleas a lean shadow at our backs, we started up the narrow trail into the territory of the Wailing One.

"What kind of beasties do you think live up here?" Puck asked a few minutes later, ducking a dead branch that poked out over the trail. Ash pushed it aside as well but held it up until I had passed beneath it. "I haven't seen any giant spiders so far, and believe me, I've been looking."

"Searching for trouble, Goodfellow?" Ash asked, continuing to hold the branch back for Keirran and Gilleas, though the tall Evenfaery nearly bent in half trying to duck beneath.

"Me, ice-boy? Never." Puck paused and looked back at Ash. "But this place is supposed to be crawling with baddies, and I'd kind of like to know what type of baddie they're crawling with. Normally, I assume giant spiders, because that's how it usually works, but I haven't seen anything around here at all. Also, I love that everything is so quiet—you can appreciate how loud the Wailing One really must be, to reach this far."

I listened to the distant howling coming down the mountain and shivered. "The Whisper said we need to find and destroy the Nightmare's core," I mused, thinking back to the conversation at the waterfall. "Gilleas, do you know anything about that?"

The tall Evenfaery scratched his bony chin. "Bits and pieces," he replied. "I never thought I was going to need to know how to kill a named Elder Nightmare. But in my research of the king and his Nightmares, cores and essences have cropped up a time or two. It is thought that the core is a physical item that holds a bit of the Nightmare's power, something not attached to the Nightmare itself, but hidden away. The 'essence' of what the Nightmare is. In mortal terms, I suppose it holds a bit of the Nightmare's soul, if Nightmares had such things."

"Oh, great," Puck said. "So, we have to find and smash a soul jar. That sounds fun."

"And this Nightmare will be unkillable until we do?" Keirran asked.

"Sounds like it," Ash muttered.

Another scream rang out, sounding far too close. For a moment, fear prickled, and I shoved it down. "I think we need a plan," I told the others. "This Nightmare isn't going to let us walk up and destroy her core. She's going to do everything she can to stop us. We might be able to sneak in, but it'll be difficult to avoid notice with nine of us, and if the Wailing One already knows we're coming, she'll be on the lookout. I think we're going to have to fight her either way."

"Some of us could distract her," Ash mused, looking thoughtful, "while the others go after the core. It'll be dangerous, but it's better than all of us running around and the Nightmare picking us off one by one."

"Sounds like a job for us, ice-boy," Puck said. "You, me, and Nyx can take on the Nightmare while everyone hunts for the soul jar. We'll just have to avoid getting squashed by the unkillable monster until then."

"I have a better idea," Varyn said abruptly.

He sounded almost angry. Surprised, I glanced at the two assassins trailing us, meeting Varyn's hard gaze. "None of you know what you're facing," he said, and gestured to himself and Other Nyx. "So, let us take care of it. We'll get in and destroy the core before the Wailing One even realizes we're there. We can even soften her up a little for you. Then, you Neverfey can come in and finish her off while she's weak."

"Varyn," Other Nyx said, her voice hard, but surprisingly, Gilleas spoke first.

"And you think you're going to take on a named Elder Nightmare by yourself?" he asked Varyn. With a snort, he shook his antlered head. "You know how powerful Elders are—named Nightmares are a hundred times worse. You will only put yourself and your mate in danger if you try to fight the Wailing One alone."

"We know how to fight Nightmares," Varyn told Gilleas. "We've done it for longer than I can remember now." He shot a glance at us, and his lip curled. "These fey don't know what they're up against. They've never had to fight battles like we have."

"You're wrong," I told him, before Puck could blurt out whatever he was about to say. I could feel his anger, and knew I had to step in before things spiraled out of control. "All of us have fought in faery wars," I told the Evenfaery. "We've battled countless monsters and have faced powerful creatures. You don't have to worry about us—we are not strangers to the battlefield."

"But you have no magic here," Varyn reminded me. "And you've never had to survive long without it." He gestured up the trail, toward the peaks soaring overhead. "This isn't a normal monster we're going to fight," he went on. "The named Elder Nightmares are the most dangerous creatures in Evenfall. The Order can stand against the Nightmares because we all trust each other and fight as a team." His eyes narrowed as he gazed around at the rest of us, his stare lingering on Nyx and Puck. "But I don't trust any of you to have my back. And that's dangerous in the lair of an Elder Nightmare."

"Varyn." Other Nyx's voice was calm, though her eyes glittered dangerously. "Stop this, right now. What do you hope to accomplish? I will not put either of us in that kind of danger, not if there are others who are willing to fight."

"Trust us or not," Ash added calmly. "We're still going to have to work together. None of us can take on the Nightmare by ourselves."

"You don't understand, Neverfaery." Varyn didn't sound quite so hostile when facing Ash; perhaps he thought that, of us all, Ash was the most warrior-like. Or perhaps he was feeling chastened by Other Nyx. "You've seen what we face," he went on. "You've seen what we have to go through just to survive. All because the Lady and a group of Neverfey decided that we didn't deserve to exist any longer. We were 'too dangerous' for her perfect vision of Faery. And I'm sorry, but I can't forgive that. I've lost too many friends to the Nightmares to forget what the Lady did. And any who served her…" His gaze flickered to Keirran and Nyx. "They are just as responsible, for not stopping her when they could."

"That's pretty hilarious," Puck said loudly. "Considering the one who betrayed Nyx in the real world—on the Lady's orders—was *you*."

Nyx closed her eyes. Varyn stared at Puck, his expression caught between anger and wary surprise. "What are you talking about?" he asked.

"It doesn't matter, Puck," Nyx whispered, but Puck shook his head.

"No, since we're throwing around accusations now, I think everyone needs to hear this." Puck's voice was unrepentant. His hard green gaze went to Varyn, narrowing angrily. "You keep dinging Nyx and Keirran for serving the Lady," he told the assassin, "when in the Nevernever, you tried to assassinate Nyx. Why? Because the Lady told you to. You chose to follow the orders of the queen you claim to hate, rather than stand with the woman you loved." He crossed his arms, still glaring. "How's that for trust issues?"

Varyn looked dumbfounded. "That's..." he began, and stopped. His gaze slid from Puck to our Nyx, who stood at the edge of the trail drawn fully into her hood. "When you said we both served the Lady in the real world," he began slowly, as if he didn't want to know the answer, "what happened to us?"

Nyx raised her head, and the flash of anguish and guilt in her golden eyes made my stomach tighten. "I killed you," she said flatly.

A cold wind moaned as it crested down the trail, carrying that sharp, bitter smell that made me grit my teeth. "Enough," I said, before anyone else could speak. "Puck, that was uncalled for." He shrugged, defiant, though his gaze flickered guiltily to our Nyx. I sighed. "We can't start turning on each other now," I said. "Every one of us is needed if we're going to face the Wailing One. We have to start working with each other, or the Nightmare is going to tear us apart."

I looked at our Nyx, sympathy and remorse curling my stomach. Her face was blank, her expression closed off. The mask was firmly in place, but I could guess at the storm of emotion roiling within. Still, she met my gaze, golden eyes giving nothing away, and nodded.

"I am still here, Iron Queen." Her voice held no emotion, and behind her, Puck winced. "I am with you, in whatever capacity you need."

Other Nyx gave a single nod as well. "We are with you as well, Iron Queen." She shot a steely look at Varyn, mouth tightening, but did not voice her thoughts about him. "The Order does not forget its promises," she said decisively. "We will be at your side when you face the Elder Nightmare. And when the battle is done, we will guide you to the palace of the Nightmare King, as we said we would."

"Good," Gilleas said, sounding impatient. "I am glad that I will not have to remind certain fey of the seriousness of the situation. Our world is fading, our king is waking up, and we could all very well vanish in the blink of an eye. But by all means, continue to squabble with each other about fey and past lives that have nothing to do with the present situation."

Varyn's fists clenched, and Puck's mouth tightened, but they didn't say anything more. We continued up the trail in somber silence, a frosty air radiating from both Nyxes and guilty expressions fixed on the faces of Puck and Varyn. I knew this wasn't over, that a confrontation was still on the horizon. I just hoped that everyone would keep it together until we had defeated the Elder Nightmare.

Thankfully, there were no more outbursts on the mountain. Partially because the journey became much more difficult.

The trail curved around a jagged corner, momentarily vanishing from sight as it snaked its way up the mountain. It had been a long, slow climb through the jagged peaks, and made harder by the cold, driving wind and the crumbling pathway. Thankfully, the trail had widened a bit, allowing two people to stand abreast of each other without crowding the path. Though it was still a sheer vertical plunge down the side of the cliff.

Ahead of us, Varyn and Other Nyx paused, looks of mild concern crossing their faces as they stared up the pathway. Keirran joined them, and the same expression crossed his features as well.

"What is it?" Ash inquired. I took a few steps forward, peering around the bend, and saw the cause of their concern. A waterfall cascaded down the side of the mountain, spilling into a river across the path. The wind shifted, and the terrible, bitter smell stung my eyes and made them water.

Puck coughed, covering his nose with his sleeve. "Okay, well, that's unpleasant." He had returned to his normal, overly cheerful self minutes after the argument with Varyn and was acting like the fight had never happened. Though Nyx was still giving him the cold shoulder. "Anyone think to bring along a bridge?"

"I usually do," Keirran said. He glanced mournfully at his open palm. "Or at least, I could make one, if I had any magic left."

"Not an option, unfortunately," Ash replied. "We're going to have to find another way across."

"Just out of curiosity," Puck said, dropping his hand. "Does anyone know what happens if we do touch the water? I mean, how bad is it? Are we talking mild-case-of-lead-poisoning bad, or melt-the-flesh-off-your-bones bad?"

"Bad enough that both the Whisper and the Pale Rider warned us not to touch the water," Gilleas said, and though his naked deer skull showed no emotion, the exasperated warning in his voice was clear. "Or did you not catch the 'unimaginable torment' part? This is not a pure mountain spring—these are the tears of the Wailing One, a named Elder Nightmare. I don't even have a nose and I can smell the wrongness in the water."

"He's right," I said, frowning at the Great Prankster, who didn't look all that concerned about sticking his hand into what might be magical acid. "No heroics, Puck. I don't want to take any chances. Just in case it *is* melt-the-flesh-off-your-bones bad."

"Fair enough, princess. But we're going to have to get across somehow."

Ash gazed around the soaring peaks. "There," he said, pointing to something over the falls. I followed his direction and saw a scraggly tree growing from a ledge in the mountainside, its roots barely clinging to the crumbling rock. It looked rather sickly; its trunk was decayed, and only a few withered leaves dotted its branches, but it was better than nothing. Trees weren't exactly in abundance along these cliff sides; the only other vegetation I could see was a few withered bushes and several clumps of grass that looked like all the color had been leached out of them.

Puck, also following the pointed finger, wrinkled his nose. "Not a very sturdy-looking bridge, ice-boy," he said. "I'd give it four out of ten stars on the safety meter. But, since we're not exactly spoiled for choice, who's gonna climb up there and get our bridge for us?"

Our Nyx stepped forward, peering up at the jutting limb. "I don't think I'll need to climb," she said, giving it a thoughtful look. "The roots don't look very stable." A curved blade appeared in her hand. "I think I can cut it down from here."

"Wait." Ash raised a hand, though his gaze wasn't on the branch overhead. He was scanning the sides of the cliffs around us with narrowed eyes. "I don't think we're alone up here."

Chilled, I looked up and saw what he was talking about. There were no Nightmares or monsters perched on the walls or ledges around the waterfall, no eyes peering down hungrily. But several large gaps and crevices had been bored into the stone. Large enough for something slim or insect-like to squeeze into.

I suddenly felt eyes on me. Or maybe that was my paranoid imagination.

Gilleas sighed. "I was going to ask a fellow intellectual what he thought of all this," he said. "But it appears he has disappeared again. Am I to assume that this is normal?"

Grimalkin had indeed vanished. Which made everyone who knew him even more wary. Puck groaned and pulled his daggers, and Ash casually stepped closer to me. "Normal, yes," Puck said. "Ideal? Never."

"Nyx," I said, and both Evenfaeries looked at me, their movements so identical, it gave me a brief surreal moment. I shook it off and nodded to the branch. "Go ahead and get that tree down. We're going to have to cross the river one way or another."

They both nodded. A moment later, two spinning blades of light flashed through the air, streaking directly toward the tree. At the last second, both blades seemed to curve and separate from each other, striking the roots attached to the rock face at different angles and cutting through the gnarled wood like it wasn't there. The tree immediately shuddered, bent over, and toppled from the cliff.

"Timber!" called Puck.

The tree plummeted. Miraculously, it hit the river precisely where we needed it to, straddling both banks, sending an impressive spray of water into the air. The crash from the falling trunk shook the ground and echoed off the surrounding peaks.

A ripple shuddered through the cliffs around us. The stirring of many bodies all at once. Hisses and high-pitched snarls rose into the air, coming from the dozens of holes and crevices in the rock, and things began emerging into the light.

"Yep, I hate it when Furball disappears." Puck sighed as a black leathery wing poked out of one of the cracks. A head followed, wrinkled and hairy, with large, tattered ears and a nose that looked like something had squashed it. Glowing white eyes with no pupils glared down at us. Then the bat-like creature gave a shriek and leaped into the air, soon joined by dozens swarming overhead.

Screaming, the bats descended, swooping from the sky in a

flurry of claws and flapping wings. One landed in front of me with a snarl, baring oversize fangs as I slashed at it. My blade cut into the sinewy body, and the bat gave a hiss as it scuttled back.

Another came at me from above; I caught a split-second glimpse of outstretched wings and grasping talons before Ash's sword sheared through the creature's body, splitting it in half. Like most things in Faery, the creature didn't crumple and die; its body burst into dozens of tiny brown bats that flew into the air and scattered.

Something grabbed the back of my shirt from behind, momentarily lifting me into the air. I lashed out, my blade striking flesh and bone, and was instantly dropped with an angry hiss. "They're trying to throw us off the mountain," one of the Nyxes warned, as I dodged the talons of another bat and jabbed it in the leg. "Don't let them get a hold of you."

"Easier said than done," Puck called back. "These things are very grabby. Hey, hey, no. Stop it." He slashed at another pair, keeping them at bay. "I'm gonna need you guys to respect my personal bubble. No, see, you're not listening. Agh! Get off! Bad bat things! No touchie!"

Looking back, I saw two of the bats holding the back of Puck's hoodie between them and flapping into the air. Puck squirmed, twisting in their grasp, and managed to stab a bat in the thigh, making it screech and let go. But the second bat lifted him higher, dragging him toward the edge of the cliff. A few paces away, Varyn sliced the neck of another bat, kicked it away from him, and glanced over his shoulder, seeing Puck struggling with the winged monster overhead. For a moment, there was a clear, open shot between Varyn and the bat.

He hesitated. Just a single heartbeat, but the bat holding Puck rose even higher into the air, flapping closer to the edge. I started forward, but Nyx threw out a hand, and a curved blade went spinning through the air, passing through the neck of the bat creature. It had just a moment to hiss in surprise before its head toppled from its skinny shoulders and its body exploded into tiny bats. They swarmed into the air with furious squeaks, and Puck dropped to the ground.

He shot Varyn a poisonous glare as he rose, but another pair of monster bats descended on him with deafening screeches, and whatever he was about to say was lost in the cacophony.

"Meghan." Ash caught my gaze through the swirl of flailing wings and claws. "Guard my back," he said, turning to impale a bat through the chest. "Don't let them get behind us."

I nodded and whirled to stand back-to-back with my husband, feeling his tense muscles against mine. A bat screeched somewhere behind my head, but I trusted Ash would not let it touch me and focused on the enemies in front of me. The bats hissed, frustrated that they couldn't sneak behind us, but it was still difficult slashing at enemies in the sky. It was like fighting a pack of wolves, only more annoying because the harrying tactics came from overhead as well as the ground.

Several bats closed in. For a few seconds, I couldn't see anything but flapping wings, fangs, and grasping talons. I parried and lashed out grimly, cutting through leathery membranes and hairy limbs, and the air surrounding us filled with tiny bodies that squeaked as they flew away.

"We're driving them back!" Keirran's voice rang out, though I couldn't tell from where. "Don't stop."

The swarm of wings and claws suddenly ceased. Panting, I looked up, seeing the remaining bat creatures flapping away, hissing and snarling down at us. But they didn't flee. All the bats rose up to perch on the walls and peaks of the mountain, still glowering at us with baleful white eyes.

"Not running away, I see," Puck observed. "You'd think they'd learn."

"They might be rallying," Ash muttered. He pressed closer to me, raising his sword and never taking his eyes from the swarm. "Keep your guard up for the next attack."

The bats did not attack. They fell silent, baring their fangs, eyes glowing in the night. Then, as one, they lifted their heads and opened their jaws as if they were screaming. At first I didn't hear anything. The swarm of bats clung to the walls, heads raised and jaws gaping, but seeming to make no sound.

My ears suddenly throbbed, making me wince. It was that weird sensation you sometimes got on an airplane, that pressure right before your ears popped. There was a faint ringing in my head, and I realized the bats *were* making noise; it was just too high-pitched for us to hear.

"Ugh, tell them to stop it," Puck said, jamming a pinkie in his ear with a grimace. "My eardrums are about to split open. What are they even doing?"

"They're calling something," Ash said grimly.

A cold breeze swept through the mountains, making me shiver. And on the wind, I heard something. It sounded like flapping wings. Only bigger. Much, much bigger.

A single enormous claw rose up to grip the top of the peak directly overhead, an onyx talon digging into the rock. A head followed, wrinkled and leathery, with the same tattered ears and jutting fangs, only a hundred times larger. Huge wings spread out to either side as the enormous dragon-size bat crawled over the mountain and let out an ear-splitting screech that shook the cliffs.

"Okay, I did not sign up to fight a dragon today. Or even a bat dragon." Puck grimaced and took a step back, gazing up at the huge creature. The monster bat hissed and crawled over the top of the peak, clinging to the side as it glared down at us. "Normally I would say, 'Hell, yeah, let's kick some dragon-bat butt,' but given the circumstances, perhaps a tactical retreat is in order?"

Ash nodded. "Everyone, across the river!" he called, sweeping his sword toward the bank on the other side. "We'll take cover in the crags—that thing is too big to follow."

That sounded like a good plan. Sheathing my sword, I bolted for the tree trunk stretching across the water. The others followed, though Ash and Puck stayed behind and made sure everyone had reached the edge before turning and sprinting after us.

With a screech, the monster bat leaped from the cliff wall and hit the ground with a crash that caused several boulders to dislodge and go tumbling down the mountainside. Baring its huge fangs, it crawled after us.

I reached the edge of the bank, where the roots of the tree curled into the air from the trunk. My stomach clenched as I gazed over the river. The trunk of the tree hovered only a foot or two over the rushing water, a narrow strip of wood between us and the tears of the Wailing One. I still didn't know what would happen if we touched the water, but now was not an ideal time to find out.

A hiss rang out behind me. The giant bat was coming, and it was either stand and fight the monstrous creature or take our chances with the river. Gritting my teeth, I grabbed a root and pulled myself onto the shaky tree bridge.

Faery reflexes, don't fail me now.

The water churned under my feet. Without thinking about it, I sprinted across the bridge, trusting my natural fey balance and hoping the trunk would not snap beneath me.

Halfway across, something cold and wet hit my face. It was just a drop, but immediately my eyes watered and my throat closed, cutting off my breath. Images flickered through my head, memories that weren't mine. Faeries dying, turning into Nightmares. The land withering and twisting into a shadow of what it was. A sense of despair, helpless rage, and utter failure. Gasping, I staggered the final few feet and leaped off the trunk to the other side, fighting the sudden urge to scream.

Okay, touching the water was *very* bad. If that had been only a drop, I shuddered to think what would happen if someone was submerged. Unfortunately, I didn't have time to warn everyone, as a high-pitched scream cut through my thoughts and a shadow fell over my side of the bank. The huge bat was in the air, leathery wings blotting out the sky, curved talons opening to strike. I clenched my fist. For a moment, silhouetted against the mountain, the bat was a huge floating target, had any of us still had our magic. One lightning bolt, ice barrage, or storm of angry ravens, and it would probably have been over.

No time for regrets, though. The others were sprinting across the bridge, Nyx and Keirran leading the way with Other Nyx, Varyn, and Gilleas close behind. Puck and Ash stood on the other side, waiting for everyone to cross, before they too, hurried to the other side.

"Keep going," Ash ordered as he dropped off the bridge to the ground. I saw Puck scrubbing at his eyes and Varyn pressing a hand to his face, and realized the water had probably splashed them, too. "If we can get under cover of the mountain, we'll stand a better chance than out in the open."

Screaming, the smaller bat creatures descended on us again, leaping off the walls and dropping from the sky, probably realizing we were about to escape. Sharp claws latched on to my arm, piercing my skin as the bat tried to fly off and take me with it. With a frustrated snarl, I drew my blade and stabbed the creature's stomach, and it dropped me with a screech.

As I landed, I saw the others also struggling with warding off the swarm. Gilleas had both arms over his head, shoulders ducked as he tried to avoid getting snatched. Keirran and Puck stood close together, guarding each other's backs. A cluster of bats had swarmed Varyn and Other Nyx, and just as my gaze landed on them, one of the bats managed to snag Varyn's arm and drag him away. I saw Puck look up as the assassin was pulled back, and a hard smirk crossed his face as he did nothing. Varyn finally twisted around, slicing himself free, but for just a moment, he stood alone.

The giant bat was nowhere in sight.

"Meghan!"

Ash's shout and the sudden falling darkness was all the warning I had before a shadow fell over us, and the giant bat landed from above with a roar. Ash lunged forward, grabbed me around the waist, and yanked me sideways as a massive claw smashed into the spot where I'd been standing, talons curling into the ground and crushing the rocks beneath it.

We all staggered back, shielding our faces as wind and stones from the giant wings pelted us. As the dust cleared, I looked up, and my heart seized in my chest. Varyn lay on the ground, pinned beneath the other talon, his body motionless as the claws curled around him. Other Nyx had been knocked back, and was lying several yards away, fending off a bat that had pounced on her. With its smaller kin still screeching and bouncing around us, the giant bat took one step forward and snaked its head down, jaws snapping. I decapitated a bat clawing at me, as Ash finished off two more and turned to face the gaping maw coming at him. His sword flashed, slicing across the monster's squashed, fleshy nose. At the same time, a streak of black and silver shot through my vision, and Other Nyx landed on the monster's head, driving her blade into its neck with a snarl.

The bat wailed. Its giant wings opened, flaring to either side, before it sprang into the air. The blast of wind from the downbeat whipped at my clothes and sent me and everyone else stumbling back, shielding our faces as rocks and dirt pelted everything in the area. The monster rose off the ground, a limp Varyn still clutched in its talons as it started to fly away.

"Varyn!" Other Nyx cried, and for the first time, she sounded frantic. A flurry of crescent blades flew through the air, striking the bat but not stopping its ascent. "No! Don't let it fly away, or we'll lose him."

As the bat gave its wings another flap, rising farther into the air, the bright form of Keirran suddenly appeared on a ledge above it. Sword in hand, he leaped onto the monster's back and brought the weapon slashing down on a wing joint, cutting through muscles and sinew and drawing an agonized shriek from the bat. It faltered in midair, desperately beating its wings, trying to stay aloft. The curved talons opened, and Varyn plummeted like a stone toward the rocky ground.

Our Nyx was suddenly there, managing to get her body between Varyn and the ground just before his head would've struck rock. I heard her exhale as she broke the Evenfaery's fall, and hopefully not any of their bones. In the next heartbeat, Other Nyx appeared, cradling Varyn's limp body to her. I saw her fingers gently brush his cheek, and his eyes opened, making her slump in relief. Our Nyx rolled to her feet and stepped back, the look on her face unreadable.

Overhead, the bat was screeching and flailing about with wings and claws. Even the smaller bats had scattered, fleeing the whirlwind of noise and erratic movements. Still clinging to its back, Keirran raised his sword and stabbed it again, plunging the weapon deep into the monster's neck.

With a final wail, the bat tried to flee. Its wings flapped desperately, once, twice, and then the creature plummeted toward the earth again. It struck the cliff where the waterfall poured over the side, and collapsed into the river. As the water crushed the monster beneath it, its wings gave one final flap and went still.

Keirran!

Heart in my throat, I sprinted toward the waterfall as Keirran heaved himself onto the bank, coughing, dripping wet, and drenched head to toe in river water.

"Keirran!"

I rushed toward him, as my son staggered away from the bank and fell to his knees, gasping. His shoulders heaved, and he clutched at his chest, as if he couldn't draw in enough air. His lips were blue, and dark veins stood out beneath his skin where the water had soaked through his clothes.

"Keirran." I knelt beside him, seeing his face streaked with tears, his eyes red as if he had spent an entire day and night sobbing without a break. "Can you hear me?"

"I can't breathe," he gasped. One hand went to his throat, his mouth gaping as he shook with ragged sobs. His entire body was locked and rigid with tension. "I can't... I can't..."

"Easy." I put a trembling hand on his back, fighting my own instincts to panic. Immediately, a flood of horror and sorrow rushed in, images and faces flickering through my mind. I recoiled with a gasp, as Gilleas and the others rushed up, their faces pale when they saw the convulsing form of the Forgotten King.

"Do not touch him!" Gilleas swept one long arm forward,

stopping our Nyx from springing to his side. "The water will affect you as well. We must get him dry. Someone, build a fire. Get him out of those clothes but avoid touching them if you can."

Ash moved forward, shrugging out of his long black coat and swirling it around Keirran's shoulders. "I'll take care of Keirran," he told me, then glanced at the others with narrowed eyes. "Someone get a fire going, now!"

"On it," Puck said, and rushed off, presumably to find wood. The others followed, scattering into the mountain, leaving me alone with my family and Gilleas.

I knelt beside Keirran as Ash deftly helped him out of his wet clothes. Occasionally, I saw Ash grimace or grit his teeth as he stripped away a piece of drenched clothing, but he continued his task with grim determination. Keirran tried to help, but he was still panting, his breaths ragged. The water streaming from his eyes left trails of darkness down his cheeks.

Reaching out, I took his hand. His skin was clammy and cold, but mostly dry. "Breathe, Keirran," I told him as he shook violently under my fingers. The sharp, bitter scent of the water made my own throat close up. I could only imagine what he was seeing, what the Wailing One's memories were showing him. I blinked away the tears starting to form in my own eyes and bit the corner of my lip, hard enough to taste blood. The pain did not completely drive away the feelings of horror and grief swirling through my chest, but it helped me focus on helping my son. "Listen to me. Calm yourself. Focus on our voices and shut out everything else."

"I can't," Keirran whispered. "The voices are so loud. Everyone is gone." One hand covered his face, his palm pressing into his left eye as if trying to pop it out. "I could feel them Fading. I knew the moment they disappeared from existence. I know them all. I can still see their faces, their spark, everything about them. My world is gone. The Evenfey..." His breath hitched, dark tears spilling from a stare that was suddenly glassy and far-away. "Forgive me, Evenfey, Forgotten… They called me their king, but I could not protect them."

My stomach twisted. Keirran was seeing the Nightmare King's past, reliving the grief and rage of the ruler of Evenfall, but for a moment, it was as if he was speaking for them both. The Nightmare King and the King of the Forgotten, both unable to save their subjects, both feeling as if they had failed them.

"I was afraid it was something like that." Gilleas peered down at us, his voice grave. "The Whisper warned not to touch the water, but she also said something else. She said that it was a poison. And poisons, at least in this world, tend to linger."

A chill of horror crawled up my spine. "What do you mean?"

He didn't answer at first, looking at Keirran instead. Ash had relieved Keirran of most of his soggy clothes, and Keirran now huddled beneath the long black coat, head bowed and shoulders trembling. "Can you hear me, Forgotten King?" Gilleas asked.

Keirran made a visible effort to compose himself. His hands clenched on the rock, and he drew in a shaky breath. For a moment, he stopped trembling, his voice calm as he answered. "I hear you."

"What is it you see, exactly?" Gilleas went on. Keirran hesitated, shivering, then took another deep breath and raised his head.

"Shadows," he said, his eyes sweeping over the area on both sides of the river. "Evenfey. I…" One hand went to his skull, fingers digging into his wet hair. "I know they're not real, that they're not really there," he choked out. "They're echoes, that's the best I can describe it. But… I see them. And they're all staring at me."

"How many?" Gilleas wondered.

"I don't know." Keirran's voice was dull. "Dozens. Hundreds. It's hard to tell. They keep fading in and out."

"And where do you see them?"

My son shivered and hunched his shoulders again. "Everywhere."

"Echoes of the king's memories." Grimalkin's voice reached my ears. The cat was perched on an overhanging rock, tail curled tightly around his feet as he peered down. "The Whisper told you not to touch the water, because it is the tears of the Wailing One. And the Wailing One is a manifestation of grief and despair, perhaps of the Nightmare King himself."

"Yes," agreed Gilleas. "Elder Nightmares, and named ones especially, can possess powers unique to anything else in Evenfall. The real danger is that the effects of the tears might not go away. I fear that this one—" he nodded at Keirran "—might see the echoes of the dead as long as he remains in Evenfall. Or possibly...longer."

Ash straightened, his voice low and dangerous. "And if we kill the Wailing One," he said in a tone that might've frozen the river if he still had his magic, "would that free Keirran from its curse?"

"I do not know," Gilleas said. "Perhaps."

A clatter over the rocks made me turn. Puck and the others had returned with firewood, and in a few minutes, a small fire crackled against the rocks, throwing back the coming darkness. Keirran was laid out in front of it, still draped in Ash's coat, and he fell into a delirious sleep. I sat beside him, holding his hand, my heart twisting at every flinch, every tiny gasp or tortured whisper, hoping the nightmare that had Keirran in its grip would eventually fade.

As night fell and a broken moon rose over the Howling Peaks, Keirran finally relaxed. His breathing grew calmer, he stopped jerking every few minutes, and his frantic muttering quieted.

Gilleas, who had also stayed close, looming over us like a gangly specter, let out a sigh and nodded. "I am no healer fey," he told me, gazing down with hollow eye sockets, "but I believe he is out of immediate danger. If the poison has not killed him by now, I do not think it will. The effects might linger, perhaps for the rest of his existence, but I do not believe your son is going to die. At least, not tonight."

Relief filled me, followed by a sudden, incomprehensible rage. I looked at Ash, who also hadn't left Keirran's side except to keep the fire going. Dark circles crouched beneath his eyes, and thin black veins had appeared on his hands; he too bore the marks of the river—not as much as Keirran, of course, but it had affected him, as well. My gaze slid past him to the dark shape of the monster bat, still lying beneath the waterfall. We would have been able to beat it far sooner had we all been working together.

My jaw clenched, and that burning rage bubbled over, liquefying in my veins before becoming like steel. I rose, turning slowly to take in my surroundings. A few yards away, the others had built another firepit closer to the river, though only Puck was seated there, tossing sticks into the flames. Everyone else had scattered about the area, respectfully staying a safe distance while being close enough to see what was happening.

Setting my jaw, I walked toward the second firepit. Immediately, the others left whatever they were doing to meet me there, but I barely noticed the Nyxes; my gaze was for two faeries in particular. Puck glanced up as I approached, firelight dancing over his skin and making his hair glow, and the faint smile creeping across his face faltered as he saw me.

"Oh, hey…princess." Puck blinked, warily leaning back as I loomed over him across the fire. "Uh, how's the princeling?"

"My son could have died today." The sound of my own voice made a tiny part of me cringe; cold and steely, it was the tone I used when dealing with the other rulers of the courts, or when I *needed* to get my point across to the most stubborn, inflexible fey. The voice of the Iron Queen. "Because of you.

"Both of you," I added, glancing at Varyn, who had joined us along with the two Nyxes. The Evenfaery stiffened, but I didn't give him a chance to speak. "Because of your stubbornness. Because the two of you cannot seem to put aside your differences, even when we are fighting for our lives. Varyn—" I looked directly at the Evenfaery, narrowing my gaze "—we are not the fey who did this to you. The Lady and her circle are long dead. The current rulers of the courts weren't even around when the First Queen rose to power. I know you have lost much, and your anger for the past is justified, but we had *nothing* to do with sealing Evenfall. Continuing to blame us is pointless and does not bring us any closer to what we are trying to accomplish.

"And that goes for you as well, Puck." I turned my glare on the Great Prankster. "The Varyn who betrayed Nyx and tried to kill her for the Lady is *centuries* dead. This is not the same faery. Different lives, different choices, different circumstances—they can all change a person. You *know* that. You are not the same Robin Goodfellow today that you were a hundred years ago, and yet you're blaming Varyn for an act he didn't commit and probably never would.

"So, this ends now," I finished, staring them both down. "Tonight. I don't care how you do it, but the two of you had better figure this out. And you'd better figure it out before we reach the Wailing One, or we're going to fail, and then there will be no one left to save Evenfall. Stop fighting," I finished, glaring at them both. "Learn to work together. We are not the enemies here."

And before either of them could respond, I whirled and stalked back to Keirran, anger still a roiling storm within. Enough was enough. I had been listening to those two go at each other for too long. Over past fears and grudges that were no longer relevant. If we couldn't even handle a giant bat without one of us nearly dying, we stood no chance against a named Elder Nightmare who was virtually unkillable. Varyn had been right about one thing: not trusting each other would be dangerous in the lair of the Wailing One. I didn't care if Puck and Varyn didn't get along, but they needed to work together if we were to have any hope of defeating this enemy.

Ash gave me a faint smile as I returned from chewing out Puck and Varyn, but he didn't say anything as I knelt beside the fire. Grimalkin, I noticed, had claimed our firepit as his own and was perched contentedly on a rock close to the embers. Golden eyes cracked open, peering up at me in subtle amusement.

"Don't say anything, Grimalkin," I warned. "I don't want to hear it."

The cat merely yawned. "I would not dream of it, Iron Queen," he purred. "Though your kind's tendency to argue about pointless issues that are long past has always baffled me. Why hold someone responsible for something that they had no part in? It makes no sense. At least now, perhaps, we can reach the Nightmare's lair sooner."

"Iron Queen."

I looked up. One of the Nyxes stood there, hood brushed back, golden eyes concerned as she gazed down at me. For a moment, I wondered which Nyx it was, but then noticed the other Nyx talking to Varyn by the fire and realized this one was ours.

"Forgive the interruption," our Nyx said with a quick glance at Grimalkin, who, I noticed, had gone back to sleep. "But... Keirran. Is he...?"

"Gilleas thinks he'll be all right," I said, and her shoulders slumped with relief. Keirran was her king, after all, as well as her friend. "He might be under a curse when he wakes up, but we don't think it will be life-threatening. It is something we'll have to keep an eye on, though."

She winced, a guilty expression crossing her face for just a moment. "I am sorry, my king," she murmured, gazing down at Keirran's sleeping form. "I swore an oath to protect you and your kingdom. But I wasn't there when I was needed."

"This isn't your fault, Nyx," I said softly. "We *all* could have done a little better."

"Yes," she agreed, sounding even more pained now. "Forgive me, Iron Queen. I should have told you about Varyn. The moment I saw him in this world, I should have told you the whole story. Not that I feared that he would betray us—the two Varyns are different people, just as I am different from the Nyx of this world. And it might be a little late, but…" She made a small, hopeless gesture with one hand. "The Lady was a cruel and fickle mistress. Serving her, carrying out her wishes…it made us all a little hollow inside. Who knows what would have happened if we had never served the First Queen, but I can't live on what-ifs. As you said yourself—the Varyn I knew is long dead. I have moved on."

I gave her a faint smile. "I think there is someone else who needs to hear that."

"I know." A corner of her lip twitched, and she rolled her eyes. "He is trying his best to be forgiven. I don't think he'll have to wait too much longer."

Behind us, Keirran let out a ragged gasp and bolted upright on the rocks.

"It's coming."

"Keirran."

Nyx and I both rushed to his side. Ash had gotten up as well, gripping Keirran's shoulder to stop him from thrashing. "Calm down," Ash ordered, his firm voice commanding obedience. "Breathe, Keirran. You're safe."

"No," Keirran panted, though his frantic struggles did stop as he recognized us. Taking a deep breath, he forced himself to speak calmly. "It's coming," he whispered. "We're not safe here. We have to move."

"What is?"

A chilling howl echoed over the mountains, sounding far closer than it had in the past. At the other firepit, Puck, Varyn, and Other Nyx looked up sharply, scanning the skies for the source of the noise.

"She knows we're here," Keirran went on. "The Wailing One. She knows what we're trying to do." He grimaced, one hand clutching at his head. "It's coming," he whispered again. "She sent something after us. It's left the tower and is coming toward us right now."

"Get everyone on their feet," Ash said, rising swiftly. "I'll take care of Keirran. Grimalkin, I assume you can find us a cave or other hiding spot in these mountains?"

The cat stretched languidly on the rock before stepping down, seemingly unconcerned. "Finding holes in mountains is not difficult," he said. "I am sure I can turn up something."

The screams pursued us into the mountains. They echoed off distant peaks and shivered through deep crags and gullies, never giving any indication as to how close or far away the source was. To make matters worse, Keirran kept stumbling, recoiling from things that weren't there, and going for his sword. His face was haggard, his eyes haunted as he continued to scan the cliffs around us.

As the screams drew discernably closer, lightning flickered from a sky that was suddenly mottled and black. A sharp, bitter wind blew into my face, making my eyes water. It smelled wrong; tainted and choking, like the scent that came off the water.

"It's going to rain," Other Nyx announced, glancing warily up at the sky. "I can't imagine that's going to be good for us."

"You would be correct," Gilleas said over the growing screams of whatever was coming. From the volume and the echoes, it sounded like it was right around the bend. "The rain will be laced with the tears of the Wailing One," Gilleas went on. "Not as potent as the water coming down from the mountain, but getting caught in the storm will not be pleasant, for any of us."

"Grimalkin," I called, looking around in vain for the cat. "Have you found us a shelter yet? Otherwise we're going to be fighting another Nightmare in a rain of tears!"

"What do you think I have been doing, Iron Queen?" Grimalkin materialized on a large boulder, his expression annoyed.

"While you all have been lamenting the weather, I have found a suitable cave. This way, and do watch your step. It is a very long fall to the bottom."

A few minutes later, we followed the cat along a narrow ledge, backs pressed against the wall, staring at the sheer drop at our feet. Clouds drifted below us, and a cold wind moaned through the ravine, tossing my hair as if to yank me from the ledge.

"Okay, someone is going to have to talk to that cat about the meaning of *suitable*," Puck commented, his voice echoing into the ravine below. "Because there is a difference between 'suitable for everyone' and 'suitable for mountain goats.' And if anyone makes a joke about me being shaggy and horny, I'm going to push them."

"You are almost there," Grimalkin said, calmly peering back at us. "Just a bit farther. The cave is right ahead."

I glanced at Keirran beside me. His eyes were glazed, his skin pale, and the haunted look still clung to him. Ash loomed on his other side, ready to grab him should he slip or fall, but worry still twisted my stomach.

My son must've felt my anxious gaze on him, because he half smiled without looking up. "I'm all right," he murmured. "If I stare straight down, I don't see their faces. Just a very long fall into nothing."

A drop of water hit my forehead and slid down my cheek. It didn't burn, not exactly, but it still felt tainted and smelled of bitterness and rage. My eyes watered, and I scrubbed a hand across my face to clear my vision.

"Hurry, if you can," Grimalkin urged from farther ahead. I looked up and saw the cat standing at the entrance to a large hole in the rock, eyes glowing in the darkness. "The storm is coming. I would advise you to shuffle faster."

We did, moving along the narrow ledge as quickly as we could. No sooner had I reached the mouth of the cave than the skies opened up with a hiss, and a curtain of rain began creeping over the mountains. I waited as Keirran ducked into the cave, followed by Ash, Puck, Nyx, Other Nyx, and finally Varyn, who ducked beneath the ledge just ahead of the rain.

Puck exhaled, leaning against the wall, watching the water sweep across the opening of the cave. "Cutting it a little close, but we made it. You know, I feel like we've done this before with Furball, and it always seems that he finds what we're looking for at the very last dramatic second."

I started to respond when a wail shivered through the air and caused dust to rain from the ceiling. A chill crawled along my spine, followed by looming anxiety that something was coming, drawing ever closer through the darkness.

"Meghan," Ash growled, his voice a warning. He hadn't moved away from the mouth of the cave, and cut a dark silhouette against the stormy sky, his coat billowing behind him in the wind. "Look."

Heart pounding, I gazed out into the storm.

The rain was picking up, turning the world colorless. It smelled wrong, like salt and bitterness and regret, burning my eyes again and clogging my throat. Before coming to Faery, I hadn't known emotions could have smells, but after living as a fey queen for many years, I now knew the scent of grief and rage. Even after all this time, I found it unsettling.

Lightning flickered, and in the flash, I glimpsed a shape in the rain, flowing through the air like a ragged cloud. Through the storm, it was blurry and indistinct, a long, pale form that trailed wisps of fog behind it. It had no wings, no arms or tail or even a head that I could see, but it was massive, nearly as large as the bat we'd fought earlier. I watched it twist and coil toward us, its bone-chilling screams echoing off the peaks, its form unclear.

And then it turned toward us, revealing a face. Peering out of a hundred other faces. My blood chilled as the ethereal form of the Nightmare solidified into a mass of anguished expressions, each a mask of grief and agony. Human faces, elven faces, goblin and troll faces, faces I couldn't recognize, faces I had never seen before and could barely fathom. All screaming. All crying out in torment, rage, sorrow, and despair. I met the glassy, teary eyes of the face in the middle, saw them widen for a fraction of a second, before every face that made up the Nightmare's terrible body turned toward me.

With a shriek that sent pain stabbing through my head, the creature twisted around and flew right at us.

Ash and I lunged back from the entrance of the cave. "Everyone, move," Ash ordered, his voice echoing off the walls. Reaching down, he pulled a hunched, huddled Keirran to his feet and shoved him toward the back of the cave. "Get farther into the tunnel. The Nightmare is coming!"

With a wail so loud it brought tears to my eyes, the mass of faces lunged into the cave. Its body distended, squeezing into the tight space with us, the shrieks threatening to bring the entire cavern down around us. My head throbbed, and my ears felt like they were bleeding, but I drew my sword and stabbed it through one of the faces as they slithered forward, the blade plunging deep into its temple.

That was a mistake.

Every face turned toward me, and each one of them was someone I knew. Ash, Puck, Keirran, Ethan, all staring at me with betrayal and anguish in their eyes, before they threw back their heads and screamed. Jaws gaped, unhinging like a snake's as they howled in unison. If the noise had been unbearable before, it was ear-splitting now. As I staggered away, feeling like my skull might explode, the walls and floor started to tremble. Rocks began dropping from the ceiling, crashing to the ground and adding to the din shaking the cave apart. The Nightmare thrashed, still screaming, and something hard stuck me in the temple, sending pain and a stab of dizziness through my head.

Deafened, half-blind, I lurched away, shielding my face, and felt a cool hand latch on to mine. Without questioning, I let it pull me back, away from the frenzied, shrieking Nightmare, as rocks continued to rain down around us.

I ducked into the tunnel with Ash, darkness closing around me as the cavern behind us collapsed with a muffled roar.

When the dust cleared, the tunnel entrance was filled with rubble and stone, the way back to the cavern blocked. The Nightmare was gone, and nothing but blessed silence throbbed in my ears.

19

DREAMS WITHIN DREAMS

"Is everyone here?"

Nyx's voice sounded distant and muffled, like she was underwater. My ears buzzed. I gave my head a shake, which was the wrong thing to do, as a jab of pain immediately shot through my skull. The ground beneath me tilted, and I put a hand on the wall to steady myself.

"I believe so." Gilleas's skull glowed faintly in the darkness as he gazed around, taking note of everyone. "No one is missing, though none of you appear very healthy. And the queen is not looking steady on her feet."

The walls were starting to spin. I clenched my jaw, feeling something warm trickle down my neck, as the ringing in my ears grew louder. Nausea rippled through my stomach. I turned to Ash, to tell him that I needed to sit down for a minute, but even that slight movement sent a wave of vertigo crashing into me, and I fell back into darkness.

I stood at the edge of a cracked, decaying stone staircase that curved up toward the entrance of the castle. Plinths and broken statues lined the stairs, most of them nothing more than shattered legs. I still could hear the Wailing One, crying her endless litany, but her voice sounded far away. Streams of water ran down the stairs, pooling in cracks before falling off the side of the mountain. I could smell the bitterness and despair that saturated even the stones of this place.

At the top of the steps, a figure wrapped in shadows waited for me.

I blinked. *This is a dream*, I realized. *But…none of this is real. How can there be a dream within a dream?*

Knowing that the answer to that question could probably twist my brain into noodles, I started walking up the steps. I took the center path, as the rivulets of tears mostly streamed down the sides. The castle loomed above me, crumbling stone towers looking fragile and almost skeletal against the slate gray of the sky.

As expected, the shadow figure didn't wait for me, but turned and vanished through the doorway before I was halfway up the steps. At the entrance to the castle, I paused, looking around, and saw it gliding up another flight of stone stairs, going higher into the keep.

Grimly, I followed, trailing it through a castle that was more shattered than whole. Entire sections of wall were destroyed, crumbled from either time or some terrible attack. Once-dazzling stained-glass windows lay in shards across the floors, glinting with razor-sharp colors. And water, the tears of the Wailing One, flowed, dripped, and trickled down nearly every wall, every surface, forming pools, waterfalls, and streams as it made its way down the mountain.

Eventually, I came to the bottom of a dilapidated tower, a flight of stairs spiraling up into the darkness. The shadow glided along the steps, toward the highest room of the keep.

All right, mysterious shadow, whatever you want me to see is on the top floor. Let's get this over with.

The stairs were soaked with tears, both flowing down the steps and trickling from the floor above. As I started up the staircase, the flow seemed to get heavier, trickles turning to water-falls and rivulets becoming streams. I avoided the water as best I could, but my narrow dry path was rapidly shrinking.

I was nearly to the top when a roar made me pause and look up. A deluge of water crested the top of the stairs and came crashing down at me. There was just enough time to brace my-self, holding my breath, before the wave engulfed me and everything went white.

Gasping, I opened my eyes.

"Easy," a low, familiar voice murmured in my ear. "I've got you. You're safe."

I slumped against Ash, feeling the surrealness of the dream fade as reality took its place. By the feel of stones beneath me, I knew we were still in a cave. Several yards away, someone had started a fire, which meant that the cavern we were in had to be fairly large, or at least not airtight. I would've turned my head to look, but dizziness still lingered, and I was feeling fairly content to lie against my husband and not move, for a few min-utes, at least.

Something felt different, and after a moment, I realized what it was. The cave, except for the faint pop and crackle of the fire, was quiet. The constant screams and wails of the Elder Night-mare had faded. I hadn't gone deaf, though my ears ached, and one felt strange, like it was full of water. Annoying, but not de-bilitating. It could have been far worse.

"How long was I out?" I asked.

"Not long," Ash assured me. "We're a little deeper into the mountain. Puck and Nyx were able to get a fire going, and ev-eryone agreed it was a good idea to rest for a while. Grim and Gilleas are both fairly certain that this chain of tunnels will bring us out close to the top of the peaks. So this might be our last stop before we reach the Wailing One."

I nodded. "How is Keirran?" I whispered.

"I'm here."

He materialized from virtually nowhere, making me wonder if he had been lurking just out of view, waiting to see if I was all right. Kneeling beside us, he took my hand. "I'm all right," he told me. "The voices have stopped, at least for now. Maybe they're tied directly to the Wailing One, and she's not crying at the moment, though we have no idea why. What about you?"

His voice echoed strangely in my ears, like he was standing across the room instead of two feet away. "Getting there," I said, giving him a wry smile. "I think I might've ruptured an eardrum, but there's nothing we can do about it now."

He returned the slightly pained smile. "Maybe we should have listened to Puck when he was talking about earplugs."

"Don't let him hear you say that," Ash murmured. "Then you'll *really* need earplugs."

I chuckled and closed my eyes, relaxing into the warmth of family. Even here, in this twisted nightmare world, Ash and Keirran were my two bright spots. My reasons to keep going.

The dream flickered into my mind, images replaying like a movie trailer. The keep at the top of the mountain. The long spiraling staircase. The mysterious shadow figure who kept just out of sight. I had been in Faery long enough to know a vision when I saw it. Something important waited at the top of that staircase, and someone wanted us to find it.

We just had to get past a shrieking, unkillable monster first.

Resolve settled through me. Setting my jaw, I eased out of Ash's embrace and stood, ignoring the moment of vertigo to stand on my own. "Call everyone together," I said, as both Ash and Keirran rose as well. "There's something I have to tell everyone."

"You had a dream?" Puck asked a few minutes later. "You mean, you were dreaming inside a dream?" His forehead scrunched, the flames of the campfire casting eerie shadows across his face. "Yeah, I'm not gonna think too hard about that or my brain will never untangle."

"I think it was more of a vision," I corrected him. "I definitely felt a presence leading me through the castle. There is something at the top of the keep, on the highest floor of the highest tower. When we reach the Wailing One's lair, that's where we have to go."

"And are you sure this presence is on our side?" Varyn asked. "Not that I'm doubting you," he added, raising his hands. "But what if it's the Wailing One? We're going into the Nightmare's lair—it could be setting a trap for us."

"It wasn't the Nightmare," Keirran said, and everyone glanced at him. He hovered a few feet away, leaning against a stalagmite with his arms crossed and his brow furrowed. "The Wailing One can't plan that far ahead," he told us. "It's far too volatile to have any semblance of clear thought or planning. It is nothing but grief and rage, and even its thoughts are...scattered." He looked away, narrowing his eyes, as if hearing something the rest of us could not. "Even now," he muttered, "I can feel her. The Nightmare she sent after us took a lot out of her, but she'll start crying again soon. As soon as she regains her voices, she'll be just as dangerous as before. But she doesn't have the capacity for traps."

"If it was not the Wailing One," Ash murmured, "what was it?"

"The Nightmare King," Other Nyx said.

Her tone was quietly confident, as if she had no doubt that she was right. "He is still fighting for us," she went on. "Even though he dreams, even though we are not real, he still wants us to live. Perhaps he can sense the presence of those who are real within his dream. It would make sense that he would reach out to you, a queen of Faery, to help his dream survive."

Beside me, Ash shook his head. "That is not the Nightmare King I have seen," he said, his eyes shadowed with memory. "That is not the voice who spoke to us in the Nevernever, right before we came to Evenfall. On that day, the Nightmare King spoke of vengeance and destruction. He had gone mad with his rage. That is why we came to Evenfall, to stop him. Because if he wakes up, it could mean the end for both Evenfall and the Nevernever."

"But…that makes no sense," Varyn broke in. "If the king has gone mad, then why are we traveling all the way to the palace to see him? Why are we risking our lives to seek him out? If he will not hear us, what is the point of any of this?"

"He will hear us," Other Nyx said firmly. "We will be able to reach him. He is angry, and he grieves his world and his people, but in my entire existence of living in this nightmare, I have never doubted the king."

Grimalkin sauntered into the firelight, leaping onto a nearby stone. "The storm is lessening," he said, gazing around the fire. "I believe the rain is letting up. If you are all finished having your pointless mortal conversations, perhaps we can move on."

"I am very much in favor of that," Gilleas said. "Listening to this babble is becoming tiresome, as is scraping my head against every low-hanging stalactite in this cavern."

"Another reason I am very happy to be a cat." Grim yawned and turned away, waving his tail. "The passageway is against the far right corner," he said. "I anticipate it will still take several minutes for everyone to actually arrive at the correct location. I will await you when you are ready."

I stood, and the others rose with me. "All right," I said. "This is the final leg of the journey. We know what we're dealing with, and what we have to do. Is everyone ready?"

"Not particularly," Puck said in a cheerful voice. "But when has that ever stopped us before? Oh yeah, never. It's never stopped us before."

"Even when it should have," said Nyx with a sigh.

We followed Grimalkin through a series of winding, narrow passageways, ducking stalactites and squeezing through tunnels that made me glad no one in the group was claustrophobic. The Wailing One remained eerily silent, which was both a relief for my aching ear and a constant worry as to when she would start up again. I kept glancing back at Keirran, but he marched doggedly forward, never complaining or lagging behind. Once, he did startle and go for his sword, as if a figure had just appeared beside him out of nowhere. But he quickly wrenched his gaze away and continued, keeping his eyes straight ahead and not looking down any adjacent tunnels.

Finally, I saw a lessening of the darkness ahead. We left the caves, emerging onto a narrow ledge with a sheer drop over the side of the mountain. Icy wind, still laced with rain and tears, tugged at my hair. And ahead of us, across a misty divide, a stark castle of broken stone rose up from the clouds, looming against the darkness.

"The Howling Keep," Gilleas breathed behind us. "Sometimes known as the Tower of Sorrows. I have read about it many times, but I never thought I would see it with my own eyes. It is…breathtaking and terrifying at the same time."

"You think our wailing friend is home?" Puck wondered.

"If she is, I don't see her," Nyx said, gazing up at the surrounding peaks. "Or hear her, which is even more troubling. We should try to reach the keep in case she spots us. If the Nightmare does attack, I would rather face her in a castle than on a crumbling mountain pass over nothing."

"Yeah, that's probably a smart idea."

With the wind howling eerily through the crags, we made our way toward the castle, eventually finding ourselves on a steep path to the shattered gates at the top. Small streams trickled down the path and flowed over the rocks, turning the air bitter and acrid.

"Almost there," Varyn muttered, craning his neck to gaze up at the towers, rising to an impossible height above us. "Relatively, anyway." His gaze slid to me. "You said we have to get to the top floor of the highest tower?"

"Yes. That's where the dream was taking me."

Our Nyx took a step back, narrowing her eyes as she stared upward. One hand rose, gesturing at something far overhead. "That's where we need to go, then."

I followed her gaze, finding a skinny, crooked tower looming over the rest of the castle. It didn't seem possible that it was still standing. Water poured from the top floor, shimmering in the moonlight as it cascaded down the sides. It was eerily beautiful, deadly as it was.

"I don't see the Nightmare, though," Other Nyx said. "Maybe, if we're lucky, we can get to the highest tower without running into her. Though that seems highly unlikely. If whatever is up there is valuable, the Wailing One won't leave it unattended."

"Also, not to freak anyone out," Puck added, "but I just saw something move. In the window up there." He pointed, and I caught a glimpse of something pale and ragged flitting across the broken glass. Beside me, Ash nodded and drew his sword.

"Stay together," he said calmly. "We don't want to get separated and picked off in this place."

"And if the Nightmare shows up, ice-boy?"

"We fight it together and give Meghan enough time to get to the top tower and do whatever she has to do."

"Sounds like a plan." Puck pulled his daggers, twirling both in his hands with a grin. "Okay, then. I am tired of having no magic. Let's do this."

20

THE HOWLING KEEP

The shattered gates loomed in front of us as we climbed the last of the crumbling steps, careful to avoid the many streams of water coming down from the top. After ducking through the gates, we entered the huge castle, a sprawling, ancient mass of broken walls, steps, and pillars that soared to immeasurable heights. Water was everywhere, dripping from the ceiling, trickling down the walls, and running across the floor. I had to be careful where I stepped, as half the keep was waterlogged with the poisonous tears that burned my nose and throat. Surprisingly, despite the state of the castle itself, the interiors were well furnished and almost pristine. Tables, sofas, chairs, rugs, all placed carefully throughout the rooms as if frozen in time. It gave the keep an eerie, almost dreamlike feel, seeing all these signs of life when the keep itself felt hauntingly empty.

Despite the flicker of movement from earlier, I didn't see anyone. Or hear anyone. Which was even worse. We knew the Nightmare was here, somewhere. Walking through the unnatural silence, I almost wished the Wailing One would show up and get it over with. The more time that passed, the more nervous I became, waiting for the moment when a mass of shrieking faces would come flying out of a dark room toward us.

"Oh wow, look at this," Puck remarked, pausing in the doorway that led to an enormous dining hall. A massive wooden table ran the length of the chamber, the remains of a great feast covering every inch of the wood. The centerpiece was the skeleton of a boar lying on a golden platter, a withered apple still clutched in bony jaws. Puck wrinkled his nose. "I don't know if this is creepy or just really, disappointingly wasteful."

"No one has touched this food," our Nyx remarked, peering over his shoulder. "It's just been left here to rot. But that means this place was once inhabited."

"Or is still inhabited," Varyn said. "By creatures other than the Wailing One. And they don't eat food anymore. Or they eat other things."

"Oh, that's a cheery thought." Puck sighed. "Are there vampires in Evenfall?"

Before Varyn could answer, a sound rose into the air, the scrape of a chair being pushed back. Everyone tensed, looking into the room again. At the far end of the table, previously hidden behind a moldering, three-layer cake, one of the dining room chairs had moved. As we watched, a pile of rags that had blended into the clutter rose from the surface, resolving into a figure covered in what looked like ragged sheets. After stepping down from the chair, it glided around the table toward us.

I gripped my sword, watching the ghostly figure approach, feeling Ash and Puck on either side of me do the same. As it drew closer, I saw the sheet was actually a tattered white dress, but so stained and torn it was barely recognizable as clothing. The figure's head was bowed, so I couldn't see its face, but dark strands of hair hung from its shoulders. Its hands were also hidden in its billowy sleeves, and I saw a glint of something shiny through the cloth.

"I think it has a weapon," I warned, just as the figure raised its head and stared at us straight-on.

My stomach twisted. The creature staring at us from the nest of rags was gaunt and skeletal, pale skin shrunk tightly over its bones. Its eyes were hollow pits of black as it stared blankly. Tears poured from the dark holes, making wet trails down its wasted cheeks. It had no mouth. No lips, no gash, not even a slit to show where a mouth might have been. The skin from its nose to its jawline was smooth, though I could almost see the outline of teeth through the nearly translucent covering.

The creature staggered toward us, the bones of its jaw working beneath its skin. I had the sudden, horrible feeling that it was trying to cry or scream, but without a mouth, it could make no sound.

"O-kay," Puck said, and gave an exaggerated shudder as he stepped back. "Suddenly that full dining table is a whole lot more horrific."

"Is this an Evenfaery?" Keirran asked.

"No." Gilleas's voice was full of horror and pity. "Perhaps it was, once. Perhaps a whole colony or race lived in this castle. But it has been too close to the Wailing One for too long. Whatever it was, it is only a Nightmare now. It cannot be saved. Nothing to do but put it out of its misery."

The creature covered its face with one hand, the other rising in front of it. Ragged sleeves fell back to reveal an arm as brittle as bird bones, fingers curled around the handle of a cleaver. Without a sound, it lunged at me, and hit both Ash's and Puck's blades as they swept forward. Puck's dagger struck the wrist that held the cleaver, dropping both hand and knife to the ground, as Ash's sword smoothly removed the head from its neck.

The creature flopped forward, collapsing like a marionette severed from its strings, making absolutely no sound as it fell. There was no blood, only the cleaver clinking against the stones before coming to rest at my feet. The rag-shrouded body shuddered once and went perfectly still.

"Well, that was awful," Puck muttered as Ash slid his blade back into its sheath. "A little too easy, though, and I mean that literally. It is never that simple. Not in a place like this." Glancing at the heap of bones and dirty cloth, he wrinkled his nose. "How much you wanna bet that this thing is gonna jump up, headless, and take a swipe at us again?"

The body on the floor rippled. For a moment, I thought it would do exactly what Puck said, but a second later the bones shivered, withered away, and turned to dust. The dress decayed rapidly, until only a few strips of ragged linen were left. A breeze swept through the room, blowing away the rags and causing the lines of dust to dissolve on the wind. In seconds, nothing remained of the Nightmare Evenfey.

"Huh." Puck sheathed his daggers. "Well, that was unexpected. Lately, Nightmare beasties seem to love coming back from the dead. I was sure we were gonna have to fight this thing again. Happy to be wrong for once."

Behind us, Nyx drew in a slow breath. "Don't be so sure, Puck," she whispered. Turning, I saw her staring with narrowed eyes at the vaulted ceiling overhead. "You might be right, after all."

Everyone looked up.

There were probably a hundred of them, crawling like huge pale spiders along the ceiling. Withered arms and long, thin legs moved as the horde shuffled lazily overhead. Gaunt faces with no mouths twisted, almost as one, to peer down at us.

Puck groaned. "I hate being right," he sighed, as the bundles of rags and withered bodies began dropping from the ceiling. They landed with barely audible thumps against the floor, then slowly rose to their feet and staggered forward.

"Everyone, move," Ash called, pointing his blade out the

door. "This isn't a good place to fight—we'll be surrounded if we stay here. Keep going!"

A ragged body dropped beside me with a muffled thud, a dagger clutched in one hand as it straightened. I lashed out, shearing through the middle of its torso, and both halves exploded into dust as they fell away.

We sprinted from the room, avoiding creatures that continued to fall from the ceiling, dodging or cutting our way through the ones on the ground. We made our way through the castle, not knowing where we were headed, just trying to stay ahead of the Nightmares.

A blast of icy wind hit me as I followed Ash and the others through an arched doorway, and suddenly, we found ourselves outside in some kind of inner courtyard, surrounded by broken walls and rising towers. Piles of stone and rubble were scattered throughout the open space, as if parts of the surrounding towers had crashed into the courtyard below. One of the walls had been flattened completely, showing a gap that plunged straight down the side of the mountain. An enormous tree, gnarled and bare of leaves, rose up from the courtyard's center, scraping the sky with twisted branches.

"Oh," Puck remarked, looking around as we moved across the open space. The mouthless horrors followed us, but at least they weren't dropping onto our heads from above. "Well, this is a lovely boss arena. What a perfect place for an epic battle, don't you think, ice-boy? Now all we need is—"

"No." Ash turned and glared at him. "Puck, I swear, do not say it—"

A wail rose into the air. Sudden and ear-splitting, it swept through the courtyard like an icy wind, causing my stomach to curl and my skin to crawl.

Keirran staggered, turning toward the spot where the wall had fallen away, the blood draining from his face. "She's coming."

I took a deep breath and raised my sword, seeing Ash and the others do the same. *All right, Wailing One,* I thought. *We're ready for you. Show yourself.*

The shriek rang out again, making my ears throb. And then, a massive, dark shape rose from beyond the shattered wall. Horns, scales, and beating, leathery wings appeared, as an all-too-familiar creature landed at the edge of the courtyard and let out a scream that made the ground tremble.

My breath caught. Out of all the frightening, terrible things we had seen, I was not expecting the Wailing One to be an actual *dragon*. Though, as I stared up at it, heart pounding and stomach twisting, I immediately realized my perceptions were wrong. The dragon had two heads, but they were not reptilian, lizard-like, or bestial in any way. Horns sprouted from the skull of a beautiful elven woman, her face twisted into a mask of anguish and despair. The other was a male face whose eyes blazed with fury. The great leathery wings unfurled, and within the folds, hundreds, perhaps thousands, of faces could be seen, melting in and out of the membranes. Hundreds of mouths opened, and a torrent of screaming anguish and despair slammed into me like a tidal wave, making me stagger back.

Keirran fell to his knees, clutching his head. Images flickered around him, shadowy figures that were there one moment, gone the next. The Wailing One screamed again, a piercing shaft of pain through my head, and lunged into the courtyard.

The male head swept down, jaws opening, and a column of fire erupted from its gaping mouth. Ash grabbed Keirran, hauled him to his feet, and yanked him out of the way as the inferno roared across the courtyard. I ducked behind a broken pillar and watched it set the tree ablaze, several mouthless Nightmares bursting into flame as the fire passed over them. Writhing and flailing, they scattered like birds or rolled about on the stones, before turning to dust and blowing away on the wind.

Peering out at the Wailing One, the named Elder Nightmare, I set my jaw. This was what we were here for, but we couldn't slay the Nightmare without destroying its essence. Heart pounding, I watched our Nyx spring over a wall, vault atop a broken pillar, and launch herself at the Nightmare. Her crescent blades flashed, striking the Wailing One in its long, coiling neck, an instantly lethal blow to anything else. A gash appeared in the Nightmare's flesh, and both heads screamed, twin voices rising in a unified wail of anger and pain. But almost immediately, the wound closed, sealing itself, and the male head roared as it spun on the Evenfaery. The dark wings flared open, faces pressing forward as they howled, only now they weren't random strangers but dozens of Varyns, all crying out in pain and rage. More faces appeared, members of her Order, silver-haired and golden-eyed, crowding Varyn as they stared at Nyx, screaming until the noise was deafening.

Nyx stumbled back, wincing. The Wailing One took a booming step toward her, wings still spread wide, and Puck dropped between them with his daggers unsheathed, smiling dangerously as the Nightmare loomed overhead.

"Man, you are not the scariest dragon I've ever faced, but you sure *are* the loudest!" I could barely hear the words over the cacophony of the Wailing One. Even though Puck was very good at making himself heard, the screams of the Nightmare nearly drowned out even his voice. "How are you not completely hoarse by now?"

The Nightmare screamed even louder in reply. Flaring its wings, it turned on Puck, the faces shifting from Varyn and the Order to some familiar and some less recognizable visages. I caught a glimpse of my own face within the folds, twisted into a horrible mask of pain and rage. I shivered, and Puck flinched back, still keeping his body between the monster and Nyx.

"Yeah, that's fine—show me my past traumas. I get it. That's not gonna stop us from taking you down right here. Meghan!" he suddenly shouted, making me jerk up. "Do you see the tower?"

I glanced at the towers rising over the courtyard, my gaze landing on the familiar crooked one. Water poured from the very top of the ruins, shimmering like curtains as it fell. "I see it."

"Go!" Puck called. "We'll keep this noisy thing busy."

Beneath the tree, the Wailing One screamed, the male head bellowing a challenge. Its jaws opened again, blasting a stream of fire down at Puck and Nyx. They leaped away, scattering in different directions, and Ash and Varyn darted in from behind. Ice blade and crescent daggers flashed, cutting deep into the Nightmare's flanks. There was no blood, though the blows did draw an enraged bellow from the Wailing One. Rearing up, wings snapping, it came down with a boom that shook the courtyard, and a ring of flame erupted around it.

I gripped my sword, feeling the edges dig into my palm. I desperately wanted to help, to join my allies and family in taking down the Nightmare. But that would be useless until we destroyed the essence. As much as I wanted to stand with my family, I had to get to the core at the top of the tower to kill this thing for good.

There was no sound beyond the terrible screams of the Wailing One, no warning except the faint prickle against my skin that alerted me to danger from behind. I spun to see a mouthless horror reaching for me with arms outstretched, but before I could react, a steel blade swept through the air, slicing into the lesser Nightmare and cutting it in two.

Keirran staggered forward, his jaw set and his eyes hard. "I'm coming with you," he told me. "I'll be of no use against the Wailing One. Every time it cries out, I can't see anything but shades pressing forward. The closer I get, the harder it is to even breathe." He shot a quick glance at the distant spire, narrowing his gaze. "I'll be more useful helping you reach the tower," he said. "At least the enemies we'll be facing there won't scream at me."

I nodded at my son. "All right," I said. "Let's get to that tower."

I spared one more glance at my friends and allies, fighting the Nightmare in the center of the courtyard. Nyx and the other two assassins were darting in and out, dodging flames and blows to strike where they could. Ash and Puck were fighting side by side, as they had hundreds of times before.

I trust you, I thought to Ash, to Puck, to all of them. *I know you'll be fine. Don't worry, I'll take care of this as quickly as I can, and then we'll finish this Nightmare for good.*

"Let's go," I told Keirran, and we went deeper into the castle, leaving the others to distract the Elder Nightmare for as long as they could.

21

THE TOWER

Hordes of mouthless horrors waited for us through every door and down every hallway, dropping from the ceilings and skittering down walls. They clawed at us with brittle fingers and slashed at us with cleavers and knives, all the while making no sound. Keirran and I cut our way through the masses, dust and rags swirling around us, fighting our way toward the highest tower that loomed ever in the distance. I could see glimpses of it, through windows and the many holes, tantalizingly close, yet just out of reach.

"This way," Keirran said, pointing to a crumbling spiral stone staircase that looped into the dark. "We have to keep going higher."

The horrors followed, climbing the stairs after us. About halfway up, Keirran grimaced, and I raised my sword. "More incoming," he warned, as another group of Nightmares came down the steps, trapping us in the center. I ducked as one swiped at my head with a carving knife, swept its legs out from under it, and plunged my blade through its center as it fell.

"We're trapped," Keirran muttered at my back. "There are more coming from above us."

"We stand here, then," I told him. "You take the ones coming down. I've got the ones coming up."

He nodded. Putting my back to Keirran's, I raised my sword as the mob of horrors came at us from both sides. For a few moments, we stood in the center of chaos, and it was nothing but claws and limbs and flashing blades. I braced myself against the horde coming up the steps, determined that none would get past me to Keirran. Thankfully, there were so many that the Nightmares got in each other's way, bumping into one another as they crowded forward. They reached for us, and I cut them down, putting all thoughts of weakness or mercy aside. I did not worry about the horde at my back. Keirran was there, and I trusted him as much as I did the one who'd taught us both.

"The ones above us are cleared out," Keirran panted.

I slashed through a reaching claw and kicked the Nightmare in the chest, sending it crashing back into the others. But more crowded into the stairwell from below, an unending flood. "Keep moving," I told him. "I'll be right behind you."

"Are you sure?"

"Yes! Go!"

He went, his presence vanishing up the stairs, and the Nightmares pressed forward. I ducked, cutting the legs from the pair in front of me, and leaped back as they went down. The ones behind them stumbled, tripping over their fellows, and I quickly turned and sprinted up the stairs after Keirran.

Wind blasted me as I reached the top and stepped onto the castle roof. Towers and battlements surrounded us, though the turrets and parapets had fallen away, leaving enormous holes in the walls. One tower had collapsed completely and now rested against the side of the roof, jutting up at a steep angle. It pointed like a finger toward our final destination: the narrow, spindly tower that rose above all the others. There was no obvious path to it, however; the battlements that must have once connected the tower to the rest of the castle had fallen. It stood alone, pouring water down its sides like a waterfall. So close, and yet...

"Where to now?" Keirran panted.

A pair of mouthless Nightmares suddenly clawed their way up the side of the wall and grabbed at my legs. I plunged my blade through the back of a neck, and Keirran swiftly kicked the other off the ledge, sending it tumbling back into space.

"There," I said, pointing out our path. "If we cross the roof, that fallen tower is very close to where we need to go. We'll have to jump at the end, but I think we can make it."

Keirran blew out a breath. "That's a lot of heights," he said. "Good thing I had tons of practice creeping across the rooftops with Razor when I wanted to get out of the Iron Palace."

I turned to him with a frown. "*That's* how you snuck out all those times?"

He gave me a brief, sheepish grin that I hadn't seen in ages. "The gliders and I were very well acquainted."

There was a thump behind us. The mouthless horrors had begun crawling up from the stairwell, and I grimaced. "I want that entire story later, but right now, let's go."

We leaped onto the roof and began the treacherous path toward the fallen tower. The roof, unsurprisingly, was full of holes, and the remaining tiles rocked and slid underfoot. Lesser Nightmares skittered after us, moving like spiders over the exposed beams. More crawled up and over the edges of the wall, and a few even slithered out of the holes in the roof beneath us. The screams of the Wailing One drifted up from below, and I hoped that Ash and the others were doing all right.

Ahead of me, Keirran cut down a Nightmare leaping for him, and the monster crashed into the roof before exploding into dust. The tiles beneath it shivered, then disappeared with a roar as an entire section of roof collapsed, taking my son and a pair of Nightmares with it.

"Keirran!"

I raced to the edge of the yawning hole, relief spiking as I saw Keirran clinging to a beam with one hand, the other still gripping his sword. The Nightmares clung to him, hanging off his back and legs, clawing wildly as all three dangled over the sheer drop to the stone below.

"Hang on, Keirran!"

Hurrying to the other side, I lay on my stomach to reach for him. Keirran clung doggedly to the beam, but his head was bowed, shoulders hunched against the Nightmare clawing at his face. Rage flickered. Pulling my sword back, I aimed carefully, then stabbed down at the monster assaulting my son. The point of the blade struck the creature in the forehead, flinging it back. It shivered into dust and rags before spiraling away into empty space.

Freed from the monster on his shoulders, Keirran raised his sword and plunged it into the horror still trying to climb his leg. It reeled back, tearing wildly at his clothes, then tumbled into the darkness without a sound.

"Keirran," I urged, extending a hand down, "give me your sword."

He did, passing it up by the hilt. I grabbed it, set it beside me on the roof, and reached for him once more. "Now your hand."

A Nightmare scuttled toward me out of nowhere and leaped for my back. It landed, disturbingly light, and then there was a blinding pain in my shoulder as it plunged something sharp into my flesh.

Clenching my jaw around a yell, I reached back with my free hand, grabbed whatever I could, and yanked the Nightmare over my head. It sailed into the void, dropping past Keirran, barely missing him as it flailed and plummeted to the stones far below.

"Keirran." I reached for him again, and this time his fingers latched on to my wrist. I dragged him out of the hole, ignoring the way my shoulder blazed with pain, and pulled him to his feet on the roof. His eyes were bright with worry as they focused on me.

"You're bleeding."

"It's not serious," I told him, handing him his blade. "Come on, we're almost there."

We continued across the roof, running along beams and leaping over holes, until we reached the spot where the fallen tower leaned against the wall. Rotting and ancient, it pointed like a finger toward the highest spot in the castle, the spire with water pouring from the top floor. I reached the base of the fallen tower and started to climb, trying to ignore the searing pain every time I used my right arm. I could feel warm wetness spreading across my back and hoped that whatever the Nightmare had stabbed me with wasn't poisoned.

Gritting my teeth, I reached for the top, and Keirran's hand gripped mine and drew me up the final few feet. As I scrambled up with him, the stones beneath me disintegrated, making me stagger, and Keirran grabbed my other arm.

His face paled as he drew his hand back, the palm and fingers stained red. "Not serious," I insisted, though his expression remained alarmed. "It won't kill me. Besides, there's no time to deal with it now." I gazed up the stone pathway before us, all the way to the turret roof, sticking out over empty air. The final spire, thin and crooked, waited for us on the other side of a deadly plunge to the bottom of the castle.

"There's quite a leap at the end," Keirran mused, judging the space between turret and tower with narrowed eyes. I stared up at it, too, noting the water pouring from the top floor, cascading to the bottom. Most of the outer walls were gone, showing the lower floors through the gaps.

Keirran and I scanned the outer wall of the tower, searching for the best way in. "If we aim for the third floor from the top," I said, "we'll avoid most of the waterfalls. I think we're going to get wet no matter where we go, but at least the floor beyond isn't waterlogged."

"What about the next one up?" Keirran replied, pointing to a hole farther up the tower. "It's a harder jump, but we'll be closer to the top—"

A scratching sound interrupted him, and he glanced back as a trio of mouthless horrors clawed their way onto the tower with us. "Never mind. Third floor it is."

We sprinted up the tower, running along the uneven path, hearing the Nightmares skittering behind us. From the corner of my eye, I caught bursts of orange light coming from the courtyard below, heard the screams of the Nightmare ringing off the towers, and prayed my family would be safe for just a little longer.

Keirran reached the end of the makeshift bridge and hurled himself into the air. I watched him soar gracefully over the gap, come down, and hit the ledge with room to spare, rolling into the tower. With the Nightmares right on my heels, I sprinted up the turret and bunched my muscles to follow.

A rumble went through the air, and the entire tower beneath me shuddered. I staggered, but the edge was right there, and I couldn't stop. I leaped into empty space, seeing a Nightmare slash at me as it flung itself off the roof as well, missing. It tumbled to the ground, bursting into dust on the stones.

Oh, this is going to be close.

I reached for the ledge, suddenly knowing I was going to miss it. But then Keirran was there, stretching out an arm and grabbing my wrist as I came down. I hit the side of the tower with a grunt that drove all the air from my lungs, but the grip on my hand didn't waver. Keirran pulled me onto the ledge before we both collapsed, gasping, on the stones.

My lungs burned, my legs shook, and my back stung with a constant, fiery pain. I wished I could lie down on the hard stones and not move for a few minutes, but I forced myself upright and gazed around. We had landed in a small, circular room with a pillar of water gushing straight down the center of the spire. A spiraling staircase, the same one I had seen in my dream, ran along the wall to the floors above.

Keirran stood as well, putting a hand on my non-wounded arm. "Are you all right?" he asked. I nodded, and his gaze rose to the stairs. "Whatever we're looking for, it has to be up there, right?"

"Let's hope so."

22

TEARS AND REGRET

The stairs were covered in tears. There was no way to traverse them without stepping in the water, which sloshed against my boots and made my eyes burn wildly. For a moment, Keirran hesitated, eyes shadowed. But then he set his jaw and followed, striding up the waterlogged steps until we both reached the top.

My throat and eyes burned. The smell of the tears was overwhelming, and the entire floor was covered in several inches of water, making it look like a small indoor pool. Nearly every wall had fallen away, showing open sky, and a swollen red moon had come out from behind the clouds. The hole in the center of the room gushed water, tears flowing through the cracks in the floor and over the sides of the tower in an unending stream of poison and despair.

Keirran coughed, holding his sleeve to his jaw as he gazed around. "So much water," he rasped. "Where is it all coming from?"

"There," I said, and pointed across the room.

A square pool, looking almost like a marble bath, sat against the wall opposite us. There were no faucets, no streams gushing into the pool, but water overflowed from every side, spilling to the floor in an endless cascade.

"Okay," I mused, breathing as shallowly as I could as water sloshed around us. "We're at the top of the tower. Where could the essence be? Do you see it, Keirran?"

"No," he replied. "But I see something else."

An arm rose out of the pool, clutching at the marble sides. It was transparent, seeming to be made of water; I could see the distorted sides of the pool through it. A body followed, watery and opaque like the attached arm, a creature of tears come to life.

Another followed, transparent forms rising from the pool. As they stepped forward, their features changed, blurring and running together. And then, like the faces I'd seen in the wings of the Nightmare, I was suddenly facing a crowd of everyone I loved. Ash, Puck, Keirran, Ethan. My entire family. Not only them, but my own Iron fey stared back at me, their faces sorrowful and accusing.

A huge man with eyes like glowing embers stared at me over the heads of the others, coils of metal dreadlocks hanging from his shoulders, and my heart gave a jolt of grief and recognition. *Ironhorse.*

The sound of sobbing filled my ears, and the bitter smell of tears and pain was overwhelming.

I shook myself. I had not failed anyone. My family lived. The Iron Kingdom was still there. I had given everything to protect my kingdom and the ones I loved, and I would still.

Beside me, Keirran let out a breath that was mostly a sob, closing his eyes and turning away from the slowly approaching horde.

"Keirran," I said softly, "get a hold of yourself. They're not real. You know this isn't real."

"I know," he rasped. "I am aware that this is the effect of the Wailing One, and what I'm seeing isn't true. But..." Tears gathered in his eyes, spilling down his face even as he took a breath. "It still feels…like I'm back there, on that day. When I lost her. When the courts exiled me from the Nevernever."

My throat closed up. "You see Annwyl."

"Everywhere," he choked. "And the Lady. And the Forgotten. And…everyone I killed during the war. Everyone I have failed or lost or betrayed. They're all right here, staring at me." His gaze rose to mine, bleak and haunted. "Even you."

Oh, Keirran. I wanted nothing more than to pull him close, to take away all the pain and guilt and grief he was still carrying, the wounds buried deep in his soul. Regardless of everything that had happened, he was my son, and I would always want to protect him. But we couldn't give in to pain and sorrow now. Across the room of past regrets and trauma, the pool beckoned. If we were going to have a chance to beat the Elder Nightmare, we would have to get to it. Somehow.

"Keirran," I said, "we're going to have to fight our way through. Can you do this?"

He took a steadying breath and nodded, raising his sword. "I am sorry," he whispered, and I was unsure who he was speaking to: Annwyl, myself, or someone else. "You don't have to remind me. I already know."

The crowd was nearly upon us. Gripping my blade, I took one step forward and found myself facing Ethan across the water. He held his twin swords in each hand, and his deep blue eyes were hard as he approached, silently reminding me of all the times I had abandoned him. All the times I had not been there after I had vanished into Faery for the last time. His mouth opened, and his voice, ugly with bitter resentment, lanced into my head.

"You left us," he accused, his voice caught between a snarl and a sob. "You left me alone with the fey who made my life hell. You never loved us. Why did you always choose Them over me?"

"You are not my brother," I growled, dodging the sword coming at my face. I blocked the twin sword cutting down at my head and stabbed up with my blade, striking the fake Ethan in the chest and sinking it deep. The words stung, but they didn't bring the crushing guilt I'd felt in the past, when he was confused and hurt, and I could not be there for him.

Ethan and I have made our peace. He was angry for a long time, but he has accepted that Faery will always be a part of our lives. I regret the years that I lost with him, but he will always be my family. You're going to have to do better than that.

As my blade sank home, the false Ethan jerked and then became transparent as he turned to water again and collapsed. The others pressed in—Ash, Puck, Ironhorse, even my human parents, but their features were all slightly blurry. Ash's double was the most transparent; he was almost see-through and did not have close to the skill that his real-life twin possessed. I still hated fighting even a weak shadow of my husband, and had to look away when I dealt the killing blow, but it was a relief when he disappeared. Of the mob crowding forward, he'd seemed the least real.

In a startling moment of clarity, I understood. Out of everyone in this room, Ash was the least of my regrets. Of course, there were always going to be some. He had gone through a lot to be with me; we had both gone through hell to defy the courts and be with each other. The fallout of our decisions still shaped the Nevernever today. But I had never regretted falling in love with a Winter prince. Not once had I second-guessed my decision to marry the youngest son of the Unseelie Queen. In this nightmare world of fear, rage, sorrow, and regret, even if it all faded away, Ash would be the last one standing at my side.

And then Keirran stepped forward, and for a moment, I had to glance over to see if the real Keirran was still there. What I saw chilled me. He stood several paces away, his sword lowered, the tip touching the ground and his head bowed. A figure stood before him, a fey girl with chestnut hair and large green eyes, watching Keirran with a look of heart-wrenching grief. Her lips were moving, and though I couldn't hear any sound, I knew Keirran caught every word.

Oh no. "Keirran!" I called, and immediately had to block as the mirror image of my son lunged and swiped at me with his blade. This Keirran was much more real than Ash had been, his strikes coming in fast and aggressive, driving me back a few steps. I blocked, parried, then spun to the left, my boots sending up sprays of water as I whirled and swept my blade at my opponent's head. From the few sparring matches I'd had with my son, I knew Keirran was quick and skilled enough to easily duck, block, or simply not be there. This one was not. The sword edge sliced through the back of his neck, and thankfully, the false Keirran turned to water as his head toppled from his shoulders, easing a bit of the horror as he died.

I whirled back, searching for the real Keirran, but the spot where he'd been standing moments before was empty. My heart clenched as I spotted him, walking steadily toward the pool at the back of the chamber. The crowds let him pass, and he paid them no mind, his gaze fixed to something at the back of the room. Annwyl, standing waist deep in the center of the pool, one hand outstretched to Keirran as she urged him forward.

"Keirran!" I shouted, but my son ignored me. I started toward him, but the imposing bulk of a long-dead Ironhorse suddenly blocked my way. Grimly, I turned to fight one of the Iron Kingdom's legends while trying to keep Keirran and Annwyl in my sights.

"Keirran, snap out of it!" I called, ducking an enormous fist that swung at my face. But Keirran didn't seem to hear me. Standing at the edge of the pool, he hesitated for a single heartbeat, then climbed over the rim into the water, joining Annwyl in the center.

Trailing a hand over his shoulders, she circled him, bringing her lips close to his ear. Keirran closed his eyes, and she eased him back, into the waters. The tears closed over his head, and Keirran was gone.

No.

Rage flared. Dodging the blow to my head, I raised my sword and brought it down on the outstretched arm with a yell, shearing through the limb completely. Ironhorse staggered, and I lunged in, driving my blade into his chest and out his back.

The rest of the horde closed in. With a scream, I hurled myself through the dissolving body and into the midst of my enemies. Faces flashed by me, familiar and recognizable. Puck, Nyx, Oberon. I cut them down, steeling myself every time they fell. They were shadows, all the regrets I'd carried with me ever since I'd walked into Faery, but they did not define me. I had not failed them, and right now, they were only obstacles between me and my son.

I slashed through an enemy and turned to find there was only one left. A body stepped toward me, tall and lean, with long metallic hair and depthless black eyes. A cloak of writhing silver cables spread from his shoulders and down his back. I hadn't seen him in ages, but I knew him instantly.

"Iron Queen," Machina the Iron King whispered. "An empty title. The Iron fey are mine. You merely stole them. You are nothing but a pretender."

I parried an iron cable that came slashing at my head, but was forced back as several more snaked around me. "A pretender," the Iron King repeated, walking steadily forward, those silver cables writhing in a hypnotic, mesmerizing pattern. "What are you without your glamour?" he whispered. "Without your knight? Without that power? *My* power." A tentacle lashed at me; I raised my sword and knocked it aside. "You are nothing," Machina went on. "You are merely human. A thief with stolen magic. You can do nothing without glamour. Look around you, child. Girl. Where are you now? *Who* are you?"

The cable came at me again. I raised my free hand and snatched it from the air, drawing a shocked look from the tall faery before me. Taking one step forward, I drove my sword into his center, ignoring the tentacles as they flailed wildly around us. Machina stared down at me, raising a long-fingered hand to gingerly touch the sword hilt in his chest.

"I am the Iron Queen," I told him simply, as his features blurred to water, and the Iron King collapsed into a puddle at my feet.

I rushed through him to the pool. Pressing both palms to the marble lip, I stared into the depths, searching for Keirran. The overwhelming bitterness stung my eyes, making them water and tear; I scrubbed at them angrily and kept looking.

A face appeared in the water, staring up at me. It rose swiftly toward the surface, making me step back as a figure broke through the water and stood before me.

"Do you hate me, Iron Queen?" Annwyl whispered, lifting sorrowful green eyes to mine. "Do you despise me for stealing Keirran away? For causing him to turn against his court and family? Or do you hate yourself, for not being able to help him?" Her gaze narrowed, a spark of anger flickering across her face for just a moment. "You and the Winter prince defied all the laws of Faery that stated you could not be together. Why couldn't it work for us? Why was your love more important than ours?"

Guilt tore at me, but I gripped my sword and tensed to lunge. *I will not stand here arguing with shadows. Not when Keirran is lying on the bottom of that pool.*

A sword suddenly exploded from the water behind Annwyl, and she jerked up, eyes going wide, as the point pierced her chest. Her mouth opened, and she rippled into water and collapsed, as Keirran burst from the pool in a spray of tears and lunged to the side.

My heart stood still. Coughing and gasping, Keirran slumped against the rim, water pouring off him in waves. I grabbed his arm, dragged him from the pool, and knelt with him on the floor, holding him steady as he coughed and hacked and emptied water from his mouth and nose.

"Keirran," I said, once the violent expulsions had calmed somewhat. "Are you all right?"

He retched, dragging a palm down his face. "Eyes...burning," he gritted out. "Feels like I just ground a bunch of salt into my face. Can't see anything."

"Breathe," I told him, and he sucked in several deep, shuddering breaths. As he did, I noticed one of his hands, clutched tightly around what looked like a glass ball. "Keirran," I said, touching the back of his hand. "Is this...?"

He coughed once more and tried opening his eyes. I winced at how red they were. "I don't know," he rasped, holding it up. "I found it at the bottom of the pool. Thought I might drown before I discovered what was down there."

Understanding dawned. "You let yourself be taken," I whispered.

"I'm sorry," he said. "I heard you calling me, but...it was hard enough keeping my focus on what I had to do. If I let my guard down for just a moment, I might've done what Annwyl wanted, which was to join her on the other side. Wherever that was."

My stomach tightened to the point of pain. "I'm glad you didn't listen."

"It was tempting," he confessed, and ran a hand down his face. "Seeing her again, even though I knew she wasn't real... the *pain* felt real. Real enough to consider letting it all go." His brow furrowed. "But Annwyl is gone. If I let myself be haunted by her, it's going to consume me." He raised his head, regarding the pool, the water flowing steadily over the sides, and his gaze hardened. "Besides, the real Annwyl would never have asked me to do that. I promised her I would live, and I still have a lot of things to set right. The least I can do is try to fix the atrocities the Lady left behind."

I released my breath in a puff. "Show me what you found."

He held up his hand, turning it over to reveal what lay in his grasp. It was…a snow globe, or something very similar. The clear crystal ball had flecks of white drifting through the glass like a miniature blizzard. "I looked as long as I could, but I didn't find anything else."

I took the globe from him, turning it over and back in my hand. The second I did, the snow swirled frantically, and faces began appearing in the glass, blinking into existence and fading away. There and gone far too quickly to see. The litany of faces continued, all different, all vanishing in a fraction of a blink. A wail arose from the tiny globe, hundreds of voices all screaming out at once. A cry of agony from countless fey that no longer existed.

An answering wail rang out horrifyingly close, and the tower beneath us trembled with the sound of beating wings.

"The Wailing One. She's coming." Keirran and I leaped to our feet as the huge, dark form of the Elder Nightmare rose into the air just beyond the edge of the tower. The faces in its wings screamed at us, as did the female head, but the male head's jaws opened, an ominous red glow blooming at the back of its throat. There was no cover at the top of the tower, and only a sheer plunge straight down to the last floor. As the column of fire swept forward, I turned and slammed into Keirran, knocking us both into the pool of tears.

The water closed over my head, and I held my breath, hearing the muffled roar of flames above me. In my hand, the globe pulsed like a heartbeat, and instead of muffling the screams, the water seemed to amplify them. A maelstrom of noise swirling around us, shrieking and howling in my ears.

To defeat a named Elder Nightmare, you must destroy the essence. The core that represents what it is.

The king's regret. That was what I held in my hands. His grief at not being able to save his people, a sorrow so great it had taken form and turned into a Nightmare. I could feel the steady throb of the globe in my fingers, the vibrations of the voices shrieking around me. I cradled the globe in both hands.

I understand. I accept your sorrow and your grief. It will become part of me, but it will not consume me. And when we finally meet, I will understand a little more.

I brought my hands together, crushing the globe and the glass.

The shards sliced into me, cutting my palms and fingers, which burned like they were on fire. A howl rose from the shattered globe, louder than anything I had heard before, making the water vibrate around us.

A surge of glamour, a powerful pulse of magic, drove away everything else. Opening my eyes, ignoring the instant burning sensation, I found myself floating beneath the surface of the pool. Keirran hung suspended beside me, his eyes still closed, his silver hair a bright cloud in the water. Faces swirled around us, a miasma of dark, roiling glamour. I extended a hand, opening myself up to the magic, and absolute rage and despair lanced through me. Was this what Ash had felt when he was tempted by the Nightmare glamour? This sensation of wanting to lash out, to take this power and use it to destroy everything in my path?

The scream of the Wailing One echoed above me. I clenched my fist, and glamour rippled along my veins, hot and powerful. I was the Iron Queen again, and this Nightmare had tormented us long enough.

I raised a hand and sent a surge of energy pulsing in all directions.

The marble pool cracked, then exploded as the energy strands slammed into it. Water and stones went flying as the pool disintegrated, draining in an instant and dumping me to the rocky floor of the tower.

I rose from the remains of the pool, gazing around. The blast of energy had not only shattered the pool; it had blown off the roof of the tower and torn through the walls, so I now stood on an empty platform high above the castle grounds. The Wailing One hovered a few feet away, leathery wings beating the air, two sets of eyes blazing down at me. The faces in its wings seemed to have vanished, though the female head still opened her mouth and screamed her sorrow and rage, buffeting me and making the very tower tremble.

Behind me, Keirran stirred, coughing, and pushed himself to his hands and knees. I saw his hands clench into fists, and the water beneath him crinkled, turning to ice.

I turned back to the Nightmare, feeling glamour surging through me once more. Raising a hand, I gathered that power to me. A glowing ball of crimson grew in my hands, the light flickering and dancing off the stones.

The Wailing One howled a challenge, and I hurled the ball of light. It crackled as it instantly became a strand of lightning and slammed into the Nightmare's chest, exploding into flickering ribbons of energy.

The Nightmare reeled back with a scream. Tendrils of darkness coiled from its chest and writhed into the air. The female head lowered, jaws gaping, and I braced myself for another ear-splitting wail. Instead, a stream of clear liquid shot from her open lips, hurling toward me. I dodged, and the stream struck the remains of the pool, which steamed and bubbled as the liquid melted through it.

Okay. Did not know she could do that.

The head sobbed and disgorged another stream of acid, spewing it over the stones toward me. I scrambled back and hurled a quick bolt of lightning, but the head twisted out of the way. The male head swept down, jaws opening, and a tornado of flame roared through the air.

It met a sudden blast of ice that stopped it in its tracks, and steam billowed as the two elements slammed into each other. Heart pounding, I looked back to see Keirran on his feet, eyes hard and one hand outstretched as he directed his own glamour at the Nightmare.

The female head whipped around, lips curling back as she spotted Keirran. She took a breath, but something streaked through the air from the side, slamming into her. A long spear of ice, the point punching through the other side of the monster's neck. She wailed, and my heart leaped in my chest.

A black cloud of screaming ravens descended from the sky, swarming around the male Nightmare, which was still breathing fire. Its flames sputtered out as it reeled back, shaking its head and snapping at the birds. Keirran raised his other arm, and layers of frost spread across the Nightmare's scaly body, solidifying into sheets of ice. The Wailing One screamed, staggering in midair. The female head swung toward Keirran again and met a spinning crescent of light that struck her in the eyes. Two more followed, hitting the Nightmare in the face, and she recoiled, blinded and reeling.

I took a deep breath, drawing the dark glamour from the air, feeling it crackle as it rushed into me. I let it build, a churning mass of power, anger, grief, and despair. My eyes blurred, poisonous tears streaming down my face. I looked up at the Nightmare, seeing exactly what it was, knowing there was nothing I could do to help it or the ones it grieved for. I raised a hand, releasing all that energy, power, emotion, and magic into the air. Above the Wailing One, the skies churned with clouds, a dark swirling vortex that flashed with crimson light.

"Everyone, get clear!" I shouted, and saw the flock of ravens disperse, scattering to different parts of the castle. The barrage of ice and moonlight blades ceased, and behind me, Keirran took a few quick steps back. Left in peace for just a moment, the two heads of the Wailing One shook themselves, glared down at me, and snarled. For a split second, the Nightmare was bathed in a sullen red glow...

And then the rain of lightning struck it dead center, trapping it in a web of flickering energy. The Wailing One jerked up as the lightning tore through it, shredding it apart. It gave one last scream, both male and female voices rising as one, before it un-raveled into writhing tendrils of shadow. Ghostly faces emerged from the cloud, trailing darkness behind them as they flew into the sky, their mournful wails growing ever more distant, and vanished into the wind.

23

THE FOREST OF MIST

I staggered back and sank to one knee on the stones, my breath coming in short gasps. The anger and grief of the Elder Nightmare still raged through me, and my eyes burned with tears. I clenched a fist on the floor and willed those emotions into check, breathing deep to find my calm. The Nightmare glamour pulsed in my ears, tangled up with emotion, but I forced it down, turning it into raw determination. With a deep breath, I rose, glancing at Keirran to make sure he was all right. He leaned against the broken wall, breathing hard, but I saw the ice spread out around him and felt the chill of his glamour in the air.

"Meghan!"

I turned as Ash strode across the floor, and a moment later his arms were around me, crushing us together. Closing my eyes, I relaxed against him, listening to his heartbeat and letting my guard down for just a moment.

"Is everyone all right?" I whispered, and felt him nod.

"We were able to keep the Nightmare distracted for a while," he murmured, still holding me close, "but then, whatever you and Keirran did caught its attention. It abandoned the fight and went charging off toward the tower. We followed it, but none of us could fly, so we had to take the long way around. A few minutes later, there was this pulse of glamour that went through the air. I assume that was you, destroying the essence or soul jar or whatever the Nightmare was guarding up here."

"Regret," I said softly. "The king's regret."

Ash's embrace tightened. "In any case," he murmured, "we were able to rejoin the battle, with magic this time."

"And man, lovebirds, let me tell you how nice it is to be able to fly again!"

Puck dropped onto the edge of the tower and stood, shaking feathers from his hair as he grinned widely at us. Reaching up, he plucked out an ebony pinfeather and twirled it between thumb and forefinger, shaking his head. "How did I ever go this long without annoying a giant monster with a really irritating flock of ravens? No wonder I wasn't feeling myself." He gave a dramatic sigh and released the feather, letting it spiral into the wind. "A Puck with no magic just isn't the same."

"You should try not to waste it, Puck." Our Nyx appeared, sliding out of a clump of shadows. "There's not a limitless source like in the Nevernever. We're going to have to make it last until we reach the Nightmare King and... What are you doing?"

Puck took a few quick steps toward the assassin, pulled her close, and kissed her. Nyx stiffened, but after a moment she relaxed, either in resignation or acceptance, and slipped an arm around his neck. Against the wall, Keirran rolled his eyes, but he was smiling, too.

Nyx drew in a slow breath as they pulled back. "Is this tradition, then?" she asked, one brow raised as she gazed up at Puck. "Something I need to prepare for every time we win a fight?"

Puck gave her a fierce grin. "Hey, I'm all for starting traditions," he said. "We just beat a huge, almost indestructible baddie, got our magic back, and no one died in the battle. I'm feeling pretty good."

"That is good to hear," said Grimalkin's voice. "And I would take the Evenfaery's advice and not waste the magic you have gleaned tonight. Because the next stop is the Nightmare King's castle."

That sobered everyone. We had defeated one enemy, but the hardest task still loomed: finding our way to the mysterious door in the throne room, past the hordes of monsters and Elder Nightmares, and confronting the Nightmare King himself.

"You can still get us there, right, Nyx?" Keirran asked.

She nodded, stepping out of Puck's arms. "Mostly. If I cannot, the others will be able to. Their memories of this world are recent, whereas mine...are still scattered."

"Where are the others?" I wondered.

"They were checking on Gilleas when I saw them last," Nyx replied. "Between us, we should be able to find the edge of the Forest of Mist. The real question is, will we be able to find the castle within the forest? Gilleas was able to make his way there, long ago. But the Forest of Mist is a fickle thing. Its borders shift, and within the forest, everything moves around—trees, rocks, even the castle. You'll rarely find anything in the same place twice."

"How far is this forest?" Ash wanted to know.

"Not far," Grimalkin said. "In fact, once we cross this mountain range, we should see the edge. Do not ask me how I know that, Goodfellow," he added, stopping Puck as he opened his mouth. "As I told you before, I was around before this world was sealed away. I remember certain things about it. And I am quite sure that I have been to the castle."

"Not to mention," Nyx added, a half smile tugging at the corner of her mouth, "he is a cat."

Puck nearly choked on his laughter. "Oh, to hear that phrase *not* come from Grimalkin," he chortled, while Grim thumped his tail and pretended not to hear. "I've never been so proud."

The Elder Nightmare was dead. We had our glamour back, or at least, we had a reserve of magic again. How long it would last, I didn't know, but hopefully it would be enough to get us to the Nightmare King's castle and through the monsters that prowled the land between us.

The trek across the mountains didn't take long, though exactly how long was impossible to tell in a land with no sunrise. However, nothing stopped us or got in our way; no giant bats or lesser Nightmares swooped out of the sky to impede our progress. When we crossed the final mountain range, I gazed down the cliff side into what looked like a sea of mist. An ocean of gray clouds, hanging over the entire valley, as far as the eye could see. Somewhere, waiting in that murky sea of fog, was the Nightmare King's castle.

And the Nightmare King himself.

We stopped to rest once more before heading down into the valley. Knowing that Nightmares and Elder Nightmares prowled the eerie forest, I didn't want us to start the last, and most dangerous, leg of the journey while we were exhausted. Staking out a flat ledge that overlooked the valley, we started a fire, took turns dozing against the rocks, and made our final preparations to confront the Nightmare King.

Though I still had no idea what we were going to do when we found him.

"I wonder what's happening in the Nevernever right now," Puck mused, poking the flames of the small fire he'd started. "You think Oberon, Titania, and Mab are still sitting where we left them, at the site of the seal?"

"They said they would be," I replied. "And if they all share Faery's memories of the Nightmare King, they know they can't pretend this isn't happening. I don't think even Titania is willing to ignore this, especially if it threatens her rule of Summer."

Puck snorted. "The Nightmare King wouldn't want the Summer Court, anyway," he said. "He'd take one look at it, go, 'Hss, too bright!' like a vampire, and then move on to Winter." He sighed, tossing the stick into the fire to be consumed by flames. "Man, I miss the sun."

Sitting beside Other Nyx, Varyn narrowed golden eyes at Puck. "And what is a vampire, that you would compare our king to one, Nevernever fey?" he asked.

"Oh, you know." Puck waved a hand. "They're broody, they creep through the shadows, they have an aversion to sunlight...kinda like you guys—ow!" He jerked and glanced at our Nyx, who raised a brow at him. "Present company excluded, of course, geez."

Gilleas moved around the fire, gliding from the darkness like a wraith. Crossing his long legs like some kind of giant insect, he lowered himself with a groan. "Tell me about the Nevernever," the Evenfaery said, turning his deer skull in my direction. "I am curious. You said it has changed since the time of the Lady and her circle. That kings and queens now rule parts of Faery in their different courts?"

"Yes," I said. "There are three official courts within the Nevernever—Summer, Winter, and Iron. The Seelie fey make up the Summer Court, which is ruled by King Oberon and Queen Titania."

"That would be my court," Puck broke in. "Obviously. Pretty nice place, too, except for the harpy known as Queen Titania, Lady of Spite. But nobody likes her. Unlike me—everybody *loves* me."

I saw a collective eye roll from nearly everyone, and bit down a smile.

"And what of the others?" Gilleas continued. "If there is a

Summer Court, then it stands to reason that there is a Winter Court."

"Queen Mab rules the Winter Court, where the Unseelie live," I went on. "Tir Na Nog is at the heart of her territory, just like Arcadia is for Summer. Then you have the Iron territories, my domain. The capital of the Iron Realm is Mag Tuiredh, where most of the Iron fey live."

Gilleas slowly shook his head in disbelief. "Iron fey," he repeated. "Has the rest of Faery changed so much? Do the Nevernever fey no longer fear the touch of iron? Have the Evenfey fallen that far behind?"

"No." This was from Ash, who had been making a snowflake dance around the fire in front of us. He'd claimed it was practice, but I think he missed his Winter glamour as much as I missed my Iron and Summer. "Iron is still deadly to all fey except those from the Iron Realm," he told Gilleas. "The fey of Summer and Winter can't cross into Meghan's territory without harming themselves. It was…interesting, trying to maintain the peace between all three courts. But nowadays, we think we have it worked out."

"What happens if a faery does not fit into any particular court?" Other Nyx wondered.

"There are the wyld fey," I answered. "The ones who live in the wyldwood, or in the Deep Wyld across the River of Dreams. They're not part of any of the courts."

"But they still must obey the kings and queens of Faery," Gilleas reasoned.

"To an extent." I shot a look at Grimalkin, who lay on a nearby rock with his feet tucked under him. His eyes were half-closed, and he didn't look remotely interested in the conversation. "It's complicated."

"Apparently." Gilleas tapped his claws against his bony chin. "And what happens to a faery who does not wish to be part of a court," he asked, "or who disobeys the king and queens?"

"They're punished," Ash answered. "It depends on the act, and what the ruler is feeling at the time, but exile or banishment from the Nevernever is the most common sentence."

"Correction, ice-boy," said Puck, holding up a finger. "They're punished only if they get caught. The rulers can't be everywhere at once, and what they don't know can't get you exiled. Thank goodness, otherwise I'd *never* be allowed back in."

"I see." Gilleas's voice gave no hint as to what he thought about all this, but I felt those hollow eyes fix on me again. "And have you ever banished anyone from the Nevernever, Iron Queen?" he asked.

My stomach clenched. On the other side of the fire, Keirran had been sitting quietly, one knee drawn to his chest, staring into the flames. He didn't look up or react as Gilleas asked his question, but a cold fist grabbed my insides and twisted them around until I thought I might be sick.

"Yes," I replied, unable to look at Keirran as I did. "I have."

Gilleas did not seem to sense the rising tension around the fire. "And what were their crimes?" he went on.

"Starting a war in the Nevernever." Keirran's voice was flat. He didn't look up as he spoke, continuing to gaze into the fire. "Siding with a usurper and attempting to bring her to power again. Killing a member of the royal family. Trying to permanently destroy the Veil, so that all humans could see the fey."

Silence fell, as Gilleas and the other Evenfey finally realized whom we were speaking of. Gilleas gazed at Keirran for a long moment, then turned and bowed his head to me. "My apologies," he offered. "I did not realize... I did not mean to open old wounds."

I wanted to tell him it was all right, that he couldn't have known the details of the last war, but I couldn't speak. Instead, I rose and walked around the fire until I reached the edge of the cliff, where the stones dropped away into an endless expanse of mist. Overhead, the full moon peeked through a few wispy clouds, lighting the sea below and turning it silver.

I heard the soft crunch of boots behind me, felt his presence step up to join mine. "I'm tired of this, Ash," I whispered, gazing down into the churning sea of gray. "I want him to come home."

"I know." Ash slipped his arms around my waist. "Me too."

"Eternal banishment is pointless," I went on, leaning into him. "It's just a slow death sentence. It's a way for the rulers of Faery to not deal with a problem. Banish the faery responsible and forget they exist. But they *do* exist. And for countless fey, once they've been banished, that's it. There's no way for them to correct what they've done, no hope to ever return to the Nevernever. Unless they're someone like Puck, who is too useful to banish forever. Or unless the rulers need them to save the courts. Again.

"Keirran will never return to Faery," I said, feeling a hollow despair as I spoke those words out loud. "He'll never get to come home. Unless there is some crisis that needs him specifically. He and the Forgotten will stay in the Between, ignored by everyone. Why?" I clenched a fist on Ash's forearm. "Because Faery doesn't like change. Because the rulers are afraid of anything different, anything that doesn't fit into their traditional version of normal. The Iron fey, the Forgotten, and now the Evenfey... but we are *all* fey. I just wish they could see it."

"Maybe you can show them," said a soft voice. Keirran's, as he stepped up to join us on the ledge. The wind gusting from below tossed his silver hair and ruffled his clothes, as he gazed down at the valley with somber eyes. "The rulers won't listen to me," he said calmly, "but if we somehow save this world, the Evenfey will need someone to speak for them when we go back to the Nevernever." He exhaled, leaning against the rock wall and putting his head back, gazing at the sky. "I just wish I could've been a better voice for the Forgotten and the Exiles," he murmured. "If I had, maybe the war with the Lady never would've happened."

My throat tightened. "Keirran…"

He glanced at us with a faint smile. "Don't worry about me," he said. "I have my own kingdom to take care of now. The Forgotten are content in the Between—or they will be, if things ever go back to normal—and I take full responsibility for what I've done." He gave his head a small shake, still holding my gaze. "I've never blamed you for having to exile me—I know that's how Faery works. And if we can save Evenfall, I can return to my kingdom knowing that I did something worthy."

I'd started to answer when Ash suddenly straightened behind me. Puzzled, I turned to gaze over the valley again as Keirran did the same, and a chill crept down my spine.

In the far distance, over the silver ocean of mist on the horizon, I could just make out a pair of towers. Tall and pointed, they rose out of the fog, gleaming under the light of the moon, where I was certain nothing had been a few seconds ago.

"Mistveil," Nyx breathed behind us. I hadn't heard her get up and leave the circle, but she walked past me to the edge of the cliff, staring out at the horizon. "The Nightmare King's castle. I remember now. We…" She paused, glancing back at the others, who had risen to their feet as well. "We were the king's protectors," she said. "We kept the castle safe from any that would threaten it and the fey who lived there. We weren't assassins. We were…defenders."

"Protectors of the castle," Other Nyx said, as if she too, had just remembered. "The Crescent Order…we were his knights, who kept watch on everything within the castle and the lands around it." A frown creased her forehead. "How could I have forgotten?"

"Perhaps the king did not want you to remember," Gilleas suggested. "Perhaps he did not want you to come looking for him. Because if you were to find him, you might realize the truth of this world."

Puck walked up beside our Nyx, gazing out at the distant keep. "Well, at least it's closer than I thought it would be," he said. "I thought we'd have to wander aimlessly for at least a day or two." He stared at the castle a moment longer, then wrinkled his nose. "I don't suppose it's going to cooperate and stay in the same spot until we get there, is it?"

Nyx gave a tiny smile. "As I recall, it did like to disappear the second you took your eyes off it," she said. "But the Order could always find their way to the castle. Maybe that still holds true."

"Let us hope so," Grimalkin said. "I do hate walking in circles."

The forest rose around us, thick and uninviting. It was impossible to see more than a few paces away, trees and bushes swallowed by opaque, drifting fog. Strangely, it wasn't as dark down here in the valley, a flat gray luminance shining through the mist, turning things surreal.

"Okay, we're here." Puck crossed his arms and looked at our Nyx. "So, where's this secret, hidden path into the castle that surely avoids all the Nightmares and super nasty beasties that are prowling through the forest?"

"I didn't say it was a path," Nyx replied. "I just said the Order could always find their way."

"Don't worry, Neverfey," Varyn chimed in, a faint smirk on his face. "The Order will keep you safe from the scary Nightmares."

"Me? Worried?" Puck scoffed. "That's laughable. You have Robin Goodfellow with you, not to mention the Iron Queen and the son of Mab. I know you guys have no idea who they are, but really, *we* should be saying something like that to *you*."

Gilleas walked forward, gazing around at the looming trees and fog. "I remember this," the Evenfaery murmured. "The last time I went looking for the king. I remember this forest. We are on the outer edges now, but farther in, there will be many Nightmares. I suggest we proceed with caution. And perhaps…" His deer skull turned in Puck's direction. "A bit of discretion."

"You are wasting your breath, I am afraid." Grimalkin sauntered past with his tail in the air. "Asking Goodfellow to be silent is like telling a dragon not to hoard gold, or a fish not to swim. It is simply not in his nature."

"Yeah, like a cat not disappearing whenever something scary pops in," Puck added.

Grimalkin didn't even turn around. "Do not be ridiculous, Goodfellow. That is simply common sense."

We ventured into the forest, which grew more tangled and eerie the farther we traveled. Tendrils of mist hung in the branches, reaching out to us like they were alive. Our footfalls made little eddies that swirled through the thick carpet at our feet before writhing away on the air. Sound was muffled, and sight was nearly nonexistent. The shapes in the fog played tricks with my mind; it was hard to tell if what I was seeing was the base of a trunk or the legs of some monstrous creature standing in the trees.

"Huh. You know, this place isn't so bad," Puck commented, after we had been walking for several minutes without running into anything that wanted to kill us. Thankfully, he kept his voice relatively low. "Misty, quiet, creepy. A lot of places in the Nevernever are like this. Oh hey, remember the forest where that coven of witches lived, ice-boy?"

Grimalkin sighed from where he appeared atop a fallen branch. "And my point stands. However, now that we are in the forest proper, I believe I know the way to the castle."

"Oh, of course you do, cat. And you were going to tell us… when?"

"Wandering about aimlessly was never the answer, Goodfellow," Grimalkin said, as if it was obvious. "Nor does the castle move around, as is the common thought. No, when you leave the forest, you leave your memories of how to reach the castle behind in the mist. That is why no one can remember how to get there once they depart the valley. The mist takes those memories and the forest holds them here, until the time when you return."

"Oh," Puck commented. "Well, that's pretty devious. Effective, I suppose. So, how do we reach the castle? Because, unlike some of you, I have no memories of this place."

Gilleas folded long fingers beneath his chin, thinking. "When I first came through," he mused, "I didn't use the front gates. They were guarded by Nightmares that would tear me apart as soon as they spotted me. But I remembered there were other ways into the castle."

"The passage," Other Nyx said suddenly. "I remember…a passageway underground. It led past the gates into the courtyard. The Order would use it when we wanted to get in and out of the castle unseen."

"In the ruins by the great tree," Nyx added. "But…wasn't that passage guarded by something?"

"It was," Varyn said. "But the Forest Sentry never bothered the Order. It knew us. And it's a better plan than trying to fight our way through the Nightmares at the gates."

"I think I might've hit my head or something," Puck said, "because I like that plan. That plan makes a lot of sense to me."

I looked at Gilleas and the three Evenfey. "Do you remember where this secret passage is?"

"I believe I do," our Nyx replied.

We continued through the forest. Gradually, the mist began to disperse, though it never went away completely. Stone ruins began appearing in the fog; towers that had fallen, crumbled stone archways, and half-erect walls soon littered the landscape. Trees had grown over many of the structures, moss and roots crawling over the stones, branches pushing out through roofs and windows. But even more eerie than the ruins and the fog were the dozens of children's toys lying scattered through the dirt. Dolls, wooden swords, jump ropes, toy trains, balls, and numerous stuffed creatures lay abandoned and forgotten by their owners.

"I remember these ruins," our Nyx said. Even her soft voice echoed in the absolute stillness of the forest. "Fey lived here, once, even before my time." She bent and picked up a cloth figure with yarn for hair and button eyes.

Puck let a yelp. "Nyx, what are you doing? Everyone knows you don't touch the creepy little dolls in the haunted forest. That's just begging them to come to life and start popping up everywhere."

"It's fine, Puck." Nyx gently placed the toy against a broken wall. "As long as you respect the forest, you'll be safe from the guardians within its boundaries. Or, that was the case when I lived at the castle. I'm not sure how much has changed."

"Right, so that means we shouldn't touch creepy dolls in a nightmare forest, just to be safe."

Ducking beneath an archway, we came to a small grove that the fog didn't seem to penetrate. An enormous tree stood in the center, twisted as if in agony, its trunk and branches bone white and barren of leaves. The ground beneath it was thick and mossy, a verdant carpet that stretched across the ground, covering ruins and tree trunks and several huge boulders scattered throughout the grove. Fat white toadstools grew everywhere, and the bones of several animals lay in bleached, broken piles in the moss.

Beneath the tree, being actively strangled in vines and the twisted, snakelike roots rising from the ground, an archway with a flight of stone steps led down into the unknown.

"Well, there's the entrance to the passageway," Gilleas said, gazing warily around the grove. "And it doesn't seem to be guarded."

Puck gave a mock gasp. "You mean we might actually get to do something easy?" he asked in fake disbelief. "Something that's not going to cause us intense bodily harm? Wow, this is a first. We might actually get to the castle without having to fight our way—ow!"

Nyx, standing quietly beside Puck, drew back an arm and smacked the back of his head. "If you finish that statement, I am going to stab you," she said calmly.

Ash's quiet laughter surprised us all. "Never let her go, Good-fellow," he chuckled. "For all our sakes."

"If the gate to the underground is clear," Gilleas said, coming forward, "we should proceed. There is no point standing around waiting for any number of forest guardians to arise." Looking around the deceptively peaceful grove, he shook his head. "Additionally, I wonder if some of our fights could have been avoided, had we simply been quieter."

"Do not waste your time wondering about that," said Grimalkin, appearing on a nearby log. "You will drive yourself to madness, knowing a thing *can* be accomplished but will simply never come to pass."

Puck blinked. "You can stop looking at me, Furball. We all know who you're talking about."

"And yet it never seems to change anything." Grimalkin sniffed and looked across the grove. "Well, shall we go, then?" He sighed. "The castle is not far now. Let us see how many fights we can avoid before we manage to find the Nightmare King."

24

THE HALL OF HEROES

The stone doors groaned horribly when we pushed against them, but they gradually swung back to reveal several wide, mossy steps down into the darkness. Stone pillars formed deteriorating archways every few feet, and the narrow recesses in the walls held aging skeletons, rags, and the occasional glint of ancient coins.

"Oh, that's great," Puck exclaimed as we came down the steps, pausing at the bottom. "A dusty crypt is totally where I wanted to be today." Several shiny beetles scuttled across the floor at the sound of his voice, and he winced. "Complete with bugs and spiders, my favorite."

Gilleas rubbed the top of his head and looked at Grimalkin. "I see what you mean," he said flatly.

Grimalkin sniffed. "It is wearying, to always be right."

"Okay, professors Gloom and Doom, you don't have to rub it in so hard." Puck crossed his arms, then looked at our Nyx. "What am I missing? What is this place?"

"These are the Catacombs of Heroes and Kings," Nyx explained, gazing down the stone passageways. "The tunnels run under the whole castle. The dead sleep here, but many are restless. Loud noises have been known to wake them up."

"Oh," Puck said in a much quieter voice, and frowned at Grimalkin. "You know, some of these facts could have been related a little earlier, if someone didn't feel the need to be an ass just to prove a point."

Grimalkin yawned. "It would have been proven regardless."

"Well." Gilleas gazed around the passageway and sighed. "I remember this passage," he murmured. "The memories are coming back now. I believe this is the route I took the first time I tried to find the king."

"Do you remember enough to get us to the throne room?" Ash wondered.

"Yes." Gilleas scanned the tunnel once more and nodded. "Yes, I remember the way. Follow me, but do know…" He raised a slender finger. "Not only are the dead restless, but the crypt keepers also prowl these halls. They do not take kindly to the living roaming the spaces of the dead."

"Of course they don't," Puck said. "Because nobody is ever okay with anything anymore. Think you're getting through that ancient temple unscathed? Nope—meet its lovely, fully armored temple guardian. Want to enjoy that peaceful grove? Nope—forest guardian wants to eat your face off. Gotta pass through some scary catacombs? Not if those crypt keepers make you dead like them." He snorted and crossed his arms. "You know, just once, I'd like to come across some keeper or guardian or ancient sentry that says, 'Welcome to my…whatever, it is so nice to see you. Please, look around and let me know if there's anything I can do to help.' I would pay a favor to have a crypt keeper tell me that this time."

I saw our Nyx and Keirran exchange a glance, and Nyx briefly rolled her eyes, making Keirran smile.

"Are you done, Goodfellow?" Ash said in a voice devoid of emotion.

"Yeah, I'm good. Let's go."

The crypt turned out to be much larger than I expected, with miles of tunnels, stone passageways, and sluiceways running beneath the earth. We passed countless skeletons resting in the stone recesses, and it was eerie how many of the skulls seemed to stare at us as we went by. As if we really had woken them up, and they had turned to give us irritated looks for disturbing them.

But even though the dead didn't seem to be rising from their graves, I didn't once think we were going to make it through without running into something.

We were walking atop a long sluiceway, passing beneath huge stone pipes that spilled water into the canal below, when I heard a noise. It sounded like...clicking. I looked around and saw what appeared to be a forty-foot centipede crawling along the opposite wall of the canal. After the initial heart attack, I looked closer and saw the upper half of the huge insect was that of a yellowed skeleton with four clawed arms, holding a scythe in one hand. It turned its skull to peer at me, a pair of enormous black mandibles curving from its bottom jaw, before it scuttled into one of the huge drainage pipes jutting from the wall and vanished into the dark.

"Gilleas," I whispered. "What was that?"

"That was a crypt keeper," Gilleas replied in a resigned voice. "They've seen us."

The clicking noise sounded again, directly below us. We all backed away from the ledge, drawing our weapons, as the creature rose into the air...and continued to rise, its segmented body swaying upward like a snake. Up close, its carapace was a shiny bloodred, the hundreds of jointed legs bright orange. Its yellow skull peered down at us, the scythe held casually in four bony hands, and it cocked its head, appearing more curious than aggressive. The curved pincers opened, and a sibilant voice emerged from the bony jaws.

"Meat and blood in the halls of the dead. Why are you here? What do you seek among bones and dust?"

For once, Puck was silent, which was admirable as he was faced with probably the scariest giant bug I had seen in my life.

Other Nyx stepped forward. "Crypt keeper," she said, bowing respectfully as the huge centipede-skeleton thing loomed over her. "We are seeking the entrance into the castle. We wish an audience with the king."

"I know you," the crypt keeper whispered. It bent down until those shiny pincers were barely a foot away from her face. "I have sensed your shadows before. You and your kin once flitted through the darkness, leaving no signs of your passing. But the bones sense the change in the air, the warmth left from a living body. Even you," it went on, turning to stare at Gilleas. "I know you, and the castle recognizes you as well. But..." It paused, rising up to tower over us again, hollow gaze now fastened on me. "It does not know this one. Because this one does not come from here. This one comes from the other place, the other side of Evenfall."

"The Nevernever," I said.

"The mortal world," the crypt keeper went on, surprising me. It angled its pincers at Ash and Puck. "This one's companions come from the mirror realm, yes. The Unseelie, the Summer faery, even the child of three worlds is more fey than mortal. But this one...this one was born in the human world and grew up believing it was human."

"How do you know all this?" I whispered.

"I am the Keeper of Heroes," the crypt keeper said. "I have been here since the first champion fell. Their bones are stored in these catacombs, a reminder to remember their deeds and sacrifice. The bones tell a story, but not all the bones buried here are from Evenfall. Some are from the Nevernever, fey who crossed into this land and made it their own. And though it has been a very long time since any mortal visited this world, several sets of human bones can be found here as well."

I felt Ash's frown beside me. "But faeries who die don't leave anything behind," he said, causing the crypt keeper to glance at him, mandibles working. "Our bodies don't wither and decay like humans do—we just cease to exist."

"In the Nevernever, that is true," the crypt keeper told him. "And here, it is much the same. But in Evenfall, the realm of fear and nightmare, true bravery is scarce, and sacrifice almost unheard of. If Evenfall recognizes a hero, their bones will appear in these halls when they finally perish. I keep their remains, and the memories of them, safe." It paused, looking around the catacombs like an artist studying a gallery of its own paintings. "Granted, there are not many who can be called true heroes," it went on. "I have been here a long, long time.

"So, I have seen many pass through these halls," the crypt keeper told us, sweeping its scythe down the tunnels. "I have witnessed the heroes whose bones finally come to rest here. I know humans, and I know Summer and Winter. I have seen mortals, Seelie, Unseelie, Evenfey and those who fit nowhere at all. And I recognize that faint, fragile aura of a hero. Many of you have it," it went on, gazing around at all of us. "That is the only reason we are standing here, speaking, the only reason your flesh bodies are not lying in pieces around me. The dead do not suffer the living well down here, but this is not the place to end your story. You will continue on, because that is what heroes do."

"Uh," Puck ventured, "hang on. This is your crypt, right? You wouldn't mind pointing us in the right direction, would you? You don't even have to say anything. Just…waggle a leg or something."

The ancient Evenfaery regarded Puck with empty, hollow

eyes. "I am not the guide of this quest," it told him. "That part of your story falls to others. In fact, I believe you have so many that they are getting in each other's way." I heard a quiet snort that I thought came from Nyx, though I couldn't be certain. "This portion of your quest is almost past," the crypt keeper went on. "The dead will not impede you, and the king awaits in his castle of dreams. But…" Its skull face turned and looked directly at Keirran, causing a fist of ice to grip my heart and squeeze. "I sense an epilogue is coming," it whispered. "A final chapter for some of you. And who am I to stand in the way of a hero's sacrifice?"

Keirran met its gaze, his expression both hopeful and resigned. "Is that what is needed for this story, then?" he asked softly. "Is it to be that type of ending?"

The crypt keeper backed away. "I will say no more." It raised a skeletal hand, as if to stop the hundreds of fears and questions rising to the surface. "The final chapter approaches, but it is yet to be written. It is unclear whether the heroes will triumph, or if everything will Fade away. I shall not influence what is to come."

And with that, the ancient crypt keeper turned and crawled up the wall of the catacombs, hundreds of legs moving together as its segmented body flowed up the bricks. Within moments, it reached the collapsed ceiling, slithered into one of the many dark holes in the roof, and disappeared.

I looked at Keirran. He stood there with his arms crossed, still wearing that thoughtful expression that made my heart seize. He didn't look troubled or anxious about anything the crypt keeper had told us. If anything, he looked almost eager.

"Keirran," I said. He glanced at me, and the flash of hope and longing I saw in his gaze was heart-wrenching. I could never express everything I was feeling right then, so I opted for a single word. "No."

The small smile he gave me did nothing to alleviate those

fears. "The ending hasn't been written yet," he said simply. "We can't know what's going to happen until we get there."

"But it is close," said Grimalkin's solemn voice. The cat leaped onto a stone block, outlined in a single ray of moonlight coming in from the ceiling. "And we cannot turn back now. We must keep moving forward." His golden eyes turned in my direction, somber and firm at the same time. "To whatever end awaits us, Iron Queen. No matter what we must do when we get there."

I didn't see much more of the catacombs after that. I knew they went on, as we followed our guides down one passageway and into another, flickering candles and forgotten lanterns lighting the way. We didn't run into any more crypt keepers, though I thought I felt eyes on me from time to time, watching us progress through the tunnels. Or maybe that was my own paranoia. I couldn't shake the feeling of dread that plagued me after meeting the crypt keeper and how he'd looked directly at Keirran when he spoke to us about sacrifice.

And Keirran…seemed all right with it. More than all right; entirely willing and ready to accept his fate, and that scared me most of all. After everything we had been through, all the wars and fighting, all the suffering and bloodshed, the anguish my whole family had through…after all that, I was not prepared to lose my only child. Even if he had grown up. Even if he was the King of the Forgotten and knew sacrifice and responsibility better than most. Even if, many years ago, a sixteen-year-old half-human girl had been willing to sacrifice herself to save a race called the Iron fey. I didn't want that for Keirran. Or Ash. Or Puck, Nyx, the Evenfey, anyone else. How much was enough? We had all given—and lost—so much already.

I didn't have to look at Ash to know he felt the same.

"We've arrived," Other Nyx said quietly.

I glanced up. We stood in a small stone chamber, a flight of steps leading down to the crypts below. I didn't even remember climbing the stairs. Before me, two enormous statues, their faces cowled and hidden, stood on either side of an ancient doorway.

I could feel something on the other side. A pulse. A heartbeat. An old, old power, waiting for us to approach.

This is it. The Nightmare King is somewhere beyond those doors. No turning back now.

I put a hand on the ancient doors, feeling cold stone under my palms, gave Ash a single nod, and pushed. The doors swung back with barely a groan, and we stepped into the castle of the Nightmare King.

PART

III

INTERLUDE

In her travels through the Nevernever, the girl met many creatures and crossed paths with many strange, frightening, and
beautiful fey. But one meeting stands out as the moment that
would change not only her life, but her entire future. Up until
that moment, the path she was on could eventually have led her
home, back to the human world. The steps sounded simple. Find
her brother. Return home. Resume a normal life.

But then, she met him. Danced with him. And stepped completely off the path that would lead her back to Normal. From
that moment on, her fate was sealed.

As it turns out, that was true for *him*, as well.

Another Elysium.
Another day wishing he were anywhere else.
Ash, third son of Mab and prince of the Unseelie Court, did
not like Elysium. He found the pomp boring, the company irritating, and the forced civility tiresome. But a prince of Winter couldn't exactly ignore the yearly gathering of the courts.

He couldn't "forget" to attend. That would embarrass Mab, Queen of the Winter Court, which would result in fates worse than anything you could imagine. Disappointing the Unseelie monarch was a risky proposition, angering her was foolish, but *embarrassing* her...that was a death sentence. So, there wasn't really another option. Ash would attend Elysium.

This year, he was more distracted than usual. He had just returned from an extremely interesting hunt where he had run into his nemesis, and the opportunity to try to kill Puck had been too good to pass up. He hadn't really expected to catch or kill Robin Goodfellow; he'd known the Summer prankster far too long, and Goodfellow always had a trick up his sleeve. Even after Ash had called in a Wild Hunt, which he normally never bothered with because of the favors involved, Puck had been too slippery and had managed to escape. He always did.

But the girl.

Ash clenched his jaw at the memory. The girl who had been with Puck had been human, there was no doubt about that. She'd lacked grace, and elegance, and the unnatural beauty of the fey. She was clearly mortal, or had lived in the mortal world most of her life.

Despite that, when he'd looked at her, for just a moment, he'd seen Ariella.

Anger filled him. How dare this mortal remind him of his lost love? And even worse, how dare she be friends with Puck, the one responsible for Ariella's death? He didn't know why Puck had brought this mortal into Faery in the first place, but it didn't matter. If she was friends with Robin Goodfellow, that meant she was Ash's enemy.

After Elysium, he decided. After Elysium, he would go looking for this girl, try to figure out why she was special. Certainly, she had the Sight. If she was hanging around Goodfellow *and* had come into Faery with him, there had to be a reason.

He would find this girl and discover her secrets. It was still uncertain if he would kill her or not.

Summers in Arcadia were unbearably warm, but Ash was used to them. He much preferred the icy chill of Tir Na Nog, but he had been to Arcadia countless times and had learned to use a tiny bit of glamour to keep the air around himself permanently cold. Following Mab and his brothers into the great Summer hall, he barely saw the crowds of Seelie fey around him. The crowds, the noise, the extravagance of the fey; it was all white noise to him. After a quick scan of the room determined there was no red-haired nemesis nearby, he grew disinterested in everything else, resigning himself to a long, boring ordeal.

And then...he saw her.

The girl from the hunt, who had been with Puck that day. Ariella's human shadow. She was *here*, at the Seelie Court.

Sitting at the same table as King Oberon and Queen Titania.

Shock rippled through him. The only ones allowed to sit with the kings and queens were the members of their own family. Ash had heard the rumors. There were whispers about King Oberon and his wandering, of his eye for talented mortals in the human realm. But that was expected of all fey. Queen Titania had been with several mortal lovers in her long life, as had Mab, and all the rulers of Faery. But this was different. It had recently been rumored that Oberon actually had a half-human daughter, hidden somewhere in the mortal world. Hidden, because if Queen Titania ever found her, she would make her life a living hell.

So that's *why you were with her, Puck. I understand now.*

Unease and a strange disappointment went through him. If this girl was indeed Oberon's long-lost daughter, *he* would not be the only one interested in her. His plans involving Goodfellow and the girl might have to wait, because he was certain Queen Mab would be intrigued, as well.

His suspicions were confirmed almost immediately.

"So, tell me of your daughter, Lord Oberon," Mab crooned after they had taken their seats. "I was not aware that she would be attending Elysium this year."

"Neither was I," the Erlking said. "Her arrival in the Nevernever was...somewhat unexpected." He sounded disinterested, almost bored, with the notion of his half-blood daughter. Knowing the Summer King, that could be either to protect the girl from interested enemies, or because he truly did not care about her. On Oberon's other side, Queen Titania gave him a look of blatant disgust, which the king pretended not to see. "But she is here," Oberon went on, "and she is under my protection, as a member of the Summer Court and the royal family."

Ash hid a smile. That was Oberon essentially telling Mab *and* Titania to leave his daughter alone or suffer the consequences. So, she really was a Summer princess, even as a half-human.

Interesting.

A snicker came from the seat to his right, and Rowan shot him a sly glance. "Well, well. So, the rumors are true," he murmured. "Oberon's half-human whelp has finally crossed over into Faery." He turned his head, giving the girl at the end of the table an appraising leer. "She's not bad-looking, for a mortal. I can think of several games to play with a half-blood Summer princess. What about you, little brother?"

Ash shrugged, keeping his voice flat and disinterested as he looked away. "It's just a human," he muttered. "I've seen them before."

Because if he showed any interest at all, that would make Rowan all the more intrigued. And strangely, he didn't want his sadistic brother anywhere near the Summer princess.

"Hmph. Well, aren't you a bore." Obviously disappointed in him, Rowan turned to the Winter Queen. "My queen," he began, speaking to Mab but raising his voice for the other rulers to hear, "isn't there a tradition where a son and a daughter of opposite courts dance with each other, to show goodwill during Elysium?"

Mab's eyes gleamed, a predatory smile crossing her face. "That is true," she purred, turning to Oberon, who looked extremely annoyed, if only for a moment. "We haven't had a dance like that in many decades. I believe a son of Winter should offer a dance to your newly discovered daughter, to welcome her to Faery. What say you, Erlking?"

Ash saw Rowan's evil smile, saw Oberon's hesitation before he nodded, and clenched his fists beneath the table. He didn't know why he spoke up then; certainly drawing attention to himself at Elysium was something he'd avoided in the past. But the thought of Rowan that close to the Summer princess caused his stomach to turn violently. And the words came out of his mouth before he could stop them.

"Isn't it also tradition," he said, "that it is the *youngest* sons and daughters that dance with each other as a show of goodwill between the courts?"

Rowan's smile faded, but Mab turned to him, looking surprised but also pleased. "It is," she said, nodding. "Although, this is surprising, prince. Are *you* offering to dance with the girl, then?"

He could feel Rowan's glare, promising retribution, but he shrugged and looked away. "If that is what is required of me."

He hoped none of them could hear his heart pounding beneath his shirt.

"So, this is Oberon's famous half-blood."

She was afraid of him.

He could sense her fear when she whirled in her seat at the high table, her large blue eyes widening with alarm. It was understandable. He had just chased her and Puck through the wyldwood and had even shot a couple arrows in their direction. True, they had been aimed at Puck, but that probably didn't matter to her. She knew him only as an enemy, as someone who should be feared.

He stood calmly beside her chair and resisted the urge to clench his fists. Up close, she looked even more like Ariella, a younger, more naive version of the Winter faery he had lost. A sudden stab of disgusted fury lanced through him. How dare he compare this human girl to Ariella? She was nothing like her.

"And to think," he went on, "I lost you that day in the forest and didn't even know what I was chasing."

She shrank back from him a little, but her eyes flashed. So, she did have some fight in her, after all. "I warn you," she said, trying not to show her fear, "that if you try anything, my father will remove your head and stick it to a plaque on his wall."

He almost smiled. Not many would openly threaten him like that, even if she was threatening him with her father. "There are worse things," he said, and watched her eyes widen in horror. Oh, she was interesting. "Don't worry, princess," he said, giving her a faint smile. "I won't break the rules of Elysium. I have no intention of facing Mab's wrath should I embarrass her. That's not why I'm here."

She eyed him warily. "Then what do you want?"

What did he want? He suddenly wanted to know more about her. He wanted to know why she was in the Nevernever. Why now, when she had lived her entire mortal life in the human world?

Catching himself, he squashed that curiosity, shoving it back where it came from. It didn't matter why she was here, he told himself. She was Oberon's daughter, a princess of the Summer Court, and his enemy. He just needed to get through this dance, and then he could return to pondering if he should kill her or not.

Stepping back, he offered a perfectly polite bow. "A dance."

"What?" She gave him a look of disbelief. "You tried to kill me!"

"Technically, I was trying to kill Puck," he said. "You just happened to be there. But yes," he admitted. "If I'd had the shot, I would have taken it."

"Then why the hell would you think I'd dance with you?"

In that moment, she seemed very human, masking fear with anger. She was just a girl, he reminded himself. A half-human girl, who knew nothing about the ways of Faery. "That was then," he said flatly. "This is now. And it's tradition in Elysium that a son and daughter of opposite territories dance with each other, to demonstrate the goodwill between the courts."

"Well, I just got here," she argued, and crossed her arms. "I don't know anything about faery traditions. So, you can forget it." She glared stubbornly. "I am not going anywhere with you."

He raised an eyebrow, not certain whether he was amused or annoyed. "Would you insult my monarch, Queen Mab, by refusing?" he asked softly. "She would take it very personally, and blame Oberon for the offense. And Mab can hold a grudge for a very, very long time."

That did it. She protested again, muttering about choice, but her hesitation faded, replaced by fear. So she did understand enough to know what angering the fey would mean, especially someone as volatile and powerful as Mab.

He held out his hand, assuring her she did, truly, have a choice, and he would not force her and would, in fact, be a perfect gentleman, at least until the night was done. And after a pause, she rose from her seat and placed her fingers in his.

That contact sent a tingle racing all the way up his arm, so much that he almost pulled his hand back. Thankfully, the girl seemed too nervous about dancing in front of a crowd of fey to notice, and he schooled his expression into a blank mask as they made their way toward the open space that would serve as the dance floor. She trembled, mumbling something that sounded like a curse and how she couldn't dance, and he tightened his grip on her hand.

"You'll be fine," he said, leading her to the center of the dance floor and deliberately not looking at her. As they bowed and curtsied to the rulers of Faery and became the focus of the courts, he could feel her shaking. He turned to her, saw those blue eyes gazing up at him, frightened but strangely trusting, and that strange shiver went through him once more. "Just follow my lead."

She *was* a terrible dancer at first. She tripped over her own feet and nearly stepped on his toes as they circled the floor, which both amused and bewildered him. How could a princess of the Summer Court, even one who was half-human, be so bad at something that came naturally to every faery? He hoped it was just the fact that she was so nervous that was causing her awkwardness; even though she was with him, this was painful.

"So." The girl paused, and nearly tripped over her own feet again. He kept a firm grip to keep her upright. "You're Queen Mab's son, right?"

"I think we've established that, yes."

"Does she like to...collect things?" He gave her a puzzled look, and she hurried on. "Humans, I mean? Does she have a lot of humans in her court?"

"A few." Apparently, talking was helping her forget her fear. He twirled her, and this time she went with it, returning to his arms as if she did it every day. "Mab usually gets bored with mortals after a few years," he explained as she gazed up at him. "She either releases them or turns them into something more interesting, depending on her mood." The girl's face went pale, and he frowned. "Why?"

"Does she have a little boy in her court?" the girl asked. "Four years old, curly brown hair, blue eyes? Quiet most of the time?"

Ah. Suddenly everything made sense. *This* was why she was here, in Faery; she was looking for someone. He knew humans could get very attached to each other, and some of the strongest bonds he had seen came from those in the same family. He didn't understand it. Neither of his siblings would risk their own life to save him unless there was a huge favor involved, or unless he would be indebted to them forever. But this girl had come into the Nevernever, completely unprepared, to look for this child.

Unfortunately, he didn't have any information for her. "I don't know," he replied. "I haven't been to court lately." Her face fell with disappointment, bringing on a pang of guilt, which made him annoyed with himself. "Even if I had," he went on, "I cannot keep track of all the mortals the queen acquires and releases over the years."

"Oh," the girl murmured, dropping her gaze. Again, that strange flicker of disappointment that he wasn't able to help coursed through him. He spun her again, and she twirled away as gracefully as any fey dancer. "But if you're not in court," she went on, gazing up at him as she returned, "where are you, then?"

Her eyes met his, and for just a moment, his heart roared in his ears. "The wyldwood," he answered with what he hoped was a chilling smile. "Hunting. I rarely let my prey escape, so be grateful that Puck is such a coward." She whirled away from him, pale hair floating around her, and he pulled her close once more, his mouth against her ear. "Although I am happy I didn't kill you then," he whispered, feeling her shiver against him. "I told you a daughter of Oberon could dance."

There was a moment of surprise, of astonishment, and then she settled confidently into his arms as they swirled around the stage. The melody rose around them, powerful and all-consuming, and for a few minutes the rest of the world disappeared, until it was only them, spinning around each other.

As the music soared and reached its crescendo, Ash pulled the girl into a final spin. And suddenly, her face was inches from his, her blue eyes gazing up at him. He could feel her heart pounding in her chest, echoing the thud of his own. It would be easy to kiss her, he realized...just before a scream shattered the night and brought the dance to an end.

★ ★ ★

If he ever told that story to anyone else, most would assume that was the moment when he started to fall for the half-blood daughter of the Summer King. They would assume wrong. He'd been intrigued by her, yes. And she had reminded him of a faery he'd loved, long ago. But truthfully, he didn't know when he began to fall in love again. It might have been at Elysium. It might have been after a conversation in an old manor house, when he had been wounded and the Summer princess had surprised him yet again with her willingness to care for someone who was supposed to be her enemy. Or it might have been her complete dedication to her lost sibling, her determination to do whatever it took to save him, that earned his admiration.

He didn't know when it had happened. Only that, one day, he'd looked at her and realized he was willing to do anything for this girl. Including following her into a realm that would kill him. Including turning his back on his court, enduring banishment to the mortal world, and finally, going to the End of the World to earn the impossible. All for her.

He didn't know when he had fallen in love. Just that he had, and despite everything he had been through, everything he had lost, learned, changed, and given up, he didn't regret a thing.

They will tell you that the fey in the Nevernever don't fall in love. That, of course, is not true. The fey actually fall in love all the time, sometimes to the point of obsession. The thing is, their attention is usually fleeting, the type of instant love that fades quickly as new distractions take its place. The love that endures, that kind that takes time and hard work, and putting another's needs above your own…*that* type of love is alien to most fey. That is why many will warn you not to fall in love with a Good Neighbor. And that *is* sound advice, for the most part.

But there are those in the Nevernever who are capable of real love. And if you do end up giving your heart to one of them, remember that love is one of the most powerful forces in the world. It can heal the coldest, most wounded of hearts, forgive the gravest of offenses, and is the reason to fight against impossible odds. Love can even change the minds and hearts of those who seem incapable of it. It can inspire them in the most subtle of ways, even if they don't realize what's happening themselves.

So, if you do find yourself imperiled in the Nevernever, do not forget those who love you, and those whom you love. It might be your salvation in the end.

25

CASTLE OF DREAMS AND NIGHTMARES

Silence.

I blinked, gazing around in amazement. The doors had opened into an enormous, overgrown courtyard surrounded by walls and soaring towers. I looked up, craning my neck back, to gaze at the dozens of turrets and spires that seemed to touch the heavens. Unlike the broken, skeletal remains of Howling Keep, the castle of the Nightmare King looked both majestic and foreboding, silhouetted against the hazy starlight. Overhead, the sky blazed with stars, and the gigantic red moon looked like it was ready to collide with the earth. It was strangely beautiful and terrible all at once.

Shivering, I looked around the courtyard itself. The ground had once been cobble and flagstone, but enormous roots, vines, and whole trees had pushed their way up through the stones, splitting rock and shoving it aside. Moss grew on walls and the handful of hooded statues standing along the paths, holding darkened lanterns in their hands.

The quiet throbbed in my ears. I had been expecting Nightmares, horrors, and monstrosities to come leaping out at us. Gilleas had said the castle had been swarming with them the last time he was here. Where were they now? Inside the halls of the castle? Or were Nightmares lurking somewhere in the shadows around us, lying in ambush? Somehow, I didn't think so. This courtyard, though not exactly peaceful, did have that quiet, solemn air of a place long forgotten.

I turned to the others. "Looks like we made it," I said, keeping my voice low. In the utter stillness of the courtyard, anything louder than a murmur would have felt wrong. The stillness reminded me of a cemetery or a cathedral, demanding reverence and respect.

Our Nyx took a step forward, but she wasn't looking at us, instead gazing at the surrounding courtyard. There was a longing in her golden eyes that made my heart hurt.

Puck had noticed, too. "Nyx?" he said quietly. "You okay?"

"It looks...exactly the same," she whispered. "The castle. The courtyard. I remember all of this. Like I never left. It feels...it feels like..."

"Home," said a quiet voice. Varyn's, surprising us all. "This was home," he said simply, glancing at Other Nyx, who nodded.

"Come." Gilleas stepped forward, and though no expression showed on his deer skull face, his voice was sympathetic. "We waste time standing here. Navigating the castle will be confusing, but with the four of us, we should be able to find our way to the throne room."

"Sorry." This was from Keirran, which surprised me as well. He stood a few paces away, brow furrowed, a puzzled look on his face as he stared at something in the courtyard. "That statue," he said as we glanced at him. "Was it always pointing that way, or am I seeing things?"

"Knock it off, princeling," Puck said. "The place is spooky enough. I don't need nightmares of creepy statues coming to... Oh crap, it is pointing now."

I turned to look at said statue, which was indeed standing there with a pale arm outstretched, one slender digit pointing directly toward the castle entrance. I hadn't seen it move, and looking at the rest of the statues in the courtyard, I noticed that all their lanterns were now lit and glowing softly against the darkness.

"Well." Puck looked at the statues, then back to the rest of us and shrugged. "I guess someone knows we've arrived."

The castle of the Nightmare King was...*surreal* was the best word I could think of. Not terrifying or nightmarish, just a quiet kind of eerie that followed you everywhere and could not be shaken. We left the courtyard and entered a vast labyrinth of dimly lit rooms, hallways, and passages. It was a huge, regal-looking castle, with arched doorways, vaulted ceilings, enormous pillars, and statues at every corner. There was nothing particularly frightening, nothing overtly hostile or menacing. The castle just felt...strange. Paintings stared at us as we went by. Hallways seemed abnormally long. Every so often, from the corner of my vision, I thought I saw one of the statues move. Nothing blatant. But it felt like being in that dream where you knew you had to be somewhere, but you couldn't find your way. You just kept wandering endlessly, passing the same thing over and over again.

"This is strange," Gilleas said at last.

"Yeah, no kidding," Puck chimed in. "I swear, if I see one more statue turn its head when it thinks I'm not looking, I'm going to find a sledgehammer."

"No," Gilleas said, sounding annoyed. "I mean it is strange that the castle is this empty. Not that I want to run into any of them, but where are the Nightmares hiding? There were dozens last time I was here. I had to use every scrap of knowledge I had about the layout of the castle, every hidden door and secret passage, to avoid them."

"Uh, but that's a good thing, though, right?" Puck asked. "Not having to fight our way through swarms of giant beasties to get to the king seems like a win to me. No complaints here."

"Perhaps. But why are they not here? It seems unlikely that something would frighten off Elder Nightmares. And if something *has* scared them away, that is even more disturbing. If there is something in the castle that has caused the Nightmares to flee…"

"That is something we do not want to run into," I finished.

"Exactly," Gilleas agreed. "So, that begs the question—where are the Nightmares, and what caused them to disappear? If the king still dreams, this is where all the Nightmares originate. There should be at least a few roaming about."

"Maybe…" Other Nyx began, and paused, her face going pale as if she just realized something.

Varyn cocked his head in her direction. "What?"

She swallowed. "Maybe…the king isn't dreaming them anymore," she finished softly.

My steps faltered, and a somber air descended over the entire group. There was nothing to say to that, to voice what that could mean, and we continued in silence.

The castle went on, one chamber or hallway flowing into another. We passed room after empty room, seeing no signs of life anywhere. No fey, no Nightmares, nothing. And the silence continued to pulse in my ears.

"It wasn't always like this," our Nyx said, pausing in an arched doorway that opened to an elegant dining hall. A long table stretched the length of the room, with hooded statues in the corners and a magnificent gold chandelier hovering overhead. The table looked pristine, plates and goblets set out for a feast, but the chairs were empty, the surface spotless. "I remember when the castle was alive," Nyx went on. "I remember grand feasts, hunts, and masquerades with a thousand different faces.

We watched over them all, always in the wings or in the shadows. Protecting them."

My vision flickered. For a moment, I saw the dining room, but everything had aged a hundred years. The chairs were overturned and broken, the chandelier lay shattered on the surface of the table, and an enormous crack had split the wall behind it. Dust motes floated on the air, and everything had darkened with rot and time.

I blinked, and the room was normal again. The dining table sat untouched, the chandelier hanging motionless above it. No cracks marred the wall, and the chairs stood silently around the table. The scene was as it was before. Except...all the statue heads had turned...and were now staring at me.

"Did anyone else see that?" Keirran muttered into the silence.

Gilleas let out a long breath. "I believe," he said slowly, gazing at the stone figures with their hollow eyes on us, "that the king knows we are here."

"Yes," Grimalkin agreed. "The only question remaining is, which king is it?"

"What do you mean, cat?" Varyn asked. "There is only one Nightmare King."

"Is there?" Grimalkin gave the Evenfaery an unreadable look. "Or are there two versions of him that have persisted throughout this journey? The Nightmare King who grieves for his world and his lost people, who has kept the memory of Evenfall alive through the sheer force of his will? Or the king who is lost to madness, who wishes revenge against the Nevernever and the fey who sealed him away from the rest of the world? They cannot exist at the same time, within the same entity. And yet, we have seen evidence of both, in Evenfall, and the Nevernever. So which persona is the real Nightmare King?"

"You're making my head hurt again, cat," Puck said, frowning. "Besides, does any of this matter? Who cares which king we get?"

"It matters," Grimalkin said, briefly lacing his ears back, "because it will determine the outcome of this entire journey. I admit, I have seen no evidence of the madness of the king while we have been in Evenfall—on the contrary, everything I have witnessed suggests that he grieves for his world and has tried to keep the memory of his people alive the only way he can. However, we cannot forget what we saw beneath InSite. That king threatened to destroy us and everything he came across once he was awake. Which king we get, as you say, is the very reason we do not have a firm plan. The reason we have been floundering from the beginning."

"We have been floundering," Keirran said, sounding almost angry, "because there has never been a good choice. Because it's not a matter of killing a tyrant to free a world, or fighting a war with a clear enemy. Evenfall—this realm and everyone in it—relies on the Nightmare King. If we kill him, the world Fades. If he wakes up, the world disappears. If he remains asleep for eternity, what then? The Evenfey are stuck here, in this living nightmare with no escape." He gave a frustrated sigh and raked a hand through his hair. "There are no happy endings here," he whispered. "No good choices."

"And yet, a choice must be made," Grimalkin returned firmly. "The status quo cannot remain." His tail lashed his flanks, and his eyes narrowed. "This world is dying. Even the Nightmare King cannot sustain it forever. That is the harsh truth, Forgotten King. Even if all decisions are unfavorable, a decision must be reached, or this entire journey will be for nothing. A true leader understands that sometimes, sacrifice is called for. The difficult part is coming to terms with what must be given up."

"Forgotten King." Other Nyx stepped forward. "Iron Queen. Everyone." She paused, glancing briefly at Varyn, who gave a tiny nod. "Varyn and I have been talking," she went on. "About the king, about Evenfall, and about everything that has happened since you arrived. We are eternally grateful that you came, that you are willing to risk so much to save Evenfall. No matter what happens, we will remember that."

Keirran's brow furrowed as he realized where this was going. "Nyx..."

"But what kind of life is this for our people?" Varyn added, sounding more resigned than I'd ever heard from him. "You said it yourself," he went on, looking at Keirran. "There are no good choices here. I thought we might save this world, but even if the king remains asleep, this is the only life we can look forward to. The only life anyone can look forward to. My brothers...all they will ever know is pain and fear and constant struggle. Fighting for an existence that will never change. Maybe it *would* be better if it all disappeared."

"We're not real," Other Nyx said, as Keirran stiffened. "Evenfall isn't real. This is just a dream, and who are we to ask the king to sleep forever? All dreams end eventually, and..." She looked back at Varyn, who gave a solemn nod. "We've accepted it."

"You shouldn't have to." Keirran shook his head, his blue eyes suddenly anguished. "It's happening again," he whispered. "Everything I tried to accomplish with the Lady, everything we touched...we destroyed the things we were trying to save. I couldn't save the Exiles or the Forgotten...or Annwyl..." He closed his eyes. "And now there is an entire world that is Fading away in front of me. Am I supposed to just watch it disappear forever?"

Gilleas, who had been standing quietly to the side, raised his head. "It is very difficult to save something that is not there, Forgotten King," he said. "Even if you knew the Lady, you were not part of the circle that sealed us away. I have watched you all fight for us, bleed for us, and promise what you could. That is more than we could have asked for, especially for a realm that is already gone. I bear you no ill thoughts. Conversely, you have saved me from a lifetime of attempting the impossible. The time I have spent traveling with this odd group has been more mem-

orable than all the years I was consumed in the library. It was…
freeing, to finally know the truth." He lifted one thin hand in
a resigned gesture. "But with the truth comes a certain realization. As Nyx said, all dreams must end eventually. That is not
to imply that I do not wish to live, to exist. But I know that our
world is Fading, and what is left is not a place I want to spend
eternity in. Perhaps it is time to let it go."

"Whatever your decision," Other Nyx continued, "whether
it's to wake the king, put him back to sleep, or kill him, you
have our support. We will back you up. So don't hesitate on
our account."

Dammit. I blinked the stinging sensation from my eyes and
took a breath to clear my voice. "We're not giving up," I said,
to the Evenfey, to Keirran, to everyone. "I know decisions have
to be made, and we will make them as they come. But we have
come all this way, fought monsters and Nightmares and everything this world could throw at us. And the Evenfey we have
met on this journey are no different from any of the fey back
home. Evenfall might be a dream, but the king remembers everyone who lived here. His memories are so real, he created his
entire world just to keep them alive. I am not prepared to let it
go. Or watch it Fade."

I caught Keirran's gaze as I finished, seeing the relief in his
eyes, as well as a grim determination. Ash stepped up beside
me, placing a brief, comforting hand on my arm as he faced
the group. "Whatever we decide," he said in a low, calm voice,
"the original plan hasn't changed. I think our first objective is
to find that door and see what lies beyond."

My vision flickered again, showing a castle ravaged by time.
Walls cracked, pillars broken and shattered, a ceiling crumbled
away. Just a split-second glimpse, before everything returned to
normal.

Gilleas straightened up and gazed around the chamber. "The
castle is as big as I remember," he mused. "But I believe we are

close to the throne room. And judging by the faces of the statues I have seen, something is expecting us."

"Yup," Puck agreed. "Well then, who's ready to go see the king?"

A pair of arched doors stood atop a flight of cascading stone steps, guarded by a pair of enormous statues. These two were different from the many robed, hooded figures we had seen throughout the castle, the ones with the disturbing habit of turning to stare when we weren't looking. They were heavily armored, with shields and massive claymores jammed into the pedestals at their feet. Their heads wore antlered helmets, but through the raised helms, the jaws, teeth, and lolling tongues of wolves protruded through the gap.

"The throne room is up those stairs," our Nyx said, gazing solemnly at the two statues flanking the entrance. "Even if you had never been to the castle before, you could never miss the twins."

"Don't tell me they come alive, too," Puck muttered, gazing up at the two massive stone creatures. "They're not going to take a swipe at me as soon as my foot hits the stairs, are they?"

Almost before he had finished speaking, reality flickered. The stairs crumbled. The walls gaped with huge cracks. One of the statues vanished entirely, and when I looked at the other, the armored warrior was gone, replaced by the stark gaze of a snarling wolf, crouched on the plinth as if it were about to lunge. More than a heartbeat passed; unlike the first few times it had happened, this version of the castle did not flicker in and out, but stayed for several heartbeats before there was a hiccup in the world, and things returned to normal.

Or, mostly normal. One of the pedestals remained empty; the other held the statue of the armored wolf, but its head was missing. Or rather, it was lying at the base of the pedestal, muzzle curled back, eyes wide and feral.

"And things just keep getting weirder," Puck remarked.

"And worse," I added. "That lasted much longer than the previous one."

"Something feels wrong." Other Nyx gazed at the remaining statue and shivered. "It's as if there are two realities fighting for dominance. The one we know and...this darker one."

We started up the staircase to the arched doors at the top. As I was walking, however, the stones under my feet felt...unstable. As if they were about to collapse beneath me. The closer we got to the doors, the shorter my breath became. My stomach twisted with nerves. I could feel something beyond those doors. Something I couldn't describe. Ancient, powerful, terrible, it was all these things, and it was larger than any of them. And I suddenly realized... I was terrified.

"Meghan?"

I blinked. I had stopped moving and was standing at the top of the steps facing the arched doors.

"I..." I clenched my fists. I was the Iron Queen; I could not be afraid. I had to be strong, for everyone. And yet I could not seem to make my feet move. My throat scratched like sandpaper, my hands were shaking, and my heart was beating too fast. A cold sweat spread across the back of my neck, and for just a second, I considered turning around and walking back the way I'd come.

Then Ash stepped in front of me, bending close. His hands gently squeezed my shoulders as he leaned in. "I'm afraid, too," he said softly. And for some reason, hearing him admit that made my eyes fill with tears of relief. "You're not alone in this. Whatever is waiting for us behind that door, I've never felt anything like it. But we are here. And we're together. I can face even a sleeping god if you and the others are with me."

I met the silver eyes of my husband and took a deep breath, banishing the terror clinging to my mind. I wasn't alone, and we had come so far. There was just one more barrier to cross before we met the one we had come all this way to see. The Nightmare King was close. This journey was almost over.

I pressed a palm to Ash's jaw, then stepped forward, joining the others at the threshold. None of them looked eager to open the doors, either. And Grimalkin, I noticed, was gone.

Puck let out a shaky breath as we stepped up. "Man," he muttered, rubbing his arms. "Those are some serious nasty vibes coming out of there. Anyone else getting goose bumps, or is it just me?"

"This...this cannot be the Nightmare King," Other Nyx whispered. Her voice shook, and she was paler than before. Whatever this terrible sense of foreboding was, the Evenfey felt it, too. "He was the ruler of Evenfall, the bringer of nightmares—it was his very nature to be frightening. Even the Evenfey feared him, but we also loved and respected our king. This..." She shook her head. "This isn't right. I remember my life at the castle. I have never felt this amount of rage coming from the throne room."

Gilleas let out a weary sigh. "I am afraid our king might have changed after all," he whispered. He stared at the looming doorway, his entire posture reluctant to take another step. "I did not encounter him in the throne room when I came here before. But if he has indeed become the mad king the Nevernever fears, nothing in either world will save us."

"We won't know until we open that door," our Nyx said. "And we certainly can't turn back now."

Puck drew in a deep breath and took Nyx's hand. "Well, whatever comes of this," he began, "and whatever we find on the other side, this has been a hell of a journey. Evenfall wasn't what I expected, but I'm glad we came. And I can say with absolute certainty that I won't forget any of it. Or any of you. So..." He glanced at Nyx, then at the doors, a defiant smirk creeping over his face. "I guess all that's left to do is throw those doors open and announce our presence to the king. Shall we do the honors, ice-boy?"

Ash nodded. Together, he and Puck stepped forward, put a hand on either of the doors, and shoved them open.

Crimson light flooded through the doorway. The room beyond was saturated in an eerie red glow, so much so that it was hard to see through the haze. Carefully, we stepped through the doors, and found ourselves in a strangely wall-less room. Or at least, I couldn't see any walls through the darkness and shadows cast by the gigantic tree in the center. The trunk was bent and gnarled with thousands upon thousands of bodies sunk into the wood, eyes closed and faces twisted with fear. As if countless souls had been trapped and petrified within the tree and were sharing one continuous nightmare. No breeze or breath of wind stirred the space we found ourselves in, but the tree's bloodred leaves fell like snowflakes, scraps of crimson drifting around us and carpeting the ground. Through the branches, which were shaped like arms and fingers grasping at each other, the night sky and full red moon peered down at us. An ominous bloodred light shone through the cracks in the trunk, pulsing like a heartbeat.

"Um." Puck's voice was soft, barely a whisper in the stillness. "Are we in the right place?" he asked Nyx. "Or did we somehow leave the castle? This doesn't look like a throne room, unless that freaky tree in the center ate it. Is this really where the Nightmare King holds court?"

"We are in the right place." It was not Nyx who answered, but Gilleas, his voice a breathless rasp as he stepped forward. "This is the throne room, and the Nightmare Tree marks the very heart of Evenfall." He peered up at the looming trunk in reverence and awe. "According to legend," he continued in a whisper, "the Nightmare Tree was the first thing to exist in Evenfall, the first thing to bloom and thrive from the fears and terrors of mortals. The king himself built his castle around the tree to protect it, and it has stood in the same place for countless millennia. This is the king's throne room, the seat of his power."

I followed the massive trunk down, past branches and faces twisted in agony, to the roots of the tree itself, and the blood in my veins turned to ice.

At the base of the tree sat a throne. Tall, elegant, made of polished obsidian, it sucked in the light and reflected the crimson glow of the tree behind it.

A body sat atop the throne. A man, tall, lean, and cloaked in black, his chin resting on his chest as he slept. The robe he wore was so dark, it was impossible to tell where it ended and the shadows began. His hair was black, his face and long, spindly hands stark white, giving him the appearance of an old photograph, something not entirely real.

A tingle of fear skittered up my back, along with a very real sense of shock. Was *this* the Nightmare King? After everything we had faced, monsters, Elder Nightmares, scenes straight out of horror movies, I was not expecting the ruler of Evenfall, the Nightmare King himself, to look like a normal, handsome, *young* man.

Even though that might've been shortsighted. Even though the rulers of the Nevernever, from Mab to Oberon to Titania, were all beautiful, ageless, and immortal, because that was how Faery worked. The Nightmare King, for all his power and ability to cause fear, was still an ageless eternal.

The world flickered.

The tree vanished. The throne disappeared. We stood in a black void, an abyss with no ground, no stars, no sky, nothing but darkness. Terror flooded my soul so completely, I couldn't breathe. What sat where the throne used to be defied description. A roiling, pulsing mass of tentacles, claws, spines, teeth, and eyes. It was oily and scaly, covered in blood and hair, chiton, bones, and exposed muscle. It was every Nightmare monstrosity somehow rolled into one horrific abomination, and just looking at it made my eyes burn.

I flinched, turning away, and when I looked back, the chamber was normal. The tree and the throne were still there, with the sleeping form of the Nightmare King sitting motionless in the obsidian seat. But my heart still pounded, cold sweat now creeping down my spine.

"The king." I didn't know who whispered the words, Nyx or Other Nyx, but they sounded as horrified as I felt. "This... this isn't right. That is not the Nightmare King."

"Are you sure?" Even Ash didn't sound as unfazed as he normally did. "If the Nightmare King is the essence of fear and terror, this certainly fits."

"She's right," said Other Nyx. "I don't know what that *thing* was, but I clearly remember who I served for countless ages. Yes, the Nightmare King can be every fear and terror mankind has dreamed throughout time. But he ruled fairly, and he loved Evenfall and all those who existed in it. He was never pure, unfiltered chaos. This...this is madness in physical form. This is not the king."

"Well, it's sitting on a throne," Puck whispered. "And it sure acts like it belongs there. If this isn't our Nightmare King, then who is playing imposter?"

"Not an imposter." Grimalkin appeared on a coil of root, eyes glowing in the eerie red luminance around us. "I believe I have the answer, though it is not one you are going to like. The person currently sitting the throne...*is* the Nightmare King, and is not the Nightmare King."

"Uh." Puck gave a very deliberate blink. "Okay, I'm pretty sure I'm speaking for all of us when I say this—*what*?"

"Oh," Gilleas breathed, as if he too, had come to a realization that had completely eluded me. "Oh, ancient cursed gods. I believe you are correct. We are still in the Dream." His hand rose, thin black fingers covering one eye socket. "Oh, gods, we might not survive this."

"What are you talking about, Grim?" I demanded.

"This is still the king's dream," Grimalkin said. "We have not found a way to the king himself. The dreamer cannot physically exist within their own dream. They may see themselves within the dream, but that ends as soon as they wake. This place, however…" He glanced up at the tree looming overhead. "This is the place where the Nightmares are born. Where they are dreamed into the world. The fact that there are no more Nightmares in the castle is indicative that the king is simply not dreaming them any longer. Because his Dream is fading. You can see it happening around you. He is losing his hold on this reality, and his Dream flickers with every breath. How much longer it will remain is uncertain, but this world is starting to fray apart. I do not believe we have much time left."

My stomach tightened, and I saw Keirran clench a fist. Strangely, though Varyn's gaze hardened, and he glanced protectively at Other Nyx, the two Evenfaeries were frighteningly accepting of their world falling apart in front of them.

"But that still doesn't tell us who is sitting on the throne," Other Nyx said. "And why Grimalkin said it is and is not the Nightmare King. That doesn't make sense."

"It does," Gilleas murmured, still sounding pale and shaken. "The cat already told you as much. This is the place where Nightmares are born, where they are dreamed into the world. It is possible to exist in your own dream—not physically of course, but how many nightmares consist of running away from something, or being lost, or falling from great heights? We have already met one, possibly two, named Elder Nightmares. And what is currently sitting the throne now…is the most powerful Nightmare of all. The king's worst fear—becoming what the Nevernever thought him to be. Driven mad by anger and vengeance, wishing destruction upon the world should he wake."

A chunk of ice settled in my stomach, spreading a chill through my insides. The worst nightmare of the Nightmare King. It would sound comedic if it wasn't completely terrifying. A named Elder Nightmare who thought he was the immortal ruler of the Evenfey.

"So, it *is* the Nightmare King," Keirran said. "Or a version of him, anyway. How powerful will he be, compared to the real one?"

"I do not know," Gilleas replied. "But he will be powerful. Extraordinarily so. He is a Nightmare, but he is also the Nightmare King. He could be just as immortal and unstoppable as the real king himself."

"Enough to actually believe he *is* the real king?" Ash wondered. "Enough to be able to speak to us through the Elder Nightmares?"

I drew in a sharp breath. "Of course," I whispered. "If this Nightmare really is that strong, *he* might be the entity we saw below InSite. The one who threatened the destruction of the Nevernever."

"Right," Puck muttered. "So, what you're saying is, we should absolutely, one hundred percent *not* wake him up. Or he's just going to go on that rampage that could end in the destruction of the Nevernever and possibly the world."

"I would very much advise against waking him up," Gilleas whispered. "Even if this is a Nightmare and not the real king, I honestly do not believe we would survive the encounter."

"What we need to do is find the door," Ash said. "Gilleas, obviously this Nightmare wasn't here the last time you came looking for the king. But do you remember where the door was located?"

"Yes." Gilleas nodded. "I remember it appearing on the other side of the trunk. If we skirt the throne and walk around the back of the Nightmare Tree, hopefully it will be there."

"All right," I said, nodding. "Let's go, then. I don't think I have to tell anyone to be as quiet as you can."

We straightened and turned back to the Nightmare Tree.

The throne was empty.

26

THE NIGHTMARE KING

*"**I** will destroy all."*
The voice echoed through the chamber, shaking the ground and rattling the branches of the great tree. We turned, drawing weapons as we searched for the voice, the ground beneath us starting to pulse and roil. The tree shook, the twisted bodies trapped in the bark writhing in fear and agony.

"Where is he?" Ash said, glaring around the room. I gazed around as well and saw nothing but shadows and the pulsing light of the Nightmare Tree.

"All will be darkness." The voice continued to echo, coming from every direction. It seemed to vibrate from the sky and the earth itself. *"All will be fear. The sun will never rise, and the shadows will consume the world. This will be the new dream. This will be the eternal nightmare."*

The voice echoed directly overhead. I looked up...and the Nightmare King descended from the black. His eyes were open, two fathomless pits that held no light, no color or remorse or sanity. His face and hands seemed to glow as he hovered there, hollow eyes staring right through us.

"The dream has ended." The king slowly raised a hand, pale fingers clenching into a fist. *"Now the nightmare begins."*

The ground beneath us heaved. It pitched like the deck of a ship, and cracks opened in the surface. I staggered as huge shapes began pushing their way through the ground, claws and antlered skulls, tentacles and writhing bodies, leathery wings, spines, bones, and teeth. Dozens of Elder Nightmares clawing their way into the open, their eyes gleaming a soulless white as they lurched to their feet.

"Oh man." Puck raised both daggers, glancing around at the tide of Elder Nightmares. "More giant monsters, yay. Why are all the nasties so huge in Evenfall?"

We have to stop this, now. I clenched a fist, feeling my magic spark to life. The air turned static, charged with energy, and thunder rippled through the blackness as lightning flickered over the head of the Nightmare King. In the heartbeat of stillness between one flash and the next, the Nightmare King turned his head, and his empty, pitch-black eyes fixed on me.

I raised a hand, and a ribbon of red-hot energy flickered from the sky overhead, striking the form of the Nightmare King square on. He burst into a cloud of black flies that swirled away in the darkness. Almost instantly, however, the swarm of insects reconverged, melding together into the Nightmare King once more. His void eyes were no longer impassive; now they burned with rage as they stared at me.

"Your world will die first." The Nightmare King slowly tilted his head at me. His lips didn't move, but the words vibrated in my ears like worms burrowing into my mind. *"I will destroy everything you love and cover your world in despair. Everything you have built will be torn away from you. Everything that matters will be buried in fear, drowned in terror, eaten alive by rage.*

Until all you see is darkness, and all you hear are the screams of those who cannot escape their endless nightmare."

"You are not the real Nightmare King!" Ash stepped in front of me, facing the terrifying creature floating overhead. The Elder Nightmares started forward, pressing in from all sides, but Ash stood firm. "You are not the real king, and you will not touch this world or the next."

"Not the real king?" The Nightmare King turned those hollow, void-dark eyes on Ash. *"You know nothing, little dream. You wish to face the true ruler of this world? Very well."*

His body rippled, then plummeted from the air, bursting open as it hit the ground, releasing hundreds of rats that scattered into the darkness.

"I will show you the face of darkness. Look upon me and know fear."

Around us, the Elder Nightmares staggered to a halt. Throwing back their heads, they screamed, their voices rising in a terrible cacophony of shrieks, wails, and roars. Their bodies frayed apart, becoming tendrils of darkness that swirled into the air, then converged into a single whirlwind that solidified, took form, and turned into the Nightmare King. But this time, he was clad in black armor made of chiton and bones. A ragged cape billowed behind him, and I could see faces trapped within the folds, twisted in silent screams.

"I am the Nightmare King." The armored figure reached back and drew forth a blade so dark it sucked in the light. He moved forward, not walking, but gliding like a wraith over the ground. *"I am all of your fears, all of your terrors and phobias and secret horrors. I am the fear of darkness, and death, and the unknown. I am every crawling, flying, slithering thing that bites, stings, burrows, and devours. I am the hand under the bed, the tapping against your window, the killer who smiles as he raises the axe. I am blood. I am bones. I am the cold certainty of the grave. You*

*cannot kill fear. You cannot defeat what is in your mind. You
will fall, and I will consume your entire world.*

"**Come then, dreams.**" He raised his blade in a grim salute.
"*Let us begin the dance of terror.*"

He flew through the air like a shadow, that obsidian blade a
blur of darkness as it swept down at me. I raised my own sword
to block, and shook from the jarring impact as the blades met.
A chilling cry rang out, coming from the black sword, causing
my stomach to clench. For a split second, the agonized scream
sounded like Keirran.

The Nightmare King's visage changed. For a moment, I saw
myself, eyes completely black, drenched in blood, mouth open
in a wail of madness, staring at me over our crossed blades. She
rose into the air like a puppet, her head hanging at an awkward
angle, but her lips still moving in a soundless scream. She slashed
at me, and I parried her blow, twisting the blade around to stab
it through her chest.

The bloody Meghan exploded, dissolving into clouds of black
insects, their wings a deafening buzz as they swirled around us.
Dozens of tiny bodies landed on me, and stinging pain coursed
over me as they began burrowing into my skin.

Cold flared as someone, either Ash or Keirran, sent a pulse
of Winter glamour through the air, dropping the temperature
in a heartbeat. Ice coated my skin and hair, and the squirming bodies stilled and fell away, becoming a carpet of half-dead
bugs all around us.

"Okay, this is gross!" Puck's voice echoed into the void around
us. He took a step back, wincing as his boot crunched into the
squirming carpet beneath. "I officially don't like this."

"*Then perhaps you should be silent.*"

The carpet of bugs rippled and abruptly slithered across the
floor toward Puck. He gave a yelp and threw himself backwards, but the half-dead insects swarmed up his legs, his chest,
his neck, until they reached the top of his head, covering him

completely. Puck flailed, and we rushed toward him, but the swarm of bugs suddenly exploded, flying into the air and vanishing into the darkness. Puck fell to his knees, one hand covering his face. His shoulders heaved, and his other hand beat the floor in a fist, making my stomach clench with alarm.

"Puck." Nyx dropped to a knee beside him, grabbing his shoulder. Muffled moans came from his hunched form, though I couldn't see any wounds on him as we crowded around. "What happened?" Nyx asked, her voice tight with worry. "Talk to me, Goodfellow. What is wrong?"

Puck raised his head, eyes wide and bulging. And I realized he had no mouth, just smooth skin between his nose and jawline. Varyn let out a soft curse.

A soft, feminine chuckle echoed around us. "Dance for me, little insects," the new voice whispered, directly at my back. I spun, lashing out with my sword, and saw it pass through a tall figure in white, her eyes as dark and empty as the void. The figure blinked out of sight the moment the blade touched her, the echo of laughter lingering in the air.

"You are all but drones in my nest. Puppets in my game." The figure flickered into view once more, a stunning faery with long black hair and an eternally young face. Shimmering wings sprouted from her back, neither feathers nor scales nor gossamer, but something in between. Both Nyxes, Varyn, and Keirran stiffened as the familiar form of the Lady—the First Queen of Faery—smiled down at them.

"My beautiful killers," she whispered. "None of you have changed." Nyx, bent over the still-moaning form of Puck, clenched a fist as the Lady threw back her head and laughed, her voice like chiming bells. "I will make you destroy everything you care for, and you will love me for it."

She raised her arms, and a flurry of projectiles came from all directions, slamming into the Lady: daggers, ice, and moonlight crescents, striking her at nearly the same time. But instead of vanishing, the Lady unraveled. Hair-thin strands of silver un-coiled, flying out in an explosion of gossamer. A scream ripped through my head, turning everything white, and for a moment, I felt myself falling.

Gasping, I raised my head, and a wave of vertigo washed over me. I might have been floating; I couldn't feel the ground under my feet. My ears throbbed, nausea and dizziness raging within. Wincing, I managed to look up...and realized I *was* floating, held off the ground by dozens of silver threads. As my senses grew clearer, I saw that the threads weren't wrapped around my limbs or binding them in any way; they seemed to go straight through my body, suspending me several feet in the air. Looking around, I saw in horror that the rest of my allies were in the same situation: suspended above the ground by threads that pierced their limbs and bodies, holding them immobile in the darkness. Ash and Keirran dangled, motionless, several feet above me. Their eyes were closed, though Ash was beginning to stir. Puck hung like a gangly marionette beside Nyx, with Other Nyx and Varyn a few feet away. Even Gilleas, his antlers tangled in gossamer, floated in the grisly spider web like some kind of monstrous insect himself.

"All my little drones. All the puppets in my web." Something pale and monstrous came through the threads. An enormous, bloated spider with the Lady's face, smiling as she crawled into the light. I jerked up, but I was barely able to move. My body felt sluggish, and pain stabbed my skin like needles where the threads came out. Clenching my jaw, I drew my magic to me, feeling it spark to life...and then vanish. Glamour drained from my body, siphoned away through the gossamer strands.

The Lady-spider creature gave me an eerie, soulless smile. "You are powerful, little queen, but this is my web. Everything trapped here is mine."

She turned, and one thin, pointed leg rose, touching one of the threads. A ripple went through the strands, and Varyn dropped from the web and hit the ground with a thump. Almost immediately, he rose to his feet, his body pulled upright as if he were still attached.

The Lady smiled.

"Varyn..." Nyx's voice, faint and breathy, drifted into the silence. Beside her, Puck struggled weakly against the strands, still unable to make a sound because he had no mouth.

"Now, my drone. Show me you still obey." The spider creature half reared up, raising its front legs, as if controlling a marionette by the strings. "Kill your allies. Starting with the one you love. Kill them all, then slice your own throat. Obey, because you are mine."

Slowly, Varyn turned, a knife appearing in one hand. His jaw was clenched, his back stiff, as if he was fighting not to move. But he took one step, then another, walking steadily toward the two Nyxes dangling helplessly in the strands.

I could sense everyone around me struggling, trying to throw off the weakness and call on their magic. But the more I tried to draw on my glamour, the faster it drained away. My sword lay on the ground several feet beneath me, out of reach. I could only watch as Varyn walked, zombielike, toward Other Nyx, the monstrous form of the Lady-spider standing behind him.

Something glimmered in the light: the thinnest strand of gossamer, spanning the distance between them like a spiderweb. It was visible for only a moment, but Puck's gaze flicked upwards, and as Varyn calmly raised the knife toward Other Nyx's throat, he jerked one arm forward, reaching not for the dagger, but the back of Varyn's skull. I saw the flare of pain through Puck's eyes as he tore his limb free and swiped at Varyn but didn't seem to touch him.

Varyn, however, jerked away with a gasp, immediately dropping the knife. It hit the ground with a clatter, and I realized Puck had severed the gossamer thread attached to Varyn's skull. As the Lady reared up with a hiss, eyes glowing in fury,

Varyn whirled and threw out his arms. Crescent blades left his hands, but they were not aimed at the Lady. Instead, they curved around and flew into the webs, slicing the strands apart. I was suddenly free, and the magic that had been siphoned from my body flooded back with a roar.

A rush of glamour filled the air, furious and deadly. The air grew frigid, lightning crackled, and the scream of a raven echoed overhead. The Lady-spider skittered back and raised her thin legs, but before the barrage of magic could be unleashed, our Nyx darted forward, leaped onto the spider's bulbous thorax, and calmly decapitated the Lady. The Evenfaery's expression, as the spider creature's skull toppled to the floor, was terrifying and triumphant.

The spider's body shivered, then dissolved into a swarm of smaller spiders that scattered in every direction. Nyx leaped down, squashing several underfoot, and was immediately crushed in an embrace by Puck. She hugged him back fiercely, and I breathed a sigh of relief, as the strands around us frayed apart and vanished, returning us to the void.

For a moment after the Lady disappeared, there was silence. Varyn and Other Nyx stood to one side, foreheads pressed together and eyes closed. Ash strode up and pulled me to him with one arm, and I relaxed against him, relieved that the ordeal was over.

"Well." It was Gilleas who spoke first, and even his calm, exasperated voice wavered a moment. "That was...extraordinarily unpleasant. I did not realize how much the Lady had affected all of us until now."

"Is everyone all right?" Keirran asked, gazing around.

"Oh, I'm just peachy, princeling." Puck's voice rang out loud and clear, making me smile. "You try having your mouth *poofed* away and see how well you like it. It ain't funny, I'll tell you that right now."

"Really?" Ash began, and Puck whirled on him, an almost feverish gleam in his green eyes.

"Ice-boy, I swear, if I hear *one thing* about this, one teensy little joke or comment or snicker, I won't stop talking at you for the next millennium. In fact, I'm pissed enough that I might do that anyway."

"Fools."

A shiver went through the air, and a wave of cold washed over us. The Nightmare King floated down from the darkness, sword in hand, a vortex of black surrounding it. He did not look any weaker; power flared around him, the sword pulsed as it sucked in the light, and the aura of terror spread out from the Nightmare King, making it hard to breathe.

"You cannot kill fear so easily."

Despair filled my heart, and I clenched a fist in Ash's shirt as his arms tightened around me. How were we going to beat him? No matter what we tried, no matter how many times we "killed" the Nightmare King, he simply vanished and reappeared as something even more terrifying. Like the Wailing One, who couldn't be slain unless…

I straightened. The Nightmare King. Of course! He was an Elder Nightmare, a *named* Elder Nightmare. Which meant, somewhere in this terrible, twisted castle, there was a core. The essence of this Nightmare.

"I grow weary of this game," the Nightmare King stated, observing us with cold indifference. *"Your fears are varied, yet you face them well. You choose to face the Nightmares together instead of alone. But there is one fear that not even the bravest can stand against. One fear that no one can escape."*

"Ash," I gasped, looking up at him. "The Nightmare King is—"

The floor beneath me vanished, and I fell into shockingly cold water that closed over my head, muffling all sound. Holding my breath, I looked around for Ash, but he was gone. Everyone was gone. Seeing a faint, blurry glow above me, I instinctively kicked for the surface and reached for that light.

My hand struck something hard and cold, making me blink in shock.

What? Ice?

The surface of the water was covered in a solid sheet of ice. I pounded on it with my fists, trying to see through the translucent barrier, but nothing happened. My lungs burned, and I slammed my fist against the ice in desperation, but it didn't even crack.

"Do you fear death, little dream?" The Nightmare King's voice echoed in the darkness around me. *"How long before the mind snaps? Before the heart seizes in terror and ceases to beat? In dreams, one has only to wake to escape the terror, but you are not asleep, are you?"*

My vision was starting to darken at the edges. With the last of my strength, I raised a hand to try to blast my way free. But my limbs were stiff with cold, and the glamour flickered weakly at my fingertips before sputtering out. The last breath left my lungs in a trail of bubbles, and the blackness at the edge of my vision flooded in.

I floated.

27

ONLY HUMAN

*W*ake up.

The voice was a whisper in my ears, barely audible. My consciousness stirred, though everything felt hazy and delirious. I had heard somewhere that, once you got past the initial panic, drowning was a peaceful death. Was I still drowning, or was I already dead?

This is the Dream, the voice whispered again, rippling through the water like the tiniest silver fish. *But you are real. You are not a part of it. Your fate can still be changed.*

"Who are you?" I asked, or maybe it was just a thought, as I was still underwater. "Have we met before?"

Once, in a vision. It does not matter now. Look to the tree. It is the essence of this nightmare. The false king waits to devour your world if you do not stop him here. Now, wake up.

My eyes flew open. My lungs still screamed. I was still drowning beneath the ice. Throwing out a hand, I released a surge of magic and desperation, feeling glamour sizzle through the water and slam into the ice overhead. There was a muffled explosion, and I kicked frantically for the surface.

I broke through the hole in the ice with a gasp, and blessed oxygen rushed into my lungs. Coughing, I heaved myself onto the surface, emptying water from my nose and mouth as quickly as I could before looking up.

The Nightmare King hovered overhead, as impassive and eternal as death. Around us, the sheet of ice spread as far as I could see until it vanished into the darkness. But across the frozen surface, the silhouette of the Nightmare Tree glowed red against the void.

Dragging myself upright, I gazed at the figure above me. Icy cold had numbed my fingers and deadened my limbs, but I forced myself to speak without trembling. "Where are the others?"

Those abyssal eyes stared down at me, expressionless. *"They will not hear you. You are alone. It is only you and I now."*

I looked around the icy landscape, and my heart stopped. Puck, eyes open and staring, his red hair in a cloud around him, floated lifelessly below the ice. I fell to my knees, pounding my fist against the barrier, but the ice didn't crack.

"Puck, hang on!"

"You cannot save him," the Nightmare King droned as I put a hand against the ice. *"What would you be without magic? Without the power to save those you care for? The only reason you are special is because of your half-faery blood. Without it, you are nothing."*

I ignored the king and took a deep breath, intending to shatter the ice beneath me to get to my best friend. But when I tried to summon my glamour as I had hundreds of times before, a yawning emptiness filled me. There was nothing there. I couldn't use my magic.

I...had no magic.

"What are you now?" The king's voice echoed in my head as

Puck's body sank beneath the water and was lost from view. *"No friends. No family. No allies. All were made possible because of your power, because you were fey. And now you have nothing."*

I knelt on the ice, staring between my splayed fingers, at the empty space where Puck had been. *He's not gone,* I told myself, fighting back the despair clawing at my insides. *None of them are. I won't believe that he's gone.*

"Futile." I looked up, and the Nightmare King was suddenly right there beside me. I went for my sword just as a blow to my face hurled me across the ice. My blade was torn from my grip and skidded away, and the terrible form of the Nightmare King continued to glide toward me.

"It is paralyzing, is it not? The knowledge that, as a human, your life would be worthless. You met your best friend because you were a faery royal. The love of your life was only interested because you were half fey. None of them loved you for you. Because humans are insignificant and evil and do nothing but destroy. Without magic, you will show them exactly what you are, and they will despise you for it."

Gasping, I put a hand to my jaw. Warm slickness met my fingers, and several drops of crimson hit the ice below me. I looked up and saw my weapon lying on the ice a few paces away. The Nightmare King continued to glide forward, his terrible black blade held loosely at his side.

"Only human now. No friends, no allies. No power. You are worthless. Weak. Alone."

Only human. I slumped against the ice, the cold, suffocating truth pressing down on me. What could I do against the ancient, immortal Nightmare King if I had no power? If I was only human? Not the Iron Queen, not the daughter of Oberon or the successor to Machina. Not even the wife of the son of Mab. Just me. Meghan Chase. A mortal.

"I will end this nightmare for you, little dream. Close your eyes and let me send you to the blissfulness of oblivion."

My eyes flickered shut. But I didn't see oblivion. I saw... them. Everyone. Ash and Puck, Keirran and Grimalkin, Nyx, Ethan, Kenzie, *everyone*. I saw the scenes of my previous life, when Faery tried taking away everything I loved. My human father. Ash. Keirran. I saw all of them clearly, felt the despair when everything seemed lost, and I remembered what had finally brought them back to me. Not magic. Not glamour or power or faery blood. Something that the Nightmare King could never understand.

I opened my eyes.

"Wait."

My voice emerged as a choked whisper. The Nightmare King paused, his terrible hollow gaze holding the emptiness of the void. Pushing myself to my hands and knees, I started crawling painfully across the ice. My hands burned with cold, and I left a trail of blood behind me, but I forced myself to keep moving. The Nightmare King watched, patient and unconcerned, as I made my torturous way, stifling gasps of fear and pain, until I reached my sword.

Wrapping bloody fingers around the hilt, I paused, taking several deep breaths. Briefly, I closed my eyes, gathering the last of my strength.

Ash, Puck, Keirran, Grimalkin. I know you're still with me. Let's do this together.

"My name is Meghan Chase." Rising to my feet, I held my head high, and faced the terrible creature hovering before me. "And it is *because* I am human that I stand here today. I first came to Faery to save my brother, and my connection to him drove every decision I made. Faery took my father, and I refused to lose hope that someday, I would find him again. I fell in love with a Winter prince, and I have never regretted it or looked back.

"Every path I have taken, all my choices and decision points and judgment calls, have been made as a human, not as a faery. As a daughter and a friend, as a wife and a mother. It is my mortal side and everything I learned as a human that makes me strong. Not my glamour or my title as faery queen. I am only human…and that is enough."

I raised my sword, feeling blood and tears stream down my face, mingling together. "Magic, strength, and power are nothing without humanity," I told the impassive form of the Nightmare King. "Hope is what keeps us going, empathy is what sets us apart, and love is what makes us human. It isn't a weakness— it's our greatest strength. It is why I will keep fighting when everything is crumbling around me. It is why I will never regret my mortal side, flaws, failings, and everything that comes with it. And it is why I am taking you down, right now!"

"Come then, dream." The Nightmare King floated down until his feet were nearly touching the ice. He lifted his sword, and the black blade gave a keening wail as he flourished it. Behind him, the Nightmare Tree pulsed red, bathing us in a sickly crimson glow as the king raised a beckoning hand. *"Let us end this nightmare. I will be merciful and send you to the eternal void, where fear and pain and despair will not be able to find you."*

I screamed a battle cry, for Ash, Keirran, Puck, Nyx, Grimalkin, *everyone*, and charged the Nightmare King. I flew across the ice, and from the corner of my vision, I caught glimpses of their faces: husband, son, eternal best friends. I felt their love and silent support as the Nightmare King loomed in front of me, raising his great black sword in one hand. I heard the shriek of the blade as it came sweeping down, and I had a split second to make a choice.

I ducked, falling to my knees as I reached the king, feeling the wind of the blade as it missed me by a finger width. Sliding past him on the ice, I leaped to my feet, sword in hand, and lunged toward the glowing silhouette of the Nightmare Tree. I could see a gash in the trunk, a place where the crying faces had separated, where red light spilled through the crack and pulsed like a heartbeat. Raising my weapon, I prepared to drive it into the tree.

"Stop!"

The king's voice hit me just as I reached the trunk, and something in the sudden desperate tone made me pause, sword point angled toward the gash. *"That is the Nightmare Tree,"* the king went on. *"The only place where Elder Nightmares are born into Evenfall. If you destroy it, there will be no more Nightmares to roam the Dream. No more glamour. No more hope. The Nightmares will vanish, and so will the Evenfey. You will be killing them all. Again."*

I bit my lip hard enough to taste blood, and the sword in my hand trembled. Could I do this? Would this be the end of Evenfall, by my own hand? I thought of everyone we had met on our journey, everything we had been through to get this far. To defeat the Nightmare King, did I have to sacrifice the very ones who helped us get here?

Nyx's voice whispered softly in my mind. *There is no such thing as false hope in Evenfall. We all hope for something better. And I will continue to hold out the hope that I will see the other side again.*

I closed my eyes. *Nyx, Varyn, everyone, I hope I'm doing the right thing. I expect to see you all at the end of this nightmare.*

I set my jaw...and drove the point of the blade into the Nightmare Tree, sinking it deep into the trunk.

The Nightmare King screamed. The faces in the trunk screamed, a cacophony of noise that roared around me like a hurricane. The world flickered, void and ice disappearing. I was suddenly back in the throne room, still at the base of the tree, with the bodies of my friends stirring on the floor. Keirran, lying on his back, groaned once, then rolled over, coughing. Ash pushed himself upright, took hold of his sword, and dragged himself to his feet. His gaze met mine across the stones, and his expression softened with relief.

The Nightmare Tree let out another wail, and the crimson

light shining between the cracks dimmed, flickered, then vanished. Within the trunk, the hundreds of faces that made up the tree stilled, eyes closing and mouths going slack. The Nightmare Tree darkened, and then shriveled in front of me, faces, arms, and hands disappearing, until all that was left was a dry, withered trunk.

The Nightmare King writhed in the air, both hands covering his face. His body seemed to fluctuate, unable to hold a specific shape. A mass of black tentacles burst from his back, flailing wildly, then became eight curved spider legs before turning to leathery wings. I looked around and saw that all my friends were on their feet now, staring in confusion and shock at the scene before them.

"Ash!" I called, and his silver eyes met mine. "The Nightmare King is weak now! The tree was the essence, and it's gone!"

Understanding dawned on his face, and he spun toward the flailing form of the Nightmare King. Winter magic pulsed around him as he drew back and hurled a storm of ice daggers at the creature in the air. The shards peppered the king, sinking deep, and he jerked as the daggers slammed into him. His eyes opened, blazing and furious, and he turned on Ash with a roar.

Another barrage of glamour struck him from behind: a spear of ice slamming into his back, hurled by a grim-faced Keirran. Like shooting stars, the crescent blades of all the assassins streaked through the air, slicing into the king.

With a cry, the Nightmare King dropped to the ground. Hunching over, his body contorted, twisting and bending as if his bones were changing shape beneath his skin. With a ripping sound, his flesh split, the visage of the Nightmare King collapsing in a bloody heap, and something huge and dark rose from the remains. A creature of tentacles and bones, spines, teeth, and jointed legs, it loomed over us like a Lovecraftian horror. Like every Nightmare creature melded into one horrific abomination. It roared, tendrils flailing, and was caught in a maelstrom as Ash's, Puck's, Keirran's, the Nyxes', and Varyn's magic slammed into it, catching it in a nexus of glamour and power. Its roar became a scream as Summer, Winter, and Iron glamour tore through it, sending billows of dark magic into the air. Rising to my feet, I took a deep breath, feeling my power stir through me once more, and raised a hand to the empty sky. The thing that was the Nightmare King let out one last howl as a crimson strand streaked from the heavens, hitting the pulsing storm and causing it to explode in every direction. Ice shards flew everywhere, wind shrieked through my hair, and lightning strands flickered along the ground. I turned away, shielding my eyes, as the maelstrom of glamour swirled around us, screaming in my ears.

At last, the winds died down, the wild storm of magic faded, and silence fell once more. Panting, I turned back to see everyone standing in a grim circle around the spot where the creature had been. Seeing that everyone was all right, I walked up beside Ash, who crushed me to him with one arm, and gazed down at the center of the circle. Only a few wisps of dark glamour curled up from a scorched, frozen patch in the stones, and nothing remained of the Nightmare King.

28

BEYOND THE DREAM

"You...beat him?"

I looked up as Gilleas's voice, thin and weak with disbelief, drifted to us from the shadows. I hadn't seen him since the Nightmare King had appeared, but I assumed that, like Grimalkin, Gilleas was adept at getting out of sight when the fighting broke out. Still, I was relieved to see his tall, lanky form, staring down at the scorched patch of earth where the Nightmare King had stood moments before.

"Incredible," he breathed, shaking his antlered head. "I would not have thought it possible. But you battled the aspect of the Nightmare King and lived. I was certain we were all going to die a very horrible, terrifying death."

"Well, I won't lie, that *was* horrible and terrifying," Puck said. "I like to skip the 'death' part of most battles, though." He looked at our Nyx, a relieved smile crossing his face. "Glad to see you decided to skip it, too."

Nyx let out a shaky breath. "I find myself wanting to survive more and more," she said, with a wry look at Puck. "I think you're a bad influence on me, Goodfellow."

"But the Nightmare Tree is gone," I whispered, clenching a fist against Ash's shirt. "I'm so sorry, Gilleas. I had to destroy it to weaken the king. Without the tree, there won't be any more Nightmares born into Evenfall."

Gilleas bowed his head. "This world is almost done, Iron Queen," he said softly. "You haven't hastened its death in any way. I believe the king—the real king—stopped dreaming his nightmares a while ago. He is likely at the end of his existence, which means his dream is nearly over."

"Then perhaps we should hurry," came Grimalkin's voice, sounding softer and much more solemn than his usual impatient tone. "After the false king fell, the door appeared," he went on, turning his head in the direction of the withered Nightmare Tree. "The real Nightmare King, the dreamer of this world, is likely waiting on the other side."

As one, we turned to the Nightmare Tree. A simple wooden door stood on its own at the roots of the trunk. It looked like a bedroom closet door, and for some reason, it reminded me of a day, long, long ago, when I left the human world for the first time and followed Robin Goodfellow into the realm of Faery.

"Yes." Gilleas nodded, sounding tired. "It is the same door. I remember." He turned his head to me, and though his face gave nothing away, I could sense a sad smile behind the mask. "Iron Queen, this is where we must part," he said softly. "You and your companions are flesh and blood, but we cannot leave the Dream." He gestured to Other Nyx and to Varyn standing close beside her. "We will not be able to follow you."

I swallowed the lump that rose to my throat, my heart twisting with the realization. The Nightmare King waited on the other side of a simple wooden door. What would we find once we stepped through? A dying ruler, on the verge of Fading? A king who was ready to finally wake up? Whatever happened, this could be the last time we saw Evenfall. The last time we spoke to the dreams that lived here. Once we stepped through that door, everything behind us could disappear.

I gazed back at the three Evenfey, sealing them into my memories forever. Before I could say anything, however, Other Nyx stepped forward. "No matter what happens," she told me, "it has been an honor, both to have known and to have traveled with you all. You gave us a reason to hope, a reason to keep fighting. Even if we disappear and the Dream ends, I am proud of the part we could play on this journey."

I ignored the stinging in my eyes and nodded. "We couldn't have done it without you."

Varyn gave us a begrudging smile. "I didn't expect any Neverfey to stand with us," he said. "I honestly thought you would run back to Faery the second things got too dangerous. I don't like admitting I was wrong, but you fight well, and you don't leave others behind. I'd trust you to guard my back any day, and that's not something I tell everyone."

"Likewise," Ash said, nodding to the assassins. "You are both skilled warriors, some of the best I've seen. I hope we can meet again one day."

"We'll see what Fate has in store for us." Varyn shrugged. "But if the Dream is almost done, this was a good last fight. In any case, you've earned this warrior's respect." His gold gaze slid to Puck, lips curling in a faint smirk. "Most of you, anyway."

"Aw, Vary." Puck returned the slightly mocking grin. "Did we just have a moment? I think we had a moment."

"The door is flickering," Grimalkin warned. "If you are going through, I would do so quickly."

I looked over and saw he was right. The door sputtered, winking in and out of reality like a candle flame. It lasted just a moment, but it sent a chill through me, turning my insides to ice. We didn't have much time left.

"All right," I said, and took a deep breath. I looked at the ones who would be going through the door with me. Ash, Puck, Keirran, Nyx, and Grimalkin. "No more delays," I said. "No more goodbyes. It's time to meet the king."

"Iron Queen," Gilleas said as we turned away. "If you would indulge me for a moment longer. I do not believe I have ever given you the respect your title deserves."

And before I could say anything, the historian of Evenfall lowered his antlered head and bowed, bending deeply at the waist. Other Nyx and Varyn followed his example, sinking to one knee and bowing their heads as well.

"We are eternally grateful that you came," Gilleas said solemnly. "For so long, Evenfall was lost, abandoned, and forgotten. But now it has seen the light of hope, if only for a moment. Do not mourn the Fading of the Dream—rejoice instead that it existed, and remember it fondly."

I blinked tears from my eyes and nodded. "We will," I told them. "We won't forget you. We will remember, always."

There was no answer from the trio before us, and nothing left to be said. Silently, we turned, and with Grimalkin leading the way, walked up to the roots of the withered Nightmare Tree, to where the simple wooden door stood beneath the trunk. I reached out, and there was no resistance at all as my fingers touched the surface and pushed it back. The door swung open without a creak, and we stepped through, out of Evenfall, out of the Dream, and into another place entirely.

Silence greeted me on the other side of the door. Silence... and cold.

We stood in another void. Another space without walls or ceilings. Without trees or structures or anything solid. The ground appeared like the surface of a still lake, and though my shoes didn't sink into the water, my footsteps still left ripples that spread out around me. Overhead, a hazy blue-black sky stretched on forever, scattered with stars that reflected the ground beneath us, making it seem like we were standing in the vastness of space. It was cold here, not icy or biting, just… empty. Like there was no warmth anywhere, no sun or fire or living creatures. Just…nothing.

I shivered, suddenly feeling very small.

"Where are we?" Keirran wondered, gazing around. His voice didn't echo. It was simply lost in the space around us. He took a step, gazing around with solemn eyes. "This feels…like the Between," he mused. "But emptier, if that's possible. At least the Between is a place—it exists between Faery and the mortal realm. This doesn't feel like anything."

"What is beyond the Between?" Grimalkin asked, appearing a few feet away. He was seated, his tail curled around himself, and his reflection in the water was crystal clear, two pairs of glowing eyes gazing across the void. "What exists beyond the borders of nothing? If Faery Fades away, what is left?"

"You're both making my head hurt," Puck muttered. His voice was subdued; the scars of the battle we'd just come through, and the allies left behind, lingered. We'd been in Evenfall only a short time, but Gilleas, Varyn, and Other Nyx had become more than acquaintances. They were more than dreams, more than the memories of a Fading king. They were friends. There was a gaping hole left behind by their loss. It didn't seem right that they had come so far, stood with us against so much, but not be here at the very end. I desperately hoped that here, on the other side of Evenfall, we would find the answer that could save everyone we had met within the Dream. I was not ready to say goodbye to this world and watch it Fade.

Ash stepped close, resting a hand on my arm. "There is a light on the horizon," he said in a quiet voice. "I don't think we're alone."

He was right. Something stood in the distance, faint and otherworldly. Too far away to make out, but I thought I could see the outline of a single pale tree against the hazy blue darkness.

It glowed against the horizon, not crimson and ominous like the Nightmare Tree; instead, the outstretched branches were lit with an almost ethereal, flickering light.

"Another tree." Puck sighed. "Never thought I'd say this, but I'm getting kind of tired of them. It can never be just a tree, can it?"

"Whatever it is," I said, "I think this is the only thing we're going to find out here. Is everyone ready?"

They nodded, and we started across the empty space, our footsteps making no sound against the surface of the water. Silent ripples spread out from our steps, making the stars reflected from overhead waver and dance. I reached out and took Ash's hand, wanting to feel something solid in this eerily empty world. He squeezed gently, and we continued across the expanse, our breaths and muffled heartbeats the only sound in the endless nothing.

For a while, it seemed that the closer we walked toward the tree, the farther it drew away. We kept a steady pace through the void, neither hurrying nor slowing down, but the tree always seemed the same distance away.

After several minutes of walking and seeing the branches continue to hover against the horizon, Puck blew out a gusty breath. "Oh, this is one of *those* nightmares," he muttered. "Where you're running toward a door or a person or a thing and it never gets any closer. Should we turn around and walk the other way? Maybe that will make it chase us, and then we can surprise it."

"Chase us?" Nyx asked, frowning slightly at Puck. "It is a tree."

"You've never been chased by a tree before?"

"It is not moving away from us," Grimalkin said, padding over the water. His paws, I noticed, made no ripples on the surface of the lake, and his eyes glowed brightly in his reflection. "If we keep walking, we will get there eventually."

"How do you know that, Furball? You've never been here before."

"I am a cat." Grimalkin glanced back at Puck, a faintly smug look crossing his feline face. "Obviously."

Keirran, walking a little behind everyone else, let out a quiet breath and stumbled to a halt. A look of confusion creased his brow, but he wasn't staring at our surroundings or the tree on the horizon, but at the mirrorlike surface at our feet.

"Keirran?"

"I...sorry." He gave his head a shake, frowning slightly as if in pain. "I thought I saw... I keep seeing...faces in the water."

I looked down but couldn't see anything beyond my own reflection and the sky overhead. "Faces?" I wondered, looking at Keirran. "Like bodies under the surface?"

"No. More like...reflections of people who aren't there. I see them beneath the water, staring down at us, like we're the ones being reflected back."

"Are they a danger?" Ash questioned softly, his grip tightening on mine. "Should we be concerned about being dragged beneath the surface?"

"No." Keirran scrubbed a hand over his scalp, raking his hair back. "They're not real," he said. "I think they're echoes of the world that was here before. Let's keep moving, though. The longer I stay in one place, the more of them I see."

We continued, and gradually, the tree on the distant horizon began to grow. The closer we got, the more I realized how big it actually was. It was just as large, if not larger, than the Nightmare Tree in the king's castle. Its pale, near-white branches spread out like a huge canopy, glowing from thousands of candles resting in the limbs.

At the base of the trunk sat a large stone chair, identical to the one in the Nightmare King's throne room. A familiar figure sat upon it, pale and dressed in black, withered hands resting on the chair arms. His eyes were closed, his chin bent to his chest. An obsidian crown, jagged and sharp, rested atop his head.

I drew in a slow breath, feeling Ash stiffen beside me. The

real Nightmare King, the ruler of Evenfall and the creator of the Dream, sat motionless upon his throne under the great tree. His body was wasted, a mere skeleton, with skin stretched tightly over his bones, so pale he was almost transparent. As we stepped closer, he didn't move, though his forehead was creased and furrowed as if in constant torment.

"You have come."

A breath shook the branches of the tree overhead, making the thousands of tiny candle flames sputter and dance. The voice was familiar, the same one I'd heard while fighting the Elder Nightmare in the other throne room. The one that had told us to destroy the tree. I glanced around for the speaker, wondering if a ghostly image of the figure on the throne would appear before us, but we remained alone under the tree.

"Look down," the voice went on, as we continued to gaze around us. *"Into the water."*

I glanced down at the mirror image of the throne beneath the tree. The king sat there, perfectly reflected in the mirrorlike surface, but his eyes were open, gazing up at us all.

"Welcome," the Nightmare King greeted us, *"to the outside of the Dream."*

I heard Nyx release a shaky breath; the Evenfaery sank to her knees in the water, bowing her head to the figure on the throne. "Nightmare King," she whispered in a trembling voice. "Forgive me. I have failed you. If I had only killed the Lady before she could enact the ritual, Evenfall might still be here."

"No," murmured the Nightmare King. *"My dear moonlight protector. It is I who have failed you all. I could not keep my world alive. I watched it Fade around me. I watched all of you disappear and could do nothing to stop it. I fell into rage and grief for a long time, and after that, I came here, to the center of my realm, and I dreamed. But my dreams were touched with anger and despair, and though I remembered all my subjects fondly, the Dream itself became twisted and dark.*

"This tree," the king went on, as the reflection turned to gaze up at the pale oak, *"is all that remains of Evenfall. And it is Fading, as I am Fading."* The reflection bowed his head, shoulders slumping. *"I am so tired,"* he whispered. *"I wish I could let go and let oblivion take me. But I must keep the tree alive, for it holds all the memories of the Evenfey. It is what keeps the Dream going. The candles are my memories; as long as they burn, Evenfall will not be completely gone."*

"Nightmare King." Keirran stepped forward, his eyes hard and his jaw set in determination. "We want to help," he said. "We have seen Evenfall and the fey who make it their home. We want to erase the damage the Lady and the fey of old did to you, so long ago. What can we do to bring Evenfall back?"

The king sighed. His eyes flickered shut, and his haggard face seemed to wither even further, making him look a thousand years old. *"So long,"* he whispered, more to himself than to us. *"It has been so long. If only they could have been here sooner. But it is no use, and there is no time to regret what cannot be. This is the world as it exists today.*

"You cannot bring Evenfall back," the Nightmare King continued in a voice of terrible finality. *"Evenfall is gone. The realm has Faded away, its magic has disappeared, and there is no returning the world to what it was. Once the Dream fades, Evenfall will vanish.*

"But the Evenfey," the king went on in a whisper, *"might still be saved. They are part of the Dream, but I have kept their memories safe here, within the tree. There is a chance, a slight chance, that the Evenfey could start life anew. However, it might take more than you are willing to give."*

Keirran looked at me, the longing in his eyes clear. He wanted to help the Evenfey; he was willing to pay whatever price, but he was not willing to make a choice that would drag others into danger with him. He had a kingdom now, as well, and people who depended on him. This was not his decision to make. At least, not alone.

I took a deep, slow breath, clearing my thoughts, and prepared myself for the worst. "What would it require?"

"Enough glamour to bring a race back from nothing," said the Nightmare King. *"Enough magic to pull them out of the Dream and into the real world again."*

"How much?" Ash said.

"A world's worth," was the answer. *"And it will take all the glamours combined to make the Evenfey whole again. Summer, Winter, Iron, Nightmare, wyld. If the Evenfey are to exist, to live, to be real once more, they must be part of the magic of the world. All its magic, wonder, imagination, fears, and dreams. Everything."*

"It's going to take all of us," I said.

"Perhaps more than you have. Almost certainly, it will be more than you can give. As the fey of the Lady's circle discovered, this is not a simple endeavor. This will drain you, all of you. You could pour so much into the ritual that you cease to exist. So, that is your choice now, Iron Queen. Would you risk not only your existence, but the existence of those you love the most, to save the Evenfey? To pull them out of the Dream, and make them real?"

I swallowed hard. So, this was it. What were we willing to sacrifice to make the Evenfey real once more? Once upon a time, I wouldn't have hesitated. Before I became the Iron Queen, I would have made the choice without a second thought. But it wasn't just me now. I *was* a queen. I had a family, and a kingdom. If I gave everything to make the Evenfey real and lost my own life in the process, what would happen to the Iron Realm?

And the others... I couldn't ask them to make this choice with me. If I lost them, any one of them... I couldn't even imagine the devastation it would bring. A world without Puck. Without Keirran. And Ash... My heart twisted violently at the thought.

If Ash disappeared in front of me, if I had to face immortality without him... I didn't know how I would keep going.

Then Nyx took a quiet breath and raised her head. "I am willing," she said softly.

Puck gave a very loud sigh. "Of course you are," he said, running a hand through his hair and making it stand on end. "And if you're going to do it, that means I'm going to do it, too. Because, one—I can't have you showing me up. And two—well, this is going to take all of us, and if I refuse, you'll either stab me in the tender bits until I agree...or you'll never forgive me, which will be even worse. So...yeah." He sighed again and gave us a wry smile. "The things I do for love. I think I've said this before somewhere, but the Fates laugh at my torment."

Nyx stepped close to Puck, put her hands on his chest, and kissed him. He immediately closed his eyes, his hands coming up to grip her shoulders. "Thank you," she whispered when they drew back, making Puck blink in shock. "I know I was ready to give up on this world. But if we can bring the Evenfey out of the Dream, if we can make them real again...even if I don't survive, it will be worth it."

"Maybe for you," Puck murmured, and shook his head. "Dammit, I always seem to fall for the hopelessly noble types. It must be a curse." He closed his eyes, pressing their foreheads together. "Just don't Fade on me," he whispered. "I will admit to being a selfish bastard sometimes, but if you disappear... I'm going to cry. And I don't wanna do that. So, unless you want me to go into an ice-boy-worthy funk for the next hundred years or so, you'll stick around. At least until I can show you the Summer Court."

Nyx pressed a palm against Puck's jaw. "You're pretty noble yourself, Robin Goodfellow," she said softly. "I would love to see the Summer Court with you. And the rest of the Nevernever as well."

"Let's get through this, then," Puck said. "That *is* the plan, right? Because if I know our royal family, they're not going to stand by and watch, either."

Keirran immediately nodded. "You already know I'll do whatever it takes," he said quietly. "The Forgotten...they've lost so much, but they know how to survive. If I don't come back, they'll be fine. But I can't speak for the rulers of the Iron Realm. They have more to lose than I do."

Everything inside me constricted. Ash turned to me, his expression somber. "I'm willing," he said simply. "But only if you are." He stepped closer, taking both my hands. "I know the danger," he said. "I can understand any hesitation you might have. This could put the Iron Realm in jeopardy, and risk everything we've worked for over the years in Faery. But you know that I will stand with you, whatever you decide."

"I don't want to lose you," I whispered. "Either of you."

It was a selfish plea, made by the part of me that was still a sixteen-year-old mortal, completely in love with a Winter prince. By a human mother who was terrified for her son. But Ash sighed, pressing closer and lowering his voice so that only I could hear.

"I know," he murmured. "I don't want to lose you or Keirran, either. The thought of going back to the Iron Realm alone..." This close, I felt the tremor that went through him, saw the flash of anguish through his silver eyes, and clenched my fingers in his shirt. "If that happened," he continued, and his voice broke just a little, "I would never recover. But..." He placed a gentle hand on my cheek, gazing down intently. "If the worst does come to pass, I want you to know that the Iron Kingdom will be safe. I will continue to protect our realm and our people as if you were there. Because I know that's what you would do."

My eyes filled with tears. That Ash would continue on, taking care of the realm and the fey he had adopted as his own, made my heart ache with relief and love.

"But I don't think that will be a danger," he went on. "Because this type of situation is all or nothing. Everyone here—you, me, Puck, Keirran, Nyx, even Grim—we're going to give all that we have. No one is going to hold back. And we will either fail together, or we will succeed as one. Unless—" he paused, his gaze becoming even more serious "—you decide the risk is too great. We've come this far but…this is asking us to give up everything. No one would blame you for deciding it's too much."

"No." I swallowed hard. "We have to do this, Ash. How can we not? There's no chance we can just walk away, not if it means bringing the Evenfey back to Faery. Everyone we've met—Gilleas, Nyx, Varyn, Anira, all of the Evenfey—they're just as real as we are. They deserve a chance to live."

"I agree," Ash said quietly. "So, we've all made the choice. We do this together. I assume you're with us, Grimalkin?"

The cait sith let out a heavy sigh. "I would not be here were I not."

"Brave souls," whispered the Nightmare King. *"You give up much, but do not make a final decision yet. One final choice remains. Perhaps the hardest decision of all."* He paused, briefly closing his eyes as if to gather his thoughts. *"The glamour itself will not be enough,"* he continued. *"Someone must remain apart to summon the Evenfey into the real world. They must be the conduit to pull them from the Dream into reality. Be warned— the amount of will and magic this requires will be greater than anything they have faced before. They must be able to withstand all the glamour and memories as the Evenfey are pulled through them into the real world. The damage this will wreak on the body and the mind will be extreme. It is almost certain they will not survive the experience."*

The ground dropped away, plunging me into a pool of despair. So, it seemed no matter what, someone was going to have to die tonight. Who would it be? Who could I ask to make that choice? My soulmate? My best friend? I looked around at my family, and on their faces, I saw what I feared. They were *all* willing to step forward and be that sacrifice. And my heart cried at the thought of losing any of them.

No. I couldn't watch that. I was the queen.

This responsibility was mine.

"You don't have to do this, Meghan," Ash said, his voice low and, though I was the only one who heard it, desperate. "It doesn't have to be you."

I closed my eyes. "I am queen," I whispered. "I can't ask anyone else to make that choice. It has to be me."

"No."

Shocked, I glanced over as Nyx stepped forward, her expression steely. "Iron Queen," she said, as Puck turned with her, the fear in his eyes clutching at my heart. "This is not your choice to make. You have a family, and a kingdom that depends on you. My Order is gone. There is no one…" She stumbled over the words, catching herself. "There are fewer who are waiting for me to come back. I would gladly sacrifice my existence to give my kin another chance to live."

"Nyx." Puck's voice was choked.

"I'm sorry, Puck," she whispered, glancing at the distraught Summer faery beside her. "I love you, but I have to do this. Please understand." She gazed up at the tree, the lights of the candles reflected in her eyes. "This was my world, and these were my kin. I am Evenfey. This decision falls to me."

"It would make sense." Grimalkin's voice echoed strangely in the expanse, deeper and somehow terrible. "However, this sacrifice is *not* yours. You are the last Evenfaery. Your glamour is required for the ritual. But more important, you cannot withstand what is needed to pull the Evenfey out of the Dream. The conduit must be able to bear all the glamours within themselves. Summer, Winter, Iron, wyld, and the Nightmare magic of Evenfall. And out of all of us, there is only one who can."

No. I clenched my fists, feeling them start to shake. *Please. I can't lose him again.*

I looked over to where he was standing, and saw a small, sad smile cross his face. Keirran raised his head and sighed. "It's me," he said simply. "That's what the crypt keeper meant. It's always been me."

"Child of three worlds." In the water, the Nightmare King turned fathomless black eyes on Keirran. *"Prodigy of the Lady. I feared you would not make it this far. I feared you might be struck down before you ever breached the seal. The creature that sat the throne, even in the Dream, was powerful. Even in sleep, he could exert some measure of control over the Elder Nightmares. He did not even know why he wanted you dead, but he sent Nightmares into the mortal world and the Between, searching for you."*

"Why?" Keirran asked. "Why destroy my city and the Forgotten just to get to me?"

"Because you bear the mark of the Lady," said the Nightmare King. *"And like the Lady, you betrayed your own. You fought for one who destroyed a realm, who caused the extinction of an entire world."*

Keirran's jaw tightened, but he gave no other sign of what he felt. "I would take it all back if I could," he said softly.

"If only we could undo the past." The Nightmare King's voice held no bitterness, just weary acceptance. *"I came here, to my throne room, as Evenfall Faded around me. And as I let sleep take me into oblivion, I heard the Nightmare Tree whisper one last time. The final prophecy for this world. It told me, 'Only one who stood at the Lady's side can bring the Evenfey out of the darkness again.' For many years, I despaired in my dreams. The Lady's circle was gone; the fey who stood beside her, who took part in sealing our world, were dead. But then, recently, I began to hear whispers from the world above in my dreams. I reached out, through the Nightmare Tree, and found the thinnest of cracks where the roots barely touched the outside world. Where the anger*

of the mortal realm, the hate and fear, reached me even in my dreams. By then, Evenfall was already gone, Faded away, but I heard whispers of the Lady's return, and the one who stood beside her. Her new champion. And so, I waited. I was on the verge of giving up, of letting myself Fade, but I held out hope that, somehow, you would make your way to Evenfall and find me. To give my people the chance to exist once more."

Keirran bowed his head. "I would be honored," he murmured, "to give the Evenfey back their lives, and correct what was done to them so long ago. To heal all the harm the Lady brought and make things right again."

The trembling had moved from my hands to my whole body. "Keirran," I breathed, and my son looked up at me, the hope, grief, and resolve in his eyes making my throat close up.

"Please," he whispered, his gaze never leaving mine. "Let me do this. For everything I've done, all the mistakes I've made. Let me finally do something that matters."

I met my son's crystal gaze, seeing all his wounds: the pain, the grief, and the past he could not forget. But beneath it all was a quiet acceptance, and a determination to set things right, once and for all.

The tears flooding my eyes spilled over my cheeks at last, and I held back a muffled sob. Beside me, Ash let out a shaky breath.

"We can't stop you, Keirran," my husband said, his own voice unsteady. "You are a king of Faery, and this is your decision. Any of us would do the same."

"I know." Keirran bowed his head, then looked at me, his gaze pleading. "But I need to hear, before I do this... Please, I need you to let me go."

The tears continued to stream down my cheeks. I let them fall, meeting the anguished gaze of my son. "I understand," I whispered, barely able to get the words out. "It's all right, Keirran. You know what you have to do." Just as I had, all those years ago. It was little comfort. Knowing I had done the same for the

Iron fey, when I had willingly traded my life for theirs that day beneath the tree, did not shatter my heart any less.

"Dammit, princeling." Puck swiped at his face, giving Keirran a look that was angry and proud all at once. "I didn't want to cry today. I don't know why your whole family feels the need to make me bawl like a baby every few decades." He sniffed loudly, managing to dredge up a shaky grin. "Ah, but it was a good run. We had some fun times, didn't we? I guess now I'll finally get to tell the story of you and me in the hydra nest."

"Try not to shock them too badly," Keirran murmured with the faintest of smiles, and held out a hand. "You're a good guy, Puck. I learned a lot."

"Not enough." Puck took the hand and yanked Keirran into a brief, one-armed hug. "Apparently, I didn't corrupt that sense of ultimate noble sacrifice that keeps plaguing your family."

"My king." Nyx raised her head as Keirran pulled back. Her normally composed face was tormented, her golden eyes haunted as she met his gaze. "I'm so sorry," she said, and looked at me and Ash as well. "This decision... It should have been me."

"No, Nyx." Keirran put a hand on her arm. "Your whole world was taken from you. That's enough loss for a lifetime. I want to give you the chance to start again." He glanced at Puck, and a faint smile crossed his face. "Find happiness together. That's my final order."

Nyx seemed on the verge of tears, but she drew herself up, composing herself with a quiet breath. "I think we can try that," she whispered.

Keirran smiled, though his own eyes were bright as he turned back to me and Ash. "I'm not afraid," he said. "I'm happy that it's me. That I'm the one who has to do this. I just..." He stammered to a halt, closing his eyes, as the tears finally spilled over. "I wish I could have gone home, one more time."

I opened my arms, and he stepped into them, clinging to me as tears streaked both our faces and a thousand memories replayed in my head. I remembered Ash holding his infant son for the first time, his eyes shining with both pride and terror as he gazed down at him. I remembered a silver-haired boy perched on the tallest ledge of the Iron palace, laughing as gremlins swarmed around him. And I remembered an icy stranger striding into a Faery council, looking me straight in the eye, and declaring war on us all. Even then, though his face had been cold and his expression completely blank as he stared at me, I hadn't seen him as anything but my son.

"I love you, Keirran," I whispered. "That has never changed."

A shiver went through him, and the arms around me tightened. "Thank you," he whispered back. "For everything. For not giving up on me, even when I deserved it. I couldn't have had a better life than the one I had in the Iron Realm. I hope… I hope this last thing I do will make you proud."

Pulling back, he turned to face his father, who immediately reached out and drew him close. "I have always been proud of you," I heard Ash murmur, causing fresh tears to burn my eyes. Keirran gave a muffled sob, bowing his head, but Ash's soft, steady voice never wavered. "We are not our past," he went on, uncaring of the streaks of moisture down his own face. "No one is unworthy of forgiveness. No one is truly so far gone that they cannot be saved. The hardest part is forgiving ourselves, and moving on."

"So people have told me," Keirran whispered. "But… I think I finally understand."

"Forgotten King." Grimalkin's deep, quiet voice drifted into the emptiness. The cat stepped forward, his usual impatience gone, his golden eyes somber as he gazed up at us. "The Dream fades," he told Keirran, who stiffened. "It is time."

29

THE END OF THE DREAM

"I'm ready."

I watched numbly as Keirran turned to the throne, gazing down at the figure in the water. With a start, I realized the real throne was already empty, and only the reflection of the king was left. Overhead in the branches, the thousands of candles flickered, growing dim, and a few winked out entirely. The Nightmare King had not said anything during our last exchange, and now gave us a solemn bow of his head.

"The Dream is almost done," he whispered. *"I cannot hold on much longer. If you are prepared, I will send the final remnants of my power into the tree. Everyone but the conduit must then pour as much glamour into the tree as they can. When it is time, when it is enough, the conduit must summon all the memories through himself and into the real world again. What happens to the Evenfey beyond that is in your hands."*

A ripple went through the still water at our feet, breaking the king's reflection. When the ripples faded away, the throne sat empty. The Nightmare King was gone.

Keirran drew in a deep breath. Silently, he walked up to the empty throne and ran his hand along the stone armrest. There was a moment of hesitation, the faintest hint of uncertainty crossing his face, before his eyes calmed and he slowly sat down on the throne.

Leaning back, he closed his eyes, and a flutter of awe went through him. "I can feel them," he whispered. "All their voices, all their memories. They're all right here. And the roots of the tree touch all parts of Evenfall. Even..."

A furrow creased his brow. "The Nevernever," he breathed. "I can feel it. There are cracks in the seal, not enough to draw glamour in, but...it's right on the other side."

For some reason, the thought of the Nevernever and home twisted my heart and caused my eyes to burn with tears once more. "All right," I choked out. "The Dream is almost over, and we know what we have to do. Let's finish this and bring everyone home. Keirran..." My throat closed on his name; I took a shaky breath to open it again. "Are you ready?"

"Yes." My son didn't open his eyes, but a small, genuine smile crossed his face as he settled further onto the throne. "I love you all," he said quietly. "The times we had, I will never forget."

As one, we spread out around the trunk, facing Keirran and the Nightmare Tree. Me, Ash, Puck, Nyx, and Grimalkin, our reflections shining clearly in the water beneath. I could see the branches of the tree spread out above and below, the candles flickering like dying stars. I saw Keirran on the throne, eyes closed, patiently waiting for the Dream to end. Suddenly I could hear voices around me, hundreds of whispers swirling through the limbs.

Ash was behind me then, arms circling my waist. I could feel him shaking against my back, and I gripped his hand, feeling his fingers tighten on mine. Several yards away, I saw Puck step forward, reach for Nyx, and take her hand. Grimalkin sat alone, tail curled tightly around himself, facing the tree. Watching him,

I wondered: Would Grimalkin be here if he knew there was a chance he could vanish? Or was he, too, risking everything to bring the Evenfey back? I supposed I would never know.

A sigh seemed to echo through the void, and for a moment, everything, both above and below, was perfectly still.

Now.

I drew in a breath and brought my glamour to life. Summer and Iron magic rose, twin whirlwinds swirling around me, snapping at my hair and causing ripples to spread out at my feet. I felt Ash's Winter magic rise to join mine, frost and icy wind mingling with the glamour of Summer and Iron. I raised one arm, seeing Ash do the same, pointing a hand at the Nightmare Tree and the figure seated below it. Not far away, Nyx and Puck stood together, eyes closed and arms also raised toward the trunk of the Nightmare Tree. On the other side, Grimalkin sat perfectly still except for his fur whipping about in the gale. Glamour swirled through the air, flashes of light and color sparking against the void, reflecting brilliantly in the water.

I drew my magic to me, feeling it pulse and tingle beneath my skin, and hurled it in one concentrated blast at the trunk of the Nightmare Tree.

The darkness around the trunk exploded with color, as five beams of light struck the tree with a roar of energy and magic. Lightning flickered, leaves spun in the wind, icicles grew and were instantly shattered in the maelstrom. The candles flared, glowing bright and adding to the brilliant luminance pushing back the darkness. On the throne, Keirran jerked, throwing his head back, as the storm of energy and glamour howled around him.

I could feel magic leaving my body, being drawn into the endless expanse of the Nightmare Tree. The void within seemed infinite, a yawning black hole lit with tiny sparks of memory and light. Overhead, the candles flickered wildly and the tree itself glowed like a beacon, but no matter how much magic I poured into it, it was swallowed instantly.

"Damn," I heard Puck breathe, his voice strained. "This is a greedy tree. How much glamour is it going to take?"

A world's worth, the Nightmare King had whispered. *Almost certainly, it will be more than you can give.*

No, I couldn't accept that. Gritting my teeth, I pushed harder, and the light flowing into the tree intensified, sending out streaks of lightning that snapped around the trunk. We had come so far, and everyone had already lost so much. For Nyx, for Keirran, and for a world that existed only in a dream, we could not fail now.

My magic sputtered, the light flickering out for just a moment. I clenched my jaw, struggling to keep it steady, feeling my arms begin to tremble with the effort. I was reaching my limit; my magic reserves were almost gone. Behind me, I could feel Ash shaking as he, too, struggled to expend the last of his glamour. And yet, even as the branches glowed and the candles flared brightly, the tree continued to drain our magic, sucking it into a never-ending void.

Not enough, I realized in despair. *It's not going to be enough.*

Puck staggered, going to one knee but still keeping a hand outstretched toward the trunk. On his other side, Nyx flickered, blinking from sight for just a moment.

No. I closed my eyes, reaching out desperately, to any who would listen. Not even knowing who I was trying to reach. *Please, we have to do this. We can't let this entire world die. Help us. We're not strong enough on our own.*

Then let us lend you our strength.

My heart skipped a beat. Was that...? That was *Oberon's* voice. Was I losing my mind? Gasping, I opened my eyes, searching beneath the branches of the tree for the Summer King, who could not possibly be here. He and the other rulers were in the Nevernever, on the other side of the seal.

We hear you, Iron Queen. An icy, familiar voice joined Oberon's. Mab, Queen of Winter and the Unseelie Court. *What was done to the Evenfey should not have been allowed to happen. And the Never-never itself was scarred by the consequences of that choice. It is time to correct the mistakes of those who came before, and make Faery whole again.*

Because apparently, you cannot do it on your own. Titania's voice now echoed through the void, as disdainful as ever. *So, we will come to your rescue once more.*

I blinked sweat and tears from my eyes, searching in vain for the owners of the voices. The perimeter around the tree was empty save for us. "Where are you?" I gasped. My legs trembled, and I fought to stay on my feet. Behind me, Ash staggered a little, but his grip around me didn't waver, keeping me upright. "I don't see..."

We are here, droned a deep, feral voice. *We are with you. Let our strength be enough to carry you through.*

Eyes glimmered in the water, shining gold and green. I looked down and saw them all—Oberon, Titania, Mab, and the imposing form of the Wolf—standing around the tree. Only their reflections; the space above the water was empty, but I saw them as clearly as if they were standing beside us.

"How...?"

We heard your voice, Mab said. *Through the cracks in the seal, your presence reached us. We heard their voices, the Evenfey, and we made our choice.*

To restore a world, Oberon added, *will take more than the magic of a few. It will take the entirety of the courts. So, the courts have come. For this one final decision, we will stand together.*

He raised a hand, splaying his fingers, and a surge of Summer glamour shot from his palm, crashing into the trunk of the Nightmare Tree. Mab and Titania did the same, their reflections lifting their palms to the tree and releasing their magic. Summer and Winter glamour swirled with ours, and the glow around the trunk grew almost blinding.

Above us, the candles flared white, then began winking out one by one. Keirran threw back his head, his jaw clenched and his hands curling into fists. Rips opened up on his body, the skin on his cheeks, arms, and forehead splitting open, light shining through the tears. "Not...enough," he gritted out, making my heart clench. "Not there yet. I can't...hold on much longer..."

Sorry I'm late, darlings.

There was a shimmer in the water, a flutter of light, and a striking faery with copper hair and a long black gown appeared in the reflection. *Meghan, my dove.* Leanansidhe greeted me with a smile. *Whatever you're doing, I can feel the ripples all the way in the Between. Restoring the Evenfey, are we? Well, I certainly can't let myself be shown up by these three.*

My eyes stung, blurring with tears, as the Dark Muse raised a hand as well, sending a brilliant flare of glamour out to join the rest. "They're all here," I whispered, and felt Ash's fingers weakly squeeze mine. "We can do this. One last push, everyone. For Evenfall."

I felt my husband gather himself, calling on the last of his strength to keep us both upright. Puck raised his head, his face haggard but his green eyes hard with determination as he pulled himself up, following Nyx as she staggered to her feet. The tree was now almost too bright to look at, candle flames nearly lost in the glow around the trunk, the luminance swallowing the throne and the figure seated atop it. Eyes streaming, I searched for Keirran within the light, but the brilliance burned my eyes, and I dropped my gaze to the reflection beneath.

My breath caught. In the water, Keirran sat on the throne with his head bowed, face tight with pain and concentration. But two figures stood on either side of him, holding his hands tightly. A girl with raven-dark hair, and a grim-faced young man, his jaw set as he gripped Keirran's shoulder, his mouth moving with words I couldn't hear. A tiny, bat-eared creature sat on Keirran's other side, glowing eyes bright with alarm.

A hand reached around the throne, gently embracing him. A face appeared, a girl with long brown hair and green eyes, who smiled at Keirran and whispered something in his ear.

The tree flared, and the last of the candle flames vanished, snuffing out in a burst of smoke. Keirran threw back his head, and with a cry that tore at my soul, vanished in an explosion of light, magic, and color that swallowed him and the Nightmare Tree completely. I turned away, pressing my face into Ash, who wrapped his arms around me as remnants of glamour swirled through the air and snapped against my skin.

Silence fell. The swirls of energy and light faded, the magic vanishing into the void, and the world grew dark. Carefully, I pulled away from Ash and turned, gazing around at what was left.

The Nightmare Tree was gone. Not even a stump or withered branch remained of the once great structure; it had truly just vanished as if it never was. The void stretched on, endless and eternal.

But now we were not alone.

Fey surrounded us, crowds of them, some blinking and gazing around in bewilderment, some standing motionless with an awed look on their face. I saw the familiar form of a Skitterfolk scratch its ear, looking around as if it had just come out of a long sleep. Beside it, a pill bug faery blinked slowly as it observed the crowds of Evenfey, its expression one of lazy surprise. Through the pain, weakness, and utter exhaustion, I felt my heart lift in wonder. The Evenfey had come out of the Dream. What were once the Faded memories of the Nightmare King were real once again.

"Outsiders?"

A slight, familiar figure approached, slipping between a Wolfling and a Skitterfolk to stand before us. "Anira," I whispered as the crow woman gazed around in awe. A black bird landed on her shoulder, gave a confused caw, and flapped off again. "I'm glad to see you."

"Are...are we...?" Anira seemed hesitant to speak the actual words. "Is this...?"

"This is the real world," I said softly, and her beady eyes went glassy with tears. "You are out of Evenfall, Anira. You won't ever have to go back."

"Human, a moment please."

A tremor went through the ground, and crowds of Evenfey parted as something huge and monstrous made its way toward us. An enormous mass of raw flesh and gleaming bone lurched through the crowds, scattering fey like startled birds. "Excuse me," the Bone Collector said, tipping his imaginary hat as he stepped around a caterpillar sentry, who went purple with terror. "Pardon me. Terribly sorry, mind your tail, there. Ah, human. There you are." The Bone Collector gave a ghastly smile as he peered down at us, pinpricks of orange light flickering in his eye sockets. He was just as terrifying, maybe even more so, in the real world. "Unless I am still dreaming," he went on, "and this would be a strange dream, even for me, it appears that you were able to accomplish what you said you would. Am I correct in hoping that we are, indeed, out of Evenfall? That the seal has at last been broken?"

I nodded. "The Dream has ended," I told the huge faery. "The Evenfey are free now, and the nightmare is over."

"Hmm." The Bone Collector scratched the side of his face with scythe-like talons. "Well, I will say I am surprised. I did not believe the small, silver-haired one when he claimed you could save Evenfall. Though I am happy to be proven wrong, and I will tell him so." The Bone Collector cocked his head, frowning slightly as he gazed around. "Er...the small silver-haired one...where is he?"

I straightened against Ash, who hadn't let me go this entire time.

Keirran.

I spun blindly, pushing my way through the crowds, to the

spot where the Nightmare Tree had once soared into the sky. It was gone, of course, faded from existence. The last remaining piece of Evenfall had finally vanished with its king. I might have felt more melancholic, but right then, my only thoughts were of Keirran.

I stepped between two fey and stumbled to a halt, staring numbly at the spot where I'd seen him last. The throne still stood there, alone in the void, but it was empty. Nyx and Puck knelt in front of it, hunched over a figure on the ground. Puck's head was bowed, Nyx had both fists clenched on her knees, and neither looked up at me.

Keirran lay motionless at the foot of the throne, eyes closed and face slack, looking like he was only sleeping.

I walked to him in a daze, barely seeing Puck and Nyx silently move aside as I knelt at the body of my son. Burns covered him, angry gashes left by lightning, fire, ice, and wind. But his face was strangely untouched, his expression serene in the hazy starlight. I gathered him in my arms, feeling myself start to shake, hearing Ash stumble to a halt beside me. I heard my husband's muffled sob as he turned away, and that released the floodgates at last.

I bent over Keirran with a cry, hugging him to me. He was limp in my arms, his skin cold, and my tears spilled down my cheeks and dripped to his shirt. I sobbed over him, uncaring of my title and who would see me break down. Keirran was gone. He had finally found a way to redeem himself, but life would never be the same again.

No. Not yet.

Breath hitching, I raised my head. I saw everyone's reflections in the water, the Evenfey around me, somber and grim. Puck and Nyx, their faces wracked with grief. I couldn't even look at Ash, but I knew he hovered like a shadow at my back. I could feel his anguish, the tears, the devastation at losing his son, and I ached for him. For both of us.

And then I met the green eyes of a girl, standing in the crowd. Unlike the others, she had no real-world counterpart casting a reflection in the water. She smiled at me, and her gaze was gentle, though it was a little sad, as well.

Not yet, she whispered, though I could not see if her lips moved or not. The crowds of fey surrounding the girl paid her no mind, as if they couldn't see or hear her at all. *It is not his time yet. He had people here to help him stay, to keep him grounded to this side. One day, we will see each other again, but I can be patient awhile longer. There is still much he can accomplish here, and many who love him.* Her green eyes shifted to the body lying against me, and a wistful smile crossed her face. *So, my dear Keirran, I am afraid that, for now, you are going to have to...wake up.*

In my arms, Keirran let out a ragged gasp, and opened his eyes.

My heart stuttered. I stared at him for a moment, hardly daring to believe, as my son coughed, took several gasping breaths, and then gazed blearily around.

"The Evenfey," he whispered, as Ash knelt across from us, the joy and relief in his own eyes squeezing my heart. "Did... did it work?"

A sob of happiness escaped me, and I nodded. "Yes," I told him. "We did it. All of us. The other rulers came as well. Somehow..." I shook my head, still in wonder of what had happened. "Somehow, they were able to hear us."

Keirran relaxed. His eyes closed, and his body slumped against me, as if releasing all the fear, sorrow, regret, and shame that had been plaguing him for so long. "It's finally over," he breathed, so soft I barely caught it. "Although..." A pained furrow creased his brow. "For just a second, I thought I heard *her* voice, telling me not to give up. Kenzie's and Ethan's, too. Even Razor's. Though I don't know how *that's* possible." He sighed, and for a moment, it was as if I was seeing him...before. Before everything happened. Before the war with the Forgotten and the Lady, before he became the Forgotten King. The Keirran I hadn't glimpsed in so long, unbowed by guilt, eyes shining with happiness and hope. "In any case," he said, "it seems I'm still here. Looks like you'll have to put up with me for a while longer."

I gave a sob and hugged him to me, feeling Ash embrace us both. Closing my eyes, I slumped against my husband, letting myself feel the contentment and utter relief sweeping through us all. My family was safe, my friends were alive, and the Evenfey had been brought out of the Dream and into the real world. There were going to be difficulties, of course. I didn't know how the rest of the Nevernever would treat the arrival of yet another race of fey. Like most of Faery, the rulers of the courts did not react well to change. Even if they agreed that bringing the Evenfey back was the right course of action, I knew they would be wary of those who had existed only in nightmares. There would be doubts, suspicions, allegations, and accusations, because nothing in Faery was easy. That was just how things were.

We would face those problems later. Right now, I could forget everything and let myself believe that we had, in fact, achieved a happily-ever-after.

"Ooh, group hug." Puck stepped close, eyes shining and face alight with his old rakish grin. "Uh, unless this is a family moment. Normally, I don't go for these things, but I think this time it would be appropriate. I just don't want to get stabbed if ice-boy objects—"

Without looking up, Ash reached back, grabbed Puck's shirt, and yanked him down with us. I wrapped an arm around my best friend, then looked up at Nyx, hovering awkwardly a few steps away.

I smiled and held out an arm to her. "Come on, Nyx. You're part of this family now, too."

"I would not presume," Nyx said, but took my hand and joined us, kneeling gracefully at my side. "This is strange," she admitted. "Being part of something again. But I could get used to it, though I feel we are missing someone."

"We are," I said, smiling. "Come on, Grim. I know you're watching us. Get out here."

"Hmph." The cat appeared, seated a pace away. His golden eyes regarded us disdainfully. "As if I would resort to—urg!"

Whatever he was about to say was lost as I reached out, snagged him around the stomach, and dragged him into my lap. His tail bristled, thumping against my legs, but he didn't dig claws into my flesh, so I considered it a win. "You realize you are going to pay for this, Iron Queen," he warned, but settled himself comfortably, curling his tail around himself. "Just because we are victorious does not mean I will lower myself to such indignities."

I smiled at his words and let myself sink into the warmth and love surrounding me. Everyone was here. We were alive. We had won.

The nightmare was finally over.

30

THE IRON VOW

"Iron Queen."

The familiar voice echoed from the mist. I rose, disentangling myself from the circle of family and friends, to look around me. A tall, dark figure had melted out of the crowds of Evenfey, his naked deer skull glowing faintly against the gloom.

My heart leaped. "Gilleas! You made it. You're here."

"I am. As are we all, it seems." The tall Evenfaery looked at the crowds surrounding us in awe. "You did it," he whispered. "We are out of the Dream. We are back in the real world once again. After all this time, I had given up hope of ever seeing the Nevernever again. I... I do not know what to say."

"I do." Like a wraith, Other Nyx appeared from the shadows, Varyn at her side. I was relieved to see them both. Unlike some faeries who would not be named, two Nyxes in the Nevernever didn't seem like a bad thing.

Without hesitation, she walked up to me and immediately knelt, bowing her head low. "We are forever in your debt, Iron Queen," the Evenfaery whispered, as Varyn followed her example. "The Order is yours to command. Whenever you have need of us, no matter what the circumstances, we will be at your side."

"You don't have to do that, Nyx," I told her, and she shook her head.

"You've given my kin their lives back," she said solemnly. "I will no longer have to watch my people struggle and die trying to exist. It is a small price to pay to be out of the endless nightmare."

"Yes," Gilleas agreed, as Ash and the rest of them came forward. Keirran leaned against his father, one arm slung over his shoulders, but he seemed to be keeping his feet well enough. "To be out of the Dream," Gilleas went on. "To be real once more, it is worth any price. But, if I may inquire...where are we?" He raised his head, gazing around the void and the mist slowly creeping forward. "This is not Evenfall," he stated. "Evenfall Faded when the king fell into his slumber. Is this Faery? Are we in the Nevernever?"

"I think we're in the Between," Keirran said. His voice was hoarse, raspy with what he'd just gone through. But he raised his head, searching the fog and coiling mist, and gave a confident nod. "This feels familiar," he murmured. "I think... I should be able to lead us all back into Faery from here."

"Let's gather everyone together, then," I said. "They need to know what has happened. Before we all stomp into the Nevernever and give the other rulers a heart attack." I gazed around at the crowds of dazed Evenfey, an entire realm's worth of faeries, and took a quick breath. "We might be here awhile."

They were waiting for us on the other side of the Between. All of them: Oberon, Titania, Mab, the Wolf, and the armies of Summer, Winter, and Iron. As the mists parted, I could see them, the grim-faced rulers awaiting our return, their forces spread out behind them. I caught a glimpse of Glitch at the head of the Iron Kingdom's forces, a stern-faced Spikerail standing behind him. Both bowed deeply as our gazes met, though not before a flash of relief crossed the face of the First Lieutenant.

They had been standing guard at the site of the broken seal, prepared to meet the vengeful Nightmare King should he make his way into the Nevernever. But now I couldn't help but think they were also waiting for the Evenfey, ready to stop them from coming any farther into Faery.

I set my jaw, sparing a glance at Ash, Puck, and Grimalkin beside me. "Ready for this?"

"I am," Ash replied somberly, and Puck bobbed his head while Grimalkin yawned in a very deliberate manner. I looked to my other side, at the quartet of Evenfey waiting there: Gilleas, Varyn, and the two Nyxes.

Our Nyx met my gaze with a single nod. "We are with you, Iron Queen."

I raised my head, drawing on the mantle of the Iron Queen, and took a deep breath. "Let's go, then."

We strode across the ruins, across the site of the battle where vicious Elder Nightmares had clawed their way out of Evenfall and clashed with the armies of Faery. That day, we had gone into Evenfall to stop the waking of the Nightmare King, believing that he was a threat that could destroy our worlds. We could not have imagined what we would find. A Fading king, a world of nightmares, and the Evenfey who were naught but dreams themselves. Who would disappear like they'd never existed, should the king wake up.

Somehow, despite the impossibility of the task, we had triumphed. We had made the Evenfey real and brought them out of the Dream. But, ironically, they weren't safe yet. The hardest task still loomed ahead, in the gazes of the three fey awaiting us at the edge of the field. Oberon, Titania, Mab.

They were not the only ones. The imposing form of the Wolf loomed off to one side and, even more shocking, a tall faery with billowy copper hair and a glimmering evening gown stood beside him. Leanansidhe the Dark Muse stood with her arms crossed and a smug smile on her face as she gazed at Titania, as if knowing her mere presence would needle the Summer monarch. I didn't know how she was here; perhaps Oberon or even Mab, facing the greatest of threats from the Nightmare King, had called another powerful fey to the forefront of battle. Leanansidhe was not the faery that we needed to convince today, but that she was here at all, defying her exile, showed just how serious the threat of the Nightmare King had been. And now, we had arrived in the Nevernever with all the subjects of the Nightmare King behind us. Even if the other rulers had agreed to bring the Evenfey out of the Dream, I doubted any of them were going to be thrilled about it.

My heart pounded, but I felt resolve spreading through me with every step I took. The Evenfey were counting on us. After all we had been through, I was not going to fail them.

"Meghan!"

I stumbled a bit, then turned as the familiar form of my brother pushed his way through the crowds and jogged up to me, Kenzie on his heels.

"Ethan," I whispered as his arms closed around me in a tight, almost angry hug. "What are you two doing here?" I asked, extending an arm to Kenzie, who also joined the embrace. On her shoulders, Razor buzzed maniacally and grinned down at us.

"Razor brought!" the gremlin cackled as we drew back. "Razor brought funny boy and pretty girl. Brought to help!"

"We heard about the Nightmare King," Kenzie said, ignoring the gremlin as he bounced frantically on her shoulders. "Glitch reached out to us and told us what was going on, said the queen's family had a right to know what was happening."

"So, obviously, we came to help," Ethan added. "Kenzie and Razor found a trod, brought us to Faery, and here we are." He gave me a faintly exasperated look. "You could've told me that you were diving into a literal nightmare world, Meghan. We would've been here a lot sooner."

I sighed. "There wasn't really time," I told him. "But I'm glad you made it."

"Where's Keirran?" Kenzie asked, gazing around the rest of the group, her eyes bright with fear. I remembered then, the image of Ethan, Kenzie, and Razor at the base of the Nightmare Tree. Bracing Keirran. Somehow giving him the strength to hold on. "Is he...?"

"He's all right," Ash assured her. "He's waiting in the Between with the Evenfey."

Kenzie relaxed. "Thank goodness," she whispered, and then seemed to notice the four Evenfaeries standing patiently behind us. "Oh, hello," she said, blinking as Gilleas peered down at her. "We heard what happened to Evenfall," she went on, as Ethan shook his head. Mackenzie Chase did not know a stranger, even a shadowy, six-foot faery with a deer skull for a face. "It sounded horrible. I'm glad that everyone made it out."

Gilleas bowed his head to her. "We are very glad to be here," he said.

Ethan turned to me again. "I suppose now you have to have a talk with the other rulers," he muttered. "Since they're all waiting for you."

I set my jaw. "Yes, and I need you to promise me something, Ethan," I began, making him raise a brow. "We have to decide what to do with the Evenfey, and what I'm going to propose isn't something the other rulers are going to like. They're going to argue. Things could get...rather heated."

My brother held up a hand. "We get it," he told me. "Don't worry, Kenzie and I will be watching quietly from the sidelines, and *not* saying anything that will piss off any faery queens. Right?"

He looked at Kenzie as he said this. She wrinkled her nose at him.

"Fine, tough guy. But who was it that got their voice taken away for annoying a faery queen? Not me."

Ethan sighed. "I'm glad you're safe," he told me, with a last quick hug. "If you need us, we'll be right over there."

"Tell Keirran to come say hi when he can," Kenzie added, as she and her husband stepped back. Razor beamed his bright grin and waved to us from her shoulder. "We'll be waiting for him."

I watched them walk away, back to where Glitch and the other Iron fey waited, and smiled. I had spent a good deal of my life trying to keep my brother away from Faery. Away from Keirran and the prophecy that might kill them both. But now I couldn't imagine Faery without Ethan, Kenzie, and the hyperactive gremlin. Our lives were intertwined, woven between Faery and the mortal realm, impossible to sever or separate. I wouldn't have it any other way.

Now there was just one last thing we had to take care of.

"Iron Queen." Oberon spoke first as we approached the waiting rulers and the huge wolf standing beside them. Behind the monarchs, Leanansidhe gave me a two-fingered wave and a knowing smile, as if she found all of this extremely amusing.

"King Oberon," I replied politely. "Queen Mab, Lady Titania." Titania ignored me, but Queen Mab offered a slight nod. "I'm glad we could meet like this, and not in the middle of a battle."

"For once," I heard Puck mutter. Everyone pretended not to hear that.

"Where are the Evenfey?" Oberon asked, his ice-green gaze sweeping over the Evenfaeries beside me. "When we agreed to help you, we expected an entire race of fey to return to the Nevernever. Surely there are more than these four."

"They are here, Lord Oberon," Ash said. "They await your decision in the Between. Since technically, they do not have permission to enter the Nevernever."

"Good," Mab said, nodding. "A wise decision. They can stay

there until we can decide where to put them. Certainly, they cannot come rampaging through Tir Na Nog. Perhaps they can find refuge in the Between—"

"The Between has been taken over by Forgotten," snapped a voice at their back. Leanansidhe strode forward, to the immediate Death Glare of Titania, whom she ignored. "It is quite crowded, and I am already sharing my territory with more than one species of fey. I would appreciate not having to deal with more. The Between is not a dumping ground for unwanted outsiders."

"Isn't the Between eternal, Dark Muse?" Mab questioned. "I am sure you can find a suitable place for these Evenfey to go—"

"No," I said.

All four stared at me, and the Wolf pricked his ears. "They're not going anywhere," I went on firmly. "We don't have to find them a new home—*this* is their home. Faery is their home. We are not going to shunt them into some isolated part of the Nevernever and forget they exist. They've suffered too much for that to happen."

"Bring them *here*?" Titania spat the words at me, and my temper flared. "Impossible! They are Evenfey, from a realm of horror and nightmare. This is not their world. They do not belong here."

"We are all fey!" I nearly shouted the words. "Neverfey, Evenfey, Forgotten, Iron fey. It doesn't matter what we're called. It doesn't matter where we came from. We are all the same. They belong here as much as any of us."

"We are born from the dreams and fears of mortals," Ash interjected in his deep, steady voice. "If we are remembered, we exist. If we are forgotten, we Fade. It is no different for the Evenfey."

"And they're no less real than we are," Puck added. "If you don't believe me, look any one of them in the eyes—" he nodded to the quartet of Evenfey beside us "—and tell me they're not real. Be careful, though," he cautioned, and smiled at Nyx. "You're likely to take a very real knife to the ribs if you do."

The Wolf rumbled a growl, but it was more thoughtful than aggressive. "You speak for these Evenfey," he said, eyeing the three faeries behind us. "But do they have their own voice? Will they speak for themselves?"

"We do have a voice." Gilleas stepped forward, bowing his head respectfully. "Rulers of the Nevernever," he said, as their narrowed gazes turned on him. "I am Gilleas, historian of Evenfall and once advisor to the Nightmare King. Allow me to alleviate your concerns about us. We the Evenfey are born of darker dreams, of mortal nightmares and their deepest fears. The Nightmare King was our monarch, and we served him in the same way that the fey of Summer or Winter serve the courts. For many eons, we existed alongside the Nevernever. Until the Lady. The Lady thought we were a threat. She was afraid of us and our king, because we were not like her. She convinced the rest of her kin that we were somehow Other. Not fey, but monsters. Alien and different.

"But we are not different. We still require glamour to live, and if we are forgotten, we Fade away. Our appearance might be strange, frightening, even dangerous, but in the end, we are all still fey."

"That remains to be seen." Oberon turned to me, his back stiff and his expression blank. "Are you proposing," he began slowly, "that we allow the Evenfey into the Nevernever, to roam at will wherever they please?"

"Not just the Evenfey," I answered. "Everyone. Evenfey, Forgotten, Exiles, half fey." I ignored the instant exclamation of horror from Titania and met the eyes of Oberon and Mab. "Lift the banishment from the Exiles," I said. "Let the Forgotten out of the Between, and give everyone a chance to come home."

A faint noise came from Leanansidhe, the slow intake of breath. I realized that lifting the banishment from all exiles meant the Dark Muse could return to the Nevernever, as well. She didn't say anything, however, perhaps afraid that any reaction on her part would cause Titania to *really* dig in her heels. I couldn't blame her, but the sudden flash of hope in the eyes of the Dark Muse made my stomach clench and only strengthened my resolve.

"That is a massive undertaking, Iron Queen," Mab said. "Allow all banished fey to return? Such a course would shift the balance of the Nevernever and cause disruptions you could not imagine."

"Maybe," I said. "And maybe there will be problems, and we'll have to deal with them as they arise. But I know that we are stronger together. This division has only weakened us and has been the source of every war and misunderstanding from the time the first Iron King rose to power."

"According to whom?" Titania demanded. "You have been queen only a few short years, mortal. What do you know of what Faery was like before?"

Grimalkin, who had been silent until now, gave a very loud sigh. "If we must argue the past," he said, "you are all being shortsighted. In case you have forgotten, Faery existed without the courts before. Before the First Queen, before Summer and Winter and Iron, there was only the Nevernever. None of you were realized then, but the splitting into different territories caused a rift in Faery and began separating magic and fey alike. I do not believe it will ever return to the way it was, but long ago, Faery was just that. One singular world, shared by all."

"Yes." The Wolf gave a single nod. "The cat is correct. I remember this world, before it became too civilized for my liking. There were no courts. There was only Faery."

"I'm not suggesting that we dissolve the courts," I said into the begrudging silence. "I know there will always be fey who call Arcadia and Tir Na Nog their home. But it's time for us to stand as one. No more exiles, no more shunning our own.

From now on, any who are fey will be welcome in Faery. That is how it should have always been."

The three rulers were silent, pondering our words. My heart raced, but I kept my expression steady. This decision between the kings and queens of Faery had to be universal. Or at least, as close to universal as we could get. I doubted Titania would ever accept such a proposal, but hopefully, she would be the only one to object. Because I wasn't asking. This was going to happen, whether the other the rulers liked it or not. Asking for their permission was a formality, and deep down, I suspected they knew as much. Still, even in this, I had to play the game. If I was too aggressive in my approach, the proud rulers of Faery would refuse, just to prove that they could not be commanded.

And then, in the most shocking of twists, Titania let out a small chuckle. "Why not?" she said, to the complete amazement of us all. "More fey in the Nevernever means more subjects to serve and worship me. I am not afraid of them, or *any* faery." She shot a look of pure poison at Leanansidhe, who gave her a viciously sweet smile in return. "Besides," the Summer Queen went on, "I will admit, the current stock of Seelie fey prancing around the court has become rather dull. Perhaps these Even-fey will prove more interesting." She smiled and waved an airy hand. "Very well. Let them come. I look forward to seeing what they can do."

"I..." For the first time since I had known him, perhaps the first time in centuries, King Oberon appeared speechless. Quickly, he composed himself, straightening and schooling his expression into a blank mask again. "Agreed," he said at last. "The Evenfey and the Forgotten will be welcome in the Nevernever. As are any who have been exiled to the mortal realm. Let us begin a new chapter in Faery, where we are stronger and can withstand anything that threatens our world."

Queen Mab gave a small, slightly predatory smile. "I sense interesting times indeed," she mused. "If these Evenfey are born from human nightmares, I wonder how my own Unseelie will fare against them. Very well, we shall see what the future holds for Faery and the Winter Court. You also have my blessing, Iron Queen. I am eager to see what becomes of this."

I drew in a slow breath, careful not to reveal my nerves or excitement. "Then let us make it official," I said, and the rulers nodded gravely. Raising my voice, I spoke the words that would bring this into law. "From this day forth," I announced, the words rising up to echo through the ruins, "all fey are welcome in the Nevernever, no matter their background or where they were born. The Evenfey are now full residents of Faery and may choose their courts or the wyld as they please. All exiles and fey banished to the mortal realm may return, and the trods that were closed to them will be open once more. And the Forgotten are no longer relegated to the Between but may enter the Nevernever freely. If this is acceptable, let all the rulers be in accord, and it shall come to pass."

"Agreed," said Oberon.

"Agreed," Mab and Titania echoed.

"Agreed," I whispered, and suddenly had to take a quick breath to keep the tears from my eyes. It was done. After so long, everyone could start over at last. The Evenfey had a new world. The Forgotten didn't have to stay in the Between any longer. And all those banished from Faery could finally come home.

I trembled, biting my cheek to keep my emotions in check. Even now, I could not afford to show weakness to the other rulers. "It's done, then," I said, keeping my voice steady, when all I wanted to do was shout in triumph. "A new beginning, for everyone."

Leanansidhe threw back her head and laughed. "Oh, Meghan my dove, you have no idea how proud I am right now." She beamed at me, her face alight with triumph. "To think, that shy, naive, lovesick human girl I first saw that day in my home has become a true queen. I knew that helping you would change everything in Faery. Somehow, I knew."

"Yes," Oberon muttered. "And let us hope Faery does not tear itself apart because of it."

I didn't have time to answer, because at that moment, all the rulers straightened, looking past me into the darkness. I turned with Ash, Puck, and the others, as Keirran stepped out of the mists. He paused, his gaze meeting each ruler one by one, then looked back and gave a tiny nod. His lips moved, and though I couldn't hear the words, I saw the phrase on his lips, and it brought a fresh stinging sensation to my eyes.

Welcome home.

And the Evenfey appeared, walking past him out of the mist, out of the Between, and into Faery.

EPILOGUE

N ow, you might be wondering: what happened to the queen and her companions after the final meeting with the Nightmare King? After the Evenfey were allowed back into Faery again? Where did everyone go? What are they doing now?

Well, the queen and her husband returned to their Iron Realm, which, thankfully, had not fallen down or exploded during the time they were away. Their kingdom was stable and secure, but they knew there was still much to be done. For the Evenfey were back in the world again, and faeries are nothing if not consistent. The Iron rulers knew there would be squabbles and fighting, as the Nevernever adjusted to the sudden influx of another race of fey. But they were confident that, with time and some minor intervention, all faeries could live together, if not peacefully, then at least in harmony. For now, they were content. Though they did get a surprise visit from none other than Leanansidhe, who appeared at the Iron Court with a protective amulet and an entire entourage of human Charleses, claiming she was on a tour of the Nevernever and visiting the rulers of the courts to see what she had missed. She did seem a bit "miffed" at the Iron rulers; now that the banished fey could return to Faery, she was no longer the Exile Queen. However, now that she was allowed back into the Nevernever, it didn't seem to bother her *that* much.

The rulers of Summer and Winter returned to their courts as well, and as far as I know, everything went back to normal, or as normal as it can be in the Nevernever. Lord Oberon still rules the Seelie Court and finds excuses to go hunting as often as he can. Queen Titania…is Queen Titania, and will continue to be so, to the dismay of everyone who knows her. Mab still rules with an icy fist, the Unseelie are still bloodthirsty and dangerous, and the two courts will continue to squabble with each other until the end of time.

In most respects, Faery has not really changed that much. Somewhere across the River of Dreams, the Wolf roams the Deep Wyld, waiting for the next exciting hunt. Grimalkin still lurks somewhere in the wyldwood, collecting favors and being a cat. I hear he keeps company with Gilleas now, the two of them discussing the history of the Nevernever and Evenfall. I can only imagine the conversations between two ancient, immortal creatures that have been around since the beginning of Faery. I hope they do not drive each other to distraction.

Puck kept his promise to Nyx, and after everything had calmed down with the Evenfey, the two of them vanished for a while. I expect they are off seeing the world together and getting into all sorts of trouble. I wish them happiness, and I hope Puck does not stir up *too* much chaos. Though if he does, Nyx is perfectly capable of rescuing them both. Other Nyx and Varyn made their way to the Between, to Touchstone, the capital of the Forgotten Kingdom, and pledged their loyalty to King Keirran. We are still unsure if some Forgotten could be Evenfey that were trapped on the opposite side of the seal, but now they have the Order of the Crescent Blades protecting them and their city. Many Forgotten seem content to stay in the Between, in their land of gloom and shadows, but they now have the option to leave should they wish it.

And the Iron Prince himself? He kept his position as King of the Forgotten and welcomed all Evenfey and exiles into his kingdom. These days, you can sometimes see him in the Nevernever, in the Iron Court or visiting the lands of Winter. As Queen Mab irately directed the Iron rulers not long after the Evenfey returned: "Tell my grandson, now that he is no longer in exile, that I expect to see him at the Winter Court more than once in a blue moon. Just because he is a king does not mean he can ignore familial responsibilities." Ash promised he would send Keirran to Tir Na Nog with a formal apology and cookies. It is always a good idea to keep the rulers appeased, especially if they are family.

And that is the story of the girl who went into Faery, fell in love, had a family, and saved the world with everyone together. I wanted to tell you, because *you'll* be a part of this world soon, and you will need to understand what has happened, the complex history you've been born into. I'm afraid your life is going to be very far from normal, but don't worry. Your faery godmother—and your entire family—will be here to make sure you're all right.

"And how does the story end?"

I looked up from my chair. Ethan stood in the doorway, smiling into the room, his gaze not on me but on what I held. I looked down at the infant in my arms and saw she was asleep, blue eyes closed and dark hair feathering over her forehead.

I smiled back. "It doesn't," I whispered. "There is no end, no happily-ever-after. There is always a next chapter, another part to the tale. The ending of one story is only the beginning of the next adventure."

"Well, hopefully not for a few years, at least." Ethan came into the room, and I rose, Alexia Meghan Chase snoozing peacefully against me, tiny hands curled into fists. Soft voices drifted into the room, and through the doorway, I could see Ash and Kenzie in the living room, sitting on the couches with two massive dogs at their feet. The scene was so surreally normal that, for a moment, I stood there and let the utter contentment and happiness wash over me. We were alive, and I was surrounded by family and the people I loved the most. Even if they weren't physically present, I would see them again. Another story had come to an end, but a new one was just beginning.

I relaxed, bending to kiss my niece's forehead as her father stepped in to claim her. Her eyes opened, two tiny crystal pools gazing up at me, and I smiled.

"I'll see you in the Nevernever soon."

★ ★ ★ ★ ★